# SNOW IN VIETNAM

## A NOVEL

### AMY M. LE

# SNOW IN VIETNAM

Copyright © 2019 by Amy M. Le

First edition May 2019

*Jacket design by Virginia McKevitt*

Manufactured in the United States of America

ISBN: 978-1-948577-97-7 (paperback)
ISBN: 978-1-948577-99-1 (hardback)
ISBN: 978-1-948577-98-4 (ebook)

# DEDICATION

This book is dedicated to the boat people of Vietnam and the refugees who left Vietnam after the fall of Saigon. In memory of my mother who sacrificed so much, this book is a tribute to her bravery and selflessness.

# PRAISE FOR SNOW IN VIETNAM

"Well-developed characters, a brave and admirable protagonist, a vivid setting and heartbreaking struggles that felt real combine to make *Snow in Vietnam* a compelling, unforgettable read."
-Alicia Dean, Award Winning Author of Heart of the Witch

"Compelling, informative and beautifully written."
-Frances Evlin, Author of Circles of Deception

"Americans who are old enough experienced (what we call) the Vietnam War in one way -- as a conflict that ripped us apart as a country, and left our national psyche wounded. But in her novel Snow in Vietnam, Amy Lee makes us privy to an intimate portrait of what that war was like from the inside. Amy does a superb job of making her characters come alive, and tell us what it was like to run for your life from a country you once called 'home'" This is an exciting read that left me treasuring the preciousness of life, and aching for those who lose it."
-Keith Madsen, Author of The Sons and Daughters of Toussaint

"I stayed up all night reading because I literally could not put it down. This book leaves you hungry for the next chapter and the next chapter and the next chapter. This is the kind of book that you can't stop thinking about after you read it because the characters just come alive and the descriptions of the settings and the activities are so vivid." -Diana LeBeau

"I love how I laugh and cry and just find myself lost in your writing."
-Courtenay Brimer

"I loved going on Snow'semotional journey and learning about the Fall of Saigon through her unique perspective." —Lisa Schumann

"Love the way you write! Can't wait to read all your stories and learn from you as well. Web Page is AWESOME!" -Frances Moore

"This novel is epic. Snow adapts and conquers; a great read."
-Michael Harmon

This book received recognition as a finalist for the 2018 PNWA literary award. Some of the comments from the judges include:

"The author does a beautiful job of keeping the reader off balance, wanting to continue to find out what happens next."

"There are many wonderful characters in this selection that help bring this story to life."

"The story presents in many charming and unexpected ways to keep reader interest."

"The opening pulls the reader in immediately and the scenes move along briskly."

"First person narrative is strong and appropriate."

"Setting and description are nicely interwoven with the plot and dialogue and Eight's internal narrative. Mood and atmosphere are established by all of the above."

"Description is abundant whether about food, clothing, how the sisters see one another, or the young men they meet. Adroitly using many fiction and memoir techniques, the author cleverly depicts life in Vietnam in the 1970s."

"Love the voice, from the character's names (Eight, Seven, Sister Six, Tree) to the back and forth between the family members. Great dynamics."

"In *Snow in Vietnam* the author has created a charming, well-constructed story that delights the reader continually with imaginative play through language, character revelations and dialogue."

"The dialogue is an integral part of the story and gives the reader insights into the characters. The dialogue and internal narrative of Eight are two great strengths of this selection, nicely detailing the dynamics of the extended family."

# CONTENTS

# ACKNOWLEDGMENTS

Thank you to my amazing husband, Joseph Walls, and my witty son, Preston Walls, for being the best cheerleaders. To my cousin, Tri Le, you are the best brother I can ever wish to have. To my incredible family, friends, and network of supporters, thank you for sharing my work, for your support, advice, and stories. A special thanks to my critique team "The Quixotics" (Ilene Birkwood, Keith Madsen, Frances Sonnabend, Tricia Corbett, and Mac MacCullough) for spending countless hours reading my manuscript and providing invaluable feedback. A heartfelt thanks to Alicia Dean and Ally Robertson, who opened my eyes to the difference between good writing and powerful writing. To Estrella Sung and Virginia McKevitt, your vision for my book cover took me in the right direction and I love you for it. C.M. Healy, I appreciate your guidance for launching this book. Finally, thank you to the readers who chose my book. It has been a labor of love and I hope the story and characters inspire you to live life with unwavering determination. Remember that grit and tenacity will take you far in life, but love and forgiveness will carry you to the finish line.

# 1 ANT SPIDERS (MAY 1973)

I never intended to marry so late. Here I am a thirty-four-year-old virgin about to marry a man I hardly know. The Paris peace treaty was signed this year and the end of the war is near. Normalcy will be restored in Việt Nam once again.

As I scrutinize myself in the mirror, I see how different I am from the other women in my hometown of Vĩnh Bình. They have long, thick black manes, straight as a runway, framing their oval faces. Then there is me, with my round face and fine head of hair, naturally speckled with cinnamon highlights left by the scorching sun. The wavy locks, tamed only by water and a barrette, are now threatening to go limp. Today, I am going for the Elizabeth Taylor look, with my pixie cut and pale skin. Most women in my town, from the young school girls to my elders, appear fragile and gaunt. Not me. Despite my small frame, my fat arms still give me away.

"Eight, what are you doing standing there?" My older sister bursts into my room, panting and looking provoked. "You and Mông Dơ can be twins." She is referring to our chicken, whose name means "Dirty Butt".

"I do not--" She never lets me finish.

Whipping me sharply around and squeezing my chubby arm, she lectures me on how to behave today. "Do not spill any tea. Bow and smile to your future in-laws and receive their gift with both hands. Under no circumstances do you show discomfort or displeasure." My sister is a bully and enjoys bossing everyone around. She is not the beauty or the brains of the family, nor is she an affectionate soul, but darn if she is not a great cook.

"Do not worry, Sister Six, I will not mess up as you did." I yank my arm away. Although I am the youngest of seven children, Eight is my name, for the parental unit is always number one. With the heat and the dread of my upcoming nuptials, I have no patience with Sister Six today.

"Do not speak until you are spoken to first. And for Heaven and Earth's sake, do something about your face!" Sister Six abruptly leaves my room.

I take a quick glance in the mirror. My skin is shiny with beads of sweat forming around my brows while the makeup is melting from the humidity. Even with all the windows open, there is no breeze. The sounds of mopeds zipping by and the familiar rasp of the old baguette lady sounding the sale of four sandwiches for twenty thousand piasters percolates through the window. From the corner of my eye, I see that Six, in her haste to exit, dropped a small photograph of my fiancé. It dances lazily to the floor, as if to convey that it, too, is in no hurry to start the day. I stare at the photo but all I can think of is Sam.

***

Two years ago in 1971, I met Sam. My niece, Tâm, who is twelve years younger than I, accompanied me on a holiday trip to the city of Tuy Hòa, northeast of Đà Lạt where I worked, some two hundred forty kilometers up the coast. We were parched from our travels and settled for some food and iced coffee with condensed milk.

"Chao Co," came a disembodied voice, gruff yet pleasant. The words were Vietnamese but the pronunciation conveyed an attempt of a three-year-old. I recognized the accent was American and pretended not to hear him, hoping he would go away. He repeated himself and I feigned interest in the live music in front by the bar, using the loud guitar chords from the band as an excuse to ignore him. I felt a reluctant tap on my shoulder.

I gazed into eyes that were pennywort green with specks of black and yellow like a ripe kiwi fruit. He was tall and his skin tan, kissed golden from the blistering sun.

"My friend and I would like to sit. May we borrow this chair?" His smile was mischievous, which made me a little nervous, but his dimple soon put me at ease. I nodded and turned my attention back to my niece. It was not long before the soldier's deep voice captivated me. Drawn in by his honeyed speech, I had to eavesdrop. My English was not bad for I had learned the language at the university.

What do you think of her, Sky?" asked the American soldier.

"C'mon, Sam. Did you see the tits on that girl?" Sam's friend also had a deep voice but not as melodic and soothing as the green-eyed soldier. I hoped they were not referring to Tâm or me.

"I prefer my women with a bigger rack, like pomelos." Sam demonstrated with his hands how big he liked them.

"Anything bigger than a mouthful is a waste in my opinion." Sky gulped down the last of his beer and ordered two more.

They watched with amusement as the owner of the watering hole pulled up a dusty canvas tarp to reveal a cooler with a big block of ice in it. He chipped a couple of big pieces into glass mugs, and in robotic synchronicity, poured two cans of warm "33" beer into their mugs. The bartender, weathered and haggard with his "555" brand cigarette dangling from his lips, adroitly handed Sky their drinks.

The two of them were quite the sight, hunched over a small table with their long legs spilling out in front of their lanky bodies like ant spiders. Sporting their M-16s, newly issued steel pot helmets and flak vests, they appeared comfortable despite the onlookers.

"Say, where are you from?" Sam took a swig of his iced beer.

"From Burien, Washington." Sky lit up a cigarette. "Born and raised in the Seattle area!"

"What?" Sam exclaimed. "Get out of here! I'm from Washington too. Bellevue, to be exact. I can't say I've been to Burien though. Pretty much stuck to the eastside."

The smell of phở brought my attention back to my table. The distinct smells of charred onions and ginger lingered in my nostrils as I took the first sip of the broth. Outside was a sweltering thirty-two degrees Celsius, but the hot soup soothed my throat.

Tâm squeezed some lime juice into her bowl. "Aunt Eight, after we eat, can we go to the beach?" I nodded as I pinched off some more basil leaves to add to my phở. "We can order more cà phê and stop to get some durian."

Again, I nodded. I was not in the mood to talk so going to the beach to relax was appealing. I was famished and debated whether to order a second bowl. The thought of gaining weight, however, quickly crushed my impulses. While my niece ordered our iced coffees, I took the opportunity to resume eavesdropping on the American GIs.

"We better get back to the truck." Sky stood up, standing almost two meters tall, and walked toward the sidewalk. "We were due back a half hour ago."

Sam was right behind him. My eyes followed them and I was bewitched by Sam's derrière. Most Vietnamese men do not have meat on them, so to see a man with a bulging behind was hypnotizing. As he walked leisurely, the fatigues wrinkled at the base of his butt, emphasizing his muscular thighs. I was so bewitched that when he turned his head to look back at me, I was paralyzed with embarrassment.

"Cam on." He winked and gave me his thanks with a smile that showed all his perfect white teeth. *What would it be like to be courted by an American?*

The sound of a man's voice, shrieking profanities, quickly jolted me back to reality. There was a lot of commotion as bystanders rushed to the street corner. Tâm and I joined them.

There was Sky, pacing back and forth, arms raised, with his rifle hitting his leg each time he pivoted to retrace his steps. "Fuck! Damn boysans stole one of our windshield wipers and ripped off our gas can!" He nodded in the direction where the thieves made their escape. His face was redder than a lychee fruit. "And this goddamn fool was asleep behind the wheel when he should have been keeping watch!" In the driver seat sat a local boy around eleven years old. Sky continued his ranting, calling the boy worthless, saying how he should have known better than to trust the "idiot". Spit frothed at the corner of his mouth. "I paid you to watch the truck and keep it safe." His posture stiffened. He clenched his teeth and demanded his money back.

The boy was terrified of this foreigner towering over him, no doubt worried the M-16 would be pointed at him. I held my breath. I anticipated Sam would commiserate with his comrade and yell like a lunatic as well.

"Calm down." Even with his brow furrowed in displeasure, Sam remained composed. He reminded me of the actor, Clint Eastwood. "Who's to say one of these faces is an unfriendly?"

During times of war, that much was true. You could never tell the "friendlies" from the "unfriendlies". They all had the same face. While both men were temporarily distracted, the young boy took the opportunity to escape and darted down the road.

Sky roared at the boy running for his life. "Yeah, you better di di mau!"

The crowd around the two soldiers dissipated. The thrill and excitement had subsided. Yet, there I stood, motionless.

My niece startled me. "Can we go?" Tâm held our iced coffees.

"Not yet," I stalled. There was something about Sam that had me fixated.

"Excuse me, sir?" The words tumbled out of my mouth before I realized I spoke. "You have enough gasoline?"

Sam and Sky took a couple steps closer. Tâm took a half step back, looking bewildered.

"I believe so. Thank you, er, miss…?" Sam fished for my name.

"Tuyết," I responded. "It means 'snow'. This is my niece, Tâm."

"Well shit, so there is snow in Vietnam!" Sky grinned from ear to ear.

"Tuy-yet! That sounds beautiful. I'm Corporal Sam Hammond of the U.S. Army, 180th Assault Support Helicopter Company. And this is Sergeant Skyler Herrington."

After a few pleasantries, Sky insisted they head back to base. We parted ways and I did not think I would see Sam again. Tâm and I were in Tuy Hòa for a short stay. Soon, we were expected back to Đà Lạt and back to work at the bank. Sam and Sky, the American ant spiders, had a war to win and a tunnel to infiltrate.

***

I analyze my reflection in the mirror and worry my eyes will betray my true age. The face that peers back at me can still be mistaken for a twenty-something year old. The naiveté and insecurities are still there despite my thirty-four-year-old eyes. Sister Six is right; I do look like our disheveled chicken, Dirty Butt. At least my áo dài, the traditional silk dress of Việt Nam, is not wrinkled. Sister Six insisted my dress be red and yellow, colors of our country's flag. The baguette lady makes her loop again, chirping four "bánh mì" for twenty thousand piasters, which is less than a U.S. dollar. I walk to the top of the staircase and grip the railing. It has been two years since I first met Sam and Sky at that

4

watering hole in Tuy Hòa. There is no time to dwell on the past now. I make my descent down the stairs.

Everyone is outside. I peek into the dining room. A cloth, red as a betel nut, adorns the long dinner table. Three chairs stand on either side, like centurions waiting for instructions, or perhaps more like the Việt Cộng, waiting for their next move. The cushions are re-upholstered in yellow silk; images of dragons carved on the backs of the chairs symbolize life and prosperity. I imagine myself sitting there and blending in, becoming invisible. Out of the kitchen window, I see poor Dirty Butt confined to her dome-shaped wire cage. I, too, am soon to be caged myself.

My nephew appears and takes my hand. "They are almost here." He leads me into the family room.

"Tree, wait with me." We sit together on the bench. Tree is not his real name, but we call him that because he is always climbing things. He is my eleven-year-old nephew, although he appears much younger. He is small, fast, and has a baby face. Despite his youthful appearance, he is muscular from years of running and scaling coconut trees to get away from my brother Seven's whipping. One time, I found him on top of a tall cabinet, out of his mother's reach. He squatted on top, knees and hips bent, with all his weight on the heels of his feet. What a funny sight to see him hunkered down, half crying and half taunting, while his mother jumped up and down trying to swat him with a broom handle.

From the window, I see the road leading to our home. I feel as if I am transported to another world. Sounds, smells, and colors beyond the house overwhelm me. Scooters zip by in disorderly fashion, their drivers honking at fellow riders who do not adhere to their side of the unmarked roads. Pedestrians yell as they jump out of the way to avoid getting hit while crossing to the other side. Babies are crying, no doubt hungry and uncomfortable with the heat. On typical days when there is not a wedding procession to gawk at, the view outside is drab. My neighbors, who usually wear the same boring polyester pants and tunic, in flat colors of brown or mustard yellow, now loiter around the front of their home drinking coffee or smoking a cigarette, and complain about losing a hand of cards. Today though, their animation shows off their youthful gait and toothless grins. Most flaunt their finest clothes and exchange the monochromatic for the loud, multi-colored patterns.

"Aunt Eight, let me know if you need anything." Tree is so many things I am not. He does not ask questions. He makes statements. He hates confinement; prefers the education learned on the streets to the teachings in school; he does not care much for anything except being one with nature. The boy does have a strong sense of family though and in the end, always comes home.

"I do not want to be alone. How is school?" I pat his head.

"School is for kids who do not know what they want in life."

"And you have your life figured out?"

"The American soldiers," Tree starts, "I hear them talk about their adventures. If it was not for my mom and dad, I would leave Vĩnh Bình, but someone has to take care of them."

"Yes, that is your responsibility." The faint smell of a roasted pig reminds me I have not eaten all morning. The anticipation of tasting the savory, juicy meat makes my mouth water. "Run along and fetch me some yogurt. It will be a couple of hours before we eat."

Tree quietly dismisses himself. I rarely have conversations with my nephew. Kids are here to work and do as we adults tell them to do. My interactions with Tree have been limited to fetch me this or tell your mom that. While I wait for Tree, I spy on my family standing in front of our house, looking magnificent in their tailored suits and dresses. It is the first time I smile all week.

In the distance, a procession of people from the groom's side of the family walks up the road toward us. A weathered, eighty-year-old man leads the procession. He represents the family. Next in line strides the groom's father, whom I had met once. He is still handsome for his age despite his stern and stoic appearance. I spot my future husband next. There he is, all 1.7 meters of him. He walks confidently like a dignitary, with his head held high, commanding respect, and his blue silk tunic clinging to his lean, muscular body. His legs are bowed, but on this day, it is not noticeable. The trousers underneath his ceremonial costume fit loosely and march in rhythm with his swagger. He looks sharp. Nine men, similarly dressed, follow him. Each carries a black lacquered box, adorned with a red embroidered cloth. My anxiety gets a hold of me. With each step they make, I feel a layer of independence being stripped from me.

The procession appears to go on and on. Two men carry a roasted pig hung from a spit. A group of women, young and old, cluck animatedly as they walk toward my family's house. All around the women are the "littles", each child oblivious to the etiquette preached to them minutes before the walk. At least thirty people approach the house.

A loud pop explodes through the air, followed by alternating crackles and pops in rapid succession. I smell smoke. Screams filter through the window. Dirty Butt flaps her wings, frantically squawking in protest. I stiffen and quickly drop to my knees. My headdress tumbles to the floor. I cover my face with my clammy hands as I kneel. My heart thumps loudly. I wish I had my rosary. *The Việt Cộng is raiding the village!*

"Here is your yog—" Tree's small hand wraps around my wrist. "Do not be afraid. Firecrackers were lit." He hands me my headdress and I carefully place it on my head. "You should fix your hair."

It takes a second to register I am not in danger. I hear laughter. My future husband and his family are inside the house. I stand up with a sigh of relief and muster the strength to hold back the tears. Not today, I tell myself. There will be no crying.

6

"Do I look like Mông Dơ?" I take a deep breath and an exaggerated exhale. Tree's silence confirms it. "There is no time. Maybe he will call off the wedding after he sees how ruffled I look."

Tree hands me the homemade yogurt that Sister Six made. After inhaling two big spoonfuls, I step into the dining room. I am overwhelmed with all the faces looking at me, but it is my father's that makes me cringe.

Father smiles but his eyes are stern and glaring. "Mr. and Mrs. Vương, may I present to you my daughter, Tuyết."

I bow to my future in-laws and greet them. "Chào bác."

"Your daughter is lovely, Mr. Lê." My future father-in-law clasps his warm hands around mine. "She indeed is as beautiful and light-skinned as snow."

"Please, do not be so formal. Call me Sáng. We will be family soon."

"Very well, Sáng. You can call me Bình. This is my father, Ngạn, my wife, Hương, and you know our son, Tý."

"Please, sit down." My father pulls out his chair and the rest follow suit. I remain standing. Bình and Hương smile at me with kind, empathetic eyes.

Sister Six floats into the dining room with the tea tray. One look at me and her smile disappears. I sense the disapproval of my appearance. She takes her seat in the matriarch chair beside Father.

All eyes are on me as I pick up the steaming hot teapot. It is heavier than I anticipated. Sister Six brewed a large pot and must have filled it to the top. I hold my breath and slowly pour my grandfather-in-law his tea. As the eldest, he receives his tea first. *Why do the cups have to be so small?* One splash and my marriage will be doomed. Next, I pour for my father.

I draw my attention to my in-laws. They are wealthier than my family. Mrs. Hương is plump. Any woman who has such a round face clearly is not starving or working hard in the rice fields. Her skin is flawless, stretched tight from the layers of fat beneath her cheeks and neck. She has on every piece of jewelry. Jade bracelets, the shade of cilantro, decorate both wrists; matching emerald stones dangle from her long earlobes and a marquise-cut emerald, eighteen-carat gold ring, show off her pudgy ring finger. Her green silk áo dài barely hold in the rolls of fat above her pants.

Her husband is the direct opposite. Mr. Bình is not ostentatious and is quite skinny. His only accessories are his wedding band and the flesh on his face that sags loosely. It is as if all the nutrients have been siphoned by Mrs. Hương. Still, he is a handsome man. I think of my in-laws as couple number ten because he is slender like the number one and she is round like the number zero. I smile at my private joke as I carefully pour the hot artichoke tea into their cups. Not a drop escapes onto the table.

With one finger pressed onto the lid of the ceramic teapot, I continue pouring flawlessly for Sister Six and my fiancé. I feel relief. Not a single drop of tea spilled. Our marriage should be a happy and lasting one.

Tý stands up and presses his hand against the small of my back. "A toast."

It is the first time we have stood this close to one another. He smells like grease, sweat, and the narcissus plant. His presence catches me off guard and surprisingly excites me. "May we be blessed with many sons!"

We all raise our teacups and sip the sweet soothing liquid. Mrs. Hương presents me with a gift. Inside the velvet box is the most exquisite twenty-four karat gold necklace I have ever seen. The chain cradles a golden phoenix with emeralds, diamonds, and rubies. "For strength and courage to always rise above." She winks at me and helps me put it on.

My wedding day goes by in a blur.

***

My wedding night is lasting forever. Tonight I lose my virtue. Other than Sam, no man has ever kissed me. As I lie here with my husband, who is grunting and fondling my body like he is prying apart a jackfruit, I recall my argument with Sister Six two winters ago.

She warned me true love did not exist. "Love is a concept for dreamers. If you do not marry soon, your shriveled prunes will do you no good."

"Sam and I are in love. He is going to marry me when his tour ends."

"You are foolish to believe your soldier will take you to America. Father will accept the first proposal he gets. You need to start a family before it is too late."

I believed arranged marriages were not for me. I was convinced life began and ended in Sam's arms. However, Sister Six was right. Love is for dreamers. I am married now.

My husband finally rolls over. "We will try again tomorrow night." His gaze wraps me in tenderness. I feel guilty for not trying to please him. In time, I know I can love him.

# 2 MY LITTLE DOLLY (JULY 1974)

My neighbor's rooster crows this morning like clockwork. It is 5:41 a.m. I roll over to see if Tý is still in bed, but he is not. I slide out of bed with my nightgown clinging to my sweaty thighs and swollen belly. Soon we will meet, my little dolly. I am convinced my baby will be a girl but Tý says she will be a boy. I walk down the hallway to the kitchen and pour a glass of iced coffee with condensed milk. Next to the bowl of sugar apples and soursop fruit is a note with my name on it.

*"Tuyết, I hope you slept well and our son did not keep you up all night. Father needs my help this morning with the cassava crops. Do not wait for me. Belly kisses. I love you."*

"How did you sleep, Aunt Eight?" Tâm's voice carries from the adjacent room.

"Like a prawn pan-fried in soy sauce." I join her on the hammock.

"That bad? This sticky heat is unbearable. Shall we go to the market and get ingredients for lunch?" Tâm grabs a basket to take to the market. "I want spring rolls."

I chuckle. "We should torture your mom by making her cook for us."

"We do that every day."

"True." I take a sip of my coffee. "No shrimp for me, though. It will make me scar. I have a feeling this baby is coming before the next sunrise."

Tâm looks at me, her mouth agape. "You are not due for another month! Besides, no shrimp during pregnancy is an old wives' tale. You are a healthy woman."

"A woman who just turned thirty-five years old."

"Well, with that face, you could still hook every creature out there, if you had not hung up your fishing net."

We laugh and link arms. "Let us go to the market," we say in unison.

As usual, the market is bustling in the city center. Vendors line the perimeters of the square, selling fabric, plastic toys, shoes, jewelry, and clothes.

In the middle of the square, fishermen and their families lay out their catch from that morning. Others sell live frogs, chicken, rice mice, and snakes. We stop at the produce section. I love the kaleidoscope of vibrant colors, each fruit vying for my approval. There are durian, rambutans, longans, dragon fruits, and other exotic produce. Squatting on her haunches, an old woman picks up a large cockroach that is scurrying behind the mangosteen cart. She bites its head off and chews her prize. Crunch. I am horrified.

"You going to buy something, or stare at my mangos?" She pops the last morsel of the insect into her mouth. Tâm and I come home with more fruits than we can consume in a week.

*** 

"Sister Six, what is for dinner?" I saunter into the kitchen. The smell of turmeric and garlic sautéing in the frying pan beckons me.

"Crepes." Oh, how I love bánh xèo! My sister has perfected her recipe. She fries the batter so that it has a nice crunch on the outside, but still soft and savory on the inside.

"Can you make all three of mine with pork belly, onions, and bean sprouts? No shrimp. Shrimp will—"

"Make you scar. Yes, I know. You seriously want three? How are you going to fit through the door when that baby comes?"

"Make it four crepes then." I stick out my tongue. "This baby is coming today. I need my strength. Oh, and make mine extra spicy to induce labor."

Six rolls her eyes at me. She is making the sauce for the crepes, combining fish sauce with lime juice, sugar, chili, garlic, and coconut water. I try to commit to memory how to make the sauce as I enjoy my iced coffee. Strangely, I have not had any strong cravings during my pregnancy. I have been eating a lot of fruits, drinking a lot of coffee, and enjoying every spicy meal Sister Six prepares. To break up the silence, I turn on the radio.

"Richard Nixon, president of the United States of America, has been following the impeachment debate closely, but when the vote came from the House Judiciary Committee, he was nowhere near a television. Instead, he was at Red Beach in Camp Pendleton Marine Base. President Nixon was with his daughter, Tricia, and son-in-law, Edward Cox, when News Secretary, Ron Ziegler, informed him of the vote."

"What are your thoughts on President Nixon's possible impeachment?" I strum my fingers on the table and steal a piece of the pork.

"I have more things to worry about than Nixon. Hand me the big frying pan." Sister Six pours some pig fat into the pan. "So many soldiers come here, get our women pregnant, and leave them. Half-breeds are popping out of the womb like bubbles in boiling water. Every day, there is death and we are all haunted by spirits."

"Do you remember the story of Captain Martinez?"

Captain Martinez served in the U.S. Air Force. He flew an AC-47 gunship, which was nicknamed Puff the Magic Dragon. Tâm spent a few months in Đà

Nẵng where she cleaned the barracks. The men called her little mama-san and referred to her as their hooch maid. Captain Martinez once told Tâm, through a translator, that he felt the pull of nationalism and volunteered for a mission in Việt Nam. He was deployed to Đà Nẵng. At night, the Việt Cộng would launch rockets into their base, so they referred to Đà Nẵng as Rocket City.

"He was one troubled soul to have demons chasing him." Sister Six pours the crepe batter into the sizzling frying pan. The smell of lard permeates the kitchen and I am salivating.

I pop another slice of fried pork belly into my mouth. "He had an angel, not a demon. Captain Martinez was on his way to his bus pick-up after midnight for his 3 a.m. mission that morning. He was strolling and heard someone call his name. 'Captain Martinez, wait.' He stopped and looked around hoping it was his co-pilot, but it was pitch black and he did not see anyone. He shook it off and picked up his pace. Out of the corner of his eye, he saw his bus, so he started to run. He heard again the loud voice scream in his ear 'Captain Martinez, WAIT'. He stopped dead in his tracks and was paralyzed by fear. The hairs on his neck and arms stood up and he was afraid to turn around. By the time he looked up, the bus was gone. Another one finally pulled up twenty-five minutes later. The driver told him he was delayed due to engine problems and had to get another bus. Otherwise, he would have been there sooner. Three-quarter of a kilometer into the ride, Captain Martinez heard an air raid warning, followed by the sound of a humongous BOOM." I take a plate and bang it hard against the table to see Sister Six jump, hoping she will pee her pants a little.

Startled, she swears, "Mother F- I have hot grease here, Eight!"

Feeling quite pleased with myself, I continue. "He looked over his shoulder and saw flames rising one-hundred-fifty meters into the air. He thought maybe a gas truck got hit. He got to his operation and found out that boom he heard thirty minutes before was his aircraft being blown up. What had happened was the crew chief had finished fueling up. There was a loud metallic click and he ran towards the shelter as the rocket flew right into the cockpit. When it blew, it took the gas truck with it." Sister Six stares at me blankly. "So you see, Sister Six, Captain Martinez had an angel—AACCCKKKK!" I wail loudly.

Sister Six jumps. "Not funny. You about gave me a heart attack."

"No, the baby. She is coming. Oh, God."

"He cannot come yet. The crepes are not done!" Sister Six zips back and forth, flailing her arms above her head. I debate whether she resembles Dirty Butt or an orangutan.

*** 

I gave birth to my daughter at 11:53 p.m. on Tuesday, July 30, 1974.

"What is wrong with her?" I can see Tý in the hallway talking to the doctor.

"Mr. Vương, your wife is fine, but your baby, well, her heart does not sound normal. We need to run some tests."

"My daughter looks so frail. There is no color in her face."

"Mr. Vương, your wife is awake. Please, go see her while we tend to your baby." The doctor quickly leaves my husband.

"Tuyết, sweetheart. You are awake. How do you feel?" Tý takes hold of my hand.

"Where is our baby?" My voice is barely above a whisper. I desperately want to see her.

"You will see her soon enough."

"I told you she would be a girl."

Tý smiles at me. "You are right. I have a name picked out for her."

"I hope it is not a common name."

"Can any daughter of ours be common?"

"I like the name Tuyết Mai. She is a part of me so I like Tuyết and Mai for the beauty of the apricot blossoms."

"That is exotic. Mai also means 'tomorrow'. She is our future, and she is beautiful like her mother and the blossoms." Tý caresses my arm.

"You said you had a name picked out?"

"Yes, Thủy-Tiên."

"Water-Angel?"

"Correct, because she is an angel sent from heaven, and like water, she will bring us new life and restore hope during this time of war and drought."

"I like that. Strong like water and pious like angels." I close my eyes.

"Rest. I will be back later." Tý kisses my forehead and exits the room.

I drift off to sleep. In my dreams, I see my baby, lying limp and pale like a little dolly. She is dying.

*** 

The sun is shining brightly. I survey the room and take inventory of the fruits and bundles of sticky rice wrapped in plantain leaves. My stomach growls. Outside my room, the voices are muffled, but one distinct voice can be heard, drowning out the rest.

"These crepes are currently golden and fresh, and unless we see our sister right now, they are going to become old, smelly, and limp crepes, and I shall name them Doctor Vũ crepes, after you." My sister's voice can sound like television static to most people, but if you listen carefully, you can decipher the subliminal message. Sister Six and Brother Seven burst into my room.

"I would still eat the Doctor Vũ crepes," Seven says.

"They are not for you," Sister Six snaps. She rushes to my bed. "I made you some crepes, extra crispy the way you like them. No shrimp."

Never did Sister Six shine more beautifully than she does at this moment. Maybe it is her skin, moist from the tiny beads of perspiration percolating to the surface, now glistening in the sunlight. Perhaps it is her untamed hair, flowing freely over her heaving bosom, which makes her appear feral and ready to fight. My stomach rumbles in protest and reminds me, yes, Sister Six is beautiful because she is holding a plate of warm, delicious crepes.

"I am starving." I eagerly wait for Brother Seven to hand me chopsticks. "Do I get to see my baby today?" Neither of them responds. Their eyes try to convey a message of positivity and joy, as their mouth and face grimace. "Go get Doctor Vũ."

Like a lieutenant following his general's order, Brother Seven is dismissed to carry out a task. There is awkward silence as I avoid eye contact with my sister and resume eating. I am no longer hungry but I fear the wrath of Six if I push my plate aside. I have always been in competition with my sister. She is a strong matriarch, with healthy children, and a strong backbone to take charge. She is always in control and effective when conveying her suggestions. She lives in the real world while I numb my feeling of inadequacy by living in a dream state.

The door opens. Doctor Vũ and Brother Seven walk in, followed by Tâm carrying two fresh coconuts. I am happy to see my niece. One breath later, a nurse comes in, holding a small bundle wrapped in a stained white cloth. My chest feels heavy and I imagine myself being crushed, one rock at a time. My stomach is in knots. There is phlegm in my throat and I suppress the urge to vomit. The nurse gently places the small bundle into my arms. My baby feels lighter than my chicken, Dirty Butt. I cradle her. She peers back at me with her dark eyes. Her pupils, black and round, remind me of longan seeds. Her translucent skin tells me she does not belong on Earth, but on another plane of existence. Her face is round and expressionless. Her blue lips are wrinkled and puckered, like an old lady coming in for a kiss. I am overwhelmed by the exquisite beauty of her ugliness. Her breathing is weak but the rise and fall of her little chest assure me she is alive. The tears fall as I feel the imprint of my baby's love, fear, curiosity, hope, and joy. Perhaps all those emotions are what I am imprinting on her as well.

"Madame, we detect a heart murmur." Doctor Vũ is addressing me, but I only stare at him blankly. "We will want to monitor Thủy-Tiên to see if the murmur resolves itself. I must tell you though that there is a chance one of her heart chambers has a hole in it, and if the murmur is a pathological one, her condition will worsen."

"What do you mean?" I push aside my plate and sit up.

"If her respiratory rate increases, if she fails to grow at a normal rate, meaning her height and weight is stunted, if her heart rate and rhythm are abnormal, and if her energy level is low or she is always fatigued…These signs mean you must take her to the hospital right away. You will need to go to Sài Gòn or perhaps Thái Lan for the surgery to repair the hole."

"Thailand? Surgery? I cannot afford this!"

"Our hospital is not equipped to handle the situation if your baby has a pathological murmur and requires surgery. If she does not get prompt treatment, she can die. Most babies will survive and be fine though, so do not worry."

"That is enough for now." Sister Six dismisses the doctor and nurse. "Let her rest. Go find someone else's spirit to break." She scowls at them as they exit.

All I can replay in my mind are his words of 'she can die' and I sob. The waves of anxiety crash in on me and I cannot breathe. Tâm wraps her arms around me and rocks me as if I am her child, not her aunt. My brother is silent. I suspect he feels oafish finding himself in unfamiliar territory. Crying women make him nervous. He is a strong disciplinarian when it comes to his family, being the man of the household, but when it comes to his two sisters, he gives us the stage.

"This is not fair!" I scream and break free of Tâm's arms. "I have done everything right in my life. I have been good to everyone, to my parents, to my family, to my neighbors, to God! I am good to animals and I never swear! I even went to college five hours from home while you all got to stay here! Instead of marrying Sam, I get an arranged marriage to a man I do not love! And now this? The one thing I want most in my life is to have a baby of my own, who will love me and be with me. My baby is supposed to be beautiful and healthy and smart. She is meant to grow up to be successful. She is supposed to outlive me, see the world, and do better than me. She will not get that chance now! Oh, Mary, Mother of God!" I wail in anguish. My siren cry alarms Brother Seven.

Sister Six strokes my hair. "Get it out of your system. Be angry and woeful. Scream, swear, cry. Do what you need to do."

This is the first time she talks to me with such tenderness and empathy. I remind myself to remember this moment the next time her sandpaper tongue scolds me.

"Fuuccckkkk! Mother Fucker!" I let loose the kraken tongue and the swear words propel. Surprisingly, I start to feel better. "Fuck. Mother Fucker. Ass…Doctor's Ass…Vũ Crepe Fucker!" I scream some more and trip over the words.

This swearing thing is new to me. The tears marathon down my cheeks to my chin. Every breath of air I grasp sends my chest and shoulders into heavy convulsions. I cling to the hope that my dolly will be fine, that she will not need surgery, and that the murmur, whatever that is, resolves itself. Time ticks on slowly until my heaving becomes rhythmic, my tears subside, and I exhale in calm defeat.

"Are you done?" Sister Six asks. I nod, letting out a big sigh. "Feel better?" I nod again. "Good." She laughs at me. I take offense at her mockery. "That is the worse windmill swearing I have ever heard! 'Vũ Crepe Fucker'? Really?"

A smile creeps up on Tâm's and Brother Seven's face. The four of us laugh hysterically.

# 3 SHE-JEKYLL (APRIL 1975)

My daughter slumps against our red, vinyl chair. Propped up beside her is a tiny doll. Today Thủy-Tiên and her doll are twins, both wearing yellow onesies. Their round face and dark eyes mirror each other. I look at both angelic faces. The doll smiles at me. Her golden locks of hair peek out from under her hoodie. She looks happy and at peace. I look at Thủy-Tiên and I see a fallen angel. Her wavy black hair tussles with the crimson cushions. For the past five minutes, she has been struggling to push herself up, but her marshmallow arms fail her. At eight months old, she is barely bigger than her doll and almost as pliant. Her body falls forward and sideways.

"You can do it, my angel. Use your legs to push yourself up against the armchair." I smile encouragingly at my daughter and hope the enthusiasm in my voice serves as arms to lift her up. Thủy-Tiên's brows crinkle with anger and she rolls off the chair.

Like watching a movie in slow motion, I see her body hit the cold surface of the tiles. Her right temple ricochets off the floor and her nose smashes into the leg of the chair. Blood drips down her face and a piercing cry sends shock waves down my body.

Tý and Tree run into the room. "What happened?" They speak in unison.

"Thủy-Tiên fell off the chair." I feel disconnected from the situation.

Tý scoops up his daughter effortlessly and takes her into the kitchen. Her screams are so loud, they can split a tree.

"You look tired." As usual, Tree does not inquire, but rather, states a fact. "I will watch Thủy-Tiên while you nap."

"Wake me up if she gets too difficult for you. There is a jar of yogurt left if she gets hungry. Tell your uncle to pick me up some chicken congee and Chinese donuts. I will be hungry when I wake."

I look forward to taking a nap on my hammock underneath the coconut

---

and banana trees. I have what Tý calls "hammock-grin" whenever I smile thinking about laying down for a nap. I walk outside to the back garden. Dirty Butt struts toward me.

"Mông Dơ, you are my best friend." I bend down and pat my chicken's head. Her beady eyes look at me blankly, but I pretend she understands. I pick her up and carry her to the outhouse with me. "Do you know what the secret to a good nap is?" I pause to give her the opportunity to answer. "Why, an empty bladder and empty bowel, of course."

I giggle as if sharing this secret with Dirty Butt makes us kindred spirits. Dirty Butt flaps her wings, perhaps in agreement, or perhaps in protest. I put her down before she uses me as a scratching post. I saunter onto the rickety boardwalk leading to the outhouse that juts three meters from the edge of the pond. The catfish swim toward the outhouse. I squat above the pond with my feet steadily balanced on top of two parallel wooden boards so as not to fall in.

The hum of Tý's scooter starts up. I recognize the rattle of the motor. "Tell your aunt I will be back in a couple hours. I have some errands to run."

"Remember the congee and donuts," yells Tree.

I hover for another minute before quickly washing myself with the bucket of water. I head to the hammock and see from the window my nephew inside the kitchen. He ladles a small amount of water over Thủy-Tiên's head and runs his fingers through her hair to spike it into a mohawk. He laughs. She looks like an emu. Fifteen minutes go by. I swing back and forth, letting the cool breeze lull me to sleep. My thoughts drift to Sam, back to December of 1971.

***

A man with a mustache appeared at the front entrance of my family's house. I did not recognize him at first. He was wearing blue jeans and a white cotton shirt that said 'God Is Our Copilot'. His eyes were covered by dark aviator sunglasses. Then he smiled and his dimple made an appearance.

"Sam!" I squealed, with a mixture of excitement and fretfulness. "What you doing here?" I wanted to run and nestle myself into his arms, but that would not have been appropriate.

"Snow, I'm on R and R!"

"What RNR?" I ushered him into the kitchen.

"Rest and recuperation." He flashed a smile that could make me swoon.

I returned his smile, not wanting him to suspect that his village girl did not understand the word 'recuperation'. We sat down at the kitchen table. "You stay to eat dinner? I have my sister make some rice and rabbit?"

"R and R! You are a clever woman. I am on leave for two weeks. Did you get my last letter?"

"No. Maybe I get soon. Please, stay."

We had the house to ourselves. Sister Six was playing cards with our neighbors, Tú and Vân, gambling as usual. Brother Seven was at work. Everyone else was at the market. I feared they would come home to find me

16

alone with a man in the house.

"So, in my letter, I wrote that I was getting transferred from Tuy Hoa to Phu Cat. Also, I was eligible for R and R and wanted to see if I could visit you during my vacation. There is no one I'd rather see."

I blushed. "I will talk to my father. You maybe stay in Tâm's room. She still in Đà Nẵng. She take care of the air force camp. She not want to work at bank anymore."

"Why? Will she come home for Christmas?" Sam inquired.

"Yes, she plan come home. She can take my room with me if my father allow you to stay."

Sam cupped his hand on top of mine. "I've missed you."

Fearing Sam could feel my trembling hand beneath his warm, calloused one, I stood up and distanced myself from him. His presence in my home made me nervous.

My words petered out as I corralled the conversation back to my niece. "Tâm not happy at bank. She want to be teller, in front, talk to customers. Ice tea?" I did not let Sam answer and mechanically poured him a cup, hoping he had not noticed the drop of amber liquid that fell to the floor. "She say only pretty girls get promotion."

"Snow, I have not been able to get you out of my mind."

"I tell Tâm she have to be good with math and speak good English."

"I want to marry you when my tour is up." He took off his sunglasses and pierced me with his pleading eyes.

"I get promotion and she quit." I waited for Sam to say something.

My lips quivered. My heart pounded so hard, it tenderized my flesh. His eyes beckoned me to come to him. I wanted to feel his lips on mine and run my fingers through his hair, but I froze. To show him physical affection was not proper etiquette. I wanted to reassure Sam that I returned his amorous feelings, but that would mean cooking for him. My cooking would kill him faster than the war would.

"You will get cross-eyed if you stare any harder." Sister Six waltzed in and focused her attention on Sam as if he was on display at the curiosity shop. She shifted her gaze over to me. "He is pretty." As abruptly and quietly as she entered the room, so Sister Six left.

Sam stayed with our family the two weeks he was on rest. Tâm came home from Đà Nẵng and brought us food she snuck out of the barracks. Sister Six prepared an amazing feast for Christmas. There we were, all eleven of us sitting together. There was my father, Sister Six, her husband Thắng, my nieces Tâm and Trinh, Brother Seven, his wife Hiền, and their two sons Tree and Tuấn. The women slaved in the kitchen for days prepping our holiday feast. I was excluded from those duties.

Sister Six pushed me out of the kitchen. "Your job is to be the interpreter between Sam and the men while they eat, drink, and tell bad jokes." In other words, my presence was a hindrance, not a help.

Sam tried to help in the kitchen as well, but my father would not have it. "Daughter, tell Sam that women cook and men drink."

My father and Sam ping-ponged between Vietnamese beliefs versus Western beliefs, good beer and bad beer, and whether the *Vespa* made by *Piaggio* was worth owning.

"Mr. Sang, the *Vespa* gets incredible gas mileage," argued Sam. "It's a beautiful Italian scooter. It's fast and fun to ride. It has good storage compartments too."

"Those mopeds are too expensive and ugly. The Italians did a sexy job with the *Maserati*, the *Ferrari*, and the *Lamborghini*, even the *Ducati*, but with the *Vespa*, they got it wrong."

My father and Sam bantered back and forth until dinner was ready. The table was adorned with roasted duck, grilled pork, pickled carrots and cucumbers, mango salad, taro soup with shrimp, steamed rice, and a couple of things I did not recognize. One plate had thin strips of reddish-brownish yellow meat, while the other plate had something that reminded me of Chinese sausages.

Seeing my curious gaze on the plates, Tâm volunteered. "I got those from the air force base. They eat this every day. There was so much, I did not think they would miss a few."

Tree grabbed a strip of meat and took a bite. His eyes lit up. "This is amazing! It is crunchy and salty, but also a little chewy and tender." He grabbed three more strips and crumbled it over his bowl of rice.

Sam was amused. "He likes the bacon. It's cured meat made from pork." Sam pointed to the sausage rolls. "This here is what we call hot dogs."

My sister dipped her bacon into the taro soup. "The bacon is very fatty. Tomorrow I will fry some rice in the lard."

I fell in love with Corporal Sam Hammond that night over bacon and hot dogs.

***

Tree's voice slices into my memories of Sam. "Thủy-Tiên is throwing up."

"Did you feed her anything?" I roll out of the hammock.

"A few spoons of yogurt like you said."

I clear the vomit out of my baby's mouth with my finger. Thủy-Tiên cries and objects to me invading her tongue and gums. She throws up again and I am unsure if it is a gag reflex or normal regurgitation after eating.

"She is throwing up again?" Tý appears at the doorway and looks concerned.

"What is wrong with her? One day she is pale, the next she is blue. She cries all the time and throws up as often as she poops." I am exasperated.

Tree walks over to Tý, takes the bag from my husband's hand, and heads towards the kitchen. "This must be the congee. I will get a bowl."

"Tree, grab a towel and clean up the vomit too." My husband takes hold of my wrist. "We need to talk." Once inside our bedroom, I put my dolly on our bed. "Sweetheart, we need to leave Vĩnh Bình." I cast him a defiant look. "The Việt Cộng and northern forces have already taken control of Ban Mê Thuột, Huế, Đà Nẵng, and Nha Trang."

"No. I cannot leave my family." I notice Thủy-Tiên is trying to suck on my hairbrush. I take it from her and she cries.

Impatience simmers in Tý's eyes. "I am your family now. Pack your bags. We leave at two in the morning. And do not tell your family."

"I cannot say goodbye to them?" I hand my daughter her doll.

"You will do as I say and not question me."

My anger brews. "At least tell me where we are going."

"Sài Gòn. It will be safe there. President Thiệu is already mobilizing his forces to protect our capital and the presidential palace."

"Are you sure? And what about your parents?" I ask.

"I talked to my mother and father this afternoon." Tý's words slap me in the face.

"So you said your goodbyes to your family and I cannot say goodbye to mine?" I cannot believe the double standard.

"Pack light. One bag. We leave at 2 a.m. sharp." Tý leaves the room.

I question who this man is that I have married. My stomach turns in knots. A combination of hunger and distress descends upon me. I did not question him when we married and lived with my family instead of his. I do not question him when he disappears for hours, sometimes days at a time. And when he surprises me with money or gifts, still, I do not question my husband. Why now, do I demand answers? Suspicion gnaws at me, yet I cannot explain the root of my feelings.

Tree clears his throat before coming into my room. "I brought you the congee and Chinese donut."

"I am not hungry." I fall to the bed next to Thủy-Tiên and force myself not to cry.

***

The long bus ride from Vĩnh Bình, in the Mekong Delta, to the big city is bumpy. Every seat is occupied by a man, woman, or child, as young as one month old to as elderly as eighty-two. We arrive in District One at six o'clock in the morning. Nostalgia engulfs me. The last time I was in Sài Gòn was 1961. I was twenty-two years old, studying mathematics and English at the university. The United States of America had elected John F. Kennedy as their president, and President Ngô Đình Diệm was re-elected to power in South Việt Nam. The Americans were mass producing military personnel and exporting them to my country. The Sài Gòn I see now is no longer the same as when I was in college. Today, I do not see many American military or government workers in the streets. They have been replaced by the Sài Gòn army. President Gerald Ford is

19

currently America's puppet master, while President Nguyễn Văn Thiệu is ours. One thing that is unchanged between 1961 and today, April 11, 1975, is the sound of motorbikes competing with street vendors, who argue over trivial details, as they set up their booth outside the Bến Thành Market.

As the bus approaches the intersection, I see the presidential palace on the left. A few days ago, a South Vietnamese Air Force pilot dropped bombs on the palace and abandoned his cause in favor of the Việt Cộng's. Surprisingly, there is not much damage to the building. Our country's flag, yellow with three horizontal red stripes, still flies high above in the center of the building. Looking equally grand and ominous, the palace appears deserted behind the iron gates.

"Where are we going?" I ask.

"We are almost there," Tý says.

It is pointless to ask again. Thủy-Tiên sleeps soundly in my arms. I am thankful she made it through the night without any incidents. As we continue on Thống Nhất Boulevard, I see a company of Vietnamese soldiers. They walk toward the palace and grip their AK-47 rifles. One of them makes eye contact with me. I immediately shift my gaze ahead. A convoy of tanks rolls by. We pass the U.S. embassy. The building is white, big, ugly, and nondescript. Outside, posted on the gate is a sign that reads: *"PETITIONERS: Only petitions for wives and children accepted now. We will inform you when a petition for other relatives will be accepted."*

"Are we leaving our country?" I glance down at Thủy-Tiên again. Her innocence warms my heart. The thought of fleeing scares me.

Tenderness returns to Tý's face. "Sweetheart, yes. Soon. The Americans are leaving. The communists are on our doorstep. Too much blood has been shed."

I am lost for words so we ride in silence. A few minutes later, the bus stops. Tý stands up and collects our bags. I follow his lead. We walk a short distance down an alley.

"Will we be staying with your brother?" I remember Tý's younger brother lives in the city. I met him at my wedding reception.

"I have a surprise for you, Sweetheart." With a twinkle in his eye and the first charming smile he has cracked in days, Tý stops to unlock and roll up a garage door. It is empty inside except for a red scooter. "Welcome home."

"Home? I thought we were leaving the country?" I am confused.

"We are. This is a temporary home. Upstairs there is a mattress for us to sleep on and the kitchen has a few basics."

"And the *Honda*?" I point to the scooter. "How did you get your hands on one of those?"

"A friend of mine. He imports parts and assembles them here. We will not be here for long, but until then, it is yours to ride." Tý winks at me. "The woman living next to us is a good woman. I have already met her and she can watch Thủy-Tiên whenever you need."

"How did you...? When did you...? Forget it. What is her name?" I walk over to the scooter and run my fingers over the sleek body.

"Mrs. Trần. She is expecting you to introduce yourself while I go to the post office." Tý gives me a kiss on the cheek and walks out.

"Wait. You are not taking the scooter?" I ask.

"Sweetheart, these calves are not muscular from riding. I was born to run."

"You are crazy. No other man lifts weights or runs for fun, except you."

"No other man has a beautiful wife to protect as I do." He can be endearing when he wants to be. "Also, maybe if you learned how to cook, I would not be running all the time to fetch you food." He dashes out the door before I can find something to throw at him.

*** 

Mrs. Trần is a nice woman if you consider being tortured with a sixty-grit sheet of sandpaper on your lady parts, nice. And if pugnacious and neurotic are acceptable, then she is the epitome of a psychotic and delusional woman. She is my sister Six, cloned one too many times, and is the annoying sliver of bok choy that is stuck in my teeth, relentlessly reminding me that she is still there, regardless of how tactfully I try to circumvent her. Despite her corkscrew demeanor, she is loving and attentive to Thủy-Tiên and flutters around my little dolly like a raptor protecting her young.

"Only ugly girls have short hair." Mrs. Trần criticizes my haircut. "It is too curly like pubic hair." Mrs. Trần's need to degrade me without any filters makes me feel like my helmet is on backward. She outwits me every time when I give her tit for tat. "I hear you cannot cook either. A handsome man like your husband can do better. Must be your big chest that has him blinded."

Today I choose to bite my tongue and remind myself, not much longer. Secretly, I hope her ripe, spotted skin spontaneously combusts. "Mrs. Trần, I am riding into the Bến Thành Market. Can I get you anything? Persimmons? Pineapples?" Mrs. Trần opens her mouth and points at her teeth. The cavern that is her mouth showcases decaying gums and rotting teeth. No doubt, it is home to a rabid bat. "I will get bananas for you then."

I kiss my baby on her forehead. One glance at Mrs. Trần and I ride off, down the alley to connect to the main street. I approach the U.S. embassy and shake my head. It is such an ugly building. The only redeeming feature on the property is the tamarind tree that stands tall and protective. I imagine how grand the building can be with a few strokes of Van Gogh's brush, as he paints the bland canvas into 'The Starry Night'. In the distance I see Tý. He stands with both hands in his pockets. He looks left and right as he negotiates when to cross. The flood of mopeds, cars, and bicycles speed by in disorderly fashion, zig-zagging around pedestrians. Most of the mopeds carry two passengers while some have pigs, ducks, or chickens strapped to the front and back, piled as high as feasible without losing balance. Tý crosses the road with ease. I plan to stop and invite him for a beer or iced coffee.

I slow down and make my way to the right side of the street. An American woman greets Tý with a hug. *Who is that?* Her fingers dovetail with his and they walk into a toy store together. I leave my shoes at the entrance, as is customary, and follow them in, careful to keep my distance. Tý and the American woman speak to the store owner.

In perfect Vietnamese, the petite woman addresses the store proprietor. "Brother Cường, will you give us a good price for this toy airplane? Our son turns five tomorrow."

"Sister Annette, consider it a gift for your son. Your husband and I have a long history together." The store owner removes the airplane from the display case and hands it to her.

She gladly accepts. "Really? You will have to tell me about it."

"Annette, another time." Tý ushers the American woman towards the exit. I quickly dash behind some big kites hanging from the ceiling. "You should get back to our son. I have business to discuss with Cường." The woman kisses Tý on the lips. "I do not like displays of affection outside of closed doors." Tý distances himself from her.

"Yes, that is the Vietnamese culture, but no one can see us except our friend Cường," she replies, again, in perfect Vietnamese. She waves to the store owner. "Thank you for the gift. Timothy will be happy with his new toy."

I am betrayed. I am angry. My knees feel weak. Who is this American woman that regards my husband with such intimacy and candor? She retrieves her shoes at the foot of the entrance and backs her scooter off the sidewalk. She is not much taller than me, perhaps one and a half meters tall. It is like discovering there is an American doppelganger version of me, except her short, wavy hair has bangs that cling to her forehead.

Tý's voice forces me to refocus. "Where is the money?" Cường hands over a child's messenger bag. Tý opens the flap and peeks inside. "If it is not all there--"

"It is all there," confirms Cường.

Tý walks out of the store. I am in disbelief at the Nixonian blow that has transpired. What lie has he been living?

I intend to find out.

***

Early the next morning, I ride to Cường's toy store. "Hello. Do you have any toy airplanes?"

"We have these two." He points to the airplanes in the glass display case behind him. I feign interest as I inspect the two models.

"How is business?" I attempt small talk to get a feel for how aggressively I should barter. He ignores my question. "How much for this one?" I intend to buy the same airplane the American woman acquired.

"One-hundred-fifty thousand piasters." He walks away from me.

"Here is eighty thousand." I put the money on the display case. I am in no mood to haggle. He is either going to take it or lose a sale. I leave the store with my purchase and ride to the Bến Thành Market to pick up pastries, barbecue pork buns, and coffee.

As soon as I get home, I hear Mrs. Trần. "Thủy-Tiên is sleeping." Mrs. Trần picks up the toy airplane. "You know you have a daughter, right?"

"Yes, Mrs. Trần." I already feel my skin pulled by her grating presence.

"My sons used to fight over toys like this airplane. I have not seen my oldest for eight years and my youngest for five years. My oldest son joined the North Vietnamese Army while my youngest joined the Republic's army. Since they were children, they always fought against each other and gave me grief, but I love my sons. Even my stupid husband...I loved him too. Now, I am an old woman, all alone."

"What happened to your husband?" My hardened heart thaws toward her. This is the first cordial conversation I have with the she-Jekyll.

"Stupidity killed him. He should have been home to celebrate Tết with me. He was out getting treats for the Lunar New Year celebration but decided to stop into work at the radio station, twenty minutes before the building exploded." Mrs. Trần slowly stands up and winces. I step toward her to assist. "Do not touch me, you stupid girl."

And there it is. Mrs. Hyde returns and casts aside the she-Jekyll. I do not understand Mrs. Trần's mood swings. I have always been taught to respect my elders and never offer an opinion. To bring honor to my parents, I had to be demurring, obedient and accommodating. Now I feel there is a Mrs. Hyde inside of me too that is begging to be let free.

"I do not understand why you hate me. I have shown you only kindness and respect. It is evident you care for my daughter and take good care of her, but, forgive me for asking, what have I done to make you bitter towards me?" I hold my breath for her reply.

"You are weak and blind. Open your eyes, you foolish girl. Your daughter is dying. Your husband is a traitor."

"What do you mean he is a traitor?"

She ignores my question. "You have everything and yet, you do not appreciate what you have. You make too many assumptions. I do not hate you, girl. I pity you, and I worry for Thủy-Tiên, to be so innocent and already cursed. There is a war going on and still, you live in a bubble." Mrs. Trần pauses and I am too stunned to speak. "I see the tears forming in your eyes. I do not give you permission to cry. One day you will be my age, and you will lose everything you hold dear, and even then, you cannot cry. You take your fears and turn them into rage. You take the energy spent on wallowing and blaze a path towards survival. In the end, you are the only person you can trust. Your tongue, not your beauty, is your greatest artillery. Say what you want. Love who you want. Take what you want. Understand?"

"I am afraid," I whisper.

At that moment, Tý walks in the door.

"Then you will teach your daughter to also live in fear." Mrs. Trần nods to Tý and takes her leave.

"What were you two talking about?" Tý sees the toy airplane and says nothing.

"I purchased a toy for Thủy-Tiên." I nod towards the airplane. "We left Vĩnh Bình so quickly, and since you only let me pack one small bag, I wanted to get her something. She misses her doll."

"Fine, but you should have bought a small ball or stuffed animal," Tý says coldly.

"Well, maybe she can play with her brother, Timothy." I brace myself for his reaction.

Tý stiffens his posture but says nothing. Instead, he grabs a bottle of alcohol from his bag and pours the clear liquid into a glass. I recognize the red label. It is *Maotai*, the official liquor the Chinese use when they want to entertain and impress distinguished guests such as foreign dignitaries. Tý hands me the glass and takes a swig from the bottle.

"That bottle costs two hundred U.S. dollars. Your parents lost their cassava farm last year from the bombs so I know their wealth is gone. How are you affording this? How did you afford the *Honda*? Did you steal all of this?"

"You are asking too many questions." Tý leans on the scooter and takes another sip from the bottle.

"I am not asking enough questions," I say.

Tý picks up the airplane. He says nothing. He sits down on the hard floor, cross-legged, and leans against the wall. "You have some nerve." He takes another drink.

"ANSWER ME!" I scream. "Who is that American woman you were with yesterday?"

"Sweetheart, you are the love of my life."

"Then who is Annette? Why was she kissing you? Why is her Vietnamese so perfect?"

"Calm down. Annette and I met a long time ago when I was in America, studying at the Milwaukee Institute of Technology. We ran into each other five years ago in Sài Gòn."

"Five years ago? Have you been together for the past five years?"

"She is a linguist and works at the embassy for the Americans as a translator. She got pregnant so we married."

I cannot believe this. "So I am your second wife and your son, Timothy, turns five today."

"You have to know, you are the love of my life."

"STOP SAYING THAT!" I shout. "Why did you marry me?"

"You were so graceful and charming. I had to make you mine."

"Are you not even going to say you are sorry? My heart already belonged to another man. I married you because you and my father made an arrangement, not because I loved you, or that I was desperate. Sam and I--"

"AND WHERE IS YOUR SAM NOW?" Tý's nostrils flare. He stands up and punches the wall. "Your soldier. Where is he now? Yes, your father told me all about your GI, how he stayed with your family for two weeks and spent Christmas with you, how he asked your father's permission to marry you after his tour ended, and how he was going to take you back to Washington state."

"Sam will always be more of a man than you. At least I was enough for him but apparently, one wife is not enough for you, is it? Any others I should know about?"

Tý lunges forward in one long stride and grips my wrist. "You were thirty-four years old with no husband and pining for a man you could never have. What man would start a family with an old virgin who burns everything she cooks? I SAVED YOU FROM YOURSELF!"

Mrs. Trần's voice creeps in my head. *I do not give you permission to cry.* I yank my arm away and free myself from his grip. "What other secrets are you keeping from me? Why did Cường give you a bag of money?" *You take your fears and turn them into rage.*

"I work for Mr. H." Tý kicks the airplane and sends it gliding across the floor. "He is one of Đại Cathay's generals."

His confession triggers my spring-loaded eyelids to open wide. "Đại was a mobster. Are you insane? You work for one of the Four Great Kings? I thought his gang disintegrated after his death in Phú Quốc?"

"No. His men still have operations underground." Ty drowns himself in more of the clear liquid.

"So you were extorting money from that store owner?"

"No. I was collecting the money from Cường, who also works for Mr. H."

"You are going to get us killed. What else?" I demand.

"You already know too much. Listen, I have exit visas for us. We leave in a week. Annette is getting us out of the country and--"

"Of course she is," I interrupt with sarcasm, "because you are her husband and we are what? The poor relatives? Does she think I am your unmarried sister, raising a child by myself? Tell me, are you the love of her life?" Mrs. Trần's message echoes in my head. *Say what you want. Take what you want. Love who you want.*

"Damn it! I have been saving my money to bribe officials to get you and Thủy-Tiên out."

"I am not going anywhere with you and I sure as hell want nothing to do with that woman."

"You are being stupid and ungrateful. Think of our daughter. It is not safe here. She will have a better chance in America, and she can get the medical attention she needs there."

I grit my teeth. "Then what? We all live together as one happy family? I am stupid to have married you, but leaving you will be the smartest thing I do." I grab the glass of *Maotai* and down half of the distilled spirit. My throat burns. I cringe at the taste but force myself to not give Tý the satisfaction of seeing me gag. I walk up the stairs to the bedroom, with my glass of Maotai in hand, to get away from him. His presence sickens me.

Tý follows me. "Sweetheart?"

"What?" I swivel around to face him from the top of the stairs.

Tý takes an envelope from his pocket and places it on the steps. "In one week, meet me in front of Cường's store at 8 a.m. We will be picked up and taken to the airport. Take this envelope with you and a small bag. Your and Thủy-Tiên's visas and paperwork are in the envelope. Do not be late."

"You do not understand. I am leaving you." I throw back the rest of the *Maotai*.

"And sweetheart, happy birthday."

How ironic that I share the same birthday as Timothy. I hurl my glass at Tý's head. It is too bad I miss. "A bottle of *Maotai* and exit visas...Yes. Happy birthday to me."

# 4 SECOND FIDDLE (APRIL 20, 1975)

A week has gone by. It is 7 a.m. A throbbing headache pulses its way from the base of my neck to my forehead and temples. I imagine the blood vessels inside my head are the Cu Chi tunnels, each harboring little Việt Cộng soldiers who pound at the walls and inflict this persistent pain. The stress of meeting Tý in an hour in front of Cường's toy store has me questioning if this is the right decision for Thủy-Tiên and me. I look at my watch. Only three minutes have gone by. I turn my attention to my sleeping baby. Her perfect little mouth quivers as if she is speaking in her dreams. Those cheeks! Oh, those perfectly round, soft, chubby little cheeks. She looks healthy and peaceful when she sleeps. Her pale skin in the morning light appears pure, as if God, Himself, was emanating His light through her wafer skin. I admire her black curly hair and the cowlick on her hairline. I caress her tiny hand. My heart swells with love and I am moved to tears. *I will always protect you, my little dolly.* I let her sleep a little longer while I gather our belongings.

From my bedroom I see Mrs. Trần sweeping the stoop that leads to the backyard of her home. She is balding. The gray wispy strands hang wildly, searching for the comfort of a bun that is not there this morning. I see her as a frail old woman, wearing her rags like a second set of skin. I hope one day her sons will come home to take care of her. I am a little sad to leave her behind. What will become of her? Her leathery feet are cracked and calloused. She shuffles around sweeping an already immaculate door front. She sets the broom aside and pulls down her pants. She is not wearing any underwear! Mrs. Trần leans forward and I can see her buttocks swaying side to side. She scowls at me for spying on her.

I dart my eyes over to Thủy-Tiên. Her small black eyes peer intently at me. She no longer looks like the angelic sleeping baby. Her pale skin is sickly yellow; her lips purse into a sour pucker. I quickly give her the toy airplane to play with.

It is now 7:28 a.m. I scoop up Thủy-Tiên and head over to Mrs. Trần's house to say goodbye.

Her door is open so I walk in and set Thủy-Tiên down on the floor. She crawls to the hammock, tugs at it, and gives me a big smile. She has hammock-grin too. I scoop her up into the hammock. She is content lying there holding her airplane while I swing her back and forth. Mrs. Trần's house smells of incense, lemongrass, and the sweet smell of overly ripe fruits. I see on her wall photos of her mother, father, mother-in-law, father-in-law, and husband. Incense burns at the "veneration of the dead" altar with an offering of cherimoya fruits and papayas. Five bowls filled with rice and grilled meats along with sets of chopsticks are also laid out. A large gold-plated figure of Buddha sits above the photos.

"Mrs. Trần?" I call out. She appears from the back room.

"Did you like the view?" She mocks me. The image of her buttocks rushes back to me.

"I came to say goodbye. I want to wish you good luck and will ask for Buddha to bestow on you peace. May you be reborn with enlightenment and good--"

"So you are leaving with him." It was a statement, not a question, and a rather bitter one.

"Yes. He is my husband and it is not safe here. Thủy-Tiên will likely need surgery and America is her best chance." I take out my handkerchief and unfold it. "I have a gift for you." I hold up the gold necklace that Tý's parents gave me on my wedding day. The ruby eyes of the phoenix pendant are especially blood-red in this light. "Tý's mother gave me this gift. She told me the phoenix is for strength and courage. I want you to have it. You need this more than I do, and if one day you find that life is too unbearable, I want you to sell it. It is worth a lot of money."

Mrs. Trần's eyes open wide. "Child, I am not worthy of such a fine gift." The tears slide down her cheek.

"I insist." I take hold of her hand and turn it palm up. I place the necklace in her small trembling hand. Despite her ratchety and abrasive personality, I understand Mrs. Trần is human after all. "Thủy-Tiên and I will always be indebted to you."

Mrs. Trần shakes her head. "Last week, I said your husband was a traitor. Let me explain." She puts the phoenix necklace into a copper coffee tin. "Tý used to serve in the South Vietnamese Army. My youngest son joined him five years ago. When your husband showed up here with you and Thủy-Tiên, living a normal civilian life, I was suspicious, because I had seen him before with an American woman and a little boy, half white, half Vietnamese. His face is square and his eyes dark, like your husband's. What am I to think, but that he is a traitor to his country, his women, and the children in his care, not to mention he abandoned my boy?"

"I see," I say coldly. I scoop up Thủy-Tiên. "I will use my documents to get to America and once I am there, I will leave my husband. I have a friend in Washington who can help me. Take care of yourself."

I return to the house, collect my bag, and put it in the compartment under the seat of my scooter. I grab the sheet off the mattress and tie a sling around my waist and shoulders. I tug at the knots to make sure they are tight and secure. "We are going for a ride, my baby. I am afraid you will have to leave your airplane, but I promise to get you a better toy."

I put Thủy-Tiên into the sling and start up the scooter. My baby cries for her airplane. Memories of Sky and Sam sweep over me. A week after Sam spent Christmas with my family and returned to base from his R and R, his letter finally arrived. I cannot believe that was over three years ago.

*"My lovely Snow,*

*We had a barbecue last night on the base to celebrate the holidays. My new CO (Commanding Officer) sent Sky and me into Tuy Hoa city to get some ice, charcoal, and lobster if we could find any. We did. I have a ¾ ton truck assigned to me now. Sky scored some dope from a boysan for cheap. All the guys were drinking, smoking a joint, and having a good time. One guy got a little too drunk and tried to kiss us. It was actually funny. He has two women back home waiting for him. He couldn't make up his mind which one he liked better and vowed he'd marry the one who was the better kisser. I guess he thought Sky and I were his girlfriends. Snow, you will never be second fiddle to anyone.*

*At the barbecue, the CO gave a speech and announced we were getting transferred to Phu Cat. I'm not happy about that, because it means I will be farther away from you. I also like being on the beach. The Viet Cong don't have a navy. I'm thankful to the man upstairs for putting me on the shores of Tuy Hoa. Anyways, my extension ends soon. I'll be on the freedom bird, getting out of the army in March next year. You and I can start our life together!*

*Tet is two months away and we've been doing drills with our M-16s. I try to keep mine oiled and cleaned in case Charlie attacks our base. I'll be one of the guys in the foxholes for a few days during Tet. Pray for me.*

*I've been granted some R and R. That means rest and recuperation. There is nowhere I'd rather be than with you. If it is all right with you and your family, I would like to come for a visit. I have a question to ask you.*

*With love and anticipation,*

*Sam (December 4, 1971)*

*P.S. There is another guy that is DEROS'ing (going home) and he is selling me his refrigerator. I can soon put my stash of Rainier beer at arm's reach. Back home in Seattle, that's all I drink because it's brewed there in Washington State. Cold beer makes me happy, but you keep me alive."*

Sam gifted me a book that Christmas, *'A Separate Reality'* by Carlos Castaneda, explaining that there was an alternate world beyond our perceived reality. He promised he would read it to me. In my bag under the seat compartment are Sam's letter, the book, two outfits each for Thủy-Tiên and me, my poncho, and the envelope containing our exit visas.

I ride through the alley and wave one last goodbye to Mrs. Trần. She waves back and gives us a sad, toothless grin. I merge onto the main road with other motorists. The sun beams down bright and hot. I squint from the glare of the light. I glance at my watch. It is five minutes to 8 a.m. I will be late. I pick up the pace. Thủy-Tiên has stopped crying. I honk my horn and speed up a little more to pass a family of three. I cannot miss the pickup in front of Cường's store. This is our chance to go to America, to start a new life. Beside me, there is another scooter. He is keeping pace with me. I slow down to let him pass but he slows down too. I speed up. He speeds up. I recognize the man as Tý's younger brother, Hải.

A boy, three years old, half black, half Vietnamese, runs out to catch his spinning top toy. Both of us swerve to avoid hitting the child. Hải falls and crashes into a tamarind tree. I feel bad, but see him get up so I keep going. Two hundred meters ahead is Cường's store. There is a silver Mercedes Sprinter van out front. I am not too late! Tý is standing on the sidewalk. He paces in circles, stops, shifts his weight to his left leg, and paces again. His blue jeans accentuate the bowness of his legs. One hand is pulling at his hair. The other hand is flailing. His head swings left, right, and left again. He is clearly agitated. I am less than one-hundred meters from the store. A slender arm extends from the van and grabs Tý's wrist. A diminutive woman steps out and pulls at him to get into the van. It is Annette. A small boy hops off the van and grabs hold of Tý's hand. I swallow a big lump in my throat. Timothy! I let off the throttle and slow down to a stop. Other than my beating heart, the only other sound I strain to hear is the muffled cry of a desperate American woman pleading to Tý to get into the van. Annette's tiny frame is no match for him as she pushes and pulls. The veins in his forearms flare prominently; the muscles on his back and neck tense and bulge. They take turns jabbing at each other in English. Cường steps out of his store. Both Annette and Cường struggle to get my strong husband into the vehicle. I freeze and hold my breath. I am not close enough to make out all the words. They yell in unison, their voices stack on top of each other like building blocks. I notice the time. It is 8:17 a.m. In my mind's eye, I see Sam's handwritten letter. I have read that letter too many times to count. *Snow, you will never be second fiddle to anyone.* I affirm from here on out, it will be only my dolly and me. We will be second fiddle to no one. Tý hangs his head down in defeat and steps into the van. The door closes. The Sprinter van distances itself from me. Cường waves and walks back into his store.

"Sister?" Tý's brother catches up to me. The expression on his face is calm. Hải is five years younger than Tý and the same age as me. His features are softer than his brother's. Whereas Tý's face is square, chiseled and quite masculine, Hải's face is more heart-shaped, with a narrower jawline and a broad forehead.

"Hải, he's gone. He left and I let him go," I say, "I am sorry you crashed and missed the van too. I should have stopped to help you."

"I was not trying to get to the van," Hải says. "I was born here, and here is where I will die. I was told to make sure you got to the van on time."

"You were following me?"

Hải casts his eyes downward as an admission of guilt. "It does not matter now. What will you and Thủy-Tiên do now?"

"Did you know about Annette and Timothy?" I challenge him with my eyes to tell the truth.

"I am sorry, sister Two, he made me promise not to tell you."

I feel my body temperature rise. My nostrils flare. My body is rigid. I want to punch him in the face. I remember Mrs. Trần telling me that my tongue is my greatest artillery. "Fuck you for being an asshole! You and your brother are worthless pieces of shit! You both are the same with your secrets." I fire off multiple rounds of verbal ammunition. "I have nothing now. My family will probably disown me for disappearing in the middle of the night and not saying goodbye. I have no money, no dignity, and no job. I have been disgraced and have brought shame upon my father's name. What am I going to do now, you ask?" I take a breath, long enough to reload my arsenal of scathing assaults. "I am going to grow me some testicles because no man here has any! Get out of my face! I never want to see you again. Both of you are dead to me. I hate you as much as I hate him! He is a liar and you are an ugly vault of steel and ice with your cold secrets."

I hold Thủy-Tiên close and ride off. Anger courses through my veins. I have no idea where I am going. I have no idea what to do next. I tell myself not to be afraid anymore. *Stand on your own two feet. You do not need a man's love to make you feel validated.*

# 5 OUR PLANKTON LIFE (APRIL 21, 1975)

A rooster sounds his alarm. My weary body slithers off the mattress. I am cognizant of the little body sleeping soundly next to me. She snores softly. I rolled my scooter through the narrow alley late last night, down to this house that Tý and I shared. I had nowhere else to go. There was a light shining from Mrs. Trần's bedroom window. Her operatic sobbing encouraged me to scurry mouse-like past her gate. The poor she-Jekyll. I had ridden aimlessly all day yesterday, asking questions that had no answers. Did he and Annette leave the country already? Did I make a mistake by staying? Will he come back for us? Should I return home to see my family? How do I get a job at the embassy as a translator? Should I go back to teaching, or maybe back to the bank? Will this war ever end? Why are we not together, Sam?

I walk down the stairs to the kitchen, too tired and dazed from yesterday's events. The toy airplane sits on the floor where I had left it. A prism of emotions runs through me. Fear. Anger. Disgust. Sadness. And hunger. Is hunger an emotion? I open the cupboard doors. Empty. I pull open the drawers. Nothing but a pair of chopsticks, two rice bowls, spoons, and cups. I turn on the stove to boil some water to drink and hope I do not start a fire. I walk to my scooter and open the seat compartment. Inside is my bag, with our clothes, documents, Sam's letter, and the book, *'A Separate Reality'*. I remember the deep dimple on Sam's cheek when I tore the wrapping off the book that Christmas. My heart aches for him now.

Thủy-Tiên cries from upstairs. I make my slow climb to the bedroom. "Hush. Mama is here." She is writhing like a hungry larva. I try to cradle her back to sleep. The cries screech louder. The teardrops flood faster and bigger. "I know you are hungry. Soon you will have some water to drink." I rock side to side and bounce her up and down. "Ssshhhh." She spews curdles of white and gray matter into my hair. I take her downstairs and check on the water. It boils angrily and a couple of droplets scald my hand. The intensity of the burn makes me jump back and lose my grip on my baby. Thủy-Tiên falls to the floor. A volcanic howl erupts from her lungs. "STOP CRYING!" I slump to the floor and pick her up. "I am sorry." I hold her close.

A loud pounding snaps me out of my haze. Mrs. Trần's small palms are rat-tat-tatting loudly on my window. She disappears, but only for a moment. She is now kicking at my garage door. I open it for her.

"Give her to me," she bellows. "What the hell is going on here?"

I obediently hand over my baby and say nothing. I zombie-shuffle up the stairs. Mrs. Trần calls my name repeatedly but her voice becomes distant. The mattress is my paramour. It beckons me to lie down.

***

I open my eyes to see a gecko scurrying across the wall. *My baby! Where is she?* I run downstairs and check the kitchen. Not there. I check the bathroom. Nothing. I dash outside. No one. *How long have I been asleep?* I fly into Mrs. Trần's house. It is eerily quiet.

"Mrs. Trần?" I sprint upstairs unladylike and check the bedrooms. She has to be home. Her door was unlocked. Sanity escapes me and I peek under the bed, behind the corner television console, even inside the dirty laundry chest. I run down and out the back door to her garden of herbs. "Mrs. Trần!" I scream desperately. Right as I plunge myself down onto a bench, the bench lifts up and Mrs. Trần's bewildered face peers out at me. She emerges from the underground passageway, which is camouflaged by weeds and watermelon vines. "Mrs. Trần! Where is Thủy-Tiên?"

"She is safe, down below." She beckons me to follow.

"You have a secret room beneath your garden, under this bench?" I lift the bench up higher and slide into the hole. The cool dirt is inviting. The smell of earth, dried fish, and sweet candy flirt with my senses. We walk down a few steps, to an opening the size of eighteen square meters. The ground is flat, partially covered by a woven, straw mat. Except for a few weeds poking up through the ground, the place is immaculate. Wooden stakes, half a meter apart, line the perimeter of the room, with sandbags on the outside of the stakes. Surprisingly, it is not musty, damp or unpleasant inside.

"My father-in-law built this bunker during the French occupation. He was a little overzealous and built this with three rows of sandbags, all around, almost two meters high, and filled the bags with soil, rice, and whatever he could find, including packages of dried anchovies, smoked fish, and other preserved foods." Mrs. Trần points to the ceiling. "He also put sandbags on top of the boards above, so it is pretty solid. Any bag marked with a red "VN" has food hidden in it."

Thủy-Tiên sits on the floor sucking a salted cuttlefish and so preoccupied with a spool of thread, that she does not even greet me.

"VN?" I inquire.

"Ay, you are not so smart! VN for Việt Nam." She kneels down beside my

33

daughter. "My father-in-law built this almost thirty years ago. He hated the French and fought for the Việt Minh."

At the risk of being called stupid again, I ask, "Is this bunker directly below your entire garden?"

Mrs. Trần smiles with pride. "Bigger."

"How do you get any ventilation?"

"There are two fake vents up above in case the enemies try to smoke us out, but the real vents are here." Mrs. Trần points to the openings in the opposite sides. "They lead to the outhouse and the hollow bamboo poles separating your house and mine."

"Clever. What about supplies? Water?"

Mrs. Trần lifts up the mattress of the bed to reveal sixteen wooden crates, each filled with water, dried cuttlefish, pickled mangos, pork pemmican, candied plums, tamarind, and ginger. "Enough for one lunar cycle…Longer if you cut into the bags marked VN."

"You made all these preserved foods?"

"How do you think an old woman like me survives in wartime, with no husband or sons? I make and sell all of these."

"Please teach me. I do not have any money of my own. I am too ashamed to go back home to my family."

Mrs. Trần laughs. "I cannot have you as my competition. Go home. Pride has no place when there are mouths to feed. Take your baby and go home. I will even buy you a bus ticket."

Maybe Mrs. Trần is right. I need to go home and face my family. I walk over to Thủy-Tiên and pick her up, bidding the she-Jekyll good evening. "Thank you for your offer. Instead of a bus ticket, can I please borrow some money? I want to keep the scooter and ride back to Vĩnh Bình."

"Come back this evening, around 6:30 p.m. I will give you money and some food to take with you for the journey. You can stay for dinner."

"Thank you. I will find a way to repay you. By the way, late last night, when I came home, I heard you crying. Is there anything I can do to help?"

"You were spying on me again?"

"No, I--"

Mrs. Trần laughs. "Those soap operas get me every time! In last night's episode, the village girl found out her husband loves another."

Embarrassed, I smile and leave the bunker with Thủy-Tiên.

***

At exactly 6:30 p.m. I saunter into Mrs. Trần's home. She swings carefree on her hammock and motions me to sit. "They have taken Xuân Lộc. It will only be a matter of time before they takes Sài Gòn. Our country will be united."

This development makes me nervous. A part of me regrets not getting on the van with Tý. "With Xuân Lộc lost to the northern army, the highway is open and clear for them to infiltrate the capital."

We watch the news in silence on her small television while Thủy-Tiên plays with her airplane. A familiar face appears on television and I am keen to hear his message. Mrs. Trần announces our president as if I need the introduction. "Nguyễn Văn Thiệu."

We tune in to what he is saying. He recaps the development of the country under his leadership in South Việt Nam, thanks our allies for fighting against the communist aggressors, and outlines the tactics the communists used to strengthen their offensive. He tells us how he had wanted both northern and southern troops to demobilize so that North Việt Nam and South Việt Nam could govern independently. However, during the peace talks in 1972, the U.S. did not demand the north withdraw its troops from South Việt Nam, and this, President Thiệu told President Nixon and Secretary of State, Dr. Henry Kissinger, he could not support. With the United States stopping aid and withdrawing their troops, he argued that the demilitarized zone and 17th parallel be respected; otherwise, South Việt Nam would crumble. *'I regret that later on, Watergate occurred in the United States. The U.S. political situation has prevented economic aid and the continuation of the Vietnamization program as well as the program to modernize the RVN armed forces. In addition, international economic changes concerning energy and food have created difficulties and contradictions among the U.S. people.'* President Thiệu continues his scathing speech about the United States' trickery, broken promises, and betrayal.

Following every sentence, my heart sinks deeper into my stomach. "Maybe one Việt Nam will be a good thing. Maybe it is best that the Americans withdraw." I try to believe my words.

Mrs. Trần exhibits no emotion. "I only want my sons home."

Desperation washes over me. I must leave my country, whatever the cost. With President Thiệu resigning, there is no government to keep Sài Gòn safe. "I still have my exit documents. Come with us, Mrs. Trần. We can use that phoenix necklace I gave you and bribe the Marines to let you come with us. We can say you are my mother."

"If the war is ending, then my sons can come home. They will not need to fight anymore. I have to be here when they return."

"And what if they do not return?"

Mrs. Trần cranks her head slowly. Her body is still, her eyes cold and menacing. Chills trickle down my spine like a scampering gecko escaping danger. I am reminded of the 'The Exorcist' movie. Like projectile vomit, Mrs. Trần screeches biles of profanities at me. "You fucking stupid girl! You heartless bitch! How dare you?"

"I am sorry. I--"

"Fool!"

"I did not mean--"

"You call yourself Vietnamese? A true Vietnamese is not a deserter! A true Vietnamese fights for her country and fights for unification and fights for peace!

A true Vietnamese believes that her sons, no matter what side they fight on, will come home, because they are strong in their convictions and brave in their hearts! How dare you suggest they are dead?" Mrs. Trần's whole body convulses as she barks at me. The she-Jekyll extends her bony finger at me and nods toward the door. The hostile rage in her eyes warns me not to come back.

I regret speaking so brazenly to her, but surely, she comprehends the tectonic landscape is shifting? That the seismic waves of change will soon disrupt our plankton life? "If you change your mind--"

"Get out! Leave! Take your daughter and get the fuck out of my country!" Mrs. Trần picks up her slipper and hurls the rubber shoe at me. It smacks my ear and brushes against Thủy-Tiên's head on the way to the floor. It startles Thủy-Tiên but she does not cry.

A flicker of compunction crosses Mrs. Trần's face, and I grasp the opportunity to speak my mind. "I feel sorry for you, that this war has turned your heart bitter. You talk about courage and conviction, peace and unification, but you have not reconciled your own fears. You once told me I was weak and blind, that you pitied me. It is you who is weak and blind." Mrs. Trần collapses to the floor on her knees. I want to hoist her up and shake the frail woman before me. "Open your eyes. Even if both of your sons make it home, do you think life will be glorious with sunshine and coconut trees? One war ends and another begins. That is the only thing our country knows. You say I am a deserter? If I have to run to feel safe, to find freedom, shit, to feel full instead of hungry, then yes, I am the poster child of a deserter!"

"Stop! No more!" Mrs. Trần pleads. "Get out of my house, you insolent cunt! I curse the day you came here!"

"I will pray for you. I do hope that both of your sons come home safely, that they can shed the terrors and whatever price they paid in the rice paddies. I hope you do not have to live the rest of your life alone, that the moonlight does not haunt you, and that the sunlight does not beat you with regrets. I hope you can forgive yourself over your husband's death. I hope that in the end, you will not find yourself all alone with nothing but your money and your bitter pride." Mrs. Trần sobs uncontrollably. Tension loosens its grip on my heart and my voice softens. "I am afraid too." I kneel down and wrap one arm around her shoulders, squeezing her tight. Mrs. Trần does not resist. I try to comfort her. "We are not that different from one another. We are both dreamers. But I am beginning to see the reality before us. Your sons may be coming home for their own funeral."

# 6 THE FALL (APRIL 29-30, 1975)

A week has passed since President Thiệu resigned and left for Taiwan. He handed the presidency over to Vice President Trần Văn Hương. In a broadcast on Saigon Television, President Hương promised his army that he would stand by them if they still wanted to fight. He declared that if the Republic of Việt Nam ceased to exist, then his pile of dry bones will lay beside the bones of his fellow soldiers. Well, after one week, he resigned, and yesterday, General Dương Văn Minh was sworn in as president of South Việt Nam. President Minh has called for a cease-fire and asked all Americans to leave within twenty-four hours. This past week has been chaotic as many of my neighbors and fellow countrymen abruptly abandoned their homes and journeyed to the port city of Vũng Tàu, planning to climb aboard any vessel they can find to leave Việt Nam and be rescued by the U.S. Thousands of desperate people rushed to Tân Sơn Nhất airport to get out. The North Vietnamese Army fired rockets at the airport early this morning, destroying the runways and forcing a closure. Sài Gòn is surrounded. There is no way out.

"Are you sure you do not want to go with us?" I ask Mrs. Trần. She and I have made our peace.

"My sons will be home soon." She remains adamant about staying.

I admire her optimism. "Good luck to you."

She contently sits on the mattress inside her bunker. As I lift the garden bench to exit the bunker, Mrs. Trần's amplified version of the national anthem of South Việt Nam gives me goosebumps.

I wrap Thủy-Tiên tight around me and make my way to the U.S. Embassy. Outside on the streets of Sài Gòn, there are trash and debris everywhere. Anarchy is upon us. People are looting stores and commissaries. Babies are crying. Parents cling tightly to their children. The elderly look confused. Dogs run in every direction seeking shelter or morsels of food. In the distance the explosive sounds of M-16s firing and the pulsating rotors of the helicopters crisscrossing over the city, gives me vertigo. A massive crowd is outside the embassy gates. Everyone is screaming and waving papers, pressing against the wall or climbing it. The moment I get off my scooter and grab my bag, someone runs off with my scooter in the opposite direction. I want to chase after the thief but getting into the embassy is of higher priority.

I run toward the embassy gate. "I have papers!" I wave my exit documents and visas. I shove my way through the crowd, past flying elbows, spit, and men blowing snot rockets out of their nostrils. With one hand, I cover Thủy-Tiên's head, and with the other, I shove people aside, ducking under arms, squeezing through gaps between sweaty bodies. The forceful shouts and desperate cries of men, women, and children, compete to be heard, while the U.S. Marines on the other side of the gate are overwhelmed and exasperated. Thủy-Tiên cries out. I recognize her cry of pain. I glance down to see blood streaming down her nose. I think of Mrs. Trần, still sitting in her bunker, singing our national anthem.

*"Oh citizens! Our country has reached the day of liberation. Of one heart we go forth, sacrificing ourselves with no regrets. For the future of the people, advance into battle. Let us make this land eternally strong. Should our bodies be left on the battlefields, the nation will be avenged with our crimson blood. In troublesome times, the Race will be rescued. We the People remain resolute in our hearts and minds. Courageously we will fight such that everywhere, the Glory of the Vietnamese forever resounds! Oh citizens! Hasten to offer yourselves under the flag! Oh citizens! Hasten to defend this land. Escape from destruction, and bask our Race in glory. Make its name shine, forever worthy of our race."*

With the song in my head, I press on. "Sir! I have visas! I have my baby." One of the soldiers makes eye contact with me. He sees the blood on my baby's face. I plead with my eyes. "My husband inside." I lie.

He signals to another soldier, nods, and together, they open the gate a sliver, to let me through. A thunderous roar of protest whips through the air. The two soldiers lash back. A piercing pain shoots through my lower back and legs. Everyone is scratching, shoving, and hitting one another as they force their way through and tailgate behind me. With them comes the revolting smell of urine, cigarette smoke, and halitosis. The horrid stench of fear emanating through their pores send me into dry heaves. I see the Marines hitting people with the butt of their rifles, smashing fingers, and yelling words that fall on deaf ears. I feel relief to be inside the gates.

"Your baby is bleeding." Cường, the toy store owner who sold me the airplane, stands before me. He is skinnier than I remember. His eyes are red as if he had been crying. He lifts Thủy-Tiên's chin up with his right index finger and examines the cut. "It is a surface wound. It looks like she got scratched at the base of her nose."

He takes a handkerchief from his pocket, wipes away the blood, and applies pressure to stop the ooze. Even though the handkerchief is soiled like it has seen the inside of a hog stall, I do not protest. At least it is a familiar face.

"Thank you," I say.

"I am Cường." He does not remember me.

"Tuyết, and this is my daughter, Thuỷ-Tiên."

"She is so cute. How old is she?" he asks.

"Nine months."

"Is that so? She is so small. I thought she was six months old. Where is her father?"

I try to decipher whether he is serious or not. "We have met before. I came into your store and purchased a toy airplane. You know my husband, Tý." Cường's eyes widen. "Remember Tý? He has an American wife named Annette? He works with you for Mr. H?" His lips twitch as if they are trying to formulate the right words to say. "Đại Cathay's general?"

"I know who Mr. H is," he says emphatically.

The helicopters flying above seduce Cường's attention away from me. He says nothing more. Only the chuk-chuk sounds of the Huey blades drown out his silence.

The smell of urine invades my nose and I feel the wetness of my baby's legs soak into my shirt. Thuỷ-Tiên pees unabashed. I search for a wash station. Thousands of hysterical people try scaling the embassy gates, their arms flailing, mouths moving, while others who have made it inside the gates, sit in the courtyard clutching their bag or each other.

I notice the swimming pool and dash in that direction. "I will be right back." I strip off Thuỷ-Tiên's pants and soak it in the pool.

"Let me help you." Cường kneels beside me. He reaches for Thuỷ-Tiên, who immediately is entertained by the strip of hair over Cường's upper lip. She pets his mustache.

With Thuỷ-Tiên's pants now smelling like chlorine, I lay it on the concrete to dry, and splash the water onto my shirt to rinse off the urine. The cool water feels good on my skin. I cup the water into my hands and splash it onto my face. The memory of my childhood washes over me, when I used to stand in the alley, naked, and let the monsoon rain pummel my skin. The rainy season always breathes life into my spirit. I have the urge to dive in and go for a swim. I reach for Thuỷ-Tiên, but she rejects me. Cường lets out a laugh. I miss the sound of a masculine laugh.

"You have made a new friend." I welcome him holding the little sack of rice. She gets heavy after a while. "People are climbing up to the roof and getting airlifted out. We should get in line."

"Yes, grab your things." Cường picks up Thuỷ-Tiên's pants and together we walk toward the end of the long line. "That is all you have?" Cường points to my bag.

"I still have my watch and my wedding ring," I say sadly.

"And a nice jade bracelet." He points at my wrist.

"Yes, I bought this three years ago as a birthday present to myself."

We wait in line for hours. Everyone's bag is inspected and documents checked. The smell of smoke permeates the air as embassy employees burn documents from the rooftop. It takes me back to being in the kitchen with Sister Six. How I miss our banter. How I miss food. My stomach rumbles obscenely. I imagine there is a loud, hungry critter inside my body, gnawing away my stomach lining and gobbling up my intestines. I am embarrassed for each loud, gurgling sound.

Cường rummages through his knapsack and hands me something wrapped in banana leaves. "Try not to eat it all at once."

I peel away the banana leaves clumsily. The smell of coconut milk makes my mouth salivate. Thủy-Tiên stares at it, ready to pounce on it if I do not feed her now. I pick off a corner of the sticky rice and give it to her. She practically bites my fingers off. The sweet taste of grilled, soft bananas inside the crunchy, chewy, sticky rice sends my taste buds to nirvana. I close my eyes and savor the first bite.

A U.S. Marine inspects my documents and waves me to the side of the building. I am instructed to wait. I step aside and wait for Cường. The marine reviews the visa, assesses Cường, hesitates, and then examines the visa again. He waves one of his comrades over for a second opinion, a tall African-American soldier with the most beautiful, flawless black skin I have ever seen. If my skin is as white as snow, his is as dark as the purest, roasted coffee bean. The coffee-bean soldier inspects the documents and smiles.

"What do you think, Bryant?" the Marine asks his comrade.

"Let him in, David." He waves Cường through.

Together we head to the building and stand by one of the pillars. Hours pass. Waves of people hustle and rush into the helicopters. A tamarind tree in the courtyard is taken down to make room for more helicopters to land. Papers fly everywhere into the parking lot of the embassy as helicopters land and take off. The three of us receive no signal that it is our turn. Still, I am hopeful. We are inside the embassy gates while many are still outside, clamoring to be let in. The primal sounds of the helicopters break the tedium of the day and numb my restless mind.

Day turns to night. The banana dessert that Cường gave me is long gone. Thủy-Tiên rests her head on Cường's knapsack. I yawn.

"Close your eyes and sleep. I will wake you when it is time." He beckons me to him and offers his thigh as a pillow. I obediently lie down, heedless of the fact that Cường and I are still strangers, thrown together during this harrowing circumstance. The thumping sound of the helicopter lulls me to sleep.

*\*\**

Cường walks toward me. "My leg was asleep and I needed to relieve myself. You and Thuỷ-Tiên were working hard bulldozing something. Was it the Berlin wall or the Great Wall of China?"

"We were snoring that loud?" I ask. "What time is it?"

"You are the one with the watch."

"It is almost four in the morning!" I scan the area. There are still a few hundred of us waiting. Everyone appears hopeful, defeated, or weary.

"It has been awhile since a helicopter came by," says Cường matter-of-factly. "We need to prepare ourselves. No one but the Việt Cộng is coming for us."

"What?" I shriek. "But we have visas. They cannot leave us!" Fear delivers a hammering blow to my gut. "You are wrong! The Americans will come back and get all of us out!" *Please come back.*

Hours pass. Still, we wait. The orange haze of dawn illuminates the sky. I am restless and realize there will be no rescue. The light of sunrise is the blanket of death. It brings news that hell on Earth is here.

"I looted the embassy!" Cường holds up plastic bags full of pilfered items. Engrossed in my own sense of doom, I did not notice he disappeared the past hour. Other people perk up and come to check out what he has in the bags. They all talk animatedly and sprint to the embassy doors. "I found these garbage bags and a lot of useful things. I have candy and this camera. I found some sweaters and shoes and some sandwiches. I even found this!" He holds up a bottle containing yellow liquid. The label says '*GALLIANO*'.

Horrified, I ask, "Is that urine?"

Cường laughs. "No, it is liquor, but if it was pee, it smells sweet!"

All around us, people run out of the embassy building carrying everything from typewriters to boxes of knick-knacks. Most return multiple times to grab more stuff. They pile their loot onto chairs and wheel them out. I give in and join them. I intend to take everything I can carry. *Those damn Americans owe me!*

With Thủy-Tiên strapped to me, I push my chair outside of the compound, feeling exhilarated with my two trashcans filled with Western medicine, coffee, snacks, a pretty silk scarf, toilet paper, and office supplies. Those who are outside of the gates storm in. There are no soldiers to stop them. Everyone is running, yelling, grabbing anything and everything worth selling, trading, or keeping. As I roll my office chair full of stuff toward our temporary house in the alley, I brace myself for the sarcasm that will surely be dished out by Mrs. Trần.

"Where are you going?" Cường strolls up beside.

In the midst of my shopping spree, I forgot about him. "I am going to check on my neighbor. You are welcome to accompany us."

Together we walk down the street, me pushing a chair and he carrying trash bags full of stuff. The roads are crowded. Bombs go off in the distance. Smoke roils the skyline above the jagged rooftops and around the buildings, while people walk in every direction, holding on to their loot.

Then the tanks roll by.

The uniforms are of the North Vietnamese Army. This can mean only one thing. It is the fall of my beloved capital.

Communism wins.

My legs give way and I collapse to the ground. My body trembles, weakened by the sight. I command the tears to pull back but they seize control. Everything unravels before me.

Someone screams. "It is over! They are going to kill us!"

All around me, the people are polarized in their cheers and cries. Some people run in fear. Some embrace each other and shake enthusiastically the hands of the North Vietnamese Army. Soldiers with the People's Army strip off their clothes, helmet, boots, and gear. They desert their belongings and walk in their underwear, head hanging down in defeat. Sympathizers from balconies throw them clothes so they can blend in with society. Hopelessness seizes my throat and metastasizes into my bones, piercing deeper with each flick of the wrist as soldiers wave the Communist flag, red with a yellow star, victoriously. I mourn the fall of Sài Gòn.

Cường lifts me to my feet and walks me to a nearby shop. There is music flowing out of the storefront. A family of three gathers around the radio, along with one American man who is a reporter with the *Associated Press.*

Music is interrupted by a news broadcast. *"This is General Dương Văn Minh. I ask that the ARVN drop their weapons and surrender unconditionally to the National Liberation Front."*

Another tank rolls by with eight people sitting on top, wearing civilian clothes and waving the yellow-starred flag. A few Việt Cộng female fighters walk alongside the tank. They smile, wave, and cheer. One of them points to the American reporter sitting with us. "Go home!"

My mouth agape, I am overwhelmed with so many emotions, it is hard to describe. There is singing now on the radio.

*"Hello, Sài Gòn. It took thirty years to have today. We sing this victorious song. The sounds of our victorious song will echo in every street and district… We sing in the name of him, Hồ Chí Minh forever, Hồ Chí Minh forever…Hello Sài Gòn. In the North, Central and South, in one house of Việt Nam, together we sing our victorious song."*

# 7 A BITTER MELON DAY (MAY 1975)

The quiet is deafening. I walk slowly down the stairs, leaving my sleeping daughter to her dreams. I get to the kitchen and nearly trip over Cường. He sleeps soundly, sprawling on the floor, with one arm across his garbage bag of loot. My eyes trace his left arm, from his shoulder down to the dirt under his long, jagged fingernails. He has a wedding band! I never noticed that before. His other hand is tucked underneath his trousers. *So, you are right-handed.*

I take a few minutes to scrutinize this dirty specimen before me, from his oily hair to the stubbles on his face and neck. His mouth is wide open and his teeth are crooked and yellow, probably from nicotine, coffee, or both. For a Vietnamese man, he is hairy, with untamed eyebrows and "peek-a-boo" nostril hairs that come out with every exhale, and disappears with every inhale. His shirt is unbuttoned all the way. There are scars on his body. *Did the mafia put those there?*

I give Cường a gentle kick in the ribs. His right hand comes out of his pants and waves in the air, before falling onto his stomach. He still sleeps. I kick him again, harder, with my lead leg, but still, he does not respond. I sit down cross-legged and rifle through one of his bags, curious to see what other items he took from the embassy yesterday. I see the yellow *'Galliano'* liquor and open the cap to see what it smells like. It definitely does not smell like pee. The sweet smell of vanilla, cinnamon, anise, and other flavors bewitch me to take a swig of the enticing yellow nectar. It is so good. I take a couple more swigs.

Inside the bag, I spy a wrapped sandwich. My eyes open wide and my mouth twitches with excitement. Yes, it is a stale ham and cheese sandwich! The lettuce is wilted and the creamy sauce has a pungent vinegar smell, but I take a large bite and pulverize it with childish delight. I wash my sandwich down with another sweet gulp of *'Galliano'.* I jump up, sandwich in hand, and run up the stairs, two steps at a time, eager to share with my baby. Aw, still asleep. I strum her lower lip a few times like a guitar chord, listening to the blips as her lower lip springs up and smacks her upper lip. She does not stir or make a sound. I lift her arms up and release, allowing them to thump against the mattress. Still, she does not object.

I let out a giggle and scoop her up to hug her tightly. "Let us go pay a visit to our old neighbor next door." I head outside into the alley. There are five people outside, setting up shop like it is business as usual. I give a couple courtesy knocks on the door and enter the familiar house. "Mrs. Trần? It is me, Tuyết, and Thủy-Tiên."

I am greeted with "What are you doing back here?"

I leap forward to hug her with my free arm. "You are all right!"

"Of course I am!" My she-Jekyll dismisses my concern. "You have tried twice to leave this country and yet you are still here! Shit, if the Americans do not want you, I sure as hell do not either!"

"Yesterday we had a country. Today, Sài Gòn is no more, and there is no South Việt Nam, no president, and no U.S. embassy." My eyes glisten but instead of crying, I laugh. "I will tell you what we do have though. We have a stale sandwich, a wonderful drink called *Galliano*, and a half-naked man on my floor next door!" I roar with laughter at the absurdity.

"Child, are you drunk or just stupid crazy?"

"Yes!" I shout.

"Hello?" A male voice speaks from the doorway. There is a soldier standing at the entrance, dressed in his faded, dark green North Vietnamese Army uniform. He holds a basket of fruits and a bag of rice. The stranger has Mrs. Trần's face, and although he is young, his face is weathered, making him look much older than he probably is. The stranger runs past me and picks up Mrs. Trần. He swings her around while she kisses every inch of his face.

Mrs. Trần lets out a shrill cry. "My son! You are home!" She kisses her son's hands, puts them to her cheeks, and weeps uncontrollably.

"Mother! I am home. The war is over. I will never leave you and Father again! I promise!"

Mrs. Trần howls louder. "Your father is dead, son."

The soldier drops to the floor like a puppet without strings. "What?" He buries his face into his mother's hip and clutches her waist. I stand here bearing witness to this difficult reunion. The louder he weeps, the harder it is for me to hold it together. With tears still meandering down his tired face, the man-child looks up at his mother's puffy face. "Where is Lopsided?"

Mrs. Trần cups her trembling hands around her son's face. "I have not seen your little brother for five years now! He joined the South Vietnamese Army."

"How could you have let him, Mother?"

She has no words of comfort for him, no answers to ease his sorrow. Together, they surrender to sadness and sob like angry babies. The two of them cling to each other and let the past unbearable years avalanche down their shoulders.

I hold Thủy-Tiên a little closer and walk out the front door. I am now sober and somber. *So, this is you oldest son who left eight years ago to fight for the other side.*

***

The journey back to Vĩnh Bình is an interesting one. I never imagined myself straddling a motorbike behind a man other than my husband. Yet here I am with my arms wrapped around a man I barely know, cruising these one-hundred kilometers through provinces, past hamlets and decaying, fallen bodies, with one-hundred thirty-one more kilometers to go. Towns on either side of us are destroyed, deserted, or teetering on the edge of extinction, on their way to becoming a distant memory.

"Sister Two, we will need to fuel up soon," yells Hải, my brother-in-law.

I nod. Hải's long hair tickles my forehead as it flutters with the breeze. To a casual observer, we are a family riding into town, with our daughter wedged between us. None of us have a helmet on, which I am glad is still not required by the new government. It would be nice to have a hat though. It is a hot, sunny day. I am grateful for my facemask, to shield against dust and bugs. For the past couple of hours, I felt free riding along the stretch of concrete and past the red, sandy desert.

"We have to stop." Hải slows down. There is a line of motorists being questioned by the police.

My heartbeat changes tempo and goes from a waltz to a swing dance. "This is new. Security checkpoint?" My body is tense, my posture straight, and my stare grim. After twenty minutes of waiting in the stale, humid heat, it is our turn.

"Hello, friends." The policeman greets us. He looks small and green in his olive-colored uniform and matching hat. "What are your names?"

Hải introduces us to the police. "I am Vương Văn Hải. This is my wife, Vương Ngọc Tuyết, and our daughter, Vương Ngọc Thủy-Tiên."

I cringe, not because it is customary in Việt Nam to provide our surname first, followed by middle name, then given name, but because he lied so matter-of-factly that I am his wife and Thủy-Tiên our daughter.

"Registration for the bike." The policeman's face becomes serious and he glares at Hải.

"We do not have any paperwork." Hải's storytelling is impressive. "Our home was destroyed. The damn American helicopters literally blew away our belongings. We do not have much left."

"Where did you come from and where are you going?" The policeman smirks at me with eyes of lust, then suspicion. "Take off your facemask." I obey.

"We left District One in Sài Gòn--"

"Hồ Chí Minh City." He corrects my "husband".

"Yes, sorry, Hồ Chí Minh City. Long live Uncle Hồ."

45

The policeman smiles. I find him repulsive. The pimples on his face are ripe for the picking, and with his green uniform, he resembles a bitter melon. However, since he is small and thin, I decide he can also pass as a diseased okra.

Hải continues. "We are on our way to see our family in the Vĩnh Bình province."

"How much gold are you carrying?"

"We do not have any gold bars, only enough money to get to our family."

"How much?" His eyes narrow and his lips tighten. If he scowls any harder, I fear all his pimples will burst like fireworks. I wish I had my facemask on.

"Twelve," Hải answers.

"Twelve thousand piasters?" The bitter melon man laughs. "Good luck, friend. You will need it. You still have another three or four hours' journey. You can travel farther with an American dollar than twelve thousand piasters!"

"Then may we be blessed by the good Buddha to find a U.S. dollar along the way." Hải plays along mirthfully.

"Get off." The policeman walks around the motorbike, pausing at various spots to inspect closely. He runs his fingers along the back of the seat and traces the letter "M" on the *Minsk*. "A Russian *Minsk*. Good motorbike." He rummages inside the storage compartment and confiscates our small watermelon. He points to my bag. I reluctantly hand it over. Inside is Sam's book with his letter tucked between the pages. I can tell he is suspicious because it is written in English.

"I was a teacher." I try to stay composed while I lie to his face. "This book was a tool I used to teach my students about..." I look at the cover with the image of a man who has a ball of light for a head. "...about a man who clears his mind to embrace new teachings. I can use it to evangelize those who oppose reunification."

The guard hands me the book but holds onto my satchel. "You are free to pass after you pay the toll."

"How much is the toll?" asks Hải.

The bitter melon man stretches out his hand. "Today, it will cost you twelve thousand piasters and your wife's bracelet." Hải takes the money from his shirt pocket and hands it over. I struggle to slide the solid jade bracelet off my wrist. Admittedly, I have no plans to give it up since I purchased it as a birthday present for myself. The policeman loses patience with me and confiscates my watch instead. "Maybe if you find that U.S. dollar, you can get your wife proper traditional clothes, not the vulgar Western garb she has on now."

We finally clear the inspection point. I am frustrated. "Now what? We do not have any money to fuel up."

Hải pulls from his socks a stack of cash. "Five hundred thousand."

I squeal with delight and impetuously kiss Hải on the neck for his cleverness. Immediately I am flushed with embarrassment. For the next hour of our journey we ride in silence, except for the occasional "are you doing all right?" and "I have to pee". Along the way, we see many police officers, stopping people indiscriminately, motorists and pedestrians, young and old, to ask questions about their business.

It will take us six hours to go from Sài Gòn to Vĩnh Bình with all the checkpoints. Riding on the motorcycle with Hải gives me a lot of solitude and time to reflect. Naturally, it is the memory of Sam that occupies my thoughts.

# 8 LET GO

Three years ago, in April 1972, I purchased a jade bracelet for myself as an early birthday present. As I exited the store, two Americans were walking towards me, one in uniform and one in civilian clothes.

"Hello, Snow!" Sergeant Skyler Herrington had a mischievous smile on his face.

"Hello, Sky! Hi Sam!" I was so excited to see them both. "Sky, why you not in uniform?"

Before Sky could respond, Sam lifted me up and kissed me. It happened so fast, I had no time to object. I was of course embarrassed by the public display of affection. I dared not make eye contact with any of the locals who were no doubt gawking in disbelief.

"Sky is on R and R and is accompanying me so that he can witness this." Sam took a hold of my hands and got down on one knee. "My lovely Snow, will you be my wife and make me the happiest man in the world?"

"My father give you blessing?"

"Of course he did," answered Sky, "and if you say yes, damn it, you will make him the happiest son-of-a-bitch!"

Even with Sam on one knee, I was not that much taller than him. "Sam Hammond--" I started.

"Wait!" Sky punched Sam on the shoulder. "The ring, man, you can't forget the damn ring!"

"Oh, bloody hell." Sam pulled out of his pocket a red velvet box with the words *"Tiệm Vàng Hạnh Phúc"* embossed on the top, meaning Happiness Jewelry Store. Inside was an eighteen-carat gold ring with a large oval-cut emerald, accented with tiny diamonds cascading around the center stone. It took my breath away.

"Oh, Sam! I make you happiest son-of-a-bitch!" I squealed.

The three of us laughed and took turns hugging each other. Sam was so elated, he hugged Sky twice. The three of us talked animatedly as we walked home, my arm linked with Sam's.

"My tour is over," Sam explained. "I was given special permission to come collect you. We only have two days to get married and then you'll be flying home to the states with me."

"I'm the best man," Sky proudly declared.

"The ceremony needs to be small and inconspicuous," says Sam.

"What that mean?" I asked.

"Discreet," answered Sky.

"Private," added Sam. "We do not want to draw any attention. There have been too many air strikes and raids recently."

"More than usual." Sky stopped to tie his shoelace. "The less attention we draw, the less likely fucking Charlie will crash the party."

On the walk home, we wanted to buy some coconut water to quench our thirst. Sam was the first to spot a beverage stand. "Over there."

There was a woman and her daughter standing on the side of the street, waving us over. As we approached, the young girl stepped from behind the cart and held high above her head a grenade. The intensity in her eyes assured us she was ready to use it.

"Fuck." Sky grabbed my arm and swung me behind him. He pulled out a .45-caliber pistol and held it steady.

Sam immediately swung his M-16 up and aimed his rifle right at the girl's head. The mother screamed and grabbed her *Mosin-Nagant* rifle and fired at us. Her first shot was too high and went over our heads. Sam pulled the trigger but the rifle jammed on him. The mother fired a second shot that hit Sam in the throat and he crumpled to the ground.

"Sam!" I leapt to aid him. Sky squeezed my arm so hard, I hissed in pain. "Let go!" Sky clenched tighter. Two more shots ricocheted through the air and then there was silence. The woman and her daughter fell to the ground. Sky loosened his grip. I ripped my arm from his talons and knelt beside Sam. The tears rained down my eyes and blurred my vision. I kept wiping them away but the waterworks were turned on. Sam's eyes rolled back a couple of times. The more he tried to focus on me and talk, the louder he gurgled as his blood geysered from his neck and the drool slid down his chin. "Do something, Sky. Save him!"

Skyler stood towering above Sam, motionless and devoid of any expression. He kept blinking away his tears and was paralyzed by grief and shock. Sam took his last breaths and then was gone.

***

"We have another hour to go before we arrive at your father's house." Hải's voice brings my thoughts back to reality. "I need to pee." We stop on the side of the road for Hải to relieve himself. "Were you crying?"

I do not want to admit I was thinking of Sam. "Mrs. Trần is on my mind."

"You have to let go, Sister Two," says Hải. "There is nothing you can do about it."

"Stop calling me 'Sister Two'. In my mind and in my heart, I am no longer your big brother's wife. You can call me Tuyết like everyone else."

"That will take me some time, but if that is your wish..."

"It is. And you must promise me that if your brother contacts you, you will not tell him where I am or anything about me – or his daughter. Never. Understand?"

"Why?"

"Because I need to let go of my past. I need to survive and take care of my baby. The last thing I need is to lament his departure. Besides, you owe me for keeping a secret from me. He was already married and you did not tell me."

Hải's eyes plead me to forgive him. We get back on the *Minsk* and ride the last stretch of the journey home. My memories ping-pong between wretched Mrs. Trần and Sam.

***

On the evening of May first, the day after the war ended, Cường and I stepped out of the house to find Mrs. Trần and her son sitting on their front steps.

"I will sell your loot for you," Cường said to me. "You know where to find me." He nodded at Mrs. Trần and her son, before walking down the alley toward his toy store, carrying the garbage bags of loot.

"You trade your husband for that one," Mrs. Trần noted sarcastically, shaking her head. "You need to upgrade, not downgrade. My son, Minh-Hoàng, would be the best upgrade."

I gave Mrs. Trần's son a weak smile, leery of his gaze on Thủy-Tiên and me. He was a communist and I did not trust him. His stare burned into me as if he was committing to memory everything about me, from my mannerisms to the way my body moved, from how I smelled, to how I spoke.

Mrs. Trần broke Minh-Hoàng's stare by springing to her feet like an agile gibbon and sounding her vocal alarm. "Oh! I cannot believe it! Ay!"

Confusion quickly sidestepped to clarity. Mrs. Trần ran down the alley with Minh-Hoàng right behind her. Both of them yelling, "Lopsided!"

A man with one leg shorter than the other quickened his pace and ran into the open arms of Mrs. Trần and Minh-Hoàng. The three of them embraced and jumped for joy, laughing and crying, talking animatedly over each other, and patting one another on the shoulders. The lopsided younger brother looked savage, like a wounded dog fighting to stay alive. It brought me to tears witnessing such a reunion. *Your sons came home after all.*

That night, Mrs. Trần invited Thủy-Tiên and me to dinner, to celebrate her sons returning from war. I had never seen her so happy, so motherly and kind, telling jokes and laughing genuinely. She was affectionate, even towards me. During that first couple of hours, any animosity I had toward Minh-Hoàng or

50

pity I felt for Lopsided, evaporated with the steamy broth of our egg noodle soup.

Urgent knocks at the door interrupted our lively dinner.

Minh-Hoàng opened the door to find two government officials standing outside. They did not wait for an invitation, but rather, crossed the threshold until they were both inside.

"We are here for Trần Trinh Huy," said the one with a mustache.

"What is your business with my brother?" asked Minh-Hoàng.

"Your brother served the South Vietnamese Army and wrote some propaganda for the enemy. He is to report to a re-education camp for reform and retraining, to get on board with the new government."

"For how long?" asked Minh-Hoàng.

"Two weeks."

"Well, he is not here."

"Your brother is standing next to your mother. If you interfere, we will be forced to arrest you."

Lopsided spoke up. "It is all right, Brother Two. I will go with them. It is only for two weeks, and I will see you and Mother again soon." He kissed Mrs. Trần's cheek. "You waited five years for this day. I will be home soon and then you will not be able to get rid of me so easily. By this time next year, you will be trying to marry me off to some poor village girl and be embarrassed by my dancing skills at my wedding."

Mrs. Trần gave her son a brave, reassuring smile. She held her youngest son tight before finally letting go. Her hands trembled as she tried to choke back the tears.

The two men left with Lopsided in their custody. The door closed behind them. The sound of silence haunted us all that night.

***

The sputtering sounds of the *Minsk* snaps me back to the present.

"What is wrong?" I ask Hải. "Are we out of fuel?"

Hai pulls over to the side of the road to check. "There is still fuel in the tank but we are low. Let me check the sparkplugs."

Hải turns the petrol filter switch to "reserve". He examines the tubes, blows on it, and checks the carburetor, the filter, the sparkplugs, and other things that I do not understand. I watch him troubleshoot the problem and feel a small attraction to him, impressed that he knows what he is doing. Hải attempts to kick start the motor a few times, but nothing happens.

"Can you fix it?" I worry we will be stuck on the side of the road.

"Yes," answers Hải, "but I have no tools. We have to walk the rest of the way. It will take us an hour."

His news exasperates me. In Việt Nam, everyone would rather ride their scooter down to the next block than walk. It is faster, easier, and cooler because the heat can be unforgiving. I dread seeing my father, who will likely scold me for leaving in the middle of the night with Tý and Thủy-Tiên, without so much as a note or a goodbye. I cringe because I know Sister Six will pinch or slap me, to inflict physical pain equal to the emotional pain I caused her. Brother Seven will probably ignore me. His silence will be worse than his yelling. I sigh. The whole family will be shocked to see me returning, not with my husband, but with my husband's younger brother. They will jump to conclusions and will have already made up their mind that I have brought scandal and dishonor to the family. I will have to let go and trust God will give me the strength to endure.

# 9 MOOR PHEEN AY (MAY-JULY 1975)

Hải, Thủy-Tiên, and I walk up the path to my father's house. It is dusk when we arrive. We are greeted by warbling sounds coming from the side of the house.

"Mông Dơ!" I run to Dirty Butt. She waddles a dance around my feet and flaps her wings, chirping animatedly. I scoop her up and give my best friend a squeeze. "You are alive, you resilient dirty thing!" I laugh and give her another squeeze as I nuzzle my cheek into her feathers. Dirty Butt lets out a sharp peep in protest.

My family runs out, with Tree leading the way, followed by my niece, Tâm, and the two youngest, Trinh and Tuấn. We hug and rejoice. Through tears of happiness I see Sister Six, Brother Seven, their spouses, and my father. I walk to them, respectfully, and know that as my elders, I cannot expect them to come to me.

"Father," I begin, "I ask for your forgiveness. I must have scared you when I left without any warning and did not try to contact you the past few weeks."

My father raises his hand to quiet me. I lower my head, ready to accept the harsh words that will rain down on me. He takes a step closer. My body seizes up and my buttocks involuntarily tense, like muscle memory from all the times I was spanked and whipped as a child. My father wraps his arms around me and squeezes. He weeps uncontrollably. I feel the weight of his body slumping against me, so I wrap my arms around him to hold him up. I do not recall a time when I have received such affection and love from my father.

And then I feel a sharp pain on my forearm. Someone pinches me hard.

"You are a big shit to disappear all this time without telling anyone, especially me! Now, you come home, expecting us to receive you with open arms?" My sister glares at me with arms folded. I can almost see the smoke coming out of her lady-dragon nostrils. They flare with seething anger. "You had us worried and going insane, speculating what happened!"

Sister Six slaps my arm a couple of times and throws a jab at my shoulder. I wince but absorb her punch. My only assurance comes from understanding that the harder she hits, the more she loves and misses me. My brother-in-law and sister-in-law take their turn hugging me. We are not an affectionate family, but on this night, we make an exception.

Brother Seven wraps one arm around my shoulder. "I see you came home with Hải. Where is Tý?"

"Why not go inside the house and talk about this," suggests Sister Six. "People might be spying on us. You all must be hungry."

"And tired. My feet hurt and I am sure Hải's arms are sore from holding Thủy-Tiên." I nod towards Hải. "We have been walking the past hour."

Tree takes my hand. "I will rub your feet."

I sit down and prop my feet up on his lap. "You are a good boy."

Tâm takes Thủy-Tiên upstairs and puts her to bed. On the way here, my poor daughter cried so much, she passed out from exhaustion. Sister Six warms up some congee and sprinkles pork floss onto the rice porridge. Both Hải and I do not wait for an invitation to eat. We dig into the hot congee and shovel a big spoonful into our mouth. In between swallows, I recap how Tý insisted we leave right away, how he secured temporary housing for us in District One, and how he had documents for us to leave the country. I tell them all about Mrs. Trần and her sons. I explain the reason I was not with Tý was that I found out he had an American wife and son, and that Tý worked for the mob. They are all shocked and angry. I recount how I got through the embassy gates but the helicopters never came for us and how Cường and I stole bags of stuff from the American embassy.

"Aiyah, how did you end up coming back here with Hải?" my sister-in-law asks.

"My brother told me where their temporary house was and wanted me to make sure they got on the van," says Hải, "but when they did not go, I offered to escort them home."

"You are welcome to stay with us as long as you want," says my father. "We do not have much, but we are happy to share what we do have."

"Thank you, Uncle." Hải bows to Father.

"So much has already changed since the Việt Cộng took over," Brother Seven chimes in. "Many of our neighbors have left and some abandoned their homes to escape on the open seas. Others were lucky enough to fly out with the Americans."

"Yes," says Sister Six, "and some of them got arrested and taken to re-education camps, like Lopsided, whom you mentioned, or they were transferred to a new economic zone to farm the land."

"Yesterday," adds Tâm, "Grandfather had me burn all our western clothes and our books. All we have are our pajamas and some traditional áo dài dresses."

My father clenches his fist. "I am not going to give them the satisfaction of taking our belongings and then fining us for such possessions."

"Or worse, imprisoning us," adds my sister-in-law, Hiền. "They want to destroy all remnants of the bourgeois culture. Aiyah, they are coming into homes and seizing valuables. It is only a matter of time before they come here and take all our food and money."

"My friend's mother was asked to spy on her neighbors in the village," says Tâm, "and to report any peculiar behaviors or suspicious actions against the government. In return, they would reward her with food and money."

"We must be proactive," says Hải. "We need to combine our money and gold, hide anything valuable, maybe sell some of it if we need to, and live conservatively." Everyone nods in agreement. "And no one better be pregnant."

"What does being pregnant have anything to do with this?" asks my brother-in-law.

"Oh, believe me, there is no more bang in my firecracker," admits Sister Six dryly.

"There is no fuse left in my firecracker, either," offers Hiền.

I chime in. "I am thirty-six now, and there is not enough powder--"

"No, no. Have you all not heard? There is a new family law that is going to take effect soon, requiring abortion," says Hải.

"Why?" we all ask in disbelief.

"I am guessing the government wants to make sure no more half-breeds are born." Hải takes a second helping of the congee and pork floss. Everyone starts talking over one another saying "this cannot be" and "how can they do this?"

"Good thing I did not lie with a Westerner!" proclaims Tâm.

"I would kill you if you got pregnant out of wedlock," threatens Sister Six.

"But what if you are already pregnant in your second or third trimester?" asks my almost thirteen-year-old nephew.

"Tree?" Brother Seven is unsure what to make of his son's question.

I, too, am suspicious of my nephew. He never asks questions, only offers statements as his own truths.

"Relax! I did not get anyone pregnant! I was only asking!" Tree responds.

"I do not know," answers Hải.

"Those bitter melon men are unpredictable," I say. "Who knows what they will do. We need to do as they say and tread carefully."

"Who are the 'bitter melon men'?" asks Hiền.

"That is what I call all the North Vietnamese government officials," I answer. "On the way here, we had to go through security checkpoints and one of the policemen who inspected us had big pimples all over his face, and because he was wearing a green uniform, he looked like a bitter melon." Tree laughs. "He took my watch!"

"I am tired." Father rises from his chair. "I am going to retire for the night.

I am happy you are home. Everyone get some sleep."

We bid him goodnight and stay up talking for another hour before finally succumbing to sleep.

***

My daughter turns one years old today, July 30, 1975. In my country, many babies die before reaching the first anniversary of their birth. For this reason, to make it to one year is a big relief for the parents and is a special milestone to be celebrated.

We have been at my father's house now for three months. The government has since changed the country's currency and replaced the piaster with the dong. I barely recognize my hometown these days. Neighbors, who were once friendly with one another, now spy on each other. The only ones we trust are our neighbors, Tú and Vân, who play cards with Sister Six.

The government incentivizes us to report suspicious activity. One family was rewarded with twice the rice and meat ration for the month because they reported overhearing another family make covert plans to flee the country. Another family was accused of harboring an uncle who served in the South Vietnamese Army and aided both the Americans and members of the old regime. The uncle was arrested and that family had their monthly monetary allowance cut in half. The couple who reported this received the other half of the monthly allowance. In a nearby village, a daughter returned home from Sài Gòn with a swollen belly and was forced to have an abortion. The mother claimed it was swollen from malnutrition, but I heard the unborn fetus was mỹ lai đen, meaning black half-breed. The daughter committed suicide and her parents were sent away to some rural, remote area.

"Spying on the neighbors?" Hải walks toward me. Dirty Butt keeps pace behind him, looking gaunt but still spirited.

I bend down to stroke my chicken's head. "I have known most of my neighbors since childhood and now, many of them are gone."

"Yes, it is distressing," comments Hải. "At least your family is together."

"I have you to thank for bringing us home safely." I smile warmly at him.

"Changing the subject... Thủy-Tiên turns one today," says Hải. "We should celebrate. We have to allow ourselves some joy."

"If we celebrate, our spying neighbors will wonder how we afford it, and then report to the communist cadres that we must be doing something illegal."

"And they would be right." Hải chuckles. "Come with me."

I pick up Dirty Butt and carry her with me to the trees by the family outhouse and pond. My nephew slides down from the mango tree and startles me. Dirty Butt is not happy about the intrusion. She hops out of my arm, flaps her wings and squawks away.

Tree and Hải walk to the other side of the pond while I follow. We stop at the stalls where my father keeps our pigs. We used to have four pigs, but now there are only two. My father sold one to make some money to survive and

56

slaughtered another so that he could feed our family. We were forbidden to give any of the animals a name, but when I started referring to our chicken as 'Dirty Butt', my sister tattled. Father got upset. "It is a chicken, not a pet! Now I cannot kill it."

"We have something to show you in the bunker," says Tree.

We walk down into the bunker and immediately I am reminded of Mrs. Trần. My father's bunker is bigger than hers. It needs to be, to fit all members of our family. It is constructed like hers, except there are no sandbags marked with the letters "VN" on them. Mrs. Trần's voice rings clearly in my head. "Ay, you are not so smart! VN for Việt Nam." I wish our bags had preserved foods. What I would not give for some smoked fish and rice right now!

"I remember when I was as young as six years old," says Tree, "I would be so fascinated with the hospital."

"The one near our house?" I ask.

Tree nods. "I would walk home from school and hear all the ambulance sirens, and then see them dump all the bodies into piles behind the hospital."

"Your grandfather was head of the school then." I reminisce with Tree. "I remember the terrible smells blanketing the air from the piles of rotting flesh."

"It still lingers." Tree looks down at his feet before continuing. "I was never afraid. I do not know why, but it fascinated me to see those decomposing bodies. It may be morbid, but I was drawn to it."

"You were always a curious child, examining things." A few seconds go by before I pipe up again. "Remember when you would always stop at that café by the hospital and bring home an iced coffee with condensed milk for me?"

"I bet you would be in heaven if you could have one of those coffees now."

"Yes, I would probably sell you off for a year's worth of indentured servitude, if I could have a taste of that coffee!"

Tree glares at me. I add a wink to lighten the mood and put him at ease.

"So, Tuyết," says Hải, "Tree found something near the hospital."

Tree pulls something out from his shorts pocket. I notice the small hole near his crotch and the thread fraying at the seams. I will have to ask Hiền to sew that up later. I read out loud the big block letters on the glass bottle. "Moor pheen ay."

"I think it is pronounced 'moor pheen'," says Hải. "It is a strong painkiller."

"This small bottle of Western medicine will sell fast on the black market," says Tree.

"How much do you think we can sell it for?" I inspect the bottle.

"Three million," responds Tree confidently.

My eyes open wide. My heart races fast and I am excited. "The government only gives each household two-hundred-thousand a month. With our combined households, we get six-hundred-thousand each month." I do some quick calculations in my head. "That is five months of government subsidy for our family in this little bottle of magic!"

"You did that math in your head so quickly!" exclaims Hải.

"I used to be a math teacher before I worked at the bank," I say proudly. "This is a day for celebration after all." I clasp my hands together and jump up and down.

"Tomorrow, I will go into the market and sell the morphine," declares Tree.

"Be careful you do not get caught by the cadres or any of our neighbors," I caution him.

"I am twelve," he retorts, "no one pays attention to me."

"Maybe there are more painkillers at the hospital." I am excited at the possibility.

"No. It has been completely looted." Tree extinguishes my hope.

"There was medicine in the loot that I took from the embassy. I gave my stuff to Cường and asked him to sell all of it for me. I do not remember what kind of medicine, but maybe there were other painkillers. We need to make a trip to Sài Gòn so I can collect."

***

Tree comes into my bedroom, his eyes wide with excitement. "Meet us in the bunker after lunch."

After a small lunch of boiled cassava root dipped in sugar, the family retires to their bedroom for a nap, while Tâm washes the pot and plates. I sneak off to the bunker, anxious to learn how much money Tree got for the morphine.

"Did anyone see you go into the bunker?" asks Hải.

"No. They are all going to take their nap. Tâm is washing the dishes and then she was going to patch the holes in Tree's shorts," I respond.

Tree sits down on the small chair in the bunker and reaches into his pocket. "I went to the market and asked around to see where I could buy Western medicine. I found a lady who took me into her fabric shop and she showed me her medicine supply. She had a lot but I do not know what they all were."

"So, did she buy what you had to sell?" I ask.

Tree smiles at me and leaves me in a moment of suspense, before responding, "Yes." He dangles a red pouch in front of me.

"For Heaven and Earth's sake, spit it out! How much?"

"She offered me two million--" Tree says.

"That is not enough!" I exclaim.

Hải pipes up. "Let him finish."

"I told her my family would beat me if I did not get at least four million for the morphine." Tree hands me the pouch. "She laughed at me and waved me off, but I lied and told her the man three stores down offered me three million. Then I left her shop. She chased after me a minute later and offered me three million five hundred. I told her it was better to have a beating on a full stomach than an empty one, and accepted her offer."

The biggest grin spreads across my face and I laugh. "Tree, you are a clever scoundrel." I open the silk clutch, embroidered with a mai flower on the front. Inside were thin, rectangular, gold bars, with the words *'Kim Thành'* embossed on them.

"Since the government froze everyone's bank accounts last month and any currency that was not exchanged became useless, we are buying gold bullions."

"Tuyết, you and I should go and buy some more gold leaves. We need to turn cash into gold quickly, before they change currency again," urges Hải.

"Yes, with all this gold and the government subsidy, our family of twelve can live conservatively for a year, without raising suspicion." I smile at him. He smiles back. Why have I never noticed how attractive he is?

We celebrate Thủy-Tiên's first birthday by getting her ears pierced.

## 10 RAGAMUFFIN CHIC (AUGUST 1976)

I wake to the sound of heavy rainfall pounding against my window. It is only 4 a.m. My two-year-old sleeps beside me. Her breathing is labored and irregular. Her skin is dark and bruised-looking. I wonder if my drinking coffee during pregnancy caused her heart to tear. Every morning, I fear I will wake up to a lifeless child. I imagine what our life would be like if Thủy-Tiên and I went to America with Tý. My daughter would have received the medical care she needed to repair her heart.

I change the story in my mind and imagine myself married to Sam. I can picture us living in his hometown of Bellevue, Washington, and I would be chasing after two beautiful Amerasian kids, with another one on the way. We would have many children, and I would call them Two, Three, Four, Five...

It has been four years since Sam's death. For so long, I carry in my heart the sound of Sam's laughter, deep and beautiful, except for when he is in an absolute uproar and no sound escapes his open mouth. His head would tilt back, his eyes in tears, his hands slapping his knees, and his mouth agape... and for a few seconds, he would laugh in silence, until he caught his breath, and let out a lion's roar. How I miss his laugh. How I miss his dimple and his kiwi-colored eyes. I wish I had a photo of Sam so that I can remember every detail of his face. At least I still have the book and his letter.

I twirl my wedding ring around. It is time to take it off. It has been one year and four months since that day Tý and Annette pulled away from Cường's store. I walk to my dresser and pull open the last drawer. It creaks and wobbles in protest, like a piglet separated from the comfort of its mother's body. I pull out from the bottom of the pile my old, black pajama pants with the big elastic waist. It is the first and only pair of pants I ever attempted to sew. Brother Seven's wife tried to teach me a few years ago but gave up.

"The waist is crooked!" Hiền had said.

"Sister Seven, you told me to zig zag the stitching!" I barked.

"Instead you zig-zagged your pants. One pant leg is wider than the other and this one is also noticeably shorter. Aiyah, Sister, the elastic at the waist is all wrong, too. And why do you have three different colors of thread?"

"I broke the black thread and then could not get another through the eye of the needle, so I started over with the red thread, but when that one broke--"

"Aiyah, you cannot pull so hard! And you are supposed to lick the end to smooth the fibers out before you thread the needle!"

"Well, if you were not so cheap and purchased stronger thread, they would not be breaking!"

"Aiyah, you are hopeless. A woman who cannot cook or sew! Let us hope you are the last of your kind!"

She made me put it on and do a fashion show for the whole family. Sister Six laughed so hard, she fell off her chair and split the seams under her right armpit, pointing as she fell. "Poor little sister, let me give you a piaster for those exquisite pants! I must have them for fashion week in Paris! Monsieur and Mademoiselle, may I proudly present this year's theme, Ragamuffin Chic!"

Now, the only thing these pants are good for is hiding precious mementos in the elastic waistband. I strip the pants inside out and search for the small hole in the waist. I find the opening and drop my wedding band into it. Clink. I remember what else is in there. My heart beats fast as my fingers work, inch by inch, to guide the small object through the length of the waist until a portion of it peeks through the hole.

In the palm of my hand lies the oval-cut emerald ring that Sam gave me, with its glorious tiny diamonds surrounding the center stone. I put it on and feel the eighteen-carat gold wrap itself around my left ring finger and imagine Sam's arms wrapped around me.

Muffled voices come from downstairs. The women are awake. I put Sam's ring back into the waistband and tuck the pants back in the bottom drawer. I join my family in the kitchen.

"I wish it would end." Hiền sits at the table twirling a chopstick.

"You wish what would end?" I ask.

"The monsoon season," Hiền responds. "Aiyah, we have two more months of rain. I cannot wait for the mid-autumn festival in a few weeks."

"I miss the old days when our husbands would let us sit with them at the table and drink all day long!" chimes in Sister Six.

"Yes, and after you nhậu all day long, I remember us kids having to clean up all the beer cans you adults threw under the table!" exclaims Tâm. "I am glad I am not a child anymore!"

"And then we would play tứ sắc all night long, and you would always lose, Sister Six." I poke her ribs playfully.

Sister Six slaps my hand away. "Because I would be drunk by then! I cannot distinguish one card from another after half a dozen beers!"

"Aiyah, do not make excuses. You are always bad at gambling. We can see right through you." Hiền points the chopstick at her. "When you lie, your left eye flutters like this." She demonstrates her left eye going into seizures.

"And when you have a good hand, you pass gas!" I form my right hand into a fake gun and aim at Tâm's shoulder. I let out two fart pops. "Bang. Bang."

Tâm pretends to fall over dead. "That, dear Mom, is how lethal your farts are when you are winning tứ sắc." Tâm blows my sister a kiss. We all laugh.

Sister Six grumbles, "I cannot help it if I get relaxed and gassy when I am excited." We laugh harder. "Keep laughing but remember who cooks for this family. You want to eat, do you not?" Sister Six threatens us with a pouty glare.

"What is so funny that you all are laughing so hard this early in the morning?" Brother Seven stands at the bottom of the staircase, dressed in his usual faded black slacks and white cotton shirt, with yellow armpit stains, ready for work. *Now that is ragamuffin chic.* "What do we have to eat?"

"Not much," responds Sister Six. "We ran out of all the gold bouillons two months ago and everything costs four times more than they used to!"

"Well, what can we sell?" he asks.

"We do not have anything else to sell."

"Look again. By tomorrow morning, I want everyone, including the children, to bring me one item we can sell."

"Aiyah, Husband, there is nothing, unless you want to sell our children!" protests Sister Seven.

"We can sell my jade bracelet," I say reluctantly. "Brother Seven, I want to go with you today. I need to see Cường and finally collect on the sale of my loot from the embassy. Our family needs the money. I also want to check in with Mrs. Trần and see how she is doing, if there is time."

"I am a truck driver, not a bus driver or your personal chauffeur. It is a long, uncomfortable six hours to Sài Gòn. It is too much of a trip for you and Thủy-Tiên."

"I will entertain her." Tree stands on the last step of the stairs in his underwear scratching his stomach. He lets out a big yawn.

"It is settled then," I say.

***

Brother Seven and I ride out at 5:30 a.m. We share a sweet potato for breakfast and save the other two for lunch and the ride back.

"Do you like being a truck driver?" I attempt to fill the silence.

"So far, it is not bad. There are worse things than driving twelve hours each day, seven days straight."

"Brother, each day, you leave before 6 a.m., get to the brewery by 12 p.m., and spend two hours eating, napping, and reloading the truck. You get home by 8 p.m., tend to the needs of your family, get five hours of sleep, and then do it all over again, with no rest. What can be worse than that?"

"For one, getting home past the 9 p.m. curfew and getting harassed by the police. And for another, listening to my wife nag for twelve hours. 'Aiyah, Husband, go help your son, Tuấn, with his bath.' Or, 'Aiyah, Tree climbed up the roof again and you need to get him down.' 'Aiyah, aiyah, aiyah.' I am one 'aiyah' away from going insane."

I chuckle. "Brother, you act stern, but I know you love her."

"I like driving despite the relentless schedule. The bitter melon men, as you call them, do not give me any trouble at the checkpoints, especially when they see I am transporting beer."

"Speaking of beer, can we can get some for the mid-autumn moon festival?" I ask.

"It depends if you get money from Cường. Do you think he sold your embassy loot and pocketed the money?"

"We will see. I want to believe that his moral compass is pointed in the right direction, but then again, he does work for the mob."

"Speaking of mob, has Tý written?"

"No."

"Is there something between you and Hải? I see how he looks at you."

"He is nothing like his brother. He is a good, selfless man, and the best ally we have. I owe Hải so much." I sigh. "I know he is in love with me. A woman knows these things, but I am still a married woman, raising a child who will grow up never knowing her father. At least I hope she will grow to be an adult. I hear in America, the streets are paved with gold. People have money and fancy cars. They have the best education and world-class doctors who can determine what is wrong with Thủy-Tiên's heart and fix it."

"You missed two opportunities to go to America and you are going to try again?" my brother asks.

"I missed three opportunities if you count my plans of marrying Sam and moving to Washington."

"I am sorry about Sam. I will help you escape if you promise to take Tree with you."

"It is too dangerous. I cannot be responsible for him. He is just a boy," I protest.

"He is almost fourteen years old. It will be he who will take responsibility for you. He can protect you, and take care of Thủy-Tiên." My brother's eyes tear up. "His chances for a happy and safe life are greater in America than here, and it is worth the risk."

"I will think about it," I promise pensively.

∗∗∗

I leave my shoes at the entrance and walk into the toy store. Behind the showcase is a weathered-looking man slumped over his stool, removing a kite from its cellophane wrap. My heart sinks. Time has aged him and he is thinner than a year ago.

"Cường?" I ask.

Cường looks up and gives me a blank stare. For a moment, I see the anguish on his face, but a flicker of life ignites in his eyes. He recognizes me.

"Tuyết!" He stands up and waves me to sit with him on the adjacent chair. "What brings you back here?"

"It has been a long time and it is presumptuous for me to ask, but I am hoping to collect my share of the money, from the sale of the stuff I got at the U.S. embassy." I hold my breath for Cường to respond, expecting him to tell me he does not have it.

"I was able to sell most of your belongings. I wrote an inventory of everything, including the chair and two trashcans. Let me get the list." Cường disappears in the back room for a few minutes and returns with a notebook. He squats back down on the stool and thumbs through the pages, stopping on a page that is written in blue ink instead of black ink. "Here, take a look." He hands me the booklet.

I scan the list. "You only got three-hundred-thousand for all this?" I am disappointed.

Cường nods. That is not much more than what the government gives each family each month. What is that in U.S. currency? Ten dollars?

"Tuyết, I sold what I could to those northerners relocating down here to Sài Gòn, I mean, Hồ Chí Minh City, and those guys are tough to bargain with."

"Tell me, do you remember if there was any Western medicine like morphine in my bag?"

"What is morphine?"

"It is an expensive painkiller and we can get a lot of money for it on the black market. My nephew found a bottle and Tý's brother, Hải, knew exactly what it was. We were able to sell it for three and a half million back home!"

Cường's eyes widen. "Maybe Vĩnh Bình is a better market for the Western drugs than they are here?"

"Maybe," I speculate. "The demand in my hometown is higher than the supply. We are in dire need of food and supplies. The Việt Cộng cut off a lot of our food supply and is forcing families to hand over everything, especially our rice crops. People are starving and resorting to stealing, lying, cheating – anything to survive and be in good favor with the new government."

"It is madness here, too. It is a daily struggle and I am hustling to take care of my sick relatives and aging parents. My wife, she could not take it anymore and took her life last year. She poisoned herself."

Cường becomes quiet. I am lost for words, unsure of how to comfort this man who is neither family nor friend. Instead, we share a moment of silence in her memory. Abruptly, Cường rushes to the back room and disappears for a couple minutes. He rummages through paper and plastic and shoves a chair aside. He comes back with a box.

"We found abandoned pallets of stuff at the port in Vũng Tàu, including this 'Bayer' bottle. Of course, we hauled everything we could grab, and came back several times. So many people had the same idea. We had to fight them off at the docks to claim the pallets that we have. So, do you know what this 'Bayer' is used for?"

"No, but I will ask Tý's brother, Hải," I answer. "There is a great demand for Western medicine in my hometown. Why not let me help you sell some of it there? Everything costs four to ten times as much as they used to and with such a short supply of medicine and other necessities, people are willing to spend money on the care they need. There are still people with money. We need to find them."

"That is fine, but we split the sale 70/30."

"What?" I shriek. "No. Equal partners, Cường. You may be the supplier but I am the one taking all the risk and doing the footwork. I have to travel twelve hours round trip each time and smother those bastards at the security checkpoints with my charm."

"Here is the deal. Take this box of *Bayer* back to Vĩnh Bình and let us see how fast you can sell it all, and how much money you can get for it. If you can get five-hundred-thousand đồng for it within a week, we will be equal partners."

"I will see you in three days with at least five hundred," I say confidently. "Now, where is my three-hundred-thousand đồng?" *What am I getting myself into?*

# 11 MOONCAKE TO FREEDOM (SEPTEMBER 1976)

It is the eve of the mid-Autumn moon festival. Brother Seven received some beer as payment for his driving, so we will be enjoying that tonight. Sister Six, Tâm, and Hiền are in the kitchen preparing for the celebratory dinner. While meats and rice are scarce, there are some fish and potatoes at our disposal. Tonight's dinner will be steamed fish, lightly salted in a pan of water, with boiled potatoes, lightly sweetened. Tree climbed our fruit trees this morning and plucked some coconuts and unripe mangos, which we will dip in fish sauce and sugar. I wish we had pea vines to stir-fry. My body is craving leafy vegetables.

"You are not helping them prepare dinner?" Hải sits down beside me on the bench in our front lanai.

"I am banned from the kitchen." I lean down and pet Dirty Butt.

Hải laughs. "Will you be going to Sài Gòn tomorrow to see Cường or Mrs. Trần?"

"No. I have been selling those drugs for two weeks now and have not been able to save nearly enough money to buy a boat or hire a captain. Cường is taking sixty percent of what I sell. I still need to save enough for Tree. My brother wants me to take him with me."

"What about your wedding ring? You still have that?"

"I do, but that will not be enough. Are you sure you do not want to go, too?"

"No, I have told you once before. I was born here, and here is where I will die."

"Well, at this rate, it will take me at least another year to have enough money to not only pay for all three of us but to afford some gold bars in reserve for when we make it to America."

It makes me sad to be leaving everyone and everything behind. "There are families pooling money together and planning their escape together." Hải lights up a cigarette.

"Yes, I know of four other families right now, willing to risk everything to leave."

Hải sits down on the stone bench outside our front porch. He rests his elbows onto his knees. "There is something I have always wanted to tell you." He makes eye contact with me and lets out a deep sigh. "Before you leave the country, I have to confess I have loved you since the day of your wedding tea ceremony."

"Hải--"

"Please, let me finish. It has taken me a long time to have enough courage to tell you. I hope you can forgive me for being so bold. I know we can never marry, but we can still have a life together. I will take care of--"

"That will never be acceptable to my family." I interrupt again.

"Stay here with me, with your family. Together, we will survive through this."

"I do not want to survive, Hải, I want to live. Thủy-Tiên needs medical care and she cannot get good medical attention here."

"Do you have any feelings for me?" It is an honest question from Hải, but one I struggle to answer. Admitting that I feel something for him would betray the light I hold for Sam and the marriage vows I gave to Tý.

"Your silence says it all," Hải says with sadness in his eyes.

"It is not that simple," I protest. "Having feelings for one another is not enough. My daughter comes first now. What kind of life will we have, if we cannot live as husband and wife, to yearn for one another, but not be able to show any affection or be accepted as a couple?"

"We can love each other behind closed doors and from afar. Side by side, I will be with you until the day I die. There are worse things than being loved. Let me love you."

"I cannot dishonor my father's house and bring more shame to the family. We invited you into this house and treat you like family. What would happen if we loved each other behind closed doors and my family finds out?"

Hải says nothing. I want to give him a tender squeeze on the arm but hold back. Instead, I leave him and go into the house to insist helping with dinner.

*** 

"Aiyah, Eight, no! You do not peel a mango that way! You will cut yourself. And all this meat still left on the skin! That is wasteful!" After this reprimand, Hiền grabs the mango from my hand. She scrapes the mango flesh off the strips of skin with her lower teeth and chews on the crunchy, unripe fruit. She peels the skin slowly to make sure I see the action. "See? Like this." She hands me the knife and a fresh mango.

An hour later, we all sit around the outdoor table. Brother Seven proudly opens a can of beer for each adult. He puts an unopened one in front of Tree. We all laugh and cheer.

My father stands up and raises his *Tiger* beer in the air. "Family, tonight we celebrate. There is no seat for Doubt or Fear at this feast tonight. We have many blessings, despite all the pains. Let me celebrate each one of you. First, to my son, Seven! You have always been the quiet one, but when you speak, the birds stop to listen. You have grown up to make this old man proud because your quiet resolve has seen this family through tough times. Your commitment has never faltered. Cheers!" Father takes a swig of his warm beer.

We all yell cheers, "Vô!" and take a drink.

Father raises his beer to Tree. "My grandson, you are like your father, sure of yourself, committed to your family, and resourceful...although, it would have been nice if you found us ice for the beers!" We all laugh. "I have witnessed your athleticism, your tenacity, and your grit over the years and I believe that without you, there would not be enough food on the table. Tonight, we toast you."

We all yell, "Vô!" and take a drink. My nephew is all smiles. He grimaces as he drinks his beer but is happy to be treated like an adult tonight. Father goes around the table and addresses each family member.

"Hải, you brought my daughter and granddaughter home safely to us. I am in your debt. You have proven to be a sound thinker and I know where your heart and loyalty lies. You have good intentions and genuinely care for my family. Cheers to you."

We all take our third gulp of beer and cheer, "Vô".

I am already feeling the effects of my *Heineken* beer, or "ken" as we like to call it. I make eye contact with Hải. He smiles. I remember our conversation earlier and his declaration of love for me. I pretend to fuss over Thủy-Tiên, who sits patiently on my lap.

My father addresses the children, Tuấn and Trinh, thanking them for being good kids and for picking up all the beer cans later, to which we all giggle, yell "vô" and take a drink. I pace myself and take a tiny sip. My stomach gurgles and I wish Father would hurry up. He says something nice to Sister Six's husband, something about his ability to stay calm, and to Brother Seven's wife, about her sewing. I drown out his speech and focus on my impatient stomach. I say "vô" on cue and drink on autopilot.

"Father, the fish and potatoes are colder than our beer," warns Sister Six.

"Six, you are a better cook than your mother ever was, and even though our food is getting cold, it will still taste like a masterpiece," Father compliments. "You nourish our spirit and give our body strength. Vô!"

"Vô!" we all parrot.

"And to my youngest child, although not a child anymore!" Father glances at me, then to Thủy-Tiên. He will likely struggle to find something nice to say. I must be a disappointment to him – the only child to turn away from Buddhism towards Catholicism, the only one to fall in love with an American GI, the only child to marry late and not be able to hold onto her husband, the only one who cannot cook or sew or do anything domesticated like a good wife can.

My body involuntarily tenses and I catch myself holding my breath.

"Father, we should eat. Sister Six prepared a nice meal for us and we should not let it--"

"Tuyết," my father says, "let me finish." Everyone is quiet. Did anyone else notice he called me Snow and not Eight? Why is he being so formal? "From the day you were born, you gave me grief." *Fantastic. Here we go.* "I was always worried that your beauty and charm were the only things you had going for you. The world fell at your feet and people fussed over you every day of your life. But, Eight..." My father's lips quiver and his eyes brim with tears. "Child, you boldly left home to get a uni education--"

"Father, the university took me away from home, where I should have been, to care for you and Mother--"

"Stop interrupting me, Eight," my father says softly. "You learned English and became a math teacher, and then earned your promotion at the bank. You are raising my granddaughter on your own without a husband, and I see the courage in how you fight for her. You know what you want and are not afraid to take chances. In this old man's eyes, I see defiance and quiet strength, not carelessness or weakness. Cheers to you."

I am speechless but Dirty Butt comes to my rescue, strutting to the beer cans at Brother Seven's feet. She clucks loudly and provides comic relief.

Everyone yells, "Vô!"

Tree takes a sip of his beer and reaches down to pet Dirty Butt's head. "Mông Dơ is ready to party."

Father invites everyone to eat and we voraciously dig into the steamed fish and potatoes. I finish my two "ken" beers and am drunk.

***

It is nearly 3 a.m. and I cannot sleep. Conversations from the evening replay in my head. It took three beers for little Tree to get drunk. I was impressed my nephew had such tolerance. We ate everything and picked at the fish until there was nothing on the bones. Everyone offered the last potato to Father, but secretly, we probably all wanted it. The coconut and mangos had never tasted more divine. Hải and I shared one coconut and he made sure I got most of it. A couple of times our hands touched or his calves grazed against my leg, but I did not pull away from him. And once, when I stood behind him to clear the plates from the table, my breasts brushed against his shoulder. An electrifying sensation coursed through my body and I was curious what it would feel like to have his mouth on them.

Still feeling a little lightheaded from the two beers I had earlier, I seek Hải out. A quick glance at Thủy-Tiên assures me she is in deep slumber. I tiptoe to Hải's room, which was once Tree's room. They were sharing the bedroom until Tree volunteered last week to sleep in the bunker, and give each other their own space. I pass Sister Six's bedroom. She is snoring loud tonight. I turn the knob slowly to Hải's bedroom and walk in, careful not to make a sound. The cool tiles feel refreshing on my bare feet. Hải's window is wide open and the temperature is pleasant. It is raining again. I stand at the foot of his bed and negotiate whether I should leave. It takes a minute for my eyes to adjust to the new darkness of the room and I can make out the outline of Hải's body. His breathing is slow and deep. He rolls over. His eyes are open.

Without a word, I unbutton my shirt slowly with trembling hands and let the shirt fall to the floor. I slip off my pants and stand before him in my underwear, feeling vulnerable and thankful for the darkness that blankets my imperfections. Hải lifts up his bedsheet and I walk toward him, my heart beating fast. I slide underneath the sheet as his arms wrap around my waist, and we kiss with passion. The masculine scent of beer on his breath and grease on his skin, from all the years of tinkering with cars, scooters, and motorbikes, draws me in. I cannot get enough of him as he tightens his grip on my hips and pulls me to him. Tonight, I feel free and let my body surrender to his touch.

After our lovemaking, Hải gets out of bed and walks to the dresser. "I have something for you." The silhouette of his naked body is beautiful with the moonlight on him. He sits on the bed and hands me a round pastry. "It is not a mid-Autumn festival without a mooncake."

My heart swells with excitement as I clasp my hands together with glee. "Is the filling bean or lotus seed paste?" I hope it is the latter. I cannot wait to sink my teeth into this delicious, thick and rich dessert.

"Lotus seed." Hải offers me the first bite. "Too bad we do not have tea to go with it."

Without shame, I take a big morsel. "It is so sweet and dense and decadent and…Wait. How did you get this?"

Hải laughs. He carefully breaks the mooncake in half so as to not break the salted egg yolk inside. It is a perfect yellowish-orange orb, round like the autumn moon. He places the yolk gently into the palm of my hand. I lift it to my mouth. "Do not eat it yet!" I stop and notice a small hole in it. How strange. Hải grabs my other hand and leads me to the window. "Look at the moon. One day, you will be looking at this same moon, but from a window in America."

I want to pop the creamy yolk into my mouth. "We can be looking at this same moon together someday, in America, if you come with us."

Hải shakes his head no. "I cannot go with you."

We stand in silence, admiring the night sky. The light of the moon illuminates our bare skin. I feel such peace and happiness but have not forgotten the yolk in my hand. I want to eat it.

Sensing my eagerness, Hải chuckles. "Go ahead and break the yolk open." I pinch the yolk with my fingers and with a light squeeze, it crumbles apart in my hand. There is a small capsule inside. "This is your mooncake to freedom. Open the capsule."

I give Hải pieces of the broken yolk and open the capsule carefully. There is a small scroll. I read the message out loud. "Rooster, 29, cyclo, bananas." I do not understand its meaning.

"On the twenty-ninth of October, when you hear the rooster crow in the morning, be ready. There will be a cyclo passing by with a bunch of bananas on it. You and Thủy-Tiên are to get in it and pretend you are going to the market. Instead, you will be taken to a secret meeting place by the river. There will be a boat to take you out to sea. I am sorry but I did not have enough to pay for Tree, and you cannot afford to wait. There may not be a better opportunity any time soon."

I am speechless. Is this happening? How did he arrange this? I lean into him and wrap my arms around his neck, kissing him fervently at first, and then caressing his mouth gently with my tongue. I ease down to his neck, to the base of his throat, and slide my lips over his clavicle. Hải exhales and pulls me close, guiding me to the floor. My legs open willingly for him and I let out a moan of pleasure as I feel him ease inside of me. Soon the sun will rise and deliver another day of challenges, but right now, there is only Hải and my mooncake to freedom.

# 12 THE TAXI PEDDLER (OCTOBER 1976)

The rooster crows the day I leave Việt Nam on the twenty-ninth of October in 1976. It is the year of the mighty dragon. I must be fearless like the dragon so that we can get to America safely. My family is still asleep although Brother Seven is stirring to get ready for work. Same routine every day for my poor brother. He will be furious when he discovers that I am gone and did not take Tree with me. I will miss Sister Six, despite her nagging and opinionated comments. Alas, I do not have time right now to dwell on what or who I am leaving behind. I have been consumed the past month with sadness, fear, excitement, anxiety, and a mix of a hundred different emotions. It is now time to look forward.

"Are you ready?" Hải stands behind me, cigarette in hand.

"I am ready," I say. "I have in my bag an extra change of clothes, some money that you gave me, some dried fruits, sugar cane, and the fried bananas Sister Six made last night. She will be mad when she finds out I took them." Hải walks with me to the end of the alley. He says nothing. "I also have my wedding ring and will sell that if I have to."

He caresses Thủy-Tiên's cheeks. "Be a good girl for your mother. No crying. You must be quiet and brave, and when you make it to America, get a good education. Take care of your heart so it beats strong and do not give your heart to anyone unless he can make your heart beat stronger. Understand?" My little dolly reaches for Hải, but he does not pick her up.

"Hải, I have gone over the plan a dozen times in my head, but when I get to the fisherman's boat, what happens next?"

He reaches for my hand but then stops, probably because someone may be spying. "The monsoon season is over. You should have calm waters for the journey." His eyes tell me to stay as he searches for the right words, but instead, he abruptly walks briskly back to the house.

I want to chase after Hải but a man's cough distracts me. "Miss, do you need a xích lô to the market this morning?" The cyclo has arrived, with bananas in the front carriage. I hop onto the bicycle taxi before I lose my courage, and with Thủy-Tiên on my lap, we ride away towards the town center. "Hold your tears."

He weaves through pedestrian traffic, choosing the alleys instead of the main roads. He stops a couple of times to sell bananas. My peddler has bouts of coughing during our fifteen-minute ride. At one point, he has a harsh coughing spell and swerves too far to the right, hitting a chili plant on the ground. We arrive at the market, now coming to life as people begin setting up for the day. He stops in front of a tailor shop.

I hop off and thank him. "Cảm ơn bạn."

"Take these and go into the shop." My taxi peddler hands me a bunch of bananas.

I leave my shoes outside on the stoop and step inside. Samples of fabric hang from the ceiling, vibrant colors of red, gold, blue and green, in a variety of designs. There are two mannequins dressed in festive wedding attire. The garments remind me of my wedding day. There is a doorway to a back room, with a lime-green curtain covering the entrance.

"Hello?" I inquire.

A young woman steps from behind the curtain and beckons me to follow her to the back room. "If anyone asks, your name is Thu."

"That is perfect since it means Autumn," I respond.

"Put these clothes on for you and your daughter." She hands me brown polyester pajamas with green paisley patterns on them. Thủy-Tiên receives a pale yellow sundress and bonnet. "With these clothes, no one will recognize you. Listen carefully, Thu. My husband is going to take you on foot to a nearby village. A casual observer will see the three of you as a poor family heading to the river to catch a fish. And walk with a limp with your head down. Understand?"

I nod. "Thank you, friend. I will not forget your kindness."

While we dress, the young woman leaves to retrieve my shoes. We exit through the back door and my "husband" waves me to follow him.

"Head down and limp," the seamstress whispers.

I immediately shift my weight over to my left leg and limp behind my guide. It dawns on me that he is the same man as the taxi peddler, only he is wearing different clothes with holes in them.

"You and your wife are so kind." I struggle to keep pace with him carrying Thủy-Tiên. "If there is anything I can do to repay you, please let me know. I will make good on my debt once I make it to America." Pretending to have an impaired leg is not an easy facade to maintain when you have to walk nearly two kilometers.

My companion slows down. "Let me carry the child." He takes Thủy-Tiên from my arms before I give him consent.

"What is your name?" I ask.

My companion coughs and spits out phlegm. He stops to hunch over and put his left hand on his knee. His breathing is laborious and he is now wheezing. I worry he will drop Thủy-Tiên. "Call me Husband." He stands up and we resume walking. "Your brother-in-law, Hải, is a good, honest man. He used to fix our scooters. We met many years ago in Thái Lan when the tuk-tuk I was riding broke down. It turned out to be bad, watered-down fuel. We crossed paths again a year later and have been friends since then." My "husband" stops to cough again. More sputum is expelled from his mouth.

"You are sick. Do you smoke?" I ask.

"No. It is probably the bad air quality and the fumes left from the airplanes, all the chemicals the Americans sprayed." He clears his throat, spits again, and then launches a gelatinous, sticky substance from his left nostril.

"I used to sell western medicine," I say. "That is how my family has been able to survive. I wish I had some to give you, but if you make it to Sài Gòn, there is a man who can get some for you. His name is Cường and he owns a toy shop near the old U.S. embassy."

"I will remember that."

We walk in silence for a while, stopping frequently when my companion has his fits of coughing or has to pee in the bushes. My limping does not help our pace either. It takes us an hour to walk almost two kilometers to the village. There is smoke rising from the shanties. The village is on fire.

***

As we approach the village, I smell gasoline, incense, and pineapples. Strangely, the scent takes me back to my home the night my mother died of cancer. My siblings and I were all lighting incense at the altar, asking our ancestors to receive our mother, and burning joss paper so that her spirit can have money in the afterlife. Many of the offerings were Mother's favorite foods, such as pineapples, sugar apples, duck noodle soup, escargot grilled in lemongrass, and coconut-mango sticky rice. The scene now before me is grim.

The villagers are dressed in rags, their clothes held together by pineapple or banana leaf fibers. Most of them are barefoot. Their homes are small, thatched huts or cottages with leaky roofs due to the heavy rainfalls. There is a small grave site near a grove of jackfruit trees, the tombs and markers knocked down by either the force of the monsoons or maybe by the communists so that families cannot mourn the dead. The Vietnamese believe desecration of graves will anger the spirits and bring harm to the living. I can only hope the destruction was done by natural causes and not by humans. Children huddle beside their parents, scratching their tender young flesh at what appears to be scabies, their skin raw and red from the rash caused by tiny mites burrowed into their bodies. There is laughter mixed in with the screaming and crying.

I see a woman on her knees, her hands clasped together in prayer, as she begs a man in uniform. "Please, have mercy and spare this old lady. I will have nothing if you burn down my home."

The officer laughs. "You remind me of my grandmother."

"Then take pity on this old grandmother as you would of your own," she beseeches.

"My grandmother was a cruel woman and stingy as hell. I bet you are like her." He mocks her and lifts up his torch.

"Stop!" I scream and run to the old woman, forgetting my limp.

My "husband" whispers, "Are you crazy?"

I kneel down in front of her, shield her from any blow the officer may strike, and wince as I prepare for a beating. "Where is your respect for your elders? This woman is not your grandmother. If you are going to harass anyone, why must it be someone feeble, who has nothing, and is not worth your energy?"

I see a glimpse of abhorrence in the officer's eyes before I feel the hard brunt of his torch handle, first in my right temple, then again in my throat. The sharp pain in the jugular notch of my neck drowns out the pain on my head. I gasp for air and cough. I reach for the old woman to stand up but she runs away. The officer kicks me in the stomach. "You look more beautiful on your knees." I crumble to the ground. Pain shoots up my spine.

I see "Husband" hand Thủy-Tiên to a teenage girl and rush to my side. Two more cadres stride up to join the party. One of them, a young man probably not more than twenty years old, drags a young woman behind him by the hair. "You found yourself a pretty one." The woman with him screams and kicks, her body writhes in pain, her shirt unbuttoned down to her navel. Around her breasts are teeth marks. My heart sinks into my stomach.

"A little older, but definitely pretty," my aggressor responds. "Maybe she can teach me a thing or two."

The three officers laugh. My taxi peddler finds his voice and points to the young man that is clutching the girl's hair in his fist. "You look familiar. You are Giáp's nephew."

The smile on the young officer's face disappears. "Who are you?"

"I am a man who peddles bananas on the streets and make my living transporting people around on my bicycle," says my "husband". He coughs a couple times before continuing. "This is my wife, Thu. In another life, I was a physician, Doctor Phạm Văn Minh. Are you not the nephew of the great General Võ Nguyên Giáp, military commander of The People's Army?"

"Speak carefully. My uncle is the Minister of National Defense and now Deputy Prime Minister for the Socialist Republic," the young assailant warns.

"Yes," my new friend, Doctor Minh, acknowledges, "your uncle was once my father's history teacher as well as a patient of mine. I was one of his physicians who treated him when he needed medical attention. Your uncle is in my debt, and I ask that you show the people of this village mercy, as an honorable act of repaying your uncle's debt."

"These villagers must be tormented and taught a lesson," the young cadre responds. "They have been harboring war criminals and helping them leave the country."

"I believe they all have learned their lesson, and if you show us all mercy now, we will tell our children about this day, how three kind officers protected us from our own demise." Minh coughs again and chokes on his saliva. He regains his composure and continues. "These villagers were wrong to help the war criminals, however, please, let my wife, my child, and I pass unharmed. We were heading to the river to catch some fish, and are not a part of this deception."

"Is that so? Then go to the river and catch us three fish. Your wife and child stay here. When you come back, she will cook us a meal, and then we will be on our way."

Panic courses through my veins. Me? Cook a meal? I plead to Minh with my eyes not to leave us. He nods and hacks some more. "Let me bring my wife to the river. It will be easier to catch fish with two people so that you all can be feasting sooner."

The third officer finally speaks up. "Let them go. We will keep their child until they return."

"Our child is only two years old. She needs her mother," says Minh, coughing again and clutching his chest. "I give you my word, we will return. My wife is the best cook in our province. You will not be disappointed."

Again, panic strikes me.

"Enough. I have no more patience with you," says the young cadre. "Your wife and child stay here. I promise them no harm, but you have one hour to bring back three fish."

I encourage Minh to leave. "Return hastily with three of the mightiest fish you can catch. We will be safe, as he promises."

Minh runs through the brush towards the river, bending over once to cough and catch his breath. I pray he will return within an hour. Three hours ago, he was a taxi peddler to me, selling bananas and taking me to his wife's tailor shop. Now, he is my pretend husband, a doctor, a fisherman, and hopefully, a hero.

I walk over to the teenage girl holding Thủy-Tiên and take my daughter from her. The three officers ignore me. They light up their cigarette and talk about their favorite Vietnamese or French cuisines. The young cadre that was holding the village girl's hair releases his grip on her ebony locks. He gives her a kick in the butt and tells her to fetch him something to drink. She runs toward the graveyard, her hands clutching her shirt close. I follow for a short distance but then the young girl runs into a dilapidated shed. I head to the cemetery instead.

I sit down on the bench with Thủy-Tiên and share one of Sister Six's fried bananas with her. I try to read some of the headstones, but most are broken. I am content to not be bothered and allow myself to relax. The throbbing pain in my throat and stomach subsides, and it is nearly an hour that passes before the sounds of footsteps disturb my tranquility. My pulse quickens as my heart pounds hard behind the inner chamber of my chest. Is Minh back?

I prepare a warm smile to greet whoever is behind me. My smile fades into shock. I catch my breath. "Minh-Hoàng." It is Mrs. Trần's oldest son.

# 13 THE CLEVER PHOENIX (OCTOBER 1976)

Minh-Hoàng stands before me with intensity in his eyes. It has been over a year, since last May, that I was silently interrogated by his eyes. Today is no different. He surveys me up and down, stopping briefly at my breasts, before finally focusing on my temple. "You are hurt. Let me see."

"I am fine." I tilt my head to the side so he can examine my injury. "How is your brother, Huy? And your mom?"

"Lopsided was taken to a re-education camp as you know. He was transferred a couple times. My mom and I visited him once before he was transferred." Minh-Hoàng falls quiet.

"Surely he is out now, perhaps married with a family of his own?" I inquire. "If I remember correctly, he was only going to be at the facility for two weeks."

"Two weeks became two months," Minh-Hoàng says matter-of-factly, "and now, we are heading on two years. I do not know which camp he is at, or if he is even alive."

"Did you try to get him out? You have connections--"

"Of course I tried!" he says curtly. "He is my brother. You have no idea how much he suffered and how terrible he was treated." Minh-Hoàng sits down on the bench and rests his head on his hands. I feel sorry for him.

"How is your mom handling this?" I am worried Mrs. Trần's heart is broken once again.

"I feel her spirit slipping away, day by day. She begs me to do something, but what can I do? I have no influence with anyone in control of the camps. I feel so helpless while my brother is forced to do hard labor. He is being starved with a small bowl of rice and a cup of water each day, and confined to a metal box no bigger than two meters high and wide."

We sit quietly for a few minutes. I have no words to comfort him and although afraid to say something that will offend him, I speak anyways. "Why are you here with those men? They terrorized those people in this hamlet, innocent people, young and old."

"Innocent?" he asks. "Are you innocent?" I dare not respond. "I am guessing you and your daughter were heading to this village to seek refuge, before meeting up with a fishing crew or someone at the river. No doubt you paid some people nicely for the voyage to the Philippines or somewhere. I guarantee you the boat is long gone or already caught. I will take you both back home to your family."

"I cannot leave without my friend, Doctor Phạm Văn Minh. Your men sent him off to the river to catch some fish for lunch. It has been over an hour but he should be returning soon."

"You are naïve. Your companion is long gone. Why would he return for you when he can escape and hide? Maybe he is on that boat already and out to sea."

The thought of abandonment and betrayal is daunting. A wave of emotions sweeps over me, changing from sadness to anger to fear and finally, joy. Maybe Minh managed to get home.

"You are not going to arrest me?" I ask with trepidation.

Minh-Hoàng laughs. "My mother would skin me alive if I let any harm come to you. She adores you."

My eyes open wide. Surely he is not referring to cranky, old Mrs. Trần, the she-Jekyll, the woman with a razor-sharp tongue and a personality coarser than a sixty-grit sheet of sandpaper?

"I am not ready to go home. I want to go to Sài Gòn to see your mother."

"It is Uncle Hồ's city now," he reminds me, "but yes, I can take you. It is a long journey. Do you want to rest tonight and leave in the morning?"

"No, I would like to see your mother tonight. Maybe I can bring her some comfort."

"How will you return to your province?" he asks.

"I have a friend who can take me," I lie, referring to Cường.

\*\*\*

The ride back to Sài Gòn in Minh-Hoàng's *Kaiser-Jeep M715* is an uncomfortable one. The utility truck only seats two, with a large battery box between the two seats. The cargo bed is austere with space for only the wheel wells and some provisions. Thủy-Tiên sits on my lap for the duration of the trip and my legs are sore. Luckily, the journey is faster and easier when you are sitting next to a communist. We drive through every security checkpoint with ease. Minh-Hoàng flashes his military credentials and receives a nod to proceed.

"Thủy-Tiên is hungry. Are you?" I offer snacks to Minh-Hoàng to be polite. "I have some dried fruits, sugar cane, and bananas in my bag."

He takes a handful of dried tamarind and pops them in his mouth, one by one, chewing and sucking on each piece slowly so as to savor the taste, before spitting the seed out. "My mother is the master of dried foods."

"I know. She showed me the bunker. I would give anything for some iced coffee with condensed milk to go with these fruits."

"There is a nice café not far from here. We can stop."

"It is too much trouble and I do not have enough money to spare."

"What about your monthly stipend?" he asks.

"I am not eligible to receive the two-hundred-thousand đồng a month. Only the heads of households get a monthly allowance and because I am a woman with no husband--"

Minh-Hoàng arches his eyebrow. "How have you been managing?"

I cannot confess to peddling western medicine on the black market. "I am living with my father under his stipend."

"You should get your own monthly allowance. You have a daughter to feed and clothe. You need to register under your maiden name, with a different address apart from your father's."

"So if I had registered under my family name as Lê Ngọc Tuyết, instead of Vương Ngọc Tuyết, I could have received money?" I am now worried that I may have shared too much with this communist, even if he is Mrs. Trần's son.

"You will begin receiving the monthly stipend. I will take care of it," he says. What ulterior motives does he have? What does he want in return?

I thank him and switch topics to something I feel is safe to discuss. "What is your mother's name? I always call her Mrs. Trần, but she never shared with me her first name."

"Diệp," he answers. "She hates her name. She said when Lopsided and I were born, she wanted to make sure our names had powerful meanings."

"So she named you the clever phoenix and your brother radiance."

"Yes, but we have yet to live up to our names," Minh-Hoàng says.

"I disagree," I offer. "You were clever enough to stay alive for eight years and return home, and Huy, well, it is clear he brought light and sunshine to your mother's life."

Minh-Hoàng pulls the truck over and kills the engine. "We are here. This café makes the strongest coffee."

Minh-Hoàng orders me a café au lait with a spoon of condensed milk. He insists I have it hot instead of my usual iced coffee with two spoons of condensed milk. Otherwise, how can I truly appreciate the coffee this café has to offer? I am not disappointed. I sip slowly and enjoy every trickle of liquid down my throat. This is so divine.

***

By 7 p.m. we drive through the streets of District One in Sài Gòn. The Bến Thành Market remains the same. Thống Nhất Boulevard, which once ran in front of the Independence Palace, has now been renamed to Lê Duẩn Street, after the Communist Party's General Secretary, who took over power after Hồ Chí Minh's death. The Independence Palace, now called the Reunification Palace, still looks the same except gone is the yellow flag with three red stripes. Here to stay is the red Republic of Việt Nam flag with a yellow star in the middle.

I am unexpectedly nervous to see Mrs. Trần again. Will she receive me with open arms, like a lost daughter who has returned, or will she have a snarky comment to belittle me for once again failing to leave this country? We walk through the familiar alley and step into Mrs. Trần's house. It is immaculate. Not a speck of dust or a fly buzzing by. Thủy-Tiên walks immediately over to the hammock and tries to crawl in by herself. It is quiet in the house. The air is stale. I was hoping to be greeted by smells of curry or caramelized sugar, hoping that she may have prepared dinner. There is no sign of Mrs. Trần. Minh-Hoàng checks upstairs while I walk outside to the back garden. I peek around and do not see any trace of her.

A gut-wrenching scream comes from upstairs. I run back inside the house and up the two flights of stairs to the top floor. I check the rooms but see no one. The cry comes again and I fly up to the landing of the roof. Clothes hang on a rod across the rooftop. I see the bottom of Minh-Hoàng's shoes and rush to his side, pushing away pants and sheets hanging on the clothesline. His deep, throaty gurgle evolves into a maniacal roar, like an insane man throwing a tantrum. He is kneeling on the ground, cupping Mrs. Trần's face in one hand and supporting her lifeless body in his other arm. His jerky movements go from shaking her body to stroking her head, back to cupping her face and then slapping her cheeks.

"Má! Má ơi!" Minh-Hoàng sobs, saying "Mother! Oh, Mother!" over and over again. He cradles her and rocks back and forth. "Mother! Oh, Mother!"

I kneel down next to Mrs. Trần and lift her limp hand. It is cold and clammy. I feel a faint heartbeat on her wrist. I wish Dr. Phạm, my taxi peddler friend, is here. He would know what to do. Mrs. Trần's body convulses. She gasps for air and her eyes pop open. I see the pupils constrict before her eyes roll up and back. She goes into cardiac arrest and seizes again. I search for clues as to what happened. I see a bottle with a chloroquine label. Would malaria pills have this effect on her?

"She poisoned herself with these pills," I say to a grief-stricken Minh-Hoàng.

He hysterically asks over and over again why she left him. "Má! Tại sao Má bỏ con?"

I run down the stairs and out the front doors. "I need a doctor!" I pound my small fist on the door across from Mrs. Trần's house. "Please, someone, help." No one answers. I dash over to the next house and rap hard on the window. "Please help. My aunt is dying. I need a doctor."

A woman opens her window. "Take her to the hospital."

"Do you have a car? Please, we only have a jeep that seats two people and there is no space in the back large enough for--"

I am cut off by the window slamming shut in my face. I am shocked but have no time to argue. Minh-Hoàng's shrill cry has me darting back inside the house as quickly as I can. Thủy-Tiên is by the hammock, oblivious to what is happening right now, and still trying to climb into the hammock.

Minh-Hoàng carries his small, lifeless mother down the stairs. Tears rain down his face. "Why?" I half expect her to answer as if this is a cruel joke she is playing. "She is gone. She has left me. I am all alone now." His knees buckle beneath him and he kneels to the floor. Minh-Hoàng bends his head down in sorrow.

My heart is heavy. My monsoon tears begin where Minh-Hoàng's ends. "I will call the temple for a monk."

# 14 STARTING OVER (NOVEMBER 1976)

Minh-Hoàng had a beautiful tomb built above ground for his mother three days after her death. She now rests in the backyard, in her garden of herbs, watermelons, and narcissus flowers. The tomb sits atop five levels of ceramic and stones, to ensure the water level never rises high enough during the monsoon season to flood it. It is a richly decorated tomb in colors of mauve and yellow. Erected at the foot of the tomb, on either corner, sits a tiger statue, to guard and protect her spirit. In the center of the headstone, there is a personalized painting, glazed in ceramic tiles, of Mrs. Trần's face. The inscription underneath reads:

*Trần Bích Diệp*
*July 20, 1914 – October 29, 1976*
*Here lies a Wood Tiger of Việt Nam, mother to many, wife to one, and slave to none.*

I can only imagine how much this cost to build. The funeral is somber, despite the food, drinks, music, and incense to celebrate Mrs. Trần's life. At her altar, joss money is burned to prepare her for the afterlife, the rebirth. Some of her favorite foods are offered, including some dried, preserved goods. There are nineteen people attending the ceremony, most of us wearing our white mourning robes and white bandanas or pointed hoods. White represents the ashes of the dead. Minh-Hoàng wants to keep it small and intimate since elaborate funerals are discouraged under the new communist rule. I could not help but secretly wonder if she had many friends or family members left. Surprisingly, Cường is here to pay his respects, even though he only met her once.

"Your mother was born the month and year of the wood tiger. My daughter is a wood tiger as well," I say to Minh-Hoàng, who is standing next to Cường.

Neither man says a word to each other, but both look relieved to see me. I hand Minh-Hoàng an envelope of money, as is the custom in Vietnamese culture for weddings and funerals, to help the family with expenses. It is most of the money I have from Hải for my escape.

"Thank you. Yes," responds Minh-Hoàng, "and like the tiger zodiac, she was independent, courageous, and confident."

"And like the wood element, she had a lot of leadership capabilities that strengthened her resolve," I add.

"I only met her once," chimes in Cường, "but she scared me."

Minh-Hoàng and I laugh.

"She scared me too," I agree.

"Try being her son," says Minh-Hoàng. "She used to beat Lopsided and me daily when we were kids. It did not stop until we left home to join the army."

"Well, tigers are known to be fierce and short-tempered," I say.

"And arrogant," adds Minh-Hoàng. "Everything always had to be the best with her, always perfect, always spotless."

Cường and I nod. Not one of us knows what to say next as we have nothing in common. Perhaps the only common thread that weaves through all of us is the one of committing illegal acts to stay alive. I never believed I would stand next to a known communist enemy and feel compassion for him. I never imagined I would stand next to a gangster whom the mob still puppeteers and trust him with my livelihood. What a great team we would make.

"What is next for you?" Cường asks me.

"I still have to find a cure for Thủy-Tiên and I am not going to find it here. Something is wrong with her heart," I say.

"If it is money you need," offers Minh-Hoàng, "I can help you. I told you I would take care of your stipend."

"And I can continue to help you as well," adds Cường.

Minh-Hoàng gives Cường a curious glance. "What do you mean?" Cường and I both bite our tongue, fearing the truth will put us both in prison. "Spit it out or else I will be forced to investigate and things will not turn out good for you both. Tell me the truth and maybe I can help or protect you."

We both continue to hold our tongue. Minh-Hoàng is agitated. Finally, I speak up. "Cường has been--"

Cường grabs me by the arm and leads me to the other side of the garden, not offering an excuse or apology to Minh-Hoàng for being abrupt. "What are you doing? Are you crazy?" Cường is seething with anger. "You cannot tell him I have been supplying you contraband drugs and that you had been selling them in the black market."

"First of all," I say, "they are not drugs that have been imported or exported illegally. They are western medicines that have been abandoned by the United States."

"It does not matter. What we are doing is not legal and we will be punished if caught. We cannot trust him."

"Then let us test him. Let me see if he is a man true to his words. Let me see if he gets me that monthly stipend."

"And then what?" Cường is still unsure.

"Let me do something illegal in front of him and make sure he sees me. We will see what he does. If he protects me and does not have me arrested, then we can trust him."

"And if you get arrested?" asks Cường.

"I will have Thủy-Tiên with me. He will not arrest me. He once told me that his mother would skin him alive if he let any harm be done to me. I believe him and I believe that he will continue to honor his mother's wishes because he loves her."

"How do you know she even said that or if she even meant it?" asks Cường. "Or if he will even hold himself accountable now that his mother is not here to beat him?"

"Well, she can still haunt him. Cường, you were not there when he found his mother. She had a broken heart and she ended the pain by overdosing on malaria pills. He cried like a tormented child. His mother was his everything. He may be a communist, but he has his convictions and his loyalties, the greatest of all were to his mother."

Cường consents. "All right, but what if he arrests me instead? I am your supplier."

"Then you tell him one of Đại Cathay's generals will come after him. Who cares if that is true or not? The threat will be real enough."

In the few days that followed, I received my two-hundred-thousand đồng stipend that Minh-Hoàng promised. He completed the application using my maiden name and the address next to his home, where Tý and I lived briefly. Thủy-Tiên and I have been staying at that house the past week since it is an abandoned home.

"Are you going to go home, back to your family?" asks Minh-Hoàng.

"Yes, but first I need to say goodbye to Cường." I sip my iced coffee. "Their coffee is not strong, but the aroma is enticing." The little café in the city center is not busy this morning. There are not enough patrons who can afford such luxuries. I cannot either, even with the small stipend I received.

"They probably diluted it with extra water to make the supply stretch," says Minh-Hoàng. "Are you going to tell me how Cường has been helping you?"

"Last year, Cường helped me sell some things I took from the U.S. embassy after the Americans abandoned it and went home. He also gave me a steep discount on a toy for Thủy-Tiên when I did not have much money. He helps when he can."

"Is he family?" Minh-Hoàng leans in and looks directly into my eyes.

"No. He was a friend of my husband's." I hold his gaze to prove I have nothing to hide.

"Why was he so nervous or upset at my mom's funeral?"

"He was not sure how you would react to us stealing from the embassy. Maybe he was a little embarrassed, also, because you might think we have a relationship."

"Do you? A married man helping another married woman, even if she is separated from her husband, only means he has feelings for her."

"Cường is a hard-working man who makes next to nothing selling toys to take care of his sick relatives and aging parents. His wife committed suicide two or three years ago. She poisoned herself."

Minh-Hoàng's eyes mist up. "I feel the pain he must still feel."

"Maybe you and Cường can be friends," I say optimistically. "The American War is over. We are one country now but we still have many enemies. The Cambodians, Laotians, and the Chinese, they all want control of our land and our waters. Life will continue to be oppressive. Our people are poor and starving, or disabled and unable to work. The government controls everything, from our food supply to the media. You may not feel the same hopelessness I feel, but you cannot deny we are not in prosperous economic times right now."

"It will get better. Why do you want to leave when your family is here and you can get medical help for your daughter here or in Thái Lan?"

"The mortality rate for children under five years old is the highest it has ever been here. I believe Thủy-Tiên will have a better chance of survival where there are better medicine and easier access to those medicines. Thái Lan is too expensive and I do not trust them, even though our two countries have established diplomatic relations. I hear people talking all the time about the Thai pirates stealing and raping women. Besides, where are all our doctors? Most of them have died, fled, or are detained in re-education camps. The ones we have left have lost their practice, lost their hospital, are in hiding or lost their will."

"I disagree with you," says Minh-Hoàng, "but do what you want." I can tell he is annoyed and getting defensive. I do not care.

"It would be helpful if there is a way I can go about my business without any trouble or detainment at the checkpoints. I want to get home as quickly as possible without any searches. Do you have the ability to help with this?"

"Give me a day or two. I will see what I can do, then you can go home."

"Thank you," I say, "and also for the coffee. I need to say goodbye to Cường now."

Minh-Hoàng nods and I take my leave with my daughter in tow. I can feel Minh-Hoàng's eyes on me as I walk away. I sway my hips a bit more to accentuate my curves, hoping my little strut will encourage him to try hard for my security clearance at the checkpoints.

***

I meet Cường at his toy store. Thủy-Tiên's eyes open wide. All the crinkly cellophane wrappers tempt her to touch them; all the colorful toys beg her for attention. She teeters as she runs from one doll to another before getting distracted by a stuffed animal or a plastic toy figure. I let her enjoy this moment and play with the toys. I see Cường finishing up with a customer and patiently wait for him to complete the sale.

"Business must be good," I say after the customer leaves.

Cường laughs. "One customer does not mean business is good."

"I had coffee with Minh-Hoàng," I report. "He got me the stipend like he promised, and he is working to ensure I have no problems with the security checkpoints to Vĩnh Bình."

"What about the checkpoints back to here?" Cường asks.

"I assume that clearance getting home would be the same as getting back to Sài Gòn."

"I hope you are right. Now we need to do the ultimate test." Cường hands me a small olive green nylon pouch with a U.S. medical department insignia on the front of the cover flap. "You have to do something illegal right before his eyes to see if he will turn the other way or arrest you."

"So what do you have for me today?" I open the snap and pull out a green plastic box. Inside are medical supplies - an assortment of dressings and bandages, a bottle of iodine water purification tablets, a bottle of disinfectant, a container of foot powder, lip balm, and some tablets, probably painkillers. "I am not going to be able to sell these items individually."

"I have five more of those bags, three *Zippo* lighters, 48 tablets of codeine, and six pills of *Dexedrine*," adds Cường.

"What do the codeine and *Dexedrine* do?"

"Codeine is for pain but I am not sure about the *Dexedrine*."

I close the snap on the plastic box and put it back into the nylon pouch. "I will be leaving either tomorrow or the following day, depending on when Minh-Hoàng gets me the license to go through the checkpoints. I hope to return in one or two weeks with your share of the money."

I scoop up Thủy-Tiên, who taps excitedly on the glass of the display case. I see the same airplane model that we had to leave behind in the old house next to Mrs. Trần's house, now Minh-Hoàng's house. Sadly, the abandoned house was robbed and everything was taken.

"Take the airplane." Cường hands it to Thủy-Tiên. "You can pay me later."

"This time, it is fifty-fifty split." I leave before he argues with me.

***

Starting over is not an easy thing to do, but this time, I feel better equipped to handle what may be coming around the river bend. I recognize now that I do not have control of anything, and for this reason, I feel prepared for everything. My escape now seems light years away. Starting over means back to selling and saving, being patient until I have more than enough money to ensure safe passage, negotiating power, and a new start in America. It means I must take charge of my own departure and not rely on Hải or anyone to do it for me. And it means making my own allies, using and beguiling my enemies, and, like Mrs.

Trần once said to me, letting my tongue be my greatest artillery.

Thủy-Tiên and I walk next door to see Minh-Hoàng. I hope he has good news for me. We find him in the garden, sitting on the bench above the bunker. "I was talking to my mother."

"I can feel her presence," I say.

"Do you believe in ghosts?" he asks.

"Yes, I had been taunted by one, a long time ago when I was at uni," I say. "I was pushed off my hammock one night when nobody was around. Another time, I woke up to sounds of people walking. There was no one there but all the slippers in the house were moving."

"My mother once told me a story about how, in a village near Cần Thơ, the sound of a woman crying by the Hậu River can be heard right before dawn breaks. Many people have heard her crying, even my mom, so she claimed. The local people were told by a fortune teller to dig up an unmarked grave near the river and bury the woman in a separate grave. At first, people dismissed the fortune teller as crazy, but after many reports of hearing the woman's cry, they dug up the grave. They found four skeletons in one grave, one of which was a woman's. They removed her bones and gave her a separate resting place. The locals said the crying stopped."

"Is your mother haunting you?" I sit down beside him and let my daughter explore.

"More like nagging me," he answers. "She wants to make sure I help you succeed in leaving, even though it is against what I think you should do. She wants the best for Thủy-Tiên."

"You should listen to her. She can still whip you."

Minh-Hoàng smiles. "Yes."

I change the subject. "Do you have an update for me?"

"I do." He springs to his feet and picks Thủy-Tiên up. "Join me for dinner and I will tell you. I am a good cook." I agree to have dinner with him and we walk back into the house to the kitchen. "You will have to earn your dinner tonight and help me cook."

My eyes open wide in protest. "What are we cooking?"

Minh-Hoàng laughs at me. "Eel congee soup with perilla leaves. You better learn now before Thủy-Tiên finds out her mother is a fraud." *Damn Mrs. Trần! This is your doing!* I wish I had not agreed to dinner. "I also have some coconuts. We can drink the juice and eat the young coconut meat to finish the palate."

The live eels squirm about in the plastic colander. They are a little longer than half a meter and quite dark, a mixture of green and black. Their skin is shiny and slimy.

I am nauseated. "I can help make the congee and wash the perilla, but I am not touching those eels."

"You are not going to trick me into believing you are sick and unable to help me cook." My host does not let me off the hook. "You are going to learn everything from beginning to end. If you want to survive on your own and take care of your daughter in the new land, you need to be self-sufficient and not rely on anyone."

I concede, only because he is right. Minh-Hoàng guides me through the process of killing the eels, cleaning them, preparing the grill in the makeshift fire pit, and cooking them.

"I thought I was helping you cook, not doing everything myself," I say sarcastically.

"How else can you take all the pride when I tell you it is delicious?" asks Minh-Hoàng. "While the eels are cooking, we will cook the rice and prepare the perilla."

"You mean, I will cook and prepare. There is no 'we' is there?" I ask.

"See? You are already learning and proud of yourself." He hands me a bowl.

"You smile more than your mom ever did." I scoop two cups of rice into the bowl and wash the rice. I drain the water and repeat until the water runs clear. "You are different from your mom."

"You are wrong. I am very much my mother's son." Minh-Hoàng puts the rice into a pot and cooks it over an open flame. "Lopsided was more like my father. My mother loved them both and showed them affection. As the oldest son, I was always on the receiving end of her vexations. At times I resented her, but I loved and respected her too. She made me resilient so that I could endure anything, and always rise up to adversities. Lopsided was weak – too much love – and look where it got him. Same with my father."

"Receiving love does not make you grow up to be weak." I take a wooden spoon and stir the rice so it does not stick to the pot. "People need affection. Love is stronger than hate."

"Is it?" Minh-Hoàng washes the perilla leaves. "Thirty years of war for our country, from the Japanese to the French to the Americans, all because hate is stronger than love. And it is not over yet. Another war with Cambodia and China is coming."

"Another reason for me to leave with Thủy-Tiên. If her failing health does not kill her first, the war with Kampuchea or China will," I affirm. "Now would be a good time for you to tell me about tomorrow. Will we be able to get home and through all the security checkpoints without any harassment?"

"Yes, but I will fill in the details over dinner." Minh-Hoàng instructs me on how to flavor the rice congee soup. He then hands me a coconut and demonstrates how to break open one without any tools. "Do not cheat by using a knife."

I mimic his actions, first by pounding the bottom of the coconut repeatedly against a big boulder. My arms feel the fatigue of repetition and absorb the shock from each knock on the rock. I then use a small, sharp rock to carve into the husk and strip away the outer layer with my hands. With the coconut first between my thighs and then later between my feet, I use all the muscles I can muster to peel the outer layer. I am sweating now. My wrist is sore. My thighs are bruised. It takes Minh-Hoàng less than thirty minutes to crack it open but takes me forty-five minutes to free the coconut from its outer casing. Minh-Hoàng tends to the eel and congee while I continue working on the coconut.

I pound the coconut against the big boulder, rotating it as I go, swearing under my breath and ready to hurl it at Minh-Hoàng's head. Finally, it cracks open big enough for me to pry it apart. The coconut oil glistens beautifully and I am overwhelmed with pride and joy. I scream with triumphant delight and take a big bite of the coconut flesh. Finally, we are ready to eat.

"Save the fibers. I can use them to make a broom or a bed for myself," he advises. "Also, we are going to eat outside with my mom in her garden."

We serve up some grilled eel, congee, perilla leaves and coconut for Mrs. Trần as an offering to let her know she is still with us. We light some incense and say a prayer, before sitting down on the ground to eat. Thủy-Tiên sits contentedly next to me, picking at the eel and slurping a spoonful of congee. She puts a purple perilla leaf in her mouth, only to pucker up at the bitterness of the herb. She spits it out and cries. Minh-Hoàng and I laugh.

"Tomorrow, when you pass the first checkpoint, hand the guard this paper." Minh-Hoàng hands me a license to transport dried goods for non-commercial sale. "Do not lose it and make sure you get it back every time."

"And what dried goods will I be transporting?" I ask.

"My mother's stock of dried fish, shrimp, squid, and whatever else she has. I will give you some. Have the supply on you at all times. Do not sell or consume them. If you get searched, show them your bag of goods. This will allow you to come and go with minimal detainment. You have to get a new license every year."

"Thank you. I am so grateful," I say sincerely. "I am even thankful to have cooked this meal for you."

"You will never starve if you can open a coconut." The clever phoenix winks and digs in to the food we prepared together. It is delicious.

# 15 OUR TRUE SELF (NOVEMBER 1976)

In the morning, Thủy-Tiên and I stop by Minh-Hoàng's house to say farewell, and to also test his trustworthiness. I have to do something illegal in front of him and see how he reacts. I find Minh-Hoàng sitting at the kitchen table clipping his toenails in his underwear and no shirt. He shows no indication of embarrassment or vulnerability when I approach. I notice the scars on his body and conjure up possible atrocities that were inflicted upon him. I wonder if they are from Mrs. Trần's beatings or from the war.

"From the war." Minh-Hoàng reads my thoughts. "You are here to say goodbye."

"Yes, and to also present you with something." I open my bag and take out some codeine tablets. I hand them to Minh-Hoàng. His brows furrow. I cannot decipher whether he is angry or worried. "Codeine to treat pain."

"I know what it is." He looks angry now. I am nervous he will take away my papers, have me arrested, and hold me hostage here.

"You look like you are always in pain and by the looks of your scars, I am betting you still have residual pain. These can help."

"My pain is not physical, and if my face displeases you, do not worry. You will not have to see me again after today."

"That is not what I mean." I wonder why he is cranky today. "I want to do a kindness for you since you have done so much for me."

His face softens. "Where did you get these?"

"I cannot tell you. Are you going to have me arrested?" I am scared of what he might say.

Minh-Hoàng stands up and walks over to his grandparents' alter. He takes out a canister from beneath the altar table. I recognize the copper coffee tin. He opens the can and takes out the phoenix necklace. "My mother told me you gave this to her right before your first attempt to leave with your husband. She said it was the greatest gift she ever received because it came with such sacrifice and was given to her so selflessly." Minh-Hoàng stares at me. I avoid his glare, partly because he is in his underwear. "This is why my mother loved you and why she made me promise to always take care of you. I am paying her debt to you." He hands me the necklace that Tý's parents gave me on my wedding day. It makes me happy to be reunited with it. "I am not going to arrest you, but I owe you nothing more."

I take the necklace and hide it in my scarf, then tie the scarf around my waist like a sash. I leave Minh-Hoàng the same way I found him, sitting by the table cutting his nails.

***

Thủy-Tiên and I board the first bus departing from Hồ Chí Minh City to Vĩnh Bình early this morning. In my bag is the loot Cường gave me, hiding underneath Minh-Hoàng's dried goods that were given to me last night after the eel dinner. I take a seat twelve rows behind the driver, anticipating if a guard boards the bus, I will have time to dispose of the bag. By sitting on the same side as the driver, I will not get singled out first, since inspectors tend to scan from left to right.

I observe out the window as others board the bus. It is going to be a long ride and a full one at that. With stops at security checkpoints and bathroom breaks, I estimate it will take eight hours to get to Vĩnh Bình, by around 3 p.m. The stink of the dried squid, shrimp, and other preserves, combined with the stench of people who have not bathed in days, compel me to sit with the window open. An elderly woman and her husband sit down behind me. The man takes off his shoes and gets comfortable.

"Put your shoes back on or else I will vomit," warns his wife.

"No," the husband simply responds.

I collect Thủy-Tiên and my bag and sit a few more rows back. The bus pulls away from the station nearly thirty minutes late, but at last, we are on the road. Along the way, we pick up more passengers and drop off some. Thủy-Tiên plays with her airplane like a good girl and lets me rest my eyes for a few minutes at a time. We drive through the first inspection point without any incident, and again, no trouble at the second station. At every hour, we are given a twenty-minute bathroom break. Thủy-Tiên and I take the opportunities to snack on some French bread or our left-over congee. Outside, the hills and the roads blend into each other. The red-orange mud and dirt in the countryside near the coast make me yearn for the sandy river beaches in Cần Thơ. Sprinkled along the journey on the side of the roads are carts selling bread, beverages, fruits, or cheap toys. Every once in a while, the bus slows down to let a herd of water buffalos or cows pass. The roads are bumpy but the ride is fairly comfortable. Surprisingly, we make it all the way to Vĩnh Bình without any trouble.

It is almost 4 p.m. when I step off the bus. I walk through the market and make a detour before heading home. I have unfinished business to resolve first.

***

I step into the familiar tailor shop with the same lime-green curtain covering the doorway to the back room. The same samples of fabric hang from the ceiling, in colors of red, gold, blue and green. The two mannequins, however, are not wearing the same festive wedding attire. Instead, they are wearing identical yellow silk pants and the traditional red áo dài, with a yellow star in the center – the flag of the new Việt Nam.

"Can I help you?" A woman's voice calls out.

I see the same woman who gave me the brown garb with green paisley patterns. She is shocked to see me. From behind the green curtains, her husband steps out.

Now it is me who is shocked. "Doctor Minh." My taxi peddler is alive and well.

"Please let me explain," he says. "Come. Let us speak in the back room." I follow him and his wife behind the curtains. Behind their shop is where they live and where Thủy-Tiên and I had changed into our peasant clothes. There is a small kitchenette, a card table and four chairs, a tiny television, and not much more. Dr. Minh pulls a chair out and sits at the card table. "Allow me to first properly introduce ourselves. This is Thủy, my wife. And my name is not Phạm Văn Minh. I was a practicing doctor, that much was true, but my real name is Nguyễn Văn Đức. We are happy to see you are safe as well."

I glance at his wife, who winks at me. How strange. She smiles and I smile back. "Đức, your name suits you. You are a morally good man." I compliment the doctor. "And Thủy, you are a skilled seamstress. The clothes you provided fit perfectly. I would love to learn how to sew from you one day."

"Of course." Thủy winks. "Can I hold your daughter? She is so cute."

"She is a frail and sick child as you can see." I put Thủy-Tiên down off my lap and she immediately walks over to Thủy. "She usually does not like to be held by anyone."

Thủy is delighted and giggles. "She likes me." Another wink from her left eye. Funny how I did not notice that the first time we met.

"We never had children," says Đức, "but we adore them. They are little adults in training and are a direct reflection of us. They are a product of how we treat them, educate them and love them. It is a shame we never had children to help with the business."

"Yes, but it is also a blessing that you do not have extra hungry mouths to feed," I say. "Đức, tell me what happened after you left the village."

"I did not make it to the river. Instead, I changed my mind and ran back to see Thủy," he says. "Together, we went into the market and while she created a diversion, I stole three fish and ran back to the village, as fast as I could, hoping I would not be too late. So you see, I am not that virtuous, as my name implies. I robbed someone of their fish and their family went hungry that night."

"We could never leave a young mother and her child in the clutches of the communists!" Thủy exclaims. "My husband did pay the debt and left some money anonymously for the family that we stole from."

"I came back to the burned village, but it was too late. You were with a different officer, in the burial grounds, and he was taking you somewhere in his jeep," Đức says. "The other three officers let me go and had one of the village girls cook up the fish."

I notice Thủy handing Thủy-Tiên a pair of chopsticks and a pan to bang on. Her left eye twitches again. She is sitting on the floor now with my daughter, playing drums and clapping. She would have made a great mother.

"Since you did not return in an hour, I did not know if you deserted us, if you left on the boat, if you got caught or stepped on a mine... I was hoping in the end that you returned to your wife. I ended up leaving with that officer to return to Sài Gòn."

"He did not hurt you, did he?" Thủy asks. The poor woman. Her left eye keeps twitching.

"No. I actually knew his mother. He mentioned his mother was not well and I asked him to take me to her."

"That was honorable but also dangerous," says Đức. "He is a communist."

"Yes, but a communist I trust, as much as anyone can trust one, and we both have an understanding. It is good to have your enemy close."

"Yes any leverage is a good one to hang on to," agrees Đức.

"I came back here to explain what happened, in case your husband did not make it back to you." I touch Thủy's arm. "He acted brave and nobly."

Thủy's eyes light up. She places her hand gently on top of her husband's. It is obvious they love each other and contrary to cultural norms, they show affection freely.

"I have to ask, Thủy, what is causing your eye to twitch like that?"

Minh answers before Thủy can respond. "It is tetany. It is due to alkalosis, where her alkaline level is at 7.45 and her body cannot absorb calcium, so the facial nerve on her left is doing cartwheels from the mineral deficiency." I nod my head but do not understand a word he says. Sensing this, Đức rephrases. "Basically, her blood ph level is too high. Stress is the cause of her tetany. It is not permanent and can be remedied."

"I am relieved to hear that," I say. Husband and wife look at each other and smile as if they have a hidden secret they are not sharing. "Since you are a doctor, I have a question for you. Can a person overdose on malaria pills and die from it?"

"It depends on the type of antimalarial drugs one takes," answers Đức. "Do you know what kind?"

"Chloroquine," I answer.

Đức's eyes open wide. He leans back in his chair, stretches out his legs, and folds his arms across his chest. "Chloroquine is a synthetic quinoline derivative and extremely toxic if overdosed. It can cause blindness, heart failure, coma, and death."

"The woman I visited in Sài Gòn was that communist officer's mother and I believe she overdosed on it."

"Intentionally or accidentally?" asks Thủy.

"I believe she committed suicide to end her suffering." I shift my posture and pivot closer to Đức. "Have you heard of the drug *Dexedrine*?"

"Yes," he answers confidently, "it is a stimulant and it helps you stay awake. Do you have any?"

I rummage through my bag and dig to the bottom, underneath the dried foods and medical supply bags. I pull out a small envelope. "There are six tablets in there."

The doctor examines the pills. "These are amphetamines. The U.S. military used them to stay awake for long missions or extended combat operations. The Americans gave these to our soldiers fighting in the south too. I have treated men with extremely high levels of *Dexedrine* in their system. My patients always described the feelings of euphoria and invincibility, and having endless energy."

"That sounds amazing. Is it dangerous? Addicting?" I ask.

"No. Whereas we smoke cigarettes to calm down and relax, these pills help us stay awake and have energy," Đức replies.

I have trouble believing that it is not addicting but I trust him.

"How much are you selling them for?" asks Thủy. "We want to buy them."

"All six tablets?" I ask in disbelief.

"All of them," confirms Đức.

"I will sell them to you at a discount. Sixty for all of them."

Thủy lifts up her tunic and pulls out sixty-thousand đồng from her money belt. She hands the money to me. "What else do you have?"

"I want to build my practice again," says Đức. "We have been helping families leave the country and organizing escape routes. We have a cousin who made it to Australia and he wrote to us about his experience. The money from our operation is good but risky, and I want to help again through medicine."

"Do you mind me asking how much you charge for helping people escape?" I ask.

Thủy's left eye twitches a couple of times. They hesitate to disclose the amount.

"It depends on what the family can afford," Thủy finally answers.

"How much did my brother-in-law pay you for my arrangements?"

Again, they both are quiet. I wait patiently for one of them to answer. Finally, Thủy breaks. "Fifty million đồng for you both."

I am speechless but recover quickly from the shock. "I want to propose we go into business together. I can help supply you with more medicine and supplies as you build up your practice again if you can help me get out of this country. It will take me some time to save enough money, but my daughter is sick and I have to get out of here."

"What is wrong with her?" Thủy asks.

"I think she has a hole in her heart or a heart murmur."

"I am not a cardiologist," Đức says, "but I can listen to her heart as soon as I get my hands on a stethoscope. You have yourself a deal."

We spend the next ten minutes finalizing the sale of five first aid kits, all forty-eight codeine tablets, and one *Zippo* lighter. As I stand up to leave, something dawns on me. "Đức, you have not coughed once since I arrived here. You must be feeling better."

"My friend," he replies with a smile, "that was all an act, like your limp was an act, and like Thủy's eye twitching is an act."

She gives me an exaggerated wink and laughs. "We pretend to be people we are not so that when the communists interrogate others, they will come intending to arrest someone who does not exist."

"Also," adds Đức, "the ones who are weak or crippled usually receive mercy or leniency, and we find people are more willing to help us when we are not fully able-bodied."

Thủy takes my hand into hers and leans forward. "Not to mention, people ignore you if you withdraw to the background and make yourself look ugly and poor. If you look poor, the communists will not seize your property, your food, your animals, or your business. They will skip past to the next place. Only to those we trust do we show our true self."

# 16 HOME AGAIN (NOVEMBER 1976)

On the walk home to my father's house from the market, I give a lot of appreciation to what my new friends Thủy and Đức said. It is a wonder that people are not who they appear to be anymore and everyone has secrets they hold deep in their hearts. I yearn for the days of my childhood and my university days. I was young and happy living in my little bubble. People were always nice to me. Neighbors did not spy on one another. We could leave the doors unlocked and never fear of being robbed. We had visitors all the time and we shared food with one another. I had many friends. I remember walking to school with them, as well as with Sister Six and Brother Seven, and their friends. We all would run home together for lunch and a nap, then return to school for another few hours. After school, we would go swimming or fishing or cheer for Brother Seven when he fought his crickets. Then we would go home to help around the house before studying and doing homework. I had two best friends, both of them named Hồng. To distinguish them apart, I called one of them Baby Hồng, because she complained about everything, and the other one Fat Hồng, because she had a sweet tooth and was always eating. Now, not only have I lost most of my friends but also my country. I am reminded that I have no husband, no home of my own, no scooter, and no respectable job. I have lost the freedom to go as I please from the city to the countryside unless I have permission or a license, and when I get home, I may not even have my family.

My heart aches for Sam and I long to hear his voice. It has been a lifetime ago since I felt alive, in love, and happy. My only happiness now is through Thủy-Tiên, and if I were to lose my daughter too, I would not be able to live another day. I stroll through the familiar streets of my hometown, in no hurry to get home and realize how much the landscape has changed. I round the corner and see a scuffle between a boy, around sixteen years old, and a couple of police officers. There is shouting between the two officers and the young boy, who resists arrest and tries to run away. His mother is on the ground crying, begging for mercy and apologizing for her son's stupidity. The father tries to pull his son into the house, yelling that they cannot take his son. One of the police officers hits the father and kicks him while the other officer runs after the boy. I hold onto Thủy-Tiên a little tighter and walk slowly.

There are a few spectators, cognizant to keep their distance and not get involved. Others run into their homes, while some check the scene from their window. I ask a bystander nearby, "Do you know what is happening?"

"The boy was caught handing out anti-communist leaflets and ridiculing Hồ Chí Minh," he responds. "The police are probably going to send him to jail for six months, maybe more."

I continue walking slowly and head down a different alley. It takes me another twenty minutes to get to my father's house. I stand at the beginning of the long walkway and remember the last time I stood here; I was waiting for my taxi peddler, for Đức. I take a deep breath and walk toward the door, afraid of what calamity awaits.

***

The smell of burnt rice assaults my nose and I run to the kitchen. To my dismay, rice is scattered all over the floor. A small pot lies on its side on the ground. I notice the house is stripped of adornments. Furniture is missing. It is disturbingly bare.

I take notice of Dirty Butt's loud, frantic clucking and am appalled with the scene before me. My family is chasing after my chicken. Everyone is yelling for my father to catch her. I see a meat cleaver in his right hand and rush out to the backyard. Poor Thủy-Tiên bobs up and down on my hip while I run outside.

"Stop!" I scream. "Do not touch Mông Dơ!"

My family freezes. Bewildered eyes reflect my own disbelief.

Sister Six is the first to speak. "What are you doing here?"

"You should have not come back!" My father lunges forward.

"Aiyah, grab the chicken!" Hiền snatches the meat cleaver from my father. "She is getting away."

"You are not going to kill my Mông Dơ." I chase after Hiền. "She is family."

"Daughter, she is a chicken." My father blocks me from catching Hiền. "Why did you have to go and give her a name? We are starving here!"

"Father, I have money. I will buy Mông Dơ from you. No one is to touch her."

"Look around you," my father beckons. "What do you see?"

I pause and survey our backyard. The bunker has not changed. The pond and the outhouse appear the same. I scan up at the fruit trees and notice not one tree has any fruit. It dawns on me that our pigs are also gone. Every face staring at me is sad and desperate. Father's expression makes him look haggard, old and defeated. Even Sister Six's determined spirit has left, leaving behind a hollow woman.

"What happened here?" I am afraid of the answer.

"The Việt Cộng came through a couple of days ago," says Hải. "They took everything -our rice, our pigs, even our potatoes and herbs. They made Tree climb up and get all the fruits." Hải points to the barren trees. I am in shock that there is not one coconut or banana left.

"And somehow Mộng Dơ managed to escape their clutches?" I ask in disbelief.

"They tried," Tree says, "but she is a clever one. They tried to shoot her when they could not catch her. She must have superpowers. They finally left and said they would leave her for all ten of us to fight over...well, nine of us."

Everyone's head bends down, their crestfallen faces say it all. I take a quick survey and realize who is missing. "Tâm! Where is she?"

Sister Six bursts into tears. Her husband holds her tight and little Trinh clings to her parents. She cries too seeing her mother cry.

"They took her," was all Brother Seven could manage to say.

I put Thủy-Tiên down and cover my mouth in horror. The floodgates open and all the tears of past rainy seasons unleash with madness. I cover my eyes and fall onto my knees. Not my niece, my sweet niece, my Tâm...my heart. Her face and her smile flash before me in my mind. I can see us walking arm in arm to the market as we had done so many mornings in the past. I can see us laughing, drinking our coffees, and trying to outwit each other with our clever jokes and innuendos. I clutch my heart. I fear deep in the core of my being that I will never see my beautiful niece again, and even if by some divine miracle we do see each other again, she will not be the same innocent and good-humored young woman I know.

"You must have had a long journey today," says Hải. "Get some rest and we will talk later this evening. We can all catch up."

I surrender to Hải's arms as he lifts me to my feet. Hiền leads me back to the house through the kitchen while Tree takes Thủy-Tiên by the hand and walks with her.

I shout over my shoulder, "Do not touch my chicken." I let sleep sweep over my fatigued body and carry me into the dark recess of my mind.

***

Sister Six and Brother Seven are arguing. I rise from the bed and walk into the kitchen. I must have slept a long time. It is dark outside and the crickets are singing.

"We have to find her." Sister Six pounds her fist on the kitchen table.

"You have to let her go," urges Brother Seven.

"How can you say that? What if it was one of your sons? Would you give up so easily?"

My poor family, all huddled together in the kitchen. My father and Hải lean against the kitchen counter, while Brother Seven stands over his wife, who is sitting on the floor, cross-legged with their son, Tuấn. Sister Six, her husband, and their daughter, Trinh, sit at the table.

Tree is holding Thủy-Tiên on his lap and is the first to notice me. "You are awake."

Seeing Sister Six's eyes swollen from crying and her nose red and dry, makes me want to hug her. "Sister, I agree with you. We cannot give up. We have to find Tâm." I try to give her hope but am unconvinced myself. She could already be dead by now. "Tell me what happened."

My brother-in-law kick starts the story. "Two days ago they came into town, asking every family questions about what our trade is, how much money we have to declare, who lives in this house. They went through the house, took everything of value, which was not much since we sold everything of value."

"They acted sweet but we suspected what they were up to," says Hải. "They asked us about our political views and whom we prayed to. Of course, we parroted what we read in their newspapers and that pleased them."

"They questioned Tâm about her profession," Hiền chimes in, "and she made the mistake of saying she worked as a maid in one of the U.S. Air Force barracks. Aiyah, stupid girl."

Sister Six shoots a scathing glare at Hiền. "They did not like that answer and accused her of betraying the government."

Hải squeezes Sister Six's forearm. "Those Việt Cộngs accused her of not supporting the Party and arrested her."

"We were all scared and did not dare to fight them," says Tree.

Sister Six busts into tears. I cannot help my tears of sorrow either, tears of longing for my niece. I rush to her side.

"What are you doing back here, Tuyết?" asks Hải. "I told the family about our clandestine plan to get you and Thủy-Tiên out of the country. Why are you back?"

I sigh and tell them all about the taxi peddler and his wife, and how Doctor Phạm Văn Minh was actually Doctor Nguyễn Văn Đức, incognito. I told them of the burning village and the assault that took place there, to which Hải was concerned about my treatment. I told them about Mrs. Trần's suicide and got a little emotional. As much of a thorn as she was in my life, she was also a mother figure, and a wood tiger that I came to understand and respect. When I got to the part about Cường and Minh-Hoàng helping me, voices erupted with disapproval and concern.

"Aiyah, sister, you cannot trust either of them," warns Hiền.

"That is too dangerous," says my father.

"You were so stupid," adds Brother Seven.

Only Sister Six defends me. "You always had beauty and now, it is good to see your brain finally catching up." Even in her pain, our grieving matriarch is strong and defiant, swimming against the current. "This is a good thing for all of us. She has a communist in the palm of her hands, not to mention a mob boss' puppet working alongside her. Can you all not see? Cường is motivated by money and greed and has her taking all the risks to sell Western medicine for him. Without her, he would have to face his boss. And Minh-Hoàng? Well, he is either in love with her or is using her as a pawn in some crazy scheme of his. Either way, Eight, you have to continue playing their game, and never let them know you are anything other than a pretty and naïve woman who was betrayed by her husband and must care for a sick child. Men like to rescue women and be in control."

"You are playing a dangerous game," says Hải.

I defend myself. "I am not playing a twisted game. I am in this for survival and freedom."

"You are going to bring suffering to us all," says Hiền. "They will find out and will come for you. They will burn our house or seize the property. They are already starving us out and controlling everyone. Aiyah, you should not have come back and endangered us all."

"Quiet, Wife," orders my brother. "How can you say that?"

"Brother, she is afraid, and I understand, but this is what they want. They want to divide families, make us spy on each other and our neighbors, and rival one another. They pretend to be nice and helpful, and yet, they restrict us to our hamlets, make our currency obsolete, take away our food, burn our villages, and steal our livelihood. We are not liberated as one country under one flag. We are the conquered people in a land that is no longer ours."

"How can we live like this much longer?" My father's stomach rumbles.

"When was the last time you ate, Father?" I ask.

"Two days ago." Father rubs his belly. "I am tempted to catch the catfish we have in the pond and cook those up to eat."

"You cannot!" I exclaim, mortified. "Those fish catch the feces from our outhouse."

"I am an old, hungry man. I am not too proud to do that to feed my children and grandchildren. Or maybe we sell the catfish and buy some food?"

I remember the dried foods I have in my bag that Minh-Hoàng gave me. Surely I can spare some to feed my family? "Father, you have your retirement money from your days of teaching, plus the monthly government subsidy, yes?"

"Yes, but they took everything. We have to start over. Besides, if I spend it freely, the communists will say we have plenty and restrict us further, but if we do not spend it for fear of suspicion, then we starve."

"We cannot win," says Hải, "but maybe if we spend it on things we can plant and grow or raise, we can avoid scrutiny."

"Yes, we have to try," I say, "and Brother Seven, you still have your truck driving and monthly subsidy, right? Sister Six, you have your family subsidy, too?" They both nod. "We will be conservative and discreet on how we spend and rotate who goes to the market each day to buy or sell on the free market. No one will be targeted or reported. Until we get paid, I have the money I received from selling to the good doctor and his wife."

"I have my subsidy too," says Hải.

"And I now have my own as well." I notice Hải shifts his weight and runs his fingers through his hair, feeling uneasy.

"Like it or not, at least Minh-Hoàng got Eight her monthly allowance and safe passage from Sài Gòn to home," reminds Sister Six.

"Tomorrow, we will start again. For now, we eat." I take out the bags of dried food Minh-Hoàng gave me and toss them on the kitchen table.

All eyes light up seeing the edible pile of gold and new hope is restored in their faces. Their eyes light up seeing the edible pile of gold. I will have to buy more or have Sister Six preserve some to replenish the supply. We tear open the dried shrimp and cuttlefish, pop open the jar of pickled mangos, and divide the candied plums, tamarind, and ginger amongst us. All of us dig in. I am happy to be home again with my family, but tonight when I go to sleep, thoughts of my niece will disrupt my slumber. I will pray for her.

*** 

I cannot sleep. Tâm's face haunts me. To settle my restlessness, I stroll outside to get some air. I now have doubts about leaving Việt Nam. I am in the twilight of my life. Staying here means a decline in quality of life, but how can I leave my family, when they are in so much pain and distress? Losing Tâm changes everything.

"This is my favorite time of day when the light from the sky glows softly and the sun is about to rise. It is peaceful." Sister Six catches up with me.

"Sister--"

She cuts me off like she usually does. "After Brother Two and all our other siblings died, it was my burden to take care of you, of Seven, and our parents. After I got married and had children, I never had any time for myself. The only peace I found was at dawn."

"You have sacrificed so much," I say, "and I admire how strong you are, how independent and self-sufficient you are."

"A part of me has always been jealous of you," my sister confesses. Alarmed, I ask her why. "You are the youngest and therefore the most loved, most cherished, and definitely, the most spoiled. You can do no wrong. I never got the love and attention that you got as a little girl. Mother and Father showed me no leniency. I always had to make sacrifices, taking the smallest portion of food or the burnt food, accepting the imperfect clothes that Mother made, being dutiful around the house...I have lived a rigid life and as a result, have cast my shadow onto my children. They are timid rule followers, all because I did not teach them to live freely."

"You were always tough on me, but I always felt your love, and after Mother died, and Father was a wreck, it was you who kept the household together. You are the woman I want to emulate."

My sister stops and squeezes my hand. "Do not underestimate your own inner strength and your resolve to find a better life. I am glad you are not rigid like me. You are adaptable and this skill will serve you well when you leave this communist hell we are in."

A rooster crows and a few dogs bark in the distance. Morning crests above the jagged rooftops. I wrap my arm around Sister Six's shoulder. "You are a good wife and a wonderful mother. And, lucky for you, my favorite sister."

She slaps my butt cheeks. "I am your only sister."

The village comes to life. Neighbors switch on their lights, open their windows, or start up their scooters. Somewhere nearby, a man is choking on his own spit as he clears his throat.

"I do not want to see our family go hungry." I pull my sister's arm and head back to the house. "I will plan on going back and forth between Sài Gòn and Vĩnh Bình for as long as it takes, to sell medicine and save money until our family has enough to sustain a comfortable life. Brother Seven wants me to take Tree to America with me, so I need to save enough money for all three of us to go."

"This is going to take you years, not months."

"Hải paid fifty million đồng for us, so I imagine it will take another twenty-five million to pay for Tree, plus have some money for emergency use. There is still a matter of finding a boat and a captain."

"This is too dangerous. What if you get arrested? I lost Tâm. I cannot lose you too."

I hold my sister's hand in mine, giving it a reassuring squeeze. "A moment ago you told me not to underestimate my inner strength and that I had the determination to get out of this communist hell."

"I know," she says. "Make sure you do it right this time. You keep leaving and then coming back like the ocean waves. Each time you do this, you strip more sand from me."

"Sister, you have more grit than anyone. A tsunami can come and try to strip away all of Việt Nam, but it will find itself absorbed by you."

My sister scowls at me. Dirty Butt warbles by and roosts in the grass on the side of the house. I notice her hackle feathers are wet. *What mischief have you gotten yourself into?*

# 17 SURRENDER TO SORROW (DECEMBER 1977)

Today is Christmas Eve, 1977. I wake up to the sound of my nephew screaming and my sister-in-law swearing. "Aiyah, what the fuck is wrong with our son?"

"We need to get Tuấn to a doctor," demands my brother. "Tree, go wake up Aunt Eight."

"I am awake." I walk over to my little nephew. "Doctor Nguyễn Văn Đức can help."

"My brother complains about stomach pains and has diarrhea," says Tree.

"He is going to throw up." I curl my fingers to catch the vomit.

My little nephew scratches his legs and buttocks and cries.

"We can all go," says Brother Seven, "since I do not have to work today or tomorrow."

On our walk to Đức's and Thủy's house, we make a quick stop at the market to buy some guavas and a papaya. We arrive at the tailor shop and leave our shoes at the stoop.

Tree gets excited. "Aunt Eight, this is the fabric store where I sold the morphine two years ago!"

"Are you sure?" I ask. He nods.

"Aiyah, this is a nice shop. I wish I could sew as skillfully as the seamstress here!" Sister Seven kicks off her shoes and rushes to the mannequins. She is distracted by their clothes and the fabrics hanging from the ceiling. She walks over to the fabric samples folded neatly on the shelves along the walls and runs her fingers over them.

"Thank you for the compliment." Thủy steps out from behind the green curtains. "Sister Tuyết, what brings you to the shop? An áo dài?"

"Aunt Eight, that is the woman I sold the morphine to!" exclaims Tree.

"I recognize you." Thủy rests her hand on Tree's shoulder.

"You purchased morphine from me a long time ago," says Tree.

"Yes, I remember!" exclaims Thủy. "Unbelievable!"

"Hello, Sister Thủy," I say. "It is good to see you. What a strange twist of fate!"

"Indeed!" she responds.

"My family and I are here to see your husband. Is Đức available?"

"Yes, he will be here soon," Thủy says. "He is out pedaling his cycle around town, selling bananas."

I nod and make the introductions. "This is my sister-in-law, Hiền, and my brother, Seven, and their two sons, Tree and Tuấn."

Hiền quickly drowns Thủy with compliments. "Aiyah, Sister Thủy, you have such beautiful attention to detail. The patterns align so perfectly; the dress drapes flawlessly on these mannequins. And the seams are so even around the bust area. And the thread! Aiyah, the thread that you used for these are the perfect color and thickness!"

Thủy laughs at Hiền's enthusiasm. "You have an eye for sewing. You must be a great seamstress as well."

"I sew, yes, but not like you," Hiền says. "I am too frugal to buy quality thread and do not have the creative patience. You, however, aiyah, can fashion a runway in Paris!"

"My wife is the best designer." Đức parks his cyclo and joins us in the shop. Husband and wife smile at each other adoringly. It makes the rest of us embarrassed to see such open affection and love. I introduce Đức to my family and explain the purpose of our visit. We follow him into the back room, to the small kitchen.

"Tuấn, how old are you?" asks Doctor Đức.

"Yes, Doctor, I am eight years old," responds my nephew respectfully.

"And tell me, what have you been experiencing?"

"Sometimes I feel dizzy and want to throw up, but I cannot."

"Anything else?" asks Doctor Đức.

"Yes, Doctor, my butt itches all the time," Tuấn answers.

Tree adds, "And he complains about his stomach hurting."

"Hmm." Đức waves my brother to follow him. "With your permission, I will examine him in the back room."

Brother Seven disappears with Đức and Tuấn behind a door. Hiền and Thủy patty-cake back and forth over áo dài designs, fashion styles, fabric textures and types of thread. I listen patiently, yearning to understand exactly what are silk threads, metallic threads, cotton threads, and wool threads, and how they differ from nylon or rayon threads, bobbin threads and designer threads mixed with different types of other threads. My head is spinning and I find it humorous the two women can banter so animatedly about fibers. Poor Tree. He is sitting next to me as stone-faced as I am.

Finally, the back door opens and Đức, Brother Seven, and Tuấn walk out.

"Aiyah, what is it? You all look like you have seen a ghost." Hiền clutches her chest.

Brother Seven's face is stark. "Our son has pinworms living inside his rectum. He may also have tapeworms."

Hiền spits out a distressed aiyah.

Đức gets right to the point. "Either the boy ate something that was contaminated and not fully cooked, or he came in contact with feces that had eggs or larvae in it. Luckily there is no infection around the anus."

"What can we do, Doctor?" asks Hiền.

"You can start by making sure your son washes his hands well with soap and water after every bowel movement, and you should keep his fingernails trimmed. Eggs can get under his nails and spread to anything he touches."

"Are there any medicine or remedies to treat the worms?" I ask.

"There are anti-parasite medicines he can take, but unfortunately, we have none. Any of you can be infected as well and not show any symptoms."

"My poor son! Aiyah, if we have no medicine, then what do we do?" asks Hiền.

"Go home and clean the whole house and wash his bed linens. Clean all his toys and pretty much anything he regularly comes in contact with. Pinworms can survive for three days without a host. Keep an eye on him and bring him back if he has any big changes in his eating habits, if his vision changes, if you find any lumps on his skin, or if he has seizures. Those are signs of eggs entering his bloodstream and hatching in his tissues."

"Tapeworms usually leave your body on their own," says Tree.

"They can, but the eggs can remain. Always wash your hands after going to the bathroom or handling food. Cook everything well, keep clothes and linens clean and take baths regularly. Garlic and coconut oil is helpful for treating this, so use the coconut oil as a topical remedy around the affected area. You can crush the garlic with the oil and apply together. I recommend he eats minced garlic or drinks it with some tea or water as well, to remove the yeast and kill the parasite. You may want to try eating a lot of carrots, papaya seeds, and cloves, too. It can help flush the worms out."

We all thank Đức and Thủy for their time. As payment, Tree presents them with the guavas and papayas we purchased at the market. I give Đức some money as well.

We spend Christmas Eve and Christmas Day cleaning the house from top to bottom. No one dares to speak of the worms and I suspect we all are a little worried we might be infected too.

# 18 A FORGOTTEN RAG DOLL (FEBRUARY 1978)

The Lunar New Year is here. Today is February 2, 1978. It is the lucky year of the horse. To welcome good fortune and health for this zodiac sign, families and businesses in our village decorate their establishments in colors of yellow and green. Those who can afford to, have fresh jasmine or calla lily flowers on the altars. The sweet aroma of these flowers can be intoxicating and when I get a whiff of one of these, it brings me so much joy and fond memories of happier times. I remember when I was a little girl; I would get new clothes and receive red envelopes with money in them from my elders. We would eat, pay tribute to our ancestors, set off firecrackers, enjoy the dragon dances, and play games. Our family celebrated for three days. There was to be no arguing and no cleaning, otherwise, bad luck could enter our home and stay for the whole year. My favorite game to play as a child was "Bầu Cua Tôm Cá", which means "Gourd Crab Shrimp Fish". It is a traditional Vietnamese gambling game using three dice. Each side of the dice shows a picture of a gourd, crab, shrimp, fish, rooster or deer. The game board has six squares; each square has a picture of one of the animals. Growing up, my siblings and I would use our new year's money to place bets. We put our money on the animals of choice and held our breath as the three dice were rolled. If the animal we bet on appeared, we got paid up to three times our bet. Sister Six usually lost and Mother usually won.

There will be no celebrations this lunar year. I have spent the last year going back and forth between Sài Gòn and Vĩnh Bình, sometimes via bus, sometimes hitching a ride with Brother Seven, to sell whatever Cường gives me – alcohol, cigarettes, writing paper, typewriters. Most recently, it is opium and marijuana. My license for selling dried goods expired a few months ago and Minh-Hoàng helped me renew it. My family has been able to stay out of trouble with the communist government and we have been lucky to keep our house. Still, no news of my niece Tâm and we still speculate each day what happened to her. Minh-Hoàng tried to help but he hit a dead end trying to find her. My fear is that she is dead. I lay awake at night imagining horrible things that may have happened to her. Was she raped? Was she beaten to death? Is she in some prison, being tortured and starved? Is she someone's sex slave? Was she forced to clear minefields and got herself blown to pieces of decomposing flesh?

In the mornings, the first thing I do when I wake is check on Thủy-Tiên. I am always afraid I will find her not breathing. She continues to get weaker with every passing year. Her breathing gets more labored. She will be four years old this July, but has not gained much weight and has barely grown since the year before. Sometimes her complexion is pale and other times, blue, especially around her lips. In the past six months, she has had a lot of fevers and does not have much interest in eating. Today, her belly is a little swollen and she is unusually tired. I take her to see Doctor Đức.

Đức takes out his stethoscope and listens to Thủy-Tiên's heart. He has her take deep breaths as he checks her chest and back. "No change since the last time you brought her to me. I still hear some fluttering when I listen to her heart." I stare intently at his face, trying to read his expressions. "With her existing heart murmur, I would say there is a problem with a heart valve or she may have a hole between the two chambers that is pumping blood in and out of her heart."

I cannot help it. The tears escape and slide down my face. "Is she going to die?"

"If she has a serious congenital murmur or an infection in the heart, and does not get surgery, she may not live past her fifth birthday. Without being able to see her heart, I am not certain what we are dealing with, but then again, I am not a cardiologist."

"I have been praying every night for her to get better," I say. "It is a miracle she is still alive."

"She is a fighter, like her mother. How are you holding up?" Đức's question was an invitation to release all my stress.

My mouth erupts and an avalanche of anxiety spills out onto his empathetic ears. "I am so lost. Every day I put my life and my family's life at risk selling illegal items on the free market, and I am only halfway where I need to be in order to leave this country; this motherland that was once our home is now a prison! My daughter is dying. My family is starving. Oh God! I would rather die than live in this communist wasteland! Everything is so expensive and the government controls it all! We cannot buy anything without a ticket. People cannot even go eat at a restaurant without a ticket. It makes no sense! My family has been planting vegetables, but it has been difficult feeding eleven mouths. The soil does not have any time to rest between harvests and our crops have been meager this past year! After my nephew recovered from the worms and expelled everything from his body, my father became ill. We tried everything for him, from drinking Chinese herbs to cupping therapy and skin coining, inhaling vapors or rubbing ointment all over his aching body, but still, he has headaches and colds that last longer and occur more frequently! We still do not know what happened to my niece and my poor sister floats through the house like a ghost. I would give anything for her to snap back to her usual self and say something condescending to me, but it is like she has gone mute. There is no life in her eyes! What if she commits suicide like Mrs. Trần?"

I sob uncontrollably. I try to talk some more and tell Đức how it is unfair that I do not have Sam, how I hate my husband for his deception, and how I am living in sin with Hải. Thankfully, I am not making any sense to him. The more I try to compose myself, the more I trip over my words. Each time I gasp for air, I skip around in my thoughts and I speak in broken sentences. I try to tell Đức that I am approaching thirty-nine years old and am too young to be having a meltdown or some mid-life crisis, but here I am, beaten and ready to die to make it all go away.

"Not yet," Đức says. "It is not your time to die. You, a Catholic, should know that suicide is not an option. Life can be cruel, but you have to accept what has happened. There are many aspects of your life that you still control."

I surrender to sorrow and weep. Fatigue sweeps over me and I sit in Đức's kitchen, slumped over like a forgotten rag doll, in my patchwork clothing made of spare scraps of cloth, my unruly hair, my stained face, and floppy body.

"I want to give Thủy-Tiên the life that I dreamt of for myself but did not get."

"It is good to keep things in perspective and remind yourself what you are fighting for. Everyone has a different fight," says Đức.

"What is your fight?" I ask.

"It is to help you, and other families like yours, find their purpose."

"You are a good man." I wipe my tears. "How many families have you helped?"

"Too many to count and many more still to come," Đức responds. "I am still working different channels to get a boat and a captain for you when you are ready. As more people leave, it is getting more expensive to bribe the right people. The risks are greater with people leaving, so desperate, they are willing to gamble with their lives out at sea. Last week I helped a family of thirteen. They had been saving for two years to buy a boat. They had a family friend who was going to captain the boat but he backed out the night of their departure, too afraid to escape. So, they took their chances and went anyways. I hope they make it."

"Me too." I hand Đức some money. "Thank you for examining Thủy-Tiên. I need to go home now and check on my sister and my father."

# 19 FISH AND SNAKE (SEPTEMBER 1978)

I sense Hải's presence behind me as I brush my hair. His arms wrap around my waist so I put the brush down. Neither of us speaks for a while. I see my father step out of the outhouse from behind the banyan tree.

"Is he...?" I ask.

"He sure is!" confirms Hải.

We both run outside. Hải grabs a towel on the way out.

"Father!" I call out to him. "You forgot your underwear."

Father notices his nakedness and places his hands on his butt cheeks. "So, I did!"

Hải wraps the towel around my father's waist. "Come, Uncle, let me help you find something to wear."

The two of them disappear into the house. I walk over to my favorite hammock and lay down, swinging it with my left leg. It makes me sad to see my father's memory deteriorating and his health declining. This man who used to be so vibrant and strong, who used to spank his children when we did something bad, can now hardly take care of himself.

"What is making you frown?" Hải returns with some peanuts to share. My brother accompanies him.

"Father." I crack open the shell and pop a peanut in my mouth. "Most parents beat their children with a belt or bamboo or rattan, but not Father. His favorite weapon was a dried, bull's penis."

Brother Seven chuckles. "That thing was a half meter long and flexible despite how hard it was. You girls were lucky, though. He never used it on you, just the boys."

"True," I acknowledge. "Mother used a wooden spoon."

"Remember that time you slipped a frying pan down your pants, hoping she would not notice? You thought you were being so clever, kneeling there straight as a pool cue, anticipating the punishment that was to be ramrodded down your backside."

I laugh. "How old was I, do you remember?"

"You were around Tuấn's age, seven or eight," answers Brother Seven.

"So what happened?" asks Hải.

"She was a little bit of a tomboy when she was younger," says Brother Seven, "and she loved tagging along with me and my friends after school. One day, I was going to fight one of my crickets but when I opened the matchbox, he jumped out and escaped. We forfeited and returned home. On the way home, there was a crowd of people yelling and getting all excited about something. She convinced me to take her over to check it out. There was a fish fight going on, so I placed a bet, and she was right beside me, placing a bet herself! It took over three hours for the fish to kill the other."

"We lost track of time and were late getting home to do our chores." I continue Brother Seven's story. "Mother yelled at me for betting and acting unladylike. I lost all of my money from the Lunar New Year on that stupid fish. And because I was not home to do my chores, my punishment was to kneel on my knees and face the corner of the wall for an hour, before accepting my spankings."

"You got off easy that day." Sister Six joins us. She takes a peanut and throws it in the air. Instead of catching it in her mouth, it bounces off her chin and falls to the ground. "Eight convinced me to get her a frying pan from the kitchen and I was shocked when she stuck it down her pants." She goes to retrieve her peanut but Dirty Butt darts from behind a bush and steals it from her.

"So you were going to shield your rear with the frying pan?" Hải roars with laughter. "You did not think your mother would notice?"

"I was seven years old. I was so scared!" I say.

"Of course Mother noticed the pan right away," says Brother Seven. "She could not contain her amusement and laughed so hard. She called every family member into the room to see, and we all laughed and mocked poor little Eight, kneeling there, facing the wall, with a round pan and the handle sticking out of her pants."

"We laughed until we cried and our stomach ached." Sister Six throws another peanut in the air and catches it in her mouth. "My dear sister achieved for the first time something that none of us ever achieved. She did not get a spanking that night."

"No," I add, "but I had to kneel for another half hour and go to bed without dinner."

"I miss those days." Sister Six's eyes mist up.

"Me too," I say. "I would give anything to have Mother here, even if it was to spank me."

"I miss her voice and how she used to sing to us," says Brother Seven.

As if on cue, the three of us sing together Mother's favorite song, "Sài Gòn Đẹp Lắm", meaning "Saigon So Beautiful":

*"In the land where the sun does not fade. Far away where the silk dresses flow. People come here to connect and delight. Sài Gòn so beautiful. Oh Sài Gòn! Oh Sài Gòn! Horses and cars like water on streets. People run, they say hello and greet. The city welcomes me to join the fun. Sài Gòn so beautiful. Oh Sài Gòn! Oh Sài Gòn! Lá la la lá la. Lá la la lá la. Laughing with the wind and drinking with joy. Lá la la lá la. Lá la la lá la. Life is beautiful like poetry."*

"You should not sing so loud." Tree walks over to us, holding both Tuấn's and Thủy-Tiên's hand. "We might get in trouble."

Sister Seven and Brother Six are right behind them. They finish the song quietly. *"A love that is worth singing about; Let love remember the distant past. May today's brightness never fade in me. Sài Gòn so beautiful. Oh Sài Gòn! Oh Sài Gòn!"*

\*\*\*

The seasons pass like a child's merry-go-round, spinning faster and faster until events become a blur. I, however, remain constant. Daily routines and familiar things continue to happen and sometimes, it is like déjà vu, but there is always some element that is a little different than the last time. The monsoon season is here again.

Hải breathes softly next to me while outside, the wind shrieks and the rain marches fanatically sideways. A small gecko scurries through a crack in the wall. The world around me is unraveling at the seams. The house is slowly rotting and the trees and vegetation outside are not thriving. Maybe that is my imagination, but the outside walls are collapsing in and my world is getting smaller.

My mind is awake so I get up and go shower in the rain before the first rooster sings. The clay floor leading to the back courtyard cools my feet. I strip off my clothes, down to my underwear, and let the raindrops fervently kiss my face and body, like a lover savoring an approaching climax. I cannot get enough of Mother Nature's tears. I cup the water from the cistern in my hands. The cool water trickles down my throat. I drink more water to appease the hunger, but I might as well be pouring salt into the sea, knowing it is useless, for no amount of water can make me satisfied.

A light illuminates one of the bedrooms a couple houses over. I grab my clothes and go inside to dress. Somewhere there must be a typhoon as the downpour is relentless. I step outside, onto the front steps of the house, and see a small shadow. The dark movement gets closer and I squint to decipher who the intruder is at this hour.

"Tree?" I call out. "Is that you?"

"Yes."

"Where have you been?"

"Fishing." He grins from ear to ear. "When it rains like this the fish wash up onto the fields." He approaches closer and I see in one hand a thick stick and in the other hand, a pillowcase slung over his shoulder.

"How many did you get?" I ask excitedly.

"One for each of us, plus a snake." He triumphantly raises his club in the air.

We spend the day cleaning and gutting the fish. Sister Six prepares the snake and steams two of the fish in soy sauce, ginger and onions for dinner tonight. The rest will be salted and preserved over the next two to three weeks. Because tonight is a special meal, the family waits for Brother Seven to come home from work, so we can all eat together.

One of our neighbors unexpectedly drops in for a visit. "We can smell the ginger and onions from our house." He stands before us, barefoot, bunions on his feet, wearing a brown tunic and faded black trousers that are a little too short for him. He is dark-skinned. His hair is long and unwashed. I notice his hands are calloused and cracked, his fingernails untrimmed and dirty. The memory of my nephew's worm incident flashes across my mind. I remember cleaning his bedsheets and scrubbing his fingers while he cried. It makes me shudder.

My brother-in-law greets him. "Brother Tú, come in." The two men shake hands. "Tree caught us some fish and a snake early this morning out in the fields."

"I see the women are busy preparing a feast for tonight." Tú smiles and I notice he is missing a few teeth. The ones remaining are stained with nicotine.

"Yes, it has been a long time since we have eaten meat," says Brother Six.

"We are in the same situation, becoming vegetarian by necessity, not by choice," says Tú.

"You must come for dinner this evening, and of course, bring your wife and son," invites Brother Six.

"We would be honored. We have a special bottle of rice wine that I made and can bring over. Maybe we can play cards as well."

The two men shake hands and our neighbor walks home. The second he is no longer in sight, Sister Six scolds her husband. "What are you doing inviting three more mouths to feed?"

Brother Six defends himself. "They are our friends. You used to play cards with his wife every week. It is our obligation to help others when we can. Besides, it will bring good karma back to us."

"God would want us to be kind to our neighbors, but your wife has a point." I rip the innards of the fish out with my bare hands. A small piece of it flies upward and hits Sister Six on the face, narrowly missing her eye. She flinches and I laugh.

"Aiyah, they can go and catch their own fish," says Hiền. "They have a son that is Tree's age. That boy is so lazy, though, not good like my son."

Father wakes up from his nap and joins us women and my brother-in-law in the kitchen. "Where did all these fish come from?" It is the second time he has asked us today.

"Father, Tree caught them early this morning in the fields," I answer.

"Oh, that is my good grandson," he says and heads to the outhouse.

"Aiyah, he is getting so forgetful these days," says Hiền.

We all nod and continue with cooking, cleaning, and preserving the fish.

\*\*\*

Our neighbors announce themselves at our doorstep before walking in. Tú is more presentable now than he was a few hours ago. I am relieved to see he clipped his fingernails and washed up. His wife, Vân, is pretty, even without makeup. Behind them is their fifteen-year-old son. He is the same age as Tree, but that is where the similarities end. The boy before me has always been immature and disrespectful. His parents come from a line of poor, uneducated families, where school takes a backseat to farming and selling food at the market. This boy is attractive, though, I will admit. It is probably the only redeeming feature I can pick out. Because he is their only child and the only son, he has been coddled and spoiled all his life. Without any siblings to rival him and no other relatives around to discipline the boy, he is lost.

My brother-in-law welcomes them. "Brother Tú, Sister Vân, please, come in."

My nephews, Tree and Tuấn, and my niece, Trinh, all run out, line up, and greet our neighbors. "Welcome, Uncle Tú. Welcome, Aunt Vân."

Our neighbors pat each one of them on the head. The three of them leave the adults and go back to finishing their chores. Tree sweeps the floor, Tuấn sets the table, and little Trinh resumes plucking gray hairs from her grandfather's head.

"Brother Thắng, as promised, I brought the rice wine." Tú hands the bottle to my brother-in-law.

"Your son has grown since a couple months ago!" Thắng exclaims. "I cannot believe how much he has grown in such a short amount of time!"

"Lộc, say hello to everyone," his mother nudges. I can see she is embarrassed by his rude manner. Lộc bows. "They cannot hear you. Speak up. Be courteous and address everyone. They are so gracious to invite us to dinner tonight, on the eve of the mid-autumn festival."

Lộc bows to each of us. "Hello, Aunt Eight. Hello, Uncle Six. Hello, Aunt Six. Hello, Uncle Seven. Hello, Uncle Hải. Hello, Aunt Seven."

"Good, now go find the elder of the house and pay your respects," Lộc's mother commands him.

"Tell our father it is time to eat and bring him out to the courtyard to join us," I call after Lộc. The boy does not acknowledge me and continues through the house.

We all walk out to the courtyard. Our table tonight is the floor. Sheets of newspaper are laid out below our feet; they stand in for a tablecloth and rest underneath teacups, bowls, and chopsticks. The courtyard is illuminated tonight by the full moon above and two lanterns on either side of our "table".

"Look at this feast." My father enters the courtyard with Tree and Lộc. We all bow and say our greetings to Father. "Who prepared this meal?"

Thắng answers, "Your daughter, Six, prepared the meal, as always, but of course, we all helped."

"Where did we get the snake and the fish?" Father asks, again.

"Father, Tree caught them early this morning," I answer patiently, "out in the fields. The fish washed ashore from the heavy rainfall and a nearby tropical storm. The river flooded the neighboring rice fields."

"What a good grandson." He pats Tree on the shoulder. "Sit. Eat."

We all sit down on the floor, cross-legged, around the newspaper table. The women choose to sit together on the far end. I notice there is one extra place setting between my sister and brother-in-law. I understand it is reserved for Tâm.

Sister Six prepared a fine meal. At either end of the table is a platter with one steamed fish, covered in soy sauce, julienned ginger, and chopped green onions. Working from the outside edge inward, there are large bowls of rice and soup on either side, then a plate of sweet potatoes, and in the center, is the snake, flavored with salt and fine chili powder, sautéed in coconut oil, and garnished with minced coriander from the garden.

Tú pours rice wine into each of our teacups. He notices the extra place setting and pours some of the wine into the cup, for Tâm. The children fill their tea cup with rainwater from one of the cisterns. We wait until Father has the first bite before we all eagerly dig in, picking morsels of food, family style, with our chopsticks. Each of us takes a small serving to be polite but Lộc helps himself to a large serving of everything. I pretend not to notice. The men talk about how Tree caught the snake this morning before switching topics to the process of making rice wine. They applaud Tú for being able to make it without detection from the police since it is now illegal to produce alcohol without a license.

On our end of the table, Vân starts up a conversation with us women. "I have never prepared snake before. Sister Six, how do you do it?"

Sister Six slurps a mouthful of soup from her bowl and swallows quickly. "You first have to make sure the snake is dead." We all laugh. "And when you cut the head off, you have to cut at least this much below the head to remove the venom glands." Sister Six shows Vân her middle finger indicating the full length of her finger as the measurement to use. I smile, understanding well that my sister is not happy our neighbors are here, intruding on our family life, eating our food, and possibly spying on us for the government. I learned from Sam many years ago that the middle finger is the symbol to go "fuck off".

My sister continues. "You have to bury the head, otherwise, it can still bite you and kill you." My sister narrows her eyes and shows her fangs, and slithers her face inches from Vân's, making the frightened woman jump and gasp. I am enjoying this interaction between my neighbor and my wonderful sister.

"Then you rip the skin off, like tearing off filthy, smelly, sweat-soaked socks from your feet. You start from where the head was severed, and you pull and tug hard until you strip it clean." Sister Six demonstrates with exaggerated gusto by pulling an imaginary sock from her foot, which is now straight up in the air at a forty-five-degree angle to her hip. I almost spit out my potato from trying not to laugh. She looks ridiculous with her left leg still crossed and her right leg in the air.

"Aiyah, Sister, put your leg down," orders Hiền, "before all the bats fly out of your cave."

I choke on my potato.

"Do you feed the snakeskin to your livestock?" asks Vân.

"No." Sister Six's eyes roll back and she laughs. "The snake is a symbol of rebirth and healing. You save the skin for medicinal purposes, not for feeding your chickens!"

The poor woman casts her eyes downward as if embarrassed. It is apparent she is from a lower class of less educated people than my family.

"Sister, you will spoil Sister Vân's appetite." I try to be polite and rescue her.

"Nonsense. Next, you put your hands into the belly of the beast and shovel out the innards like this." My sister cups her hand into a bowl and scoops imaginary guts. Her nose wrinkles. "The smell is foul, especially if you cut too deep into the stomach." Our guest's eyes open wide and she covers her mouth. Her face is frozen with disgust. I can tell Sister Six is relishing the moment. "It takes a long time for rigor mortis to set in so the fresh kill will writhe and twitch for hours." My sister thrashes about like a demon-possessed woman. "The heart still pumps in the headless snake, and--"

"Enough, Sister," Hiền pleads.

"Fine." Sister Six takes a bite of the snake. She and I exchange a secret glance and a mischievous smile. Tonight's dinner has been entertaining.

Father stands up to loosen his pants. "I am so full. I need to unbutton to make room for more food." He pulls down his pants to his knees.

Hải jumps up. "Uncle, how about we have you change into loose pants with an elastic waist?"

"Good idea." Father goes with Hải inside the house.

As soon as they are out of sight, I address Hiền and Sister Six. "What is it with Father lately, not wanting to wear pants?"

Hiền shrugs. "He is going senile."

The rest of our evening is cordial and light. The rice wine helps to keep us loose. The alcohol reminds me of the mid-autumn festival two years ago when Hải gave me a mooncake.

# 20 FURY (SEPTEMBER 1978)

A series of loud knocks rap at the door. I run to the foyer and see Sister Six beat me to it. She opens the door and stumbles backward as three cadres enter the house.

"Who is the head of the household here?" The oldest one asks.

"Our father." Sister Six's voice is barely audible. Her lips quiver.

"We must speak to him."

I walk to Father's room to fetch him. I return to see our whole household has gathered by Sister Six. I see the fear in my sister's face and am guessing she is reliving the day Tâm was taken. This is the first time I have seen her so afraid.

"Elder, we received a tip that your family has stolen government property," the oldest cadre accuses. "We will search your house now and take back what is rightfully the property of the Socialist Republic of Việt Nam."

"My family is innocent," answers Father. "You will find nothing stolen here."

The three officials disperse to different areas of the house. They leave every room in disarray like a tornado had ransacked the area.

"Here!" yells one of the cadres. We all run outside to the back of the house and into the garden. He holds a jar which contains brine and snakeskin. "I also found the fish." He points to the nine fish soaking in salt water.

"We caught those during the rainstorm when the fish washed onto the fields from the river." I cannot believe they are accusing us of stealing. "And my nephew caught that snake. We did not steal anything."

"You took these from the field without the government's permission." The oldest cadre collects our fish and the jar. "Everything belongs to the government."

"Please, we are under the protection of one of your cadres, Trần Minh-Hoàng." I lie and hope that in a sea of communist officials, Minh-Hoàng's name will mean something to these men. "I ask that you please spare our family by leaving us at least a couple of fish. We have young children who are hungry."

"That name means nothing to me," says the oldest cadre.

"I served with him in the army," says the young cadre holding the jar with the snakeskin. "If she says they are under his care, I believe her."

"What is your relation to Minh-Hoàng?" the oldest one asks me.

Again, I lie. "I was his mother's caretaker. Mrs. Trần loved me like a daughter."

The oldest cadre gives me a lurking grin. I smirk back but feel violated with his eyes piercing through my clothes. The cadre takes a step towards me but I stand firm, ready to challenge him.

Hải quickly steps in front of me. "You have what you came here for. Take the fish and the snakeskin and go." My father stands defiantly beside Hải. His scowl challenges the cadre.

"Step aside, old man." The cadre pushes my father to the ground. Father loses his balance and crashes to the floor. He lands on his hip and braces his fall with his elbow. He winces.

I immediately kneel down to tend to him. "Father, are you hurt?"

The cadre advances forward to grab my arm and roughly pull me to my feet. Hải punches the cadre in the face and chaos erupts. Sister Six and I help Father up but Hải falls back. He slams into me with such force that I crumble to the floor, taking Father with me. Father cries out in pain. His head hits the ground. In the middle of this scuffle, Dirty Butt squawks in protest and runs to the back of the banyan tree.

One of the other cadres, the ugliest one, chases after her. "They have a chicken!"

Sister Six tends to Father while I chase after the third cadre. "You leave my chicken in peace or else I will feed you to her for dinner!" I threaten.

A gunshot fires and I halt in my tracks. A hushed groan escapes my throat. The children cry out in fear. Hiền cries one of her "aiyahs".

The young cadre who found the fish and snakeskin waves his pistol in the air. "Stop where you are and kneel with your hands behind your back!"

We all do as we are told.

"You are all stupid to first steal from the government and then dare to challenge us," says the oldest cadre. "We can fine you and take away your government subsidy. How would you like that? Or we can take your house, and declare it a meeting house for us. How does that sound? Maybe, we arrest you all and separate you so that you will never see each other again. We can put the children in orphanages, or send them to rural areas to farm the land." The cadre continues his speech, threatening us with torture and even death.

With our heads bent down and our eyes focused on the floor, we have no choice but to listen. Hiền whimpers softly inside the house. Somehow, it is not fear but rage that bubbles to the surface. The longer the cadre talks, the more it fuels my anger. He finally stops talking and rounds us up in the courtyard. We huddle in silence, waiting for our sentence. I cannot help but be suspicious of our neighbors. Perhaps they were spies and reported us. Who else could it be?

"Because this is the year of the horse, and I was born under this sign, I will show you compassion. You can keep your house for now." He pauses to let the weight of his message sink in. "We are taking everything else you own, including one member of this family. I will let you determine who will get arrested today."

Cries of protest escape from each of us. This cannot be happening! One of the cadres, the ugly one, ties us up with rope. We sit helpless as they haul away the salted fish, the snakeskin in brine, and my beloved Dirty Butt. My heart anchors into my stomach knowing the fate that awaits her. They remove our hammocks, rip up our plants, and take our clothes hanging on the clothesline. They take our pots and pans, our cooking and eating utensils, even our mattress and the bicycles. We are scared and deeply dejected.

"Have you decided who is leaving with us today?" asks the oldest cadre. We can no more choose than pierce a dagger into each other's heart. It is a cruel demand.

Father stands up. "Arrest me. I am old and have lived a long life."

"No, that is not happening," I say. "Take me."

"I will not let you sacrifice yourself," says Sister Six. "You have a daughter."

"Take me," says Hải. "I am the one who punched you."

"No!" I search for Hải's hands. "There has to be another way."

"There is no other way." A tear hangs on to the corner of Hải's eye.

I mouth the words "I love you" and lean in to rest my head on his shoulder. My tears stain his shirt.

"It has been decided then," says the cadre. "Come."

"No!" I refuse to let go of Hải's hands. He pulls Hải to his feet but my grip tightens around Hải's wrist. "No!" I scream again. The cadre pries our hands apart and kicks me in the ribs. I claw at his legs and try to trip him. He escorts Hải into the house. I struggle to stand up with my hands tied behind my back and run after them. "No! Please! No!"

Outside the front of our house, I see our belongings loaded onto a truck. They even take the Buddha on our ancestors' altar. I run to Hải and beg them not to take him. The young cadre shoves Hải into the truck. The ugly cadre pushes me to the ground. They all jump in the truck and start up the engine.

I scream at the top of my lungs with the fury of a deranged lunatic. "Fuck you all to hell! I curse each of you a life of misery and pain! I will conjure up the dead to haunt and possess you, and torture you until the day you meet Satan!"

The truck speeds away and I chase after it. I see Hải's head bobbing up and down. We lock eyes and for one second, time freezes. Then, the truck screeches around the corner and is gone. I fall to the ground and succumb to grief. My world shatters.

*** 

119

"How is my father doing?" I ask Đức.

The good doctor shakes his head. "There is a severe hematoma on his thigh."

"What does that mean, exactly?" I bite my lower lip.

"He has a big bruise where he fell. The swelling and pain should go away in a few weeks. The best thing he can do is rest, keep his leg elevated, and apply ice or anything cold on it. Hopefully, it will not clot as the blockage can cut off blood flow and cause major damage."

"And his elbow? His head? What about his hips?"

"His elbow is scraped. He is lucky he did not break his hips. It will be tender for a while but he is not complaining, so that is reassuring. His head is where I have the most concern. There is a big bump there. It is possible he has a contusion or even a concussion."

"Meaning what, exactly?" I pace back and forth. "I am sorry, but I do not understand all the medical terms and how serious they are or what complications can arise."

"No need to apologize," says Đức, "but keep vigilant over the next few days. If he complains of persistent headaches, dizziness, or blurred vision, or if you notice his speech is slurred and he is confused or has trouble remembering things, they can be signs that there is bleeding in his head, in which case, the blood can fill his brain and suffocate the brain tissue."

"Thank you for coming." I walk Doctor Đức out the door. He pedals off on his cyclo. I run back into the house and grab Sister Six by the arm. "We are going over there now!"

"I am coming with you," insists Brother Thắng. The three of us storm into the house located behind ours.

"Where are you?" I yell out to our neighbors. "You cannot hide from us!"
"Brother Tú, Sister Vân," my brother-in-law calls out.

"My parents are not home." The expression on Lộc's face says it all. I lunge at him and grab him by the ear. The boy wails in pain and slaps my hand away.

Sister Six holds me back before I can sink my nails into his flesh. "He is only fifteen."

"We cannot make assumptions and false accusations," says Brother Thắng.

"How can you both be so calm and rational?" I demand. "It is obvious he is the traitor."

"What are you talking about?" Lộc looks past me to avoid eye contact.

"Do not play games with me, you liar." I am seething with so much anger that my voice shakes and my hands tremble.

"Did you tell anyone about our dinner together?" asks my brother-in-law.
"No," Lộc stammers.
"You are deceitful," I tell him.

My sister advances over to the boy. He steps back until he is pinned against the wall. Sister Six's breathing matches his, breath for breath. She stares at him. Her eyes take hold of his. They are nearly the same height. I wait to see what she will do next. Sister Six clocks her head side to side. Tick tock. Her eyes hold the boy prisoner. A smirk crosses her lips and then she blows hard into his open eyes. "Confess, or else I will see to it that they come knocking on your door next."

Lộc yells in shock and pain. "I told my friend; that is all. I was jealous. Please, I meant no harm. He must have repeated it--"

"Or maybe your friend is a communist!" I scream. "Your mouth caused my family to lose everything! They came and took all our possessions, even our furniture! We are eating and sleeping on the floor. My father is badly hurt and has to SLEEP ON THE FUCKING FLOOR!" I pound my fist on the wall next to his head. "They arrested Uncle Hải. Your mouth cost our family so much, you stupid boy."

Exasperated, we depart our neighbor's house and leave Lộc to his misery. There is nothing we can do or say to undo the damage that has already taken place.

# 21 GOODBYE, BEAUTIFUL SÀI GÒN

A new dawn scatters across the sky. To stay warm, I wear several layers of clothes. At least the cadres left us some clothes and a few miscellaneous things that were not worth their time or could not fit into the truck. Not surprisingly, they did not take my crooked pants with the uneven pant legs. I check the elastic waist and am relieved Sam's emerald and diamond ring is still there, along with the phoenix necklace. I take off my wedding ring and put it in the elastic waistband as well. It is too painful to love. A rooster announces the rising sun and the pangs of guilt amplify my longing to hold Dirty Butt. My poor little chicken. Of all the chicks, there was something about her that stole my heart. I gave her more love than any chicken has ever known and saved her from an early death. In the end, I could not save her from fate; instead, I prolonged the inevitable.

I enter my father's room to check on him. His leg is propped up on Tree, who sleeps on his side to keep his grandfather's leg as high as it can be. Lying on either side of Father are little Trinh and Tuấn. Their little bodies give off enough heat to keep Father warm. Even Thủy-Tiên wanted to do her part and keep Grandfather warm. She lies by his head, curled into a ball; her little butt pressed against his temple. My heart swells with so much love for them. My thoughts meander to Tâm and I let the tears stream down my face. I let out a long sigh and walk outside.

"You are awake," I say to Sister Six.

"I told you this was my favorite time of day," she says. "The only time I have to myself before the rest of the world wakes. Sometimes, it is also my least favorite time of the day. I have only my opinions to keep me company, and right now, my opinion is that life is bleak."

"I need to go to the city today and get more things from Cường," I say. "This will be my last run. I am going to say my goodbyes to him and to Minh-

Hoàng, and once I sell the last of this supply, I should have enough to leave."

"I wish I could leave with you," my sister says, "but I have to stay and take care of Father." This is the first I have heard of her wanting to leave.

"Let Brother Seven and Hiền take care of Father. Come with me," I say.

"Brother Seven can barely take care of himself and his family. With his truck driving schedule, he is never home. And we both know our sister-in-law does not have the backbone to do this all by herself."

"Hiền would rise to the occasion if she had to," I say, "but you are probably right, our sister-in-law would not be able to handle the stress for long before she goes crazy."

"I have to stay, in case Tâm comes back one day."

"Maybe when I get to America and settle in, get a job, I can send home some money. And when Tâm comes home one day, I can sponsor the whole family--"

"That would be a dream come true. I fear it is getting more dangerous every day to live here," Sister Six says. "Ever since the Khmer Rouge slaughtered our people in Ba Chúc five months ago, it will be a matter of time before our military counterstrikes with a massacre of their own."

"All our country knows is war," I say.

"Are you taking the bus into Sài Gòn, or--"

"Catching a ride," I say. "Can you watch Thủy-Tiên for me?"

*\*\**

We ride in silence into the city. Brother Seven and I do not have much to say this morning. We approach the last checkpoint before entering Sài Gòn. Brother Seven shows the guard his papers. The uniformed officer checks the truck before handing the documents back to him. We pull away from the gate.

"Stop!" The guard's face reappears in front of us.

My brother steps on the brakes. "Is there a problem?"

"Who is the woman with you? What is her business?"

"I sell dried goods," I say. "Squid, shrimp, mushrooms…fruits."

He glares at me. "I was speaking to him, not you. Know your place."

Brother Seven mirrors my response. "My companion sells dried squid, shrimp--"

"Shut up." The guard nods to me. "Show me your license." I hand him my papers. "This license expires today. Where is your new one?"

"I am heading home now to District One to pick it up." I force myself to show composure and hope he believes my lie. How did I forget it was expiring?

"Show me your product," he barks.

Sensing my panic, Brother Seven answers, "She sold the last of it in the last village."

The guard is satisfied with Brother Seven's response and waives us through. We both let out a sigh of relief. The cadres who arrested Hải had also taken all my dried foods. I have been so preoccupied with everything that I overlooked this detail.

***

I step into the familiar toy store and see Cường faithfully perched on his stool, waiting for a customer. He smiles but I do not smile back.

"What is wrong?" he asks. I pile it on thick, starting with the snake dinner, climaxing with Hải's arrest, and finishing with my father's condition. "Such bad luck. What about the money from the last supply I gave you?"

"I have your share." I hand him the gold bar. "I had them hidden in our bunker. This is my last supply run. I will steal a boat if I have to, but I must leave soon. I cannot wait another year."

Cường disappears momentarily behind the store and comes back with a bag. "It may take you a while to sell them."

Seeing the contents, my body temperature rises. "How the hell am I going to sell these? You seriously want me to sell these rhinoceros horns?"

"You say this is your last run, why not make it a big one? There is a high demand for these."

"African rhinoceros parts have been banned since last year," I remind him.

"Horns sold in our country have not been prohibited yet. International commercial trade of African horns has been banned but these are Asian horns and they are stronger," argues Cường.

"My journey with you ends here. I am not going to sell these."

"Do not be a fool. You can sell these for eight hundred U.S. dollars per kilogram. With your share, you can easily set your family up comfortably before you leave. Not to mention, these horns have medicinal powers and can help your father's ailments." Cường can be convincing. He hands me the bag. Maybe he is right. If I can sell these by Christmas, I can be out of the country before New Year's Day.

"Thank you, Cường, for everything. Take care of yourself," I say. "And so you know, there are no medicinal powers in any of the rhinoceros horns." I walk out of his store empty-handed.

***

My walk to Minh-Hoàng's house is bittersweet. This city that is so much a part of my heart and mind will never be the same. The sunlight does not shine the same. The trees no longer present themselves as strong and wise. The shops have lost their appeal. I am a small child in this familiar, yet strange, city. Gone are the happy days when I was a university student here. Will Sài Gòn ever reclaim her glory again? If I ever return, will this city welcome me back? Or am I dead to her now? Are we both lost to each other? Goodbye, beautiful Sài Gòn. I will never forget you.

I knock on Minh-Hoàng's door. No one answers. I call out his name but hear nothing. I peek in the window and see no one. I walk to the back of the house and see him sitting next to his mother's tomb. There are cans of "333 Premium" beer, once named "33" beer until the communists took over, lying all

124

over the garden.

"You are drunk," I say to him.

"I am lonely…and drunk." Minh-Hoàng takes a big gulp of beer.

"Come into the shade." I reach for his arm.

He slaps my hand away. "Why are you here?"

"I came to ask for your help."

"Favors. All you ask are favors. Never show gratitude. You give me nothing in return."

"I am sorry. I have asked a lot of you, especially with trying to find my niece."

"What do you want now?" Minh-Hoàng wobbles back and forth and takes another swig of his beer. He tosses it carelessly on Mrs. Trần's tomb and pops open another can. "I have given you money, and food, and a permit…" He hiccups. "…to come and go as you please."

"I need some more of your mother's dried squid and shrimp, or anything you can spare. I promise this is the last thing I ask of you. My permit expires today and I will not be renewing it."

Minh-Hoàng stands up and meanders toward me. "Why not be…why will you renew…not renewing it?" He slurs his words. His breath is foul with the smell of cigarettes and beer. Beads of sweat pour profusely down his neck. Has he even bathed these past few days?

"My father is ill and requires my full devotion to his care," I say. "I plan to stay in Vĩnh Bình for as long as he needs me."

"Why does everyone leave me?" He yells and spits droplets of beer on my face. "All I ever wanted from you is respect and gratitude."

I take a step back. Minh-Hoàng wraps one arm around my waist and pulls me close. The beer in his left hand sloshes out onto the ground. I push his chest but he holds me tighter. His lips press hard against mine and his wet, clumsy tongue thrusts deep into my mouth. I choke and slap him hard on the face. The sting of his hand cuts across my cheek. I am stunned for a moment. He takes the opportunity to grab my hair and pull my head back. He groans and kisses my neck. His hot breath on my ear and the urgency of his desire make me want to throw up. He drops his beer and with his free hand, fondles my breast.

My heart races fast and I am frightened. "Stop!" I cry out. I push harder against his body but that only excites him more. Minh-Hoàng tugs at my shirt. *Oh God, this cannot be happening!* I stomp on his bare toes.

Minh-Hoàng shrieks in pain. "Mother Fucker! You bitch!"

I run but a tightness digs into my stomach and holds me hostage. Minh-Hoàng's talons seize hold of my pants and jolt me back. My body slams into his. The hardness of his penis against the small of my back disgusts me. He picks me up around the waist and carries me inside the house. I kick and scream and throw my head back to thrust a blow to his head. It does not faze him. He throws me to the floor and straddles himself on top of me. The full weight of his body bearing down on my abdomen and hips hurt my ego more than my physical being.

"Minh-Hoàng, please, stop!" I try to reason with him. "This is your mother's house. You are dishonoring her if you continue."

He laughs. "This is my house now and she is dead."

He rips open my shirt and slides both sides of my bra straps down, exposing my flesh to his hungry eyes. I say a prayer for God to give me strength. Instead, He sends me a loud, thunderous explosion. Outside, women and children scream. The house shakes and the windows rattle. A vase falls over and shatters to the floor. I grab a fragment and dig it deep into Minh-Hoàng's throat. He howls in pain and rolls over. His erection quickly deflates. I spring to my feet and give him a powerful kick to his testicles before running out the door.

Outside is chaos. A nearby building is ablaze with fire and smoke. Ash is falling from the sky. I run in the opposite direction of the building. I am afraid that if I look back, I will see Minh-Hoàng chasing me. I clutch my shirt tight with one hand and catch a falling ash with the other. I do not stop until I see Brother Seven.

## 22 FATHER (SEPTEMBER 1978)

The long ride back to Vĩnh Bình is bumpy and loud. Without any dried merchandise to sell or a renewed license to show, Brother Seven agrees to hide me in the back of the truck behind the hundreds of cases of beer. We arrive back home shortly after 8 p.m. Brother Seven quickly unloads half of the beer until he sees my anxious face. I jump out of the truck and run frantically to the outhouse. My bladder burns like it is on fire and going to burst. I squat down with my feet planted on the slats and wait for relief. It takes some time before I can pee.

I walk inside and see my family's defeated faces.

"I am hungry," says Trinh.

"I want food," says Thủy-Tiên.

"Me too," says Tuấn. "When can we eat?"

My sister shakes her head.

I usher the children to the cistern. "Fill your stomachs with water and go to bed. We will have food tomorrow morning."

My daughter, niece, and nephew do as they are told, but complain the entire time, until they lie down next to Father in his room.

"How is Father doing?" I ask.

"Aiyah, Sister, he has been sleeping all day," says Hiền. "He woke up a couple of times and stayed awake to talk a little bit, but then he fell asleep again to the sound of his stomach crying out for food."

"Brother Seven, you get some sleep. You have to drive again tomorrow morning," I say. He slithers off to the bedroom. "Brother Six, can you load the cases of beer back onto the truck? Brother Seven has to deliver them to Phú Quốc tomorrow." My brother-in-law nods. "Sister Hiền, please keep an eye on the children and Father." I toss Sister Six a bucket. She does not even try to catch it. "And you, dear sister, are going to catch lizards. Fill a spray bottle with cold water. If you see one, spray it to slow it down and trap it with a bucket. With luck, you will catch some and fry them up to eat."

"Why do I have to catch geckos?" She picks up the bucket. "What about the money you saved up from selling your medicines? Why not use some of it to buy food?"

"I have not had the chance to convert it to gold bullions yet. It would be too suspicious if we went to market with large bills."

"Fine. What are you and Tree going to do while I catch chameleons and geckos?"

"We are going to get us a bird," I say. "Tree, grab your slingshots. It might rain later tonight, in which case, we will see if we can catch some frogs too."

My sister grumbles. "Who made you boss?"

***

Tree and I return to the house at midnight. We did not take down a bird although there were a few perched on some trees. They taunted us before flying off. We did catch four nocturnal frogs that came out thanks to the rainfall. Tree captured three and I caught my first one.

"Do you think Aunt Six caught any lizards?" I ask Tree.

"No," he responds.

"I do not either. Good job tonight. Get some sleep."

Tree walks off and I head to Father's room. Thủy-Tiên, Trinh, Tuấn, and Father are all sleeping soundly. I walk to my room and put on two layers of clothes to keep warm through the night. I lay down on the cold, hard floor, exhausted. The memory of Minh-Hoàng forcing himself on me earlier today has me crying quietly in my room. This is a burden I will carry alone.

***

Brother Seven's truck is not outside. My guess is he left for Phú Quốc hours ago. I remember the frogs that Tree and I caught last night and walk over to check on them. They are still moving in the bag. Father will be pleased.

I enter Father's room to wake up the children and him. I sit on the floor and scoop Thủy-Tiên onto my lap. Her eyes open and she smiles at me. I poke at my niece and nephew. They grumble and plead to be left alone. I tickle them and before long, their giggles fill the room.

"Time to wake Grandfather up," I say. "Do you think he is ticklish?" All three of them nod and wiggle their fingers across Father's feet, neck and ears. It does not work. "Try again, maybe his ribs." The four of us tickle, poke and scratch at Father's ribs, but he does not stir. I fear something is wrong. "Father?" I touch his hand and it is cool. "No, no, no, no." I notice his mottled skin appears marbled in hues of red, purple and blue. "You cannot be dead!" I yell at his lifeless body. I search for a pulse and find none. "Father, wake up!" I shake his shoulders. "Father! Wake up! Wake up!"

I throw myself over his torso and once again, surrender to the pain.

***

Although the tears did not make a public appearance with my taciturn sister, I believe inside, her heart is breaking into a million pieces. She is exhausted from staying up the past two days cooking to cater the funeral service herself.

"I am going to prepare everything that Father likes," she says, "the way he liked them, and I do not want any help."

If doing everything herself will keep her distracted so that she does not have time to cry, I support her wishes. Brother Seven and my brother-in-law, Thắng, handle the tomb arrangements. My sister-in-law, Hiền, calls for a monk to chant and say prayers. Tree helps me notify extended relatives and trusted friends in our hamlet, while I write letters to those who live too far to come.

Today, my brother's sunken eyes, weary movements, and gaunt figure make him age ten years older. Brother Seven is taking it the hardest, perhaps because he has loved Father longer than any of us. Thủy-Tiên is the only one here with dry eyes. She does not quite understand what is happening and what death means. Her face shows curiosity. One day, she will understand the pain of losing a parent. For now, I am thankful she is innocent and not burdened with sadness.

We lay Father to rest in a tomb next to Mother. Most of the money I saved up from selling on the black market went to building the tomb and paying for the funeral service. Like Minh-Hoàng's service for his mother, Father's service is also simple, with only a handful of people in attendance, including our neighbors, Tú and Vân, who came to pay their respects.

Sister Six still holds a grudge. "They came to eat free food."

"Bite your tongue," I say. "Today is already a sad day, and we are here to honor and celebrate Father."

"Who invited them?" Sister Six asks but does not expect an answer. "I cannot believe they had the audacity to come to the funeral."

"Sister, it takes bravery to come and pay their respects, especially since their son brought shame and embarrassment to them. They can barely look at our family because their son's carelessness cost us so much."

"They are misers," she continues. "They never share anything with us and Vân rarely loses at cards. I know she cheats."

"They are poor. Let forgiveness enter your heart before you turn into a chicory root."

"Why are you not bitter?" she asks.

"I am, but not at them," I say. It is the Communist Party and people like the bitter melon man who has me all twisted inside.

# 23 THIS IS IT (JANUARY 1979)

Hiền hands me a letter. "Hurry and open it." I stare at the envelope. "Aiyah, open it!" It is from a prison. "Read it out loud."

My hands tremble as I hold the unopened letter addressed to me. For the past three months, I questioned whether Hải was still alive. I sit down and open the letter.

"My lovely Tuyết," I read, "I hope this letter finds its way to you. I am taking a big risk to smuggle this out. I am being held at the Thủ Đức prison in Bình Thuận Province."

"That is one-hundred-forty kilometers north of Sài Gòn," says Hiền.

"I am told I will be here for three to five years as punishment for hitting a police officer," I continue reading, "and I hope I survive that long. The conditions here are deplorable. My small cell is shared with many others. It is humid and putrid here and there is urine on the walls. Water leaks down from the ceiling and it is uncomfortable to sleep. I am either too hot during the day or too cold at night. My body aches from the hard physical labor they force on us prisoners. Every night we have to sit and listen to their teachings and give confessions. We only get a little bit of rice to eat each day and I am hungry all the time. Anything that moves becomes food if I can catch it. When we see a dog or a cat, we all howl and salivate, wishing we could catch it. If you get this letter, maybe you can send me some food. There are all kinds of people here, men and women, from religious and political leaders to artists and scholars. I keep hoping I will see Tâm amongst the women prisoners here but am disappointed every time. My memory of you and the script I write in my mind's eye of our future together help me persevere. Do not try to visit me. It is too far of a journey and will only make us both sad. Remember the mooncake to freedom and let that be your focus. Freedom. Do not underestimate yourself and the power of the human spirit. Please send my love to your family. I dream of the day I can see you and TT again. With love from your greatest admirer…faithfully and forever yours, Hải."

My sister-in-law cries. "At least he is alive."

"Yes." The energy drains from my body. Tears of guilt threaten to roll. "We should send him a few things."

"Should we send him something of Father's?" asks Hiền.

"Hải would like that. I am going to the market. We can include some food for him. Can you see what is left of Father's belongings and find the thickest sweater, comfortable pants, and a pair of shoes? Father still has a pair of those plastic shoes for wearing in the rain and mud."

Hiền nods and scurries off on her mission. I am relieved to have a moment of silence to myself. I reread Hải's letter. This time, the tears flow freely.

***

I walk slowly to the market with my old school satchel slung over my shoulders. Hải's letter is tucked safely inside along with all my valuables. Five meters in front of me is a jewelry store. As I approach the store, a beggar tugs at my arm. I am alarmed by his touch and jump aside with a gasp. The condition of his skin is appalling. Mosquito bites cover his body from head to toe. Fresh claw marks scorch the areas where he scratched himself hoping for relief but only feeling fire. He is sunburned and his flesh raw.

He clasps his hands together in prayer. "Sister, please, can you spare some food? I have not eaten for days. They took everything from me."

Begging is now forbidden and helping a beggar is against government policy. I notice a few eyes on me, including the jewelry store owner. I take a deep breath and ignore the man. I keep walking but he keeps begging. I shove him away. "I am so sorry, Brother."

I step inside the jewelry store. The owner approaches me. "You did the right thing. If you help him, you would be helping a parasite."

I open my mouth to respond but am interrupted by the loudspeaker. "Citizens, today we celebrate! Two weeks ago, our military forces marched into Kampuchea and took down the Khmer Rouge army. They were no match for our mighty forces and today marks the first day of our occupation and reign. The war is over."

The jewelry store owner and I are speechless. Cheers erupt in the market and people disperse to run home to their families.

"We must cheer," says the jeweler, "otherwise they will arrest us for not being patriotic."

She and I jump up and down and hug each other. It is the strangest feeling to pretend to be loyal and nationalistic and to share enthusiastic cheers with a stranger. I am a live puppet in my own country. A few firecrackers set off in the square. Some people shake hands and talk wildly about the news, while others continue their business. I recognize the fake smiles on their faces. They are smiles of pain and suffering.

I take out of the satchel my wedding ring and the phoenix necklace. "I would like to sell these."

"This is exquisite." The jeweler perks up as she examines the necklace. "Where did you have this made?"

"It was a gift on my wedding day."

"And is this your wedding ring?"

"Yes. My husband died over three years ago." I watch her weigh the wedding ring and hope my sad story appeals to her maternal heart. "I need to sell these so I can feed my children."

"You are lucky they did not find these and confiscate them. Concealing things is considered unpatriotic and can get you arrested." I say nothing. "I will give you twenty million for both."

"The necklace alone is worth over twenty million đồng," I say matter-of-factly.

"Wake up, my friend," she says. "People are not exactly buying a lot of luxuries right now."

I counter. "Twenty-five million for both the necklace and ring. Our war with Kampuchea ended. Prosperous times are coming. I can sell these tomorrow and get my asking price without any negotiations, or I can sell them to you right now, and you will be the only jeweler with this unique and sought-after necklace."

The jeweler hesitates. "We meet in the middle."

I have hooked her. "I am firm on twenty-five million. In the days to come, you can sell this necklace for over twenty million and the ring for another ten million."

"No, twenty-two and a half is my final offer." She is stubborn.

"Fine," I say. I see her shoulders relax and a smile creeps up her face. "I will take my jewelry to another shop tomorrow." Her smile disappears. I gather up my necklace and ring, wrap them up slowly in my handkerchief to give her a chance to stop me, and place them back into the satchel. "I am sorry we could not come to an agreement." I turn to leave.

"Fine. Stay. I will give you twenty-five million for both."

"In gold coins, please." I smile sweetly at her.

She hands me twenty grams of gold and the remainder in paper money. I use the cash to buy a few dried fish to send to Hải. Before walking to Thủy's and Đức's tailor shop, I walk past the beggar and "accidentally" drop one of the dried fish at his feet. I walk a few paces and glance over my shoulder. The beggar drops to his knees and picks up the fish.

"Arrêt." A police officer approaches me and demands I stop. My legs tense up and I halt in mid-stride. "Show me your hands." I spread out my fingers, palms facing up. My heart is clapping frantically. I remain unemotional and refuse to meet his gaze directly, lest he feels challenged. "Turn your hands over." I do as I am told. He takes out nail clippers from his back pocket.

Grabbing hold of my left hand, he trims my fingernails, then does the same with my right hand. "Coquetry is prohibited." He lets me off with a warning and walks off.

I let out a big sigh of relief. *Thank you, Lord.*

***

Inside the familiar tailor shop, Thủy greets me warmly. "Come in. How have you been?"

"I have been slowly picking up the pieces." I make myself comfortable in the back room. "This whole country is under constant surveillance. There are suspicion and hypocrisy around every corner. I am so sick of it."

"With the news of us defeating Pol Pot's army and stripping the Khmer Rouge's reign in Kampuchea, peace is imminent," believes Đức.

"There will never be peace until we are free from the communist regime," says Thủy.

"I believe that to be true as well," I say, "and that is why I plan to leave soon. I received a letter from Hải. He is in a prison north of Sài Gòn. I came into the market to buy some dried fish so we can send them to him."

Đức hands me a bag of fried banana chips from the cupboard. "Send him these too, from us. You should send them quickly. I hear they transfer the prisoners around every few months so the prisoners cannot form friendships. The guards fear the bond would lead to uprisings. This also prevents the family from keeping track of their relative and hence, cannot send them aide. The prisoners become weak and completely dependent on the guards. They do as they are told out of fear."

"I cannot believe the world we live in, here in our own country." I take the gold coins out of my satchel and hand them to Đức. "This should be enough. How soon can I leave?"

"The Lunar New Year falls on January twenty-eight this year," Đức says. "There is a group scheduled to leave that night from Ba Động Beach. Do you want to join them?"

"Yes, the sooner the better."

"Perfect," Thủy chimes in. "Soon it will be the year of the goat. People will be wearing lucky colors of red, purple, and green. While celebrations are taking place, you all can slip out. Make sure you wear layers in these colors to blend in."

"Normally, we would advise you to wear old, dirty clothes to look poor and ordinary," says Đức, "but because of the celebrations, even the poor will be wearing their best clothes."

"I do not have any nice clothes or clothes in those colors," I say, "but maybe I can find something that belongs to my sister."

Thủy springs to her feet and walks briskly to her mannequins. She removes the green silk tunic from one of them and hands it to me. "Take this. We are family now. Do you have black pants to compliment the tunic?"

133

I nod. "Thank you."

"New Years is two weeks away," says Đức. "That will give me time to finalize some details and secure your seats. I will pedal to your house on the morning of January twenty-six. You can buy some bananas from me. I will place a message inside one of them for you."

"Be ready," says Thủy. "This is it."

"There will be other families joining yours so you will not be alone," says Đức.

"Remember to wear layers and bring only a small bag, like this satchel is perfect." Thủy points to my bag.

"Pack some food that does not spoil, like nuts and dried fruits," says Đức.

"Yes," says Thủy, "but also bring some things to quench your thirst, like cucumbers, lemons, and coconut water."

"And bring matches or a lighter," says Đức. "Fire and water will be your most prized possessions."

We finish our conversation with hugs and tears. I rush home, anxious to put my plans in motion to leave this country once and for all.

# 24 THE LOTUS FLOWER (JANUARY 1979)

Out in the courtyard, I survey my surroundings. The banyan tree stands big and bold. I remember how Tree loved to climb up on it and take naps. The stillness of the pond and the outhouse reminds me of Father standing there without his underwear. A big lump forms in my throat. My chest caves from the weight of these memories. Way in the back is the bunker, where Tree told me about selling morphine on the black market. It reminds me also of Mrs. Trần and her bunker. I hope my niece is out there somewhere, alive and safe, and that she will return home one day. I sit down cross-legged and remember Sister Six's snake dinner. A smile escapes my lips recalling her demonstration to Vân how to strip the skin from a snake, with her leg in the air. My thoughts sweep over to Cường. I am in his debt and will be forever grateful to him for getting me this far.

Brother Seven steps into the courtyard. I see from his red eyes that he has not stopped crying. His presence adds another few pounds of brick onto my crushed heart. His tears race faster down his face. I stand up to hug him. He weeps like a child in my arms. "I want you to stay."

My sister, hearing our cries, comes out to the courtyard. Then my brother-in-law comes, and finally, my sister-in-law. Their hugs become layers of concrete that crush my body and suffocate my desire to leave. My family gathers around me. I am afraid to say the words goodbye, for fear it would be too final.

Tree comes into the courtyard. "No crying. It is New Year's!"

Brother Thắng puts on a brave face. "These are tears of joy."

Brother Seven straightens up. "You are right." He puts his hand on his son's shoulder. "Go collect extra sets of clothes. You are going to escort your aunt and Thủy-Tiên to the shores of Ba Động beach and then help them to Bạc Liêu Province."

Tree does not move. "Today is Sunday and it is almost 9 a.m. It is bad luck to travel on New Year's Day."

"Who told you that?" snaps Sister Six.

"Do as you are told." Brother Seven puts on his stern face. "You will be back soon." As soon as Tree leaves, he cries again.

"You have to tell him," I urge. "This is his chance to say goodbye."

"If I tell him, he will not go," says Brother Seven. "No, he needs to go to America. There is no life for him here. And he can help you."

Tree comes back with a plastic bag and shoves his clothes into the bag. "I am ready."

Sister Seven hugs her son close. "Be careful and stay safe. Keep alert and protect your aunt and little cousin."

"I will be back soon, Mother," says Tree.

"Aiyah, I know. I will miss you. I am being a silly woman." Hiền hugs him again and runs into the house to conceal the torrential downpour brimming in her eyes.

Tree points to the front door. "Doctor Đức is here."

I put on my straw hat and hug my family one last time. It takes all my will not to cry and abandon my plans to leave. Thủy-Tiên kisses her aunts and uncles and hugs her cousins, Trinh and Tuấn. The three of us climb into the cyclo and wave our goodbyes.

"I do not understand why everyone is so sad," says Tree. "I am only escorting you to Bạc Liêu to help you settle in, and then I will return in one, maybe two, weeks."

"This is the first time you have been away from home," I say. "It is natural for your parents to worry."

"I am sixteen years old now, not four like Thủy-Tiên."

"One day when you are a father, you will understand what it is like to worry about your children."

"They are worried about you too and you are almost forty years old. You are going to another village for a teaching job and it does not even start until next week. They act as if they will never see us again."

Đức joins our conversation as he pedals his cyclo through the town to the other side of the market. "It proves that no matter how old you get, family always worry about family."

"Is it bad luck to travel on New Year's Day?" I am nervous and excited at the same time. "I know it is bad luck to argue or work or do housecleaning--"

"It should be a day for resting and spending time with family," reminds Tree. "We should be eating, drinking, gambling, and celebrating, so yes, traveling is a bad idea. I do not understand why we did not delay your travels until after all the celebrations."

"When will we get there?" asks Thủy-Tiên.

"It will take us a couple of hours to get to the beach," I say.

"I am hungry," my daughter declares.

Đức stops pedaling and reaches into his basket. "Have some deliciously dried bananas."

Thủy-Tiên eagerly takes the bananas. "Thank you, Uncle Đức."

Tree offers to pedal. "Let me know when you get tired."

"We can switch in twenty or thirty minutes," says Đức. "I will escort you to the Quan Chánh Bố canal."

We ride through several hamlets. Tree and Đức switch every few miles. Thủy-Tiên and I remain in the buggy. I offer to pedal but Đức says people will be suspicious seeing a woman dressed in a nice silk tunic transferring two men and a child. We continue through the countryside. Every home is different as we ride through the dirt roads. The poor live next to the rich. Thatched roof homes made of bamboo, banana leaves, straw, clay, or palm stand beside three-story homes built from brick, tile, wood, or stone. Some homes are modestly decorated for the Lunar New Year while others are lavishly adorned with banners, flowers, lucky red envelopes, and firecrackers. Despite the economic differences from one house to the next, all of them have hammocks outside or on the balconies.

"Múa Lân!" Thủy-Tiên squeals excitedly and points ahead.

"Yes, my dolly, a dragon dance," I say.

There is a large celebration commencing at this hamlet. The beat of the drums resonates through the streets into the cheering crowd. There are two sets of dragon costumes, one in red, and the other in green, with men underneath the shiny dragon cloth tapping their feet and marching to the beats. A cymbal chimes and the dancers holding the head of the dragons jump into the air to stand on the shoulder of the man behind him. The dragons pretend to grab the lucky red envelop hanging from the storefronts. I see a hand extend from one of the dragon's mouth and snatch the envelope. Firecrackers pop nonstop leaving a trail of red paper confetti. Smoke rises and swirls around the dancers. A person dressed as the happy Buddha with an oversized paper mâché mask prances around the dragons and wiggles his butt to the crowd. Everyone laughs. It is nice to hear genuine laughter in the streets again. The dragons bow to the store owner with gratitude and the happy Buddha waves his fan to cool off the store owners. The people chuckle and cheer. They clap with enthusiasm. Three young men carry colorful red, green, and purple flags that represent their school. They march on to the next business for more New Year's envelopes.

Thủy-Tiên tugs at my shirt. "Do I get a red money envelope?"

Đức comes to the rescue. "If you be a good girl, tomorrow, you will get many red envelopes with a lot of money in them."

My daughter is reassured by his promise. "I will be good."

"Another thirty minutes and we will arrive at the canal," says Đức. "There will be someone to take you across so you can continue your journey."

I nod and continue viewing the scenery. In the distance, there is a large, two-level wood house on stilts with a palm-leaf roof and a fish pond. The pond is covered with aquatic plants, including bright lotus blossoms, in ombre colors of pink and yellow. It looks peaceful.

"Those sun-kissed water lilies are so pretty," says Tree.

"The spirits are with us, Tree," I say. "This is a good sign that we are seeing these blooms."

"There is so much mystery around these flowers," says Đức. "Their roots live in the mud underneath murky water and every night, they submerge to rest, awakening every morning to re-bloom. Yet, there is no mud or any residue on the petals."

"It is a symbol of rebirth and is truly miraculous," I say.

"I feel spiritual right now," says Tree.

"You should. It is not every day that we get to experience such beauty." I squeeze his hand. "This flower can live in such filthy conditions, surrounded by grime and pesky bugs, but every morning, it wakes and revives unscathed, to grace mankind with its purity."

"The lotus flower is resilient and has a strong will to live. A lotus seed can survive hundreds of years without water," adds Đức.

"I feel like we are lotus flowers," says Tree. "We are still here despite living in murky waters."

"Yes, but some of us are prettier than others." I give my daughter a gentle pinch on the cheeks. "The prettiest one being Thủy-Tiên."

Her smile brightens my world. We ride the rest of the way in silence. With every full rotation of the tires, I am closer to the dreadful goodbye to Đức and to my country.

# 25 VIỆT NAM ECLIPSES (JANUARY 1979)

The Quan Chánh Bố canal was dug in the 1800s and now connects to the Hậu River. It flows along Highway fifty-three and spills into the East Việt Nam Sea. It can support vessels carrying up to ten-thousand tons of cargo. I sense crossing the channel of water will be the easiest part of our journey.

Đức makes an abrupt stop at the end of the provincial road. "This is where my journey ends and yours begins." I hop off the buggy and adjust my hat. My black pants and green tunic stick to me from the humidity. Đức leans close and whispers in my ear. "Things will get difficult, and when they do, remind yourself that the struggle here in Việt Nam eclipses any adversity you will face on your search for freedom in America. This will all be worth it."

I nod. "Take care of yourself. Send my love to your wife. Thank you for everything."

Tree offers his back to Thủy-Tiên who monkey jumps happily onto him and wraps her arms and legs around her cousin. He collects his plastic bag of clothes and my satchel.

Đức pats Tree on the arm and hands him a red envelope. "Happy New Year."

Tree receives the envelope with two hands. "Thank you, Uncle. May the new year bring you good health, prosperity, and great purpose."

Thủy-Tiên slides off Tree's back and jumps up and down excitedly. "I wish you love and happiness."

Đức laughs and bends down on one knee. "Very good." He hands Thủy-Tiên a red envelope. She opens it and proudly shows me her money. He hugs the three of us and pedals back down the same road. We watch until he is out of sight.

Tree taps my shoulder. "Here comes our guide."

I see an old, weathered-looking man walking towards us. He is barefoot.

He slows down and nods at us. "The road conditions are terrible with cracks and potholes." He searches my face for a response.

"And no bridges so we must go around."

He gives me a toothless grin. "Follow me."

Tree raises his eyebrows. "That made no sense."

"Do not worry," I say. "He spoke in code to make sure we were his guests. My response assured him we were."

"He should have said, 'Hello, I am your liaison. Are you Tuyết?'"

I smile at my nephew. Poor thing has no idea. After tonight, he will no longer be a citizen of Việt Nam. We follow quietly behind our guide. For an old man, he scurries quickly and with agility, easily jumping over fallen trees, stepping over big rocks, and dodging intrusive brush. I keep alert, watchful for any police and being mindful of where I step, in case there are snakes. We walk along the channel and cut through a jungle. Tree and I alternate carrying Thủy-Tiên on our back.

"Is it much farther?" I ask.

The old man points to a river. "We cross there."

"Where is the boat? Is there a canoe?"

"No, we cross over on that." The old man points to a fallen acacia tree, less than a meter wide and twenty-one meters long. "I will go first." He steps up onto the fallen tree and spreads his arms out for balance. With his toes gripping the bark, the old man walks slowly across.

Immediately my pulse quickens. "You and Thủy-Tiên go next. Do not be afraid. Go slow and be careful." The river is wide and the stream is steady, but the tree is narrow.

"I am not afraid," answers Thủy-Tiên. "We are going on an adventure. If I am a good girl, I will get more envelopes tomorrow."

"Hold on tight and be still, like a statue, otherwise, you will fall into cold water."

Tree takes off his shoes, puts them in the plastic bag, and steps up onto the acacia. He steadies himself and once balanced, he takes his first step with Thủy-Tiên clinging to his neck. He is ten paces behind our guide.

I take off my shoes and put them in my satchel. I sling it over my shoulder like a cross-body bag. I take a deep breath and do a quick Trinitarian sign of the cross on my forehead, chest, and shoulders. Our guide is almost all the way across. My nephew and daughter are not too far behind him. I step up slowly and take a moment to get familiar with the texture of the tree. It is dry and rough at the base. Step by calculated step, I inch across the narrow beam of wood, praying there are no rot or ants on the tree. I concentrate on my movements for fear of losing my balance. The sap sticks to my toes and gives me some security I will not fall. The smell of the tannins from the remaining leaves is pungent. Below me, the river rushes past. I blink a few times to maintain depth perception and not let the moving rapids become a blur. I am almost halfway to the other side.

A vibration under my feet signals to me that they have made it to the end and jumped off. I continue to focus and am now shuffling my feet instead of picking them up one in front of the other. I see some moth larvae squirming in one of the divots of the tree and scrunch my face in disgust. Taking another deep breath, I shuffle along and quickly erase the image of those translucent yellow grubs.

I hear Tree encouraging me. "You are almost at the end."

"Almost to the end, Mama." Thủy-Tiên's voice comforts me.

"Another six or seven meters," says the old guide. "Nice and steady."

I continue to glide my feet across the tree, but a piercing pain shoots up my toe. I scream in agony. I lose my balance and struggle to regain composure, but gravity takes control. I give in to the pull of the water.

"Mama!" Thủy-Tiên shrieks.

I fall in with great force. The cold river stabs me with its icy fingers. The current is deceptively fast. I gasp for air and try to swim to the bank of the river but the water sweeps me down before I can close the distance. My straw hat floats away. The old man, Tree, and Thủy-Tiên run with me downstream.

"Get on your back and keep your feet and head above water," yells the old man. "Look downstream and stay calm." I do as he tells me although the shock of the cold rapids impairs my motor functions. "Breathe, and try not to swallow too much water." *Old man, of course I am not trying to swallow the whole river!* "There is a calm area coming up. When you get there, turn over and swim over here, diagonally, and not against the current."

The rapids ease up and I realize I am in calmer waters. I flip over and swim diagonally downstream. Tree holds out a long branch for me to grab. Together, all three of them pull me up. Thủy-Tiên flings her arms around my neck and squeezes tight. Little tears slide down her cheeks.

I cough from her choking me. "I am sorry I scared you, my little dolly." I hug and kiss my daughter. "I am safe now."

An acacia thorn is burrowed deep inside my big toe. The throbbing causes me to wince. Tree kneels down and without warning, removes the thorn. I screech, more from surprise than from the discomfort.

"Can you walk?" The old man extends his hand to assist.

"Yes." I hobble along taking great care not to put any weight on the injured toe. I am distraught that Sam's book, as well as his letter and Hải's letter, are wet inside my satchel. We walk for forty-five minutes before coming to a clearing. By now, my clothes are almost dry. The village is small with only a dozen or so huts.

Our guide takes us into one of the homes made of leaves and straws. "This is my wife. You can call her Aunt Five."

An old woman greets us warmly with hugs. "Sit. Eat. You can rest for a few hours." She hands us a small bowl of porridge salted with fish sauce.

I bow to Aunt Five and wish her happy new year. Right away, I like her. We make small talk while we eat. Honestly, we are all too tired to have meaningful conversations with our kind hosts. Aunt Five wraps my big toe with strips of cloth and puts a fresh sock over my foot. I am grateful to her for nursing me.

The old man hands me a towel. "Change into something less festive after you eat."

Tree leans in close to me. "They took us in the wrong direction."

I hesitate before telling him the truth. "We are not going to Bạc Liêu."

"But your teaching job is in the Bạc Liêu province."

"There is no teaching job," I say. "We all lied to you."

My nephew's face becomes pale. He stares through me like a ghost. He stands up and walks out the door.

"Let me talk to the boy," says Uncle Five.

I stand up and walk over to the entryway to eavesdrop on their conversation. I hear a match strike and then an exhale. The smell of cigarette smoke permeates the air and wafts through the open doorway. A second match strikes and then a dry cough from Tree. He is smoking!

Aunt Five shakes her head. "Let them be."

I remain with my ear pressed against the straws that are humbly holding the roof up over our heads. Thủy-Tiên is content slurping the porridge and keeping the old woman company.

Tree takes another amateur puff and coughs again. "I want to go back."

"You cannot go back," says Uncle Five. "Your aunt and little cousin need you. It is not safe for them to travel alone."

"My family needs me," says Tree. "I know the way back to the river. I can cross it and find my way back home."

"If your parents told you, would you have gone?"

"Of course not," Tree answers. "I am going to be seventeen years old this year. I stopped going to school when I was thirteen and we lost our country. There is nothing for me in America. I cannot even speak the language and it will be too difficult to learn."

"You will find your purpose there," says Uncle Five. "Right now, your purpose is to grow up and be a man, to escort your aunt safely to a new home abroad. They cannot do this without you."

"It all makes sense now why everyone was crying when we left." The sadness is unmistakable in my nephew's voice. He takes another drag from the cigarette and does not cough this time. "I wish I had the chance to say goodbye."

"One day, you will get the chance to say 'hello' and they will be ecstatic that you made it." They finish smoking their cigarettes and come back into the house.

"Tree," I say, "your father insisted that I take you. He wants you to have a better life."

"I understand," Tree says, "but I thought you did not have enough money yet, after paying for Grandfather's funeral."

"I sold my wedding ring and the necklace I got on my wedding day. Do you remember the phoenix necklace?"

Tree nods, and for the next couple of hours, he is lost in his own thoughts.

## 26 SLANTY-EYES

It is almost 3 p.m. Aunt Five has already retired to her hammock for a nap. The wait for another escort to guide us to the beach makes the time drag on. I put on a fresh romper for Thủy-Tiên while she sleeps. Her belly is full of porridge and she is not disturbed by my intrusion. I undress and change out of my silk tunic and trousers. I put on the crooked black pants that I sewed myself, with the elastic waist hiding the only jewelry I have left...Sam's emerald and diamond ring. I look ragamuffin chic, all right, with my zigzag pants and pajama top. Tree changes into a different pair of shorts and an avocado-green cotton shirt.

Uncle Five springs out of his hammock. I am again amazed at how nimble he is for such an old man. He peeks outside. "It is time." He walks over to the round dining table and shows me a small bottle. "This is my last one and there is half left, but you will need this for your daughter. It is medicine made from valerian root and will help her calm down and sleep if she gets anxious."

"Uncle Five, I do not have any money--"

"Your money is no good here." He puts the bottle in my pocket. "You should go to the toilet. You have a long journey ahead of you."

Tree steps outside and finds a secluded spot to urinate. There is no outhouse so I, too, find a hidden area to squat down in. I am definitely in the rural countryside.

Back inside the hut, I lift Thủy-Tiên up into my arms. She remains asleep and is dead weight like a sack of rice. A young man around thirty years old appears at the doorway. He is covered in dirt and his pants are wet from the knees down.

"This is my son, Slanty-Eyes," says Uncle Five. "He will take you to Ba Động beach."

"This is my nephew, Tree, and--" I start to introduce my family.

"He is hard of hearing," says Uncle Five. "He lost his hearing a long time ago when a bomb blew close to him out in the rice paddies. He has a sixth sense, though, and is extremely alert. Of our thirteen children, he is the only one left."

"Oh, I am so sorry," I say. "Can he read my lips?"

"Most of the time. Ever since the police confiscated our writing paper, we have been getting by with gestures or writing with animal blood. Do not bother talking to him. He speaks but chooses not to."

Slanty-Eyes beckons us to follow him. We bid farewell and leave the abode. Again on foot, we traipse through the dense terrain. Our journey is short. We make it to the Hậu River where a woven basket canoe awaits. The canoe seats six people and has a wood canopy partially covering it. We climb in. Slanty-Eyes points to the canopy and gestures us to hide underneath. I am glad Thủy-Tiên is asleep during this transition.

Slanty-Eyes pushes the canoe into the river and climbs in. He rows in silence. I cannot see anything from my crouched position underneath the wood canopy but can hear the sounds of the paddle rubbing against the canoe each time our escort rows. The riverboat glides smoothly and effortlessly. I close my eyes and listen. I hear Tree breathing and the crinkle of his plastic bag when he shifts his weight. I hear the delightful soft buzz of Thủy-Tiên's snores while she slumbers soundly. Boat engines rumble by, a little too close to our canoe for my comfort. I eavesdrop on a conversation nearby from some people on a fishing boat. It sounds like they did not catch much this morning. Slanty-Eyes rows the boat for what amounts to forever. Occasionally, he rests his arms, but not for long before he resumes again.

"My foot is asleep." Tree shifts and tries to get comfortable.

"Mine too, and I have a cramp in my left leg." I reposition as well.

Slanty-Eyes' face conveys the message clearly: Be quiet.

Two hours pass. Thủy-Tiên stirs and opens her eyes. "I am thirsty."

"You will have to wait." I tell her we are playing a game and challenge her to be as quiet and immobile as a pangolin. The game interests her for only five minutes.

Tree tries to distract her. "Can you guess how many fingers I am showing behind my back?"

"Five!" She shows her hand with all five fingers spread apart.

"Shhh." Slanty-Eyes scowls at Thủy-Tiên.

She scowls back and mimics him. "Shhh."

He bribes her silence with a tamarind candy. Day gives way to night. We have been on the water for nearly four hours. My body aches. I am tired, thirsty, and hungry. We finally slow down and Slanty-Eyes gives us the signal that it is safe to come out. We climb out of the canoe and stretch our whole body. I survey our surroundings and see only water all around us. The soft haze of the moon illuminates the shimmering river. In a faraway place, the crackle of firecrackers, the blare of music, and the talent of someone singing resonates in the air. People are celebrating the year of the goat. Once again, we are asked to follow Slanty-Eyes. He takes us through a path with brush and trees on both side, and soft dirt beneath our feet. We come to a small clearing and I see fifteen people sitting around. Our guide bows to me and motions us to sit with the rest of the group. He pats Thủy-Tiên on the head, smiles, and disappears. *Where the hell are we?*

***

I study the woman sitting next to me. She is younger than me and Chinese. Her long hair is tangled and matted. Her eyes are closed, her lips open, and her head shakes side to side. She moans in distress. She takes out a menthol ointment and rubs it on her temples. She swipes some more cream from the tiny container and lathers it on her lower abdomen.

"Would you be willing to share that *Tiger Balm*?" I ask.

She opens her eyes and hands over the analgesic ointment. "What is your ailment?"

"My toe is throbbing and my legs are cramping. Yours?"

"I am a week away from having my monthly cycle. I suffer from cramps and headaches right before my period."

I rub the menthol on my calves and hand it back to her. "Do you know where we are?"

"We are at some peninsula," she responds.

"How long have you been waiting?"

"My brother and I have been here for an hour, maybe more. Every twenty or thirty minutes, more people come, in pairs or groups of three and four. Small groups mean less risk of getting caught. They come from different directions and are escorted by different people. When we arrived, there were already eight people here, including a one-year-old baby."

"Where is your brother?" I ask.

She lifts up her bony finger and points. "The one without a shirt is my little brother, Tùng, and I am Hồng-Mai." Her brother stands wearing shorts and sandals, with his shirt tucked behind his back like a tail. He is talking to another man.

"I am traveling with my nephew, Tree, and my daughter, Thủy-Tiên," I say. "My name is Tuyết."

"My youngest sister and her husband left a year ago and made it to Australia. That is where we want to go. Our parents did not join us. What is your story?"

"It is a long one," I say. "Who is the man your brother is talking to?"

"He is the co-sponsor of this operation. My brother is coming back this way. He will tell us." My new friend Hồng-Mai introduces us to her brother.

Tùng sits down with us and reports his findings. "That man I was talking to is Sơn. He and his friend are the ones who organized this escape."

"Where is his friend?" I ask.

"At home apparently," answers Tùng. "He is waiting for everyone to arrive here before heading out to meet us. Sơn said he is expecting twenty-five more people and does not expect his partner to show up until after midnight."

"That is over three hours from now!" exclaims Hồng-Mai. "He is probably celebrating the new year getting drunk!"

"He better not," says Tùng, "he is the captain of our boat."

"Your sister is probably right," I say. "He is probably spending all the money we paid him on eating and drinking, or gambling."

More time elapses and more people arrive, from different directions like Hồng-Mai said. Night brings with it mosquitos and other creatures. The collective sound of thousands of mosquitos buzzing around my head is deafening. Tree grabs a handful of mosquitos in the dark. He clenches his hand into a fist and crushes them. The pesky insects appear in droves. There is nothing we can do to escape them.

Our group has grown in size to thirty people. One would think we were all mental patients as we flail our arms and swat at the mosquitos, or slap each other to crush the ones that have landed to drain our blood. There are five children in our group...six if you count Tree. The youngest is only two months old while the other children are younger than my daughter. The poor babes cry out and their parents try to hush them. Thủy-Tiên is not immune to the blood-suckers either. Her skin is on fire each time she scratches herself. I take out the valerian root medicine that Uncle Five gave me and give Thủy-Tiên a sip, hoping it will put her to sleep and ease her suffering. Her tender flesh is inflamed and red from the allergic reaction to all the bites.

Mothers and fathers smother their babies' mouth to muffle the cries, for fear of being heard by the maritime police. This only makes them more delirious. I walk to each family with a child and offer a sip of the medicine. Every parent consents. We are all desperate for them to be quiet.

It takes another half hour for the cries to die down. The valerian root goes into effect and the children finally find relief in sleep. I hold my four-year-old and rock her back and forth. The mosquitos are still relentless but I barely feel them now. Tree still expends all his energy trying to mass murder them, one fistful at a time.

The loud rat-tat-tat sound of an AK-47 fires nearby and stuns everyone motionless. Tùng whispers, "Get down! If they see us, they will kill us all!" People scramble to hide and lie down.

"Where are they?" a voice yells out in the dark.

A woman moans, her voice barely audible. "I do not know."

A flashlight illuminates enough light for me to make out the silhouettes of two men, one woman, and a small child.

"Kneel." One of the men hit the woman on the head with the butt of the rifle. She yelps and falls to the ground like a beaten dog.

"Mama!" yells the child.

"On your knees, boy! Hands behind your head. Both of you!" The man with the flashlight shoves the child to the ground.

"Open your mouth." It is too dark to determine which one of the men is talking. The man with the flashlight crumples up something and shoves it into the woman's mouth. She cries and resists, thrusting her head side to side.

"You want to leave this country? You love money and those westerners that much? Here, eat these bills. This is the price you will pay. This is what it will cost you and your son."

The other man with a shrill voice screams, "Chew, old hag. I want to see you swallow every đồng!"

The boy cries uncontrollably and the woman gags on the money. Rounds of bullets pelt the woman's body and pummel the boy's head. They both slump to the ground, dead.

"Throw them in the water. We will go back and question the captain where they are hiding."

I am paralyzed by what I witnessed. An eerie silence blankets the forest for a brief second until the thunderous taunts of mosquitos slap me back to reality.

***

We sit together in silence and wait. A few more people arrive and I count a total of thirty-six adults, five children, and one teenager. Forty-two. How many more will show up? It has been two hours since the incident with the woman and her son being murdered at close range.

Distressed and fearful, I lean on Tree. "How are you?"

"Itchy," he answers.

"Are you afraid?" I ask.

"No. I miss home, though." Tree scratches his calves.

"Me too."

Just when I relax a little, searchlights now illuminate the darkness. I hold my breath pondering if there are more people joining our party, or more police searching with the thirst for blood.

"Lay down!" says Sơn, the co-sponsor of this trip and leader in our group.

We wait quietly. Only the thick swarm of mosquitos and our loud beating hearts give us comfort that we are still alive. The searchlights scan the area for nearly an hour. Hồng-Mai pants and resists the urge to cry out in agony from the pain of her cramps. If she is in this much pain now, I cannot imagine the misery she will face when her menstrual cycle flows. The voices coming from the boat are loud and clear. They are close. Despite the size of the peninsula, they search exactly in the general area. I assume they beat the information out of the captain of our boat, who foolishly waited at home to join us after everyone has arrived. My thoughts circle back to the woman and boy who were killed hours ago. Were they the captain's wife and son? Were they unfortunate souls who paid a high price to escape with the rest of us? It makes me sad. What if it were us who got caught and killed? I shudder.

"I do not see anything," says one of the maritime policemen.

"That bastard lied to us," says another policeman.

"He is a dead man. Let us go back to his house."

"After we kill him, I need a few beers. It is Lunar New Year."

"I am ready to get drunk."

The searchlights get dimmer and the sound of the boat's engine becomes distant. We all stand up and breathe a sigh of relief.

Sơn motions everyone to gather around him. "We were supposed to have forty-six people in our group, but we have lost our captain and two of our passengers."

"I counted forty-two people earlier," I say. "Where is the last person?"

"We cannot wait for the last person," says one of the men in the group. "We need to leave now before the police return." I cannot get a good glimpse at him in the dark from the other side of the circle. His voice, however, is distinct, with a northern accent, and quite deep.

"The last person is the one who will be bringing our boat before dawn," says Sơn. "Is there anyone here who can operate a fishing boat for us and take us out to sea?"

No one speaks up.

"What about the person delivering the boat at dawn?" asks Tùng.

"He is too young and inexperienced," answers Sơn.

The same man with the deep northern accent speaks up. "I have navigated rivers most of my life but never out in the ocean."

"You are our best chance then," says Sơn. "What is your name?"

"Nguyễn Minh-Tú," he responds.

"Listen, everyone," says Sơn. "Brother Minh-Tú will steer and operate the boat for us. You all have come this far. Now you must choose to put your trust in Minh-Tú or to stay here."

"If we stay, how do we get back to shore from the peninsula?" asks a voice in the dark.

"If you stay, you are on your own and will have to find a way back."

"What about our money that we paid you?" asks a woman in our group.

"The money is gone. Your money paid for the boat, the guides who led you here, the fuel, the food and shelter in the villages, and for the boat captain and me."

The group erupts with everyone talking over each other. Some want to press on, others want to turn back. Many are afraid and unsure.

I grow impatient with the squabble. "Listen, Brothers and Sisters. We all took the same risks and have sacrificed greatly to get to this point. There were never any guarantees. If you choose this direction," I point to the shores of Ba Động Beach, "you will be choosing to suffer for the rest of your life, however long that may be, and if you choose that direction," I point to the sea, "then you have a chance of living, a chance for freedom."

"She is right. I will give you five minutes to decide," says Sơn. "Those who wish to go can stand next to me. Those who wish to stay can stand next to that banana tree."

We deliberate amongst our families and travel companions. Slowly, people make their decision. Many walk toward Sơn to stand with him, including Hồng-Mai and her brother, Tùng. Our new boat captain, Minh-Tú, crosses the circle to stand beside Sơn. I hold Thủy-Tiên's hand and join them. No one is standing beside the banana tree.

My nephew stops and glances at the tree, then at me. I plead with my eyes for him to come with us, but he is motionless. I realize he cannot see my face so I walk to him. "Tree, we need you to come with us."

"But my parents and my little brother are in that direction." Tree points to the beach.

I try to reason with him. "This is what your parents wanted. If anything happens to you on the way back, we may never know, and your parents will never forgive me."

"I know how to navigate through the streets and the jungles, Aunt Eight, and I know how to survive and stay out of trouble."

"You are so smart and resourceful. Unlike me, you know what to do when you find that bottle of morphine and you know how to hunt for snakes and fish during the monsoon. Please, help us get to America, and after we get there, I will do everything I can to get you reunited with your family."

Tree weighs his options. He is clearly conflicted. He finally picks Thủy-Tiên up and walks toward the group standing by Sơn. I let out a private sigh of relief.

# 27 NESTLINGS AND FLEDGLINGS

At 4 a.m. the chug of a small boat announces its arrival at the peninsula. I hold my breath, fearful the police are back for another early morning search.

"The boat is here." Sơn whistles. "Minh-Tú and Tùng, help me carry these canisters of gasoline."

The three men swoop down to grab the fuel containers and hustle to the boat. The rest of us follow. I am exhausted from staying awake all night, but manage to run to the boat. What a vision the pastel green shrimp trawler makes with its blue hull and the numbers '93752' painted in dark red. The beautiful sun, large and brazen, glows in the distance and kisses our little blue boat with its golden rays. It is not larger than ten meters long from bow to stern, and with forty-three people fighting for space; it is going to be an uncomfortable voyage. Still, the wait is finally over and we are about to embark on the greatest escape of our life. Inside the boat is a teenage boy. He maneuvers as close to shore as possible and waves us in.

Thủy-Tiên tugs at my shirt. "Mama, do I get my red envelopes?"

"There are no red envelopes." I grab hold of her hand. She pulls her hand away and stands still. The excitement and eagerness in her face drains and her eyes mist up. I notice the large welts on her skin from the mosquito bites and the blood on her neck where her nails furiously dug for relief. My face softens. I gently take hold of her little hand. "You have been a good girl and you deserve something better than red envelopes." The wetness around her eyes recedes. She searches my face for clues as to what can possibly be better than a lot of money envelopes. "Come with me and I will show you a secret."

With excitement, Thủy-Tiên laces her fingers through mine and walks with me through the elephant grass. We come to a spot far enough to not be seen, but close enough that I can hear the group.

"First, we need to pee before we get on the boat," I say. "Do you have to

151

pee?"

My daughter nods and squats down to relieve herself. I join her. Her face squints. The sun is rising and shining brightly into her eyes. Thủy-Tiên grunts and I realize she is doing more than peeing. I find a couple of large banana leaves. I strip some of the fibers off and tell her to wipe her bottom.

"My butt is still dirty," she says.

"Take off your pants. We can wash our hands and your butt in the water, and while you are doing that, I will show you the secret." I inch around the elastic waist of my pants in search for Sam's ring. I feel the hardness of the gems and squeeze it toward the small opening in the front by my belly button. Thủy-Tiên's face is all smiles when she sees the emerald poking through my pants. "This is our little secret. This ring is worth millions of red envelopes and it is yours to keep when we get to America. And you cannot tell anybody, not even the animals or the plants. They will all get jealous and steal your ring."

"How can plants steal my ring?" she asks.

"The plants have snakes and birds living among them and they might overhear you telling them your secret."

She nods and promises not to tell a single soul.

"Aunt Eight, we are leaving!" yells Tree.

Thủy-Tiên and I run and climb in to the crowded boat. I step on at least one person's hand. People curse at me. An elderly man gives me a dirty look but he has such an endearing face that I forgive him.

I make my way to the rear to join Tree. "Did I miss anything?"

"We filled the motor with fuel and refilled the canisters with water." Tree scoots over an inch for me to squeeze down beside him.

Minh-Tú fires up the engine and pulls away from the peninsula. We all cheer. There is no turning back now. All forty-three of us are in this together.

***

The sunrise is breathtaking and with the soft breeze caressing my hair, my energy is restored and my hope renewed.

Our leader stands up and makes a speech. "Everyone, I need your attention. We still have to clear the border so I need everyone to cram below and hide. Only Brother Minh-Tú and I will be visible as if we are heading out to fish. Right now, it is 5 a.m. and we should clear in thirty or forty minutes. We will let you know when it is safe to come up."

"Do you know where you are going?" someone asks.

"We have a compass and the stars to navigate us. The plan is to steer towards the Philippines and stay away from the Gulf of Thailand. There have been stories of Thai pirates stealing from refugees like ourselves, or raping women and kidnapping people to sell into slavery."

Women gasp and Hồng-Mai speaks up. "How fast can we make it to the Philippines?"

"Do we have enough fuel to cross the South China Sea?" asks Tùng.

"What happens after we get to the Philippines?" another person asks.

"Everyone, please," says Sơn, "I do not have all the answers, but--"

"But you are our guide!" says one person.

"We paid you a lot of money!" cries out another angry person.

"Turn back!" demands another.

Sơn remains calm. "I know you are all scared and you have questions, but right now, I need everyone to go below the cabin. Stay hidden and quiet. If we are spotted, we will die."

"Once we clear the border, we can figure things out," I say.

"Right," says Sơn. "The police have no problems shooting without asking questions."

Begrudgingly, people squeeze down below to the hull and the engine compartment. We all sit with our knees up and arms wrapped around our legs. Thủy-Tiên sits next to me with her legs bent too. Parents hold their babies the best they can and fight for space to make sure no elbows or knees bump into their baby's head. The air is stifling below. The residual smell of fish and shrimp suffocates me. I cannot see anything other than the tired and nervous faces of those around me. The boat skates across the water for fifteen minutes. Other than the rumble of the engine and an occasional cough, all is quiet.

"Shit!" exclaims Minh-Tú. Pop. Pop. Pop. Rat-tat-tat-tat.

"Speed up," exclaims Sơn. Rat-tat-tat. "Keep going! Do not stop!"

The children scream. Hồng-Mai yelps and purses her lips tight. She closes her eyes and covers her ears. I am reminded of the "three wise monkeys" statue that Tâm purchased at the Bến Thành Market. The figurine represents "Speak No Evil, Hear No Evil, and See No Evil". Thủy-Tiên hunkers close to me and leans into my arm. I wrap my arm around her and squeeze. The unmistakable sound of AK-47s firing at us has everybody tense. The foul smell of people's breath assaults my nose as the screams of panic penetrate the dank and musty cabin. I catch a whiff of gasoline brewing in the still air. The boat is going fast and the ride is choppy. One of the elders in our group is seasick. Not a second later, vomit permeates from her mouth. She tries to hold it back and swallow it, but liquid oozes from her lips. Her vomiting sparks a chain reaction.

I challenge Tree to be strong. "This is not permission for you to throw up too."

The stink is so rancid that I find it hard to keep it together. I plug my nose. Smell no evil. The faster our boat goes, the bumpier the ride. A mixture of tears, saliva, and sweat are added to the mixture. The stench is unbearable.

The boat finally slows down and eases into a steady purr.

"It is safe now," says Sơn.

We all clamor over each other and climb out of the filth to breathe in the fresh air. Men leapfrog over women. The strong shove aside the weak. The biggest amongst us step on the smallest of us. We are desperate for relief and pure oxygen.

"We made it." Minh-Tú slaps Sơn on the shoulder.

Cheers ripple across our little boat and despite the turmoil we experienced, everyone is in good spirits.

Sơn steps onto a wooden crate. "Listen, everyone. By tomorrow, with some luck, we will come across a ship that will rescue us and take us to safety."

"That is true," says Tùng. "My sister and her family made it safely to Australia last year. They wrote to us and told us about a ship that was circling the international waters rescuing our fellow countrymen."

"Yes," pipes in Hồng-Mai, "we will be rescued by humanitarian organizations."

"Even if that is true, we need to conserve our energy, our water, and our food," declares Sơn. "I have on the boat some jicama that we all can share today. I wish I had more but I had to travel light to avoid suspicion. Each person gets one-fourth of a jicama. There is also a little bit of rice and I have enough rice balls for everyone. Also, each person can have one capful of water per day from this fuel canister."

"That is not enough," yells out a man by the cabin.

"You were told to bring provisions for yourself as well," answers Sơn firmly.

"What about the extra jicama?" I ask. "You were expecting forty-six people but since we lost our captain and the police murdered that woman and her son..."

Sơn frowns at me. "I will distribute with discretion." He passes out the already-peeled and quartered jicamas to each one of us, including the children. Some of the people who do not have children argue that the kids should share since they do not eat as much, but Sơn disagrees. "Every person here paid the same amount of money, regardless of age, profession, or connections. If you are Chinese, Cambodian, Vietnamese or Laotian...It does not matter."

With our hands outstretched to receive food and water, we are helpless baby birds. Those without their shirts on, like Tùng, are like hungry, featherless nestlings, while the rest of us are fledglings. The water makes its way to me, finally, and I pour a capful for Thủy-Tiên to drink.

"I want more, Mama," she says. "I am thirsty." I pour another capful and give it to her.

"Wait!" The teenager who had navigated the boat to the peninsula this morning stands up. "She gave her daughter two capfuls of water!"

All eyes are on me. One hand pulls the canister of water away from me. Another person shoves me and yells, "I get two capfuls, then!"

"We all should get two a day!" cries out another voice. "One is not enough."

"She should not get any water tomorrow," yells someone behind me.

"Quiet!" I scream. "I am giving my daughter my share! I was not planning on taking any! You all shut the hell up!" I point at the person who shoved me.

"If you touch me again like that or my family, I will shove you over this boat myself." To my accuser, I ask, "What is your name?" He looks at me defiantly and does not respond. "Where are your manners, boy? Have you lost your respect for your elders as well as your tongue?" Still, he does not answer me but rather, shoots a scathing sneer in my direction. I am embarrassing him. "Fine, I will call you 'Snitch'. If you were my son or nephew, I would spank you until your ass is as red as the rising sun." I hand the water can to Tree and sit back down. I am so upset, I am shaking.

***

Hours pass and we see nothing for miles in every direction. The scorching sun is slow-roasting us for a scavenger's feast. If only I had my straw hat. There are no other boats in sight, nor land or skyline to speak of. There is nothing to do but torture oneself with narrations of what will happen to the family left behind. My emotions scatter through the prism of the rolling saltwater. The waves beckon me to remember the peaceful, fun times of my youth spent with friends and family on the beach. I remember holding my daughter in my arms when she was a baby. She was so alien yet so magnificent. And then there was Sam, with his dimple and green eyes, that beautiful smile with those gorgeous white teeth and full lips.

I see a water snake swim by and think of my dear sister, who always made sure I ate well, from the crepes to the field snake, from the fried bananas to the coconut mango sticky rice. Her love surpassed all boundaries and she showed it through food. I was such an ungrateful and selfish brat to her all my life. I cannot help but feel responsible somehow for my family's suffering, with Father's death, Hải's punishment, Tâm's arrest…even my failed marriage to Tý. Darkness falls upon us as the night chill sets in. Stars raid the sky and the blackness of the sea pollutes my emotions, turning them from remorse to emptiness and despair. What if this is all for nothing and we die right here, right now? What if we are not rescued tomorrow but must endure days or weeks wandering hopelessly in this vast shimmer? I close my eyes and pray, tuning in to God's voice. Only the sounds of eerie silence echoes back. Too tired, weak and hungry, I invite sleep to come, but even that is too much to ask.

The longest ten minutes go by. Tree breaks the strange quietness by peeing over the side of the boat. One by one, people pop up to relieve themselves into the sea. Grunts, groans, and farts orchestrate our movements. At least we are still alive.

And then the climactic ending to our symphony…The engine sputters.

# 28 MY NEW FAMILY

Hồng-Mai lets out a sharp, screeching sound. Tùng rushes to his sister's side. "What is the matter?"

"My cramps are getting worse." She takes out the *Tiger Balm* salve and spreads it on her stomach.

"Rub it on your feet. Your feet have more pores and the menthol will absorb faster," I say. "A doctor once told me that."

The smell of menthol, eucalyptus and wintergreen oils remind me of my injured toe. I remove my sock and the bandage to inspect it. My big toe is white and wrinkled but is otherwise fine. The engine sputters again. Minh-Tú takes the key out of the ignition and disappears to pour the last canister of fuel into the boat. It roars back to life and we continue our journey toward the Philippines.

Snitch perks up like a meerkat. "A ship!"

My eyes follow in the direction where his finger is pointing. I stand up and wave my arms wildly. Sơn climbs onto the cabin top and waves our old Vietnamese flag. Tree takes off his shirt and joins Sơn. He ties the shirt sleeves around the bottom end of the flagpole, sets it on fire, and waves it in the air. He jumps up and down to get their attention. All able-bodied passengers on our boat are now on their feet, hollering, waving and jumping to flag the other boat's attention. It is unclear to me whether the boat is getting closer to us or farther away. A couple people whistle while others bang loudly against the boat to amplify our SOS. Minh-Tú blares our boat's horn repeatedly to signal our distress. It is no use. We might as well have been debating with Slanty-Eyes over some political issue because our pleas fell on deaf ears. The ship gets smaller and disappears off the face of the Earth.

Our forlorn efforts go unnoticed. I sit down and open my satchel. I take out Sam's book and the letters.

Tree stops me from opening them. "Stop torturing yourself. You always cry when you read their letters. Uncle Hải and Sam are gone. You need to let them go."

The ink on the airmail paper is smeared from me falling into the river. The thin sheets are warped and crunchy. The pages of the book are bent and the cover does not close all the way. I put them away and soothe my disappointment with some cucumbers that Sister Six packed.

I hand Thủy-Tiên a small cucumber. "If you chew slowly, you will trick your stomach into thinking you have a lot of food and it will feel full. It is a trick that your grandfather taught me."

We munch on our cucumbers slowly to savor the taste and prolong the supply. Tree stops eating and gives his piece to Thủy-Tiên. "I miss Grandfather."

"You are a lot like him in that you are resourceful," I say. "Before he was the principal of your school, he taught French. We lived on his pension. He raised seven children on his pension!"

"I remember my mom used to hand out money in the morning before school. I would buy pastries and treats, and Grandfather always asked me what I bought at the school."

"His favorite was the bánh bao chỉ," we say in unison.

Tree laughs. "I would give anything to have a taste of that glutinous rice mochi, filled with sweet mung bean paste and rolled in shredded coconut!"

"Your aunt Six makes the best desserts. She needs to write her recipes down. In Đà Lạt, where I taught mathematics, she would sometimes visit me and bring her latest experiments. My favorite was the yogurt. It was the right balance of sweet and tangy."

"Tell me about my other aunts and uncles," says Tree. "I do not remember them."

"Uncle Two died during the revolution against the French. Uncle Three was drafted to the military and died in the early part of the American War. Aunt Four and Uncle Five were twins and they died from pneumonia."

"A lot of deaths in our family," says Tree. "I remember when I was younger, like eight or nine years old, I saw oxcarts full of dead bodies behind the hospital by our house. The swollen bodies would be washed and dressed right there outside in the back and sometimes, they could not get to the bodies fast enough. More and more bodies got dumped, some without heads, most missing a limb. Days would go by and their flesh would smell ripe and the rot attracted all sorts of insects and rodents. It did not scare me though. I was curious and fascinated."

"That explains why you always ran toward the hospital when you heard the sirens!"

"I especially liked the interesting smell of dead bodies combined with the aroma of the coffee from the café across the road."

"You are a strange human being," I say. "The war was not so long ago yet I have managed to suppress its gravity. There was a time when we all ran to the bunker and hid when there was fighting or gunshots or bombings. The sounds of those AK-47s and M-16s were like a thousand bubble wraps popping at once."

"I liked the American GIs though," says Tree. "They are funny. One time, it was raining and I was kicking the soccer ball around in the house. I heard some yelling outside and was amused to see a group of soldiers running and jumping on each other, yelling and chasing after a man that had a ball. They were covered in mud and looked crazy tackling each other over a small ball."

Tree and I continue reminiscing about life in our home country. We talk for hours and enjoy our rice that has been hand-packed into small balls. Before long, omnipresent clouds roll across the sky and the sun runs off to hide. Our little boat prepares to host the uninvited guests. Thunder and lightning burst onto the scene. A few people seek shelter under the deck and some, including Tree and me, pull a tarp over our head. The rain pelts it's vengeance onto the plastic cover and gives us front row tickets to the loudest concert we have ever attended. Sơn opens the gas containers to catch the rain. We are all wet and cold. Our small boat is tossed around like an egg and us its yolk.

Below deck, people are thrown side to side, getting seasick and throwing up. I grab hold of Thủy-Tiên and tightly cling to the cleats bolted to the boat's toe rail. Relentlessly, the storm continues all through the night, and I take advantage of the rain to pee my pants where I sit.

***

Day three. Sơn does a head count to make sure we did not lose anyone during the storm. "All forty-three of us are still here. The rain last night spared us and replenished our water supply."

"We barely survived!" says a woman sitting behind Sơn. I notice her belly is swollen and realize she is pregnant. "You said we would be rescued after a day, but we have only seen one boat!"

"We are all going to starve to death and die out here," says a man next to her.

"You were instructed to pack some food," says Sơn. "I provided you with water, rice, and jicamas. After the water is gone, we are all on our own."

"We ate what we brought already," says the man. "My wife is six months pregnant."

"She can drink some water and take what she needs, but it is not my fault you did not bring enough food or paced yourselves, and it certainly is not my fault that you risked your wife's and unborn child's life!" says Sơn.

The man lunges at Sơn and takes a swing at his face. Sơn falls back and gets entangled with other people's arms and legs. The two of them try to throw punches but are too weak to cause any damage. It becomes a shoving and blaming contest.

Despite the distraction, I catch Snitch taking big gulps of water from the canister. "You are drinking all the water!" Others do the same and pass the three canisters around to their family members.

"Give me that," demands the pregnant woman. Her husband grabs one of the canisters and trips over a toddler.

I try to subdue the situation before it gets out of control. "Stop! Everyone, we are wasting our energy fighting. We came here together and we will either die together or survive together. I propose we combine whatever food or drinks we have and share equally amongst ourselves, as we did with the jicamas and the rice."

"Who made you the boss?" yells a man behind me.

"That is a good idea," says the pregnant woman.

Snitch sneers at the pregnant woman. "Of course you would say that, but what do you have to contribute?"

"Do you speak to your family this way?" I ask the boy. "We have to take care of each other. Right now, we are each other's family. We have a pregnant woman who needs our strength. We have a boy," and I point at Snitch, "who is traveling alone without his family and he risked his life to bring us this boat. I have a sick daughter who needs medical attention for her heart. We all are running away from the same thing and we all have the same dreams of freedom."

"Sister Tuyết is right," says Hồng-Mai. "We are in this together. My brother and I do not have much, but we will share with our new family what we have." She takes out the *Tiger Balm* ointment, sanitary napkins, two mangos, a small knife, some dried, shredded squid, and a small loaf of stale bread, and places the items on her lap.

"Hồng-Mai, thank you," I say. "My family is adding to this community pile a jar of sliced lemons soaked in water and sugar, what is left of the valerian root medicine, a bag of peanuts, dried bananas, coconut meat, coconut water, and glow sticks."

"I have some jackfruit, two cans of beer, a bottle of cognac, and a bottle of *Malathion*." Minh-Tú shrugs. "This is my suicide kit."

I stare at him in disbelief. "What is *Malathion*?"

"Insecticide," he answers.

"Keep that poison away from my daughter." I place a protective hand on Thủy-Tiên.

"We can put everything, except for the pesticide, in here." Sơn hands Hồng-Mai a burgundy duffel bag. "I have a few pieces of the jicama to add. Since this was Sister Tuyết's idea, she can be in charge of distribution."

The bag gets passed around and everyone contributes what they have. The husband and wife who are expecting a baby throw money into the bag.

"Since we are now family, we should all introduce ourselves." Tùng's optimism and energy is infectious. "I can start."

The rest of the day we share our stories and introduce ourselves. I learn that Snitch's real name is Thành and that he is thirteen years old. His family committed suicide a year after the fall of Sài Gòn by poisoning themselves, but he survived. To stay alive, he did odd jobs for Sơn, who lived in the same hamlet.

Sơn was in the army and after the war ended, he reported to the police station to serve his mandatory few weeks of re-education. However, he was there for over a year. After he got out, he and his friend, who was going to captain this boat before he got caught, attempted to leave the country five times. They first had a raft but that quickly fell apart. They tried stealing an old woman's boat but she caught them and her husband tried to shoot them. Other attempts were made but they all failed for one reason or another.

I learn that the pregnant woman's name is Tiền and that the baby is due end of April. Her husband's name is Trương, and he hopes their first baby is a boy. They used to have a large rice production company but the government seized their property and sent them packing to one of the new economic zones.

Hồng-Mai and Tùng are Chinese. They left their parents behind to join their sister and her family in Australia, with the hopes of sponsoring their parents over later.

Minh-Tú was a farmer and a fisherman. He and his wife had eleven children. He and his three sons were arrested and spent two years in a re-education camp, because they provided food and shelter to the South Vietnamese army. His sons died in the prisons and he was released because he was so close to death, the guards were convinced he was going to die anyway. He recovered but discovered his wife and daughters replaced him with another man. He is on this journey alone, adrift with a broken heart.

Everyone's story is unique yet heartrending. To lighten the mood, we sing some songs, recite poems, tell jokes, and even re-enact some scenes from a famous Chinese movie. By nightfall, we brace ourselves for another storm, but it does not come.

# 29 DIRE STRAITS

"We are out of fuel." I open my eyes and see Minh-Tú.

"How long have we been drifting?" I ask.

"I am not sure," he answers. "It must have happened during the night when we were all sleeping. I have no idea where we are."

"I thought Snitch, I mean Thành, was helping you navigate."

"He was, but he fell asleep."

Tree lifts up one of the fuel containers and surveys what is inside. "Everyone is going to panic once they wake up and realize what is happening." He tilts the container back and sucks out what is left of the contents.

"I thought they were all empty," I say.

Tree cringes and chokes. "They are, but there was a sliver of water floating above the oil."

"You drank the gasoline?" I ask in shock.

"Aunt Eight, I am so parched and dehydrated. I checked the bag and all the coconut water and lemons were gone – rinds, seeds, everything. Even the beer cans are empty. The only thing left is the cognac."

"Nothing else?" asks Sơn.

"Only things we cannot eat, like the money that aunt Tiền and uncle Trương threw in, the feminine napkins, medicine…The only things that can be consumed are the cognac and sunflower seeds. Someone stole the rest of the jicama." I throw a suspicious glance at Snitch.

"If we are going to die out here, it is better to die drunk than die back home from starvation, malnutrition and under communist control," says Minh-Tú.

"If we see any fishing boats, maybe we can buy some fish with the money and the cognac. Thủy-Tiên received forty thousand đồng in her red envelope from Doctor Đức. How much did he give you?" I ask Tree.

"One-hundred," says Tree.

"Wake everybody up and we will distribute the last of the sunflower seeds," says Sơn.

*\*\*\**

We drift aimlessly all day with the heat of the sun beating down with such malice and contempt. Many of the elderly, the women, and the children take refuge down below to escape the intensity of the rays. It is not any better down there with the rancid smells of urine, vomit, and bad body odor. Hour by hour, we get weaker and more delirious. I see Tree scoop up some ocean water to drink. I try to tell him it will make it worse, but I am too late.

Another day makes an encore. We have been on the run for five nights and four days, battling everything from the mosquitos on the peninsula to the storm at sea, and now, the cruelest punisher of all, nothingness. We are all too ill from the big waves, the hot days and cold nights. Those below deck vomit and pee where they sit and pass out from the stale air and foul smells. I sit here contemplating if I should eat the money that is in the red envelopes. Will that help the hunger pains subside? I pray for some rain but none comes. We are in dire straits. Thủy-Tiên sleeps beside me with the green silk tunic covering her head.

"Boat," whispers Tree. He points.

I sit up and sure enough, there is a boat. We siphon the last ounce of energy left and try to get the boat's attention. It turns and heads toward us, getting bigger and bigger. I am ecstatic.

After ten minutes, the elation is replaced with fear. Two vessels, both with Thai flags, pull up and tether our boat to theirs. I count seven dark-skinned, shirtless men, armed with knives, hammers, and rifles. Five of them board our boat while the other two stay with their vessel. Their sinister faces are premonitions of what is to come. The women on our boat yell and scream in fear. Some of them try to make themselves hideous by tousling their hair and rubbing grease on their face or vomit on their body. Like me, they have heard stories of girls getting brutally raped or kidnapped by the Thai pirates. They continue to be assaulted by gangs of fishermen, even after the girls hemorrhage out and die. Others get sold into slavery or deposited onto a deserted island, only to be repeatedly violated at the mercy of these men's whims.

One of the pirates, the shortest one with curly hair, wearing a sarong and a headband, speaks to his crew. I am guessing he is the operator behind this. I cannot understand anything he says. Stricken with fear and wasted from lack of food, we all stand or sit in our place, immobile. I wrap my protective talons around Thủy-Tiên and avoid eye contact.

The same pirate speaks to us in English. "Men over here. Women over there."

They separate us, even the babies and children. The leader rummages through our belongings and searches the boat for valuables, finding gold, jewelry, money and the bottle of cognac. Two of the pirates stand guard in front of our men, threatening them with guns and machetes. The other two pirates walk to our group of women and hold us hostage. There are fifteen of us women, ranging from twenty-three years old to seventy years old, a two-month-old infant, and my daughter, age four. The pirate with the curly hair lifts my chin with his knife to get a good look at my face. He smiles at me before diverting his attention to Tiền, the woman who is six months pregnant. His eyes scan down to her swollen belly before diverting his attention to a young mother holding her two-month-old daughter. He grabs her wrist and drags her toward his boat. She cries out and resists. The rest of us try to protect her and pull her back, but his companions punch us in the face and hit us with hammers. The young woman's husband screams for mercy and begs them to leave his wife alone. He receives a blow to the head with the butt of a rifle for his outcry. They throw him overboard. One of the pirates uses a pole to jab him and keep him submerged. The pirate laughs like it is a game. The young woman is lifted up onto one of the vessels. She kicks and screams while still holding her baby tight. Four more women get separated from us and taken aboard the other boats. The rest of us are forced below deck with the hatch locked. The anguished screams of women getting raped, while the baby cries and the pirates cheer, haunt me. Sơn, Minh-Tú, Tree, and Tùng try to break open the hatch.

An hour goes by and the cries have stopped. There is splashing in the water and moments later, the engines fire up and the two boats drive off. I am stunned. I close my eyes and pray, letting the tears escape. I smell something burning and realize our boat is on fire. There is panic below deck and screams coming from both inside the boat and outside in the water. The men take turns trying to force the hatch open and finally are able to break free. We clamber out and work together to smother the fire.

I grab one of the fuel canisters to fill it up with water and spot the five women in the ocean. "Tree, Snitch, help them into the boat!"

As the women are being pulled into the boat, the rest of us fill up the three canisters and douse the fire. We stomp on the flames and beat it back with our shirts. Finally, the fire is extinguished.

We all weep, relieved that the boat is still intact. I stumble to the women who were raped. All of them are shaking. One of them is hysterical. I realize her baby is not with her. I rush to the port and starboard of the boat. My eyes dart side to side, far and near, praying for a miracle. I run to the stern, and the miracle I was hoping for appeared. The young husband treads closer to the boat and in his arm is his infant daughter. His face shows pain and exhaustion. I take the baby from him. As soon as the baby is in my arms, the young man slips underneath the water. Tree dives in and lifts him back up to keep his head above water. Sơn and Minh-Tú pull him into the boat and lend a hand to my nephew.

All forty-three of us are alive and back on the boat…Safe for now.

# 30 GLOW IN THE WATER

The young husband and wife with their two-month-old daughter are now safe, but brewing underneath their tears of relief is pain. This experience will surely leave them scarred for the rest of their lives. I pray it will not tear their family apart.

I notice there are red whip lashes on the young husband's leg. "What is your name again?"

The young husband is barely audible. "Tú."

"I had a neighbor also named Tú," I share.

"My wife's name is Thảo and our daughter is Mỹ-Linh."

"I am Tuyết," I say. "You are in pain."

"There were some jellyfish in the water," Tú responds. "My leg is tingling and itchy. There is intense pain all over the area I got stung."

"Hopefully the burning sensation will go away in a few hours. As soon as we find land, we will see if that can get treated."

"Can you check on my wife? She will not talk to me or acknowledge my existence." Tú breaks down and sobs. "I could not protect them."

"Give her time. She went through something horrific. You saved your daughter and kept yourself alive for your family. You are a hero in my opinion." I make my way to the five who were victimized.

Hồng-Mai and some of the elders tend to the traumatized women. They are shivering but not because it is cold. Nothing can make things right or better. I am afraid to touch them and comfort them as they may find my presence repulsive. I cannot give them water or even cognac to soothe them. I sit in front of Thảo. She clutches her daughter so tight that the baby cries.

"Sister Thảo, let me take care of Mỹ-Linh," I say. "She is crying because you are crushing her and she cannot breathe."

Thảo loosens her grip but does not voluntarily hand the baby over to me. I gently ease my arms around Mỹ-Linh and slowly pull her into my lap. Thảo does not object. I rock the baby and hush her until she is calm. If only the heavens could open up right now and send milk down to our little blue boat.

We drift aimlessly for hours and I stare into the vast distance, dazed by the cruel and perilous events of today. I realize that if our boat was attacked by Thai fishermen then we are no longer heading east toward the Philippines. Without fuel to steer the trawler, we have drifted south near the Gulf of Thailand. This could mean more pirate attacks. We are like fish in a barrel for these pirates to do as they please without any consequences, without any police to patrol the area and protect us.

Tree states the obvious to me. "We cannot go back to Việt Nam and we are not heading towards the Philippines." My nephew sits down next to me with Thủy-Tiên in his arms. "If we are lucky, we will end up in Malaysia." My daughter leans over to kiss me on the cheek and then kisses the baby's head. What an empathetic and tender child. I lean down to kiss her on the head.

"Tree, eventually we will see land and when we do, we need to get Uncle Tú medicine for his stings and these women examined," I say. "I will need your help."

"I know," he responds.

Thảo sits completely still, her eyes closed. The faint rise and fall of her chest reassure me she is sleeping. I lean against Tree, back to back, and drift off to sleep to pass the time.

I dream that my stomach has come to life and is eating itself. I become an emaciated zombie with a hole in my lower torso. My hunger for meat has me tearing into my boat companions' flesh, biting down to the layer of fat. I relish the taste and am hungry for more. I see a four-year-old girl, her skin is smooth and white, her arms plump and juicy. She screams from my first bite.

"Wake up." Tree shakes me vigorously.

I open my eyes. Thủy-Tiên is screaming. Tú, Sơn, and Minh-Tú peer over the side of the boat. They are in a panic. The rest of the crew is powerless to do anything. Mỹ-Linh is not in my arms and Thảo is not sitting in front of me. I lean over the boat. There is only darkness in the water. Tú jumps into the ocean and dives down, in desperate search for his wife and daughter.

"Someone go with him!" I urge. "He was stung by jellyfish earlier. He will not last long in the freezing water."

No one jumps in to brave a rescue. There are many creatures lurking beneath the calm darkness of the sea. Before I can plead my case to Tree, my nephew takes off his shoes and simply says, "I know."

"Take this with you." I take out a *Cyalume* light stick from the duffel bag. I tear the wrapper away, bend the tube until it snaps, and then shake the stick until it illuminates. "Cường gave me these military glow sticks to sell and I ended up keeping them for myself."

"It looks like a giant firefly." Tree dives into the menacing abyss. He disappears for a couple minutes at a time before coming up for air.

Sơn and Minh-Tú jump in as well. I give them both a glow stick. The three of them are now searching for Thảo, Tú and their daughter Mỹ-Linh. Their heads bob up like musical notes but never in sync. As soon as one disappears, another one reappears.

"Watch Thủy-Tiên." I hand over my satchel to Snitch. "I am going to help. They are getting tired."

"It is no use," he protests. "They are gone."

"We have to try." I jump into the cold water with another glow stick.

The view under the water is incredible. Below I see some exotic aquatic life, mostly different varieties of coral, fish of all sizes, an eel and some starfish. I keep hoping I will find Thảo and her husband, Tú, and their baby, Mỹ-Linh, but my gut tells me Thành is right. Their bodies have probably been claimed by the sea. Their spirits will never embrace peace. A breathtaking blue glow in the water catches my attention and seduces me to come closer. Someone touch my arm. Tree points up toward the surface. We swim up and catch our breath.

"Did you find them?" I cling to the side of the boat.

Tree shakes his head. "We should not venture farther."

I nod in agreement. We climb back into the boat where Sơn and Minh-Tú are already waiting.

"What should we do now?" asks Sơn. "Three people in our group committed suicide. Should we say a prayer?"

"We all should pay our respects silently." I shiver and wrap my arms around myself. "When we reach land, I want to have a veneration service in their memory."

"Did you see the stretch of blue lights glowing in the distance?" Tree asks. "It is so beautiful."

"Yes. The last time I saw the sea sparkle like that was when I was in Hạ Long Bay," I say.

"You saw bioluminescence?" Minh-Tú jumps with excitement. "We are close to land!"

"What makes you think that?" I ask.

"Every time I witness these blue lights, the view is always from a coast," he answers.

"Well, since you have only navigated rivers, never oceans, of course you would only see them from shore," I say.

Minh-Tú sits down and ponders what I said. We all settle into our spot and try to get some sleep. It is hard to reconcile straight when you are hungry, cold, and tired. Some of the people on the boat have not stirred since the pirate attack earlier today. They are too weak, too famished, or too seasick. Left with only my self-sabotaging thoughts to keep me company, I ask God how much longer we will drift. Will it be days or weeks? How many more pirate attacks can our group take? Will we survive another one? I imagine Thủy-Tiên dying in my arms in the middle of nowhere, below the deceptively peaceful sky, and above the mighty waves of this ocean. How much longer will her heart beat before it, too, gives up on life? I remember my crazy dream of resorting to cannibalism to stay alive. Who would I eat first? Or perhaps I would be somebody's supper? I am getting delirious. I close my eyes and try to conjure an image of Sam's face. That was a lifetime ago.

"I see trees," says Snitch.

"Me too," says Tree.

I open my eyes and see silhouettes far away, poking out from the horizon.

"Land!" cries out Sơn.

"We should drop our anchor," suggests Minh-Tú. "Get a good night's rest and then, in the morning, figure out how to safely get to shore."

\*\*\*

The sun's warm glow rouses me awake. I stand up to stretch and am greeted by stark, unapologetic stares from eight sets of black eyes. Dark-skinned men sitting in kayaks and canoes with fishing nets greet me with curiosity. They smile and wave. I conclude they are non-threatening.

"Hello," I say in Vietnamese. "We need help getting to shore. Can you help us?"

Some of them speak but I do not understand them. I repeat myself in English, but they once again respond in their native tongue. None of them understand me.

Minh-Tú tries to communicate to the fishermen that we want to get to shore. He points at our boat and then points to the shore. Sơn joins in the charade. He points to them and mimics them pulling a rope. I put my hands together and wave it side to side, to imitate a fish swimming.

"Ya, ya," says one of them.

"I think they finally understand our gestures." I breathe a sigh of relief and jump with jubilation. I pick Thủy-Tiên up and wrap my arms around Tree's shoulder. The soft breeze of the early morning caresses the hair tendrils away from my ears and the warmth of the sun kisses my face. It is good to be alive. Sơn pulls up the anchor and Minh-Tú throws down our ropes to the fishermen.

"Are we in America?" asks Thủy-Tiên.

"No, my dolly, we are in Indonesia. See the flag on that man's kayak?" I point to the last green boat leaving the coast. "These men are helping us to shore. They are pulling us in slowly so we do not crash into the big reefs. If we approach too fast, the reef below can split our boat." I point down to the water, as smooth and clear as glass, so she can see.

"Those are so big, like the size of a house," she says.

"The water is still quite deep and we are still far from shore. You can stand here but hold my hand or Brother Tree's. I do not have the energy to swim right now if you fall in."

The islanders work their magic, pulling and guiding our small boat towards the shoreline. We weave around the reefs and Minh-Tú expertly and patiently maneuvers the trawler over and around large rocks. We get as close to shore as possible to disembark. Those who have energy to swim jump off and do so. Those who do not know how to swim or are too weak, hold onto a plank of wood and are pulled by a fellow swimmer. I lift Thủy-Tiên onto my hip. I make eye contact with one of the fishermen. I point to my daughter, then to his canoe, hoping he understands my request for a ride.

He nods. "Ya."

I ease my daughter down. She dangles from my arms while the fisherman lifts up his arms to receive her.

"Stop!" A uniformed official approaches us in a canoe, taxied by another fisherman. He speaks authoritatively in English through a megaphone. "You cannot stay on this island."

I hoist my daughter back into the boat. Those of us on the boat who understand English are up in arms and visibly upset. The hell we have been through is unexpectedly extended, making previous moments of mercy only teasers.

Hồng-Mai joins me by my side. "What is he saying?" I translate for her and watch the blood drain from her face.

"This island only has four hundred people and is not a refugee camp," the official says. "You need to go to the bigger island, another six hours journey." He points to the sea behind us, but to no defining direction. "You cannot stay here. We can provide you some fuel and sustenance before helping you back out to sea."

The official ignores our pleas. He speaks to the fishermen in their native tongue and one by one, the canoes leave. The men head out to sea to resume their fishing plans for the morning. Twenty minutes later, a small boat comes to retrieve us. It makes multiple trips to bring all forty of us to shore. At last, I am sitting on a beach, thankful to be on land, and am elated for the hospitality, despite the temporary extension. Shortly afterwards, food, water, and fuel are brought to us. Men dressed in olive green uniforms hand out bowls of rice, canned sardines, fresh mangosteens, sugar apples, and passion fruit.

I go straight for the water. "This is the sweetest, most divine water I have ever drunk." The cold liquid trickles down my throat but does not satiate the thirst.

Thủy-Tiên buries her face in the cup and asks for more water. We turn our attention to the food and dive in with our fingers, picking up every morsel like wild island monkeys. I try to savor each bite and eat like a lady, but after the first two pinches of rice and sardines, I give in to the animalistic hunger. *Forget it.* I scarf the food down.

After our thirst is quenched and our bellies satisfied, we sit and socialize with each other like civilized and polite members of the extended family. I laugh with Thủy-Tiên, Tree, Minh-Tú, Sơn, Snitch, Hồng-Mai and Tùng. The stress from being out at sea for five days evaporates through my pores. Even my big toe that was injured by the acacia thorn is unburdened and feeling nourished. The four women who were raped by pirates show some signs of renewed life and hope. They eat and speak with Trương and his pregnant wife, Tiền. The group relaxes and takes full advantage of the hospitality for a few hours.

Later in the afternoon, a boat approaches. It is a wood boat similar to ours, but much bigger. The official tells us it is time to leave. And with one sweep of his arm and a flick of his wrist, he rewinds our journey. Once more, we load onto a small boat and are taken back to our trawler. Three trips back and forth before we are all onboard the tiny boat that represent both freedom and a death sentence. We load the canister of fuel, a jug of water, and some plain, cooked rice that was donated to us by the Indonesian officials, onto our boat. As the big boat pulls our smaller boat out to sea, I notice the officials have quickly disappeared. The beach clears and is deserted. Empty, like we were never there. Funny thing about human existence - One day we exist in this world. We breathe, we laugh, and we love. We experience hardships, we go to work, and we enjoy our time with friends, family, and other passions. And then, our bodies slow down. We age, we die, and then we are invisible to those who loved us and talked to us every day. The farther I get from the sandy shores, the more distant and withdrawn my spirit becomes, and the stress of life reenters the pores of my skin.

The larger boat picks up speed and causes big waves that jostle our little boat. It thrashes up and down uncontrollably. We are air born for a few seconds before crashing down on the hard surface of the sea. Over and over we helplessly bob up and down, powerless to change our fate. People are getting seasick now and some are throwing up the food they ate. We yell out and ask them to slow down but the people on the mightier boat cannot hear us, nor can they understand us.

"Our boat is getting battered." Sơn can no longer handle the bumpy ride and cuts the ropes. The large boat slows down and circles back to us. Sơn waves this appreciation. "We can go alone from here."

The captain of the mightier boat points in the distance. "Galang". The big boat returns to its point of origin and is soon a speck on the horizon.

Minh-Tú steers our boat slowly. "It is another six hours before we get to Galang Island and that is assuming we are heading in the right direction."

"Now that we have seen land and been on one of the Riau islands, I do not want to risk our lives back out at sea," says Sơn.

"There is no guarantee that we will not be boarded by pirates again or that our engine will not fail on us," I say.

"We will surely die out there if Galang does not receive us or if we are not rescued by another boat along the way," says Tùng.

Hồng-Mai whispers to me. "My menstrual cycle started. All the jumping waves unplugged the dam."

I address Sơn and Minh-Tú. "We have to return to the island and beg for temporary asylum. The Indonesians will have to figure out what to do with us."

Sơn agrees. "We will keep sight of the island and circle slowly around. We can wait until nightfall and make our way back undetected."

"I will not take us far," says Minh-Tú. "We are already vulnerable this far out."

# 31 TRAWLER 93752

The stars get brighter and the moon relieves the sun from duty. Under cover of night, our boat heads back to the island.

"I have seared into my memory how to get us back and mapped out in my mind how to navigate around the reefs to get close to shore." Minh-Tú puts his hands on his waist.

"We should burn our boat and force them to let us stay," says Sơn. "That will buy us some time."

"Anything is better than staying out here another night," adds Snitch.

Hồng-Mai scoots over to me. "The blood flow is getting heavier. I fear it will soak through my pants."

I hand her a pair of socks. "Tuck this in your underwear to absorb the blood. You can wash your handkerchief and let it dry to reuse."

"Now?" she asks.

"No. Wait until we get to shore, otherwise we will become dinner for the sharks."

Sơn interrupts our conversation. "When we get close enough, the last person off the boat needs to set it on fire."

Minh-Tú volunteers. "I will do it."

I remind myself of Dr. Đức's message, that no matter how difficult things get, the struggle back home eclipses any adversity I will face on my journey for freedom in America. This will all be worth it.

Sơn surveys our group. "Who cannot swim?"

Three adults raise their hand plus one four-year-old child…mine.

I kneel down and hug my daughter. "Little dolly, we will use a plank of wood from the hatch for you. You can sit on it, and I will push you to shore."

"What about the babies?" asks one of the mothers on board. "How do we get the babies to shore?"

"We will get the boat as close as possible and hopefully if the water is shallow, you can walk to shore with your baby in your arms," answers Sơn.

"But what if it is too deep?" she asks.

"We can use the planks of wood and set the children on top, and push them to shore as we swim beside it. Do not worry, we are all here to help one another," I say.

"But I cannot swim and I am too big to sit on a piece of wood." An elderly man, wafer thin and weighing only forty-five kilograms at most, voices his concern.

"If you cannot swim, find a partner who can. Then hold on tight to their neck," says Sơn.

"But try not to strangle them or you both will drown," warns Minh-Tú.

The non-swimmers plead with fellow passengers and try to convince others to give them a ride on his or her water-taxi backs. They finally sort it out and we approach the shore feeling assured on what to do. That is, until we are greeted by AK-47s.

Warning shots fire near our boat. Bullets plunge into the water around us and whiz by our heads. I cover Thủy-Tiên's head and duck down. People take cover where they can - below deck, behind the engine compartment, inside the cabin, or flat on the deck. Some of us have nowhere to go so we lie on top of other people and pile up two or three people high. The bullets hit our boat. Splinters of wood shatter and separate from the deck and prow. I cover my head and yell Tree's name.

He answers back. "I would gladly trade these bullets for mosquitos!"

A couple of people who are sitting on the roof of the cabin get hit from stray bullets that ricochet off the stern. Our boat crashes into a big rock and a loud noise ripples through the dark. The impediment to the forward momentum of our boat thrusts everyone forward. Screams of fright bring shivers up and down my body and raise the hairs on my neck. Terror crosses Thủy-Tiên's face and I hug her close. A bullet grazes Minh-Tú's ear. He groans and hunkers down.

"There is an oil leak," someone yells out.

"The boat is broken," yells Sơn. "Everyone jump off and swim!"

More bullets blaze by. I scramble to get the wood from the hatch and grab it. A woman tries to pry it from my hands. It is fight or flight time. I step on her foot and tear the plank of wood from her grip. She cries out. I throw the piece of wood into the water, swoop Thủy-Tiên up in one arm, and jump. I aim for the driftwood and grab it. Thủy-Tiên climbs on. She sits cross-legged and bends down to hold onto the sides. Her left cheek rests on the wet surface. Her eyes seize mine.

"Keep your eyes on Mama, and do not let go," I say. She nods.

Others jump in, one by one or in pairs. A bright light illuminates the dark sky. Our little fishing boat is ablaze. Red and orange flames dance sacrificially upward while below in the sea, heads of black hair bob up and down. Cries blend in with the sounds of AK-47s ripping through the night. I weep for the little trawler, sad that it is dying a slow, painful death, yet grateful that it got us this far.

The shooting stops. I swim to shore, pushing the plank of wood, while Tree swims on the other side of us.

A man howls in pain. "I stepped on a damn sea urchin." He wades to shore, wincing and hobbling as he goes.

The Indonesian military waits for us on the beach. Their leader speaks to us in English. "My name is Abu and I am in charge here. Kneel with your hands behind your back." His men force us all on our knees. No one in the group dares to speak. The injured stifle their pain. "Who set the boat on fire?" We are all mute. Abu asks again and once more, we choke back our fears. He bends down and thrusts his face inches from Minh-Tú's. "Was it you?"

Minh-Tú says nothing. Abu kneels down to Sơn's level and asks Sơn the same question, but Sơn shakes his head. The commander goes down the line and stops in front of the poor man who stepped on a sea urchin. He tries to intimidate the man by staring into his eyes, challenging him to confess. The man whimpers in pain.

Frustrated, the commander orders his men to incentivize us. The cadres attack the men in our group with kicks to the face, punches to the body, or rifle butts to the head. Young or old, every man is beaten. They spare the women and children, including Tree and Snitch. The men do not fight back. I am afraid for their life. Still, no one speaks up.

Abu calls for a halt. "I have shown you nothing but hospitality. We showed you how to get to the nearest refugee camp but instead, you spit at our help. Your defiance deserves punishment. Let us see how long you survive on your own here without our help."

The military leaves us. I let out a big sigh, thankful they are gone. I stand up and mourn our pathetic little boat, still on fire and putting on a show for the waxing crescent in the sky. Below our feet, the sand is speckled with blood from the beatings and bullet wounds. Above us, the bright stars are like a million alien eyes peeking through peepholes of a black curtain; they witness our sad scene. Thủy-Tiên holds my hand. Together we witness our boat burning in the distance. I shall never forget this picture.

"We should find a place to sleep." Tree digs a sandpit and fills it with branches, leaves, and whatever he can find in the brush, including a dirty, torn, plastic poncho and a pair of mismatched flip-flops. Hồng-Mai and her brother settle in next to us.

"How is your stomach?" I ask Hồng-Mai.

"I almost forgot about my cramps from this ordeal," she answers.

"I forgot my satchel on the boat." I am miserable that Sam's book, his letter, and Hải's letter are gone forever.

"What was in it?"

"A book and some letters." I roll over and turn my back to her. "Get some sleep."

"Going to sleep in wet clothes while your uterus bleeds out is no fun."

I turn back over and face her. "On the hopeful side, maybe your menstruation will turn the sea red and Moses will appear to lead us to the Promised Land." I joke wryly, but she gives me a curious expression.

I tell her the biblical story of Moses leading the Israelites out of slavery by parting the Red Sea with his staff, how the Egyptians all drowned, and how they came to the land of Canaan safely, as God promised.

"Buddha teaches us to have perseverance. Only then can we overcome our obstacles," says Hồng-Mai, "although, I am willing to believe in your God if it means by tomorrow we are delivered to the promised land."

We chat some more until our eyelids anchor us into slumber. The boat people of trawler 93752 finally surrender to sleep.

*** 

As exhausted as I am, I am restless most of the night. I flounder around, trying to steal heat from Thủy-Tiên's little body or Tree's. My dreams race back to distant memories and catalog all my experiences, from the zenith of my happiness to the nadir of my miseries, and everything in between. My university days were when I was happiest, studying with my friends, going to the cafes or the beach, daydreaming about my future spouse that I had yet to find.

A rustling sound brings me back to consciousness. I blink a couple times to let my eyes adjust to the darkness. I see four men from the Indonesian military snooping around our sleeping bodies searching for valuables. One of them finds nothing and walks toward Hồng-Mai and me. I close my eyes and pretend to sleep.

Hồng-Mai cries out. "No!" I open my eyes to see her gripping the waist of her pants while the cadre is tugging at them. Hồng-Mai sees that I am awake and begs me to help. "Sister, please tell him not to hurt me."

I cannot pretend I am asleep anymore and must do something. I see Mrs. Trần in my mind's eye and she reminds me that my tongue is my greatest artillery. "This woman on her monthly cycle."

My English startles the cadre. He stops. His face leaves me breathless. I want to hate him but he is the most handsome Asian man I have ever seen. There is something exotic and masculine about his symmetrical features. His face is perfectly shaped by a strong, defined jawline and the bridge of his nose is high and strong. Even his ears are perfect in size and shape and stick out the right amount, level with his almond-shaped eyes. He regards me inquisitively, as if I am familiar to him, like a long-lost lover. What captivates me most are his full lips and the thick strands of blue-black hair on his head. The character lines on his face do not make him appear old, but rather, distinguished and mature. He is beautiful.

He breaks the gaze and speaks. "She is hiding something in her clothes." He tries to lift up her shirt so that he can pull down her pants. "She is hiding gold."

Hồng-Mai cries out in protest.

"Gold take by Thai pirates," I say. "The boat and sea take everything. We have nothing."

"You are lying," he says. "She is hiding something. They are always hiding something."

"Not her. You only find blood." The man continues to tug at Hồng-Mai's pants. "What will your leader, Abu, say tomorrow when he find out?"

The man pauses. "You will not tell him anything."

I notice the name stitched on his uniform and address him boldly. "No, Ommo, I will not tell if you take your friends and leave now."

I hold my breath and tense my muscles firm. I challenge him with my eyes. My heart is pounding fast. I am afraid of what he might do next, but I channel all the strength of Mrs. Trần and Sister Six into my psyche. I imagine them with me and together, we are an army ready for battle.

He relents and stands up to leave. He waves his men to go with him. He is taller than the other three men. His physique is lean and even under the dull glow of the moon and stars, I can see the muscles pressed against his cotton shirt and the tattoo peeking out from the short sleeves. I wait for them to disappear out of sight and then let out a long sigh of relief. Hồng-Mai hugs me. We both tremble.

*** 

In the early morning, I see some of the Indonesian fishermen paddle out with their kayaks and canoes. What a sight we must be to them, vagabonds loitering on the beach with nowhere to go and nothing to do. Thủy-Tiên, Hồng-Mai, and her brother Tùng, are still asleep. Tree, however, is missing. I panic and stand up to see if he is with any of the others. I see Snitch stand up and stretch. My excitement sinks realizing that he is not Tree. I am distraught and count to see if anyone is missing. Thirty-nine people are accounted for and Tree is the only one missing.

"Have you seen my nephew?" I ask the man who stepped on a sea urchin last night. He shakes his head.

I ask several others who are nearby and awake but they have not seen Tree. I gently nudge Tùng and Hồng-Mai to wake up.

"I will go find him." Tùng takes off along the stretch of sand and asks anyone who is awake, including a couple of fishermen getting ready to head out in their woven boats. He cuts through the brush and disappears.

Thirty minutes pass and I see men appear from behind the dense brush. The Indonesian military are back. I recognize one of the men, but it is not Tùng or my nephew. It is Ommo from last night.

The commanding officer, Abu, addresses our group. "Who speaks

English?"

I wait for someone to volunteer, but none of the men speak up after their beating last night. None of the women dare to speak, unsure of what will happen to them if they do confess.

I catch Ommo gawking at me. He knows I speak English and am afraid he will say something. However, informing on me would also blow his cover to the commander. Ommo leans in and whispers in Abu's ear.

Abu nods. "I need a translator so if you speak English, raise your hand, and I promise no harm will come to you."

Sơn raises his hand and so does the injured sea-urchin man. I raise my hand as well. Abu waves us over. I ask Hồng-Mai to keep an eye on Thủy-Tiên. The three of us walk over to Abu and his legion of men.

"What is your name?" Abu asks the injured man.

"Biện," he answers.

"Why are you limping?"

"I step on sea urchin last night," Biện answers.

"I overheard a rumor this morning that some of my men visited your group late last night," says Abu. "Is this true?"

Biện shakes his head. "I no see no one."

"What about you?" Abu questions Sơn.

He shakes his head. "No, sir, I sleeping. I see nothing."

Abu steps close to me. "And you? Did you see any of my men here last night?"

"No, sir Abu. It was peaceful night," I respond.

"You can tell the truth," he urges. "You will not be harmed."

"If I tell you, will you give my people some rice?" I ask.

Ommo pleads with his eyes not to say anything. I ignore him.

"What is your name?" Abu asks.

"Snow," I say. "Do we agree?"

"Snow, I promise to extend to your people the same hospitality as before if you tell me everything truthfully."

"Same hospitality as before?" I inquire. "Do you mean AK-47 hospitality or rice and sardines hospitality?"

Abu laughs. "You are a smart woman. I will have to keep my eyes on you. I promise you rice and sardines."

"That is good." I give him a sweet smile, still not trusting that he is a man of his word. "Last night, I hear sounds from the bushes and trees. I was scared." A glimpse of nervousness comes from Ommo.

"Well, who was it? Can you point to identify them? Are any of those men here right now?"

"No. I only see saltwater crocodile come out of bushes and monkeys in trees."

"That is all?" Abu asks.

"Bats too," I say, "but that is all."

He drops the inquiry and calls out some orders to his men. They disperse. "My men will bring back some food," says Abu. "Ommo and Gus will stay here to make sure there is no trouble."

"Thank you sir Abu." I walk back to where Hồng-Mai and Thủy-Tiên are sitting.

Hồng-Mai leaps up and grabs a hold of my wrist. "What did he say?" I replay the conversation. Hồng-Mai is not happy with how I handled the situation. "Why did you not tell him what his men did? Why did you protect them?" She wants the four men punished.

"What is more important? For their commander to punish them or for us to eat and survive another day?" I pick up Thủy-Tiên and put her in my lap. "They did not harm us last night and they could have. They were only after gold. Because of what I did, we all get a meal and now Ommo and his bandits owe me. You see? I have a little leverage now."

"Use your leverage wisely then," Hồng-Mai says.

"I am worried about Tree. Where the hell is he?" The question barely escapes my lips when I see in the distance my nephew running towards the group wearing his underwear and carrying a bucket.

Thủy-Tiên is excited to see him. "Brother Tree!" She hops out of my lap to meet up with him. The two of them talk animatedly as he shows her what is in the bucket. She claps her hands and skips in the sand back to Hồng-Mai and me.

Tree stands before me dripping wet. I stand up and grab him by his right ear and pull him aside a couple meters. "Where did you go? I was so worried. You were gone a long time. What were you doing?"

Tree flinches. "You are hurting me."

"Do not interrupt." I pinch his arm. "You are my responsibility. You cannot leave without telling me where you are going."

"I did not want to wake you."

I slap his shoulder. "I said do not interrupt me. What if something happened to you? What if when you came back we were gone?"

"Where would you go?"

I punch him in the arm. "If you interrupt me again, Tree, I would be justified to give you a beating."

"You are turning into Aunt Six."

I spank my nephew. Tree opens his mouth to say something but I give him the meanest, most serious expression I can, and he closes his mouth. "You better have a good explanation for disappearing. Brother Tùng went searching for you and he has not come back yet. What if something happens to him? How would you feel? You scared us. I have enough worries and after everything that we have been through, I cannot take any more. Never do that again. Do you understand?" Tree says nothing. "You can answer now."

"Yes, I understand and I am sorry. It will not happen again," he says.

177

"Look what I have in the bucket!"

We walk back to where Hồng-Mai and Thủy-Tiên are squatting. I peer inside the bucket to see two coconuts and ten crabs.

"Can we keep them Mama?" asks Thủy-Tiên. "So pretty. We can give them names."

"They are food," I say. "We cannot give them names. It would not be right to eat our pets."

"But you gave your chicken a name!" Thủy-Tiên scrunches her face up to cry.

"Let her keep one, Aunt Eight." Tree pats her head. "There are many more I can catch. This morning I woke up early because I could not sleep. I planned on being back before you woke up. I found some coconut trees way down there and climbed one. Then I got hot and went for a swim to cool off. There were blue crabs everywhere! If you go down the beach far enough, there are villagers living by the beach. I asked one of them if I can borrow their pot and some matches to cook these in exchange for some crabs. I gave them the female crabs and they invited me back when we are ready to cook them."

I grab Tree and give him an affectionate slap on the head. "So you speak Indonesian now? You are forgiven. Thủy-Tiên, you can pick one for a pet and give him a name."

My dolly selects the largest male crab in the bucket, twenty-two centimeters wide. His brilliant blue markings have elements of purple in them near the claws and his white spots resemble large swirls of condensed milk. He is missing one of the back paddle legs.

"I am going to name him King," she says.

"Make sure you keep King in the water otherwise he will die," I say to my daughter.

"I am going to swim out and grab what is left of our trawler. There are some pieces of wood we can burn after they dry up." Tree wades into the water and swims out to our boat. There is not much left of trawler 93752. The once pastel green boat with its pretty blue hull and number painted in deep red now resembles a large lump of black coal floating in the water.

"We should have a veneration ceremony tonight for Brother Tú, Sister Thảo, and their baby, Mỹ-Linh," I say to Hồng-Mai. She agrees.

"You have upgraded from sardines to blue swimmer crabs." A distinct voice interrupts us. I find Ommo's presence unnerving.

Hồng-Mai takes her leave, muttering something about finding her brother. I find myself paralyzed by his Adonis face and have trouble grasping for words.

# 32 OMMO

He stands with his arms crossed in his camel-colored uniform and black beret. His rifle hangs loosely at his side. The veins on his forearm protrude and disappear under the sleeves. His aviator sunglasses hide his eyes and I cannot decipher his mood. I have no desire to engage so I am quiet.

"Why did you not tell my commander what happened last night?" Ommo breaks the silence.

"I tell him I see saltwater crocodile come from bushes--"

"Yes, and monkeys and bats," finishes Ommo. "Am I the crocodile and my friends the monkeys and bats?" I ignore his question and pretend I am concerned for Tree swimming out to sea. I step aside to get a view of my nephew. "Is this your daughter?" Still, I say nothing to him. I pick Thủy-Tiên up and walk toward the water. She protests and runs back to King, her pet crab. Ommo walks with me. "I want to thank you, Snow, for not saying anything. I did not mean to scare you or your friend. We were looking for valuables."

"In her vagina?" I snap. "You try to pull her pants and rape her."

"What? No!" Ommo defends himself. "We always have boat people like you wash up on our shores like beached baby seals. They hide jewelry and gold in their clothes, sewn inside the pockets or tucked in the hem."

"You take advantage of helpless people. Hit them on head with guns and kick us."

"I do what my commanding officer orders me to do. I am trying to tell you I am sorry and grateful for your silence. Do not disrespect me in front of others or I will be forced to put you in your place."

I bite my tongue and wait for Tree to swim back. He carries a few planks of wood with him. I walk with my nephew back to where Thủy-Tiên is squatting with the bucket of crabs and coconuts. Ommo joins his companion, Gus, and leaves us alone.

Within the hour, the military returns. Coincidentally, so does Hồng-Mai with her brother. As promised, Abu and his men hand out rice, sardines, water, and fruits for us to enjoy. The subject of conversation this morning amongst the group is not how wonderful the food is, but how I negotiated the meal for everyone. People come by to chat and say thank you. They drool over the blue crabs and coconuts that Tree collected.

The rest of the day is uneventful. The military leaves us and tells us we are on our own until they arrange for us to get off the island. The group works together to prepare a memorial service. Tree and Tùng go for a swim in search of more crabs and take their catch to a villager's home to cook. I show Sơn and Minh-Tú how to open the coconuts, drawing from my lesson from Minh-Hoàng. The three of us take turns pounding the coconuts against rocks and strip the fibers. Others collect branches, litter and anything they can find to build a bonfire.

The evening breeze rolls in. We honor the family that died at sea by sitting around the bonfire, saying prayers and chants, sharing stories of family honor and bond, eating morsels of the ten blue crabs that Tree and Tùng caught this afternoon. A few local Indonesians join us and share their picnic food with us. A man with a hat sits down beside me underneath the palm tree and plays a musical instrument for the group. I have never seen this type of instrument before. The closest instrument I can think of is a guitar crossed with a violin, but this one only has two strings that run from the two tuning picks down to the bottom of the instrument. He stands the instrument up and strokes the two strings with a bow, pressing his fingers at various intervals on the strings. The melody is nice and soothing. He finishes and we all clap. Thủy-Tiên is especially fascinated by this new toy. She glides her fingers over the strings. The man hands her the bow and she slides it across the instrument. It screeches and we all laugh.

"Your daughter can use some lessons." His voice screeches over me like the bow. I recognize the voice and my body immediately becomes tense. I get a good look at the islander sitting beside me and recognize those almond-shaped eyes.

"What you doing here?" I ask Ommo. "You check on baby seals in distress?"

"I like to come down to the beach and play my rebab whenever I feel sad or lonely. It calms me and lifts the stress."

"Why you have to come to my beach?" I feel hostile and territorial.

He chuckles. "Your beach is a thousand meters from my mother's house and this island is small, so there is only one. You chose the nicest part of the beach to burn your boat."

"We not set boat on fire. Your bullets hit our boat and the oil leak--"

"It does not matter." Ommo dismisses my rantings. It only irritates me more. "What matters is I have not learned of your daughter's name yet." I glance across to Hồng-Mai, who shoots me a warning look. "I already know yours, which I have to say, I have never seen snow in Indonesia before. Now I have."

His comments make me miss Skyler Herrington. "Aw, so there is snow in Vietnam!" he had said.

I hesitate but answer him. "My daughter name is Dolly."

"Dolly huh? Pretty, like her mother," Ommo responds.

I blush and change the subject. "Tell me about your instrument."

"This rebab was my father's. It is made from a sapodilla tree."

"Sapodillas? The fruit is so sweet, like candy on a tree," I comment.

"This was handmade by my father. It is one string that starts from the highest tuning pick, goes down the body and then back up again. The bow is from horse hair. There are two essential scales when you play gamelan music, slendro and pélog. You hold the bow with your right hand and pull the hairs tight with the third finger, like this." Ommo demonstrates the proper way of holding the bow. He plays another melody for the group. They clap for him and demand for more. If only they realize this is the same man who tried to steal their valuables while we slept and who abused our men when we washed up on shore. I remember him mistreating my new family and it makes me mad. I shoot up and grab hold of Thủy-Tiên's hand to take her back to our sleeping area on the beach.

"I want to stay." Thủy-Tiên emphatically sits down and crosses her arms. She throws me a pout and casts her resentful eyes.

"No, it is time to sleep." I wrap both arms tightly around her arms and thighs like a straitjacket and jerk her up off the ground. I am embarrassed by her defiance. I leave the circle without saying goodbye or giving Ommo another thought.

\*\*\*

For the next twelve days, the beach is our home. Every day, we eat blue crabs and coconut. Tree goes out every morning and evening for a swim and catches crabs for us to eat. He feels for them with his feet and pries them up out of their safe, sandy haven. Sometimes he sees them skipping sideways along the shallow surface and pins them down with his feet. He has gotten good at catching them, filling a five-gallon bucket in ninety minutes. We use the saltwater to boil the crabs and borrow cooking supplies from the natives nearby. Thủy-Tiên's pet, King, died on the second day. King's death hit her hard and so begins the lessons of loss, mourning, and healing. She is on her fifth pet crab, named King the Fifth.

Every day I search for coconuts that have fallen from the tree and spend hours trying to pry one open. My arms are getting strong. I am sick of eating crabs and coconuts. Sometimes arguments break out amongst our group over who sees the coconut first. We share our food with the elders but tell everyone else they are on their own. Tree and Snitch have become good friends. I treat Snitch like my own nephew, bossing him around and telling him to find sticks for fire or fetch some matches from locals who take pity on us. He never complains. The Indonesian military has not come back to check on us and true to his word, Abu and his men have not given us any more food or support. Some days, I think they have forgotten us, but then Ommo shows up, always in the evening, and I believe he is their spy.

Today, he comes to the beach carrying a bag slung over his shoulders. "I have a gift for you."

"Why you keep coming here?" I ask.

"You are still mad?" He smiles and dumps out the contents of the bag onto the sand.

"Sapodillas!" I exclaim.

"I had to wait ten days for them to ripen. They are from my mother's tree."

A few people gather around us. Ommo takes out a knife and cuts the fruit in half. He hands Thủy-Tiên and me the fruit. He then cuts up the rest into small slices and hands everyone in our group a piece.

I bite into the flesh of the sapodilla and savor the delicious meat. "Why you being so nice?" I am in heaven. "You here five times now, always in the evening."

"You have been counting," he says. "You must miss me when I do not come." I dismiss his narcissist remark. "I have two more presents for you." He hands me two ponchos. "It is supposed to rain late tonight."

"Last time you bring us blanket. Before that you bring tarp. Other time you come and play your rebab. Does your commander send you to spy on us?" I find Ommo annoying, like he is trying to buy my forgiveness.

"Why should I tell you? You never told me why you did not tell my commander about that night."

If he did not bring us much needed things or was not so distracting to look at, I would despise him. "You said two presents. These two ponchos our presents or is there more?"

He laughs at me. "You are greedy." I take another bite of my fruit to avoid saying something he might not like. "Tomorrow afternoon there will be a Norwegian ship coming at one o'clock to take this group to the island of Galang. They have rescued others out at sea who have left Vietnam and are transporting them to the refugee camp. Abu has arranged for them to come here and take you to Galang, where you will stay until you get relocated to a country willing to sponsor your family."

I cannot believe the news and jump up and down with happiness. Biện, the man who stepped on the sea urchin but has since recovered from the pain, walks over to ask why I am so happy. I tell him the good news and tell him to spread the word.

"I see you will not miss me," says Ommo.

"I not know you well to miss you, but thank you for being kind to my family," I say sincerely.

"You are welcome. Stay dry tonight and be careful of the crocodiles, monkeys, and bats," says Ommo.

"And snakes," I say. "Many snakes here."

Ommo laughs. "And snakes." He leaves without saying goodbye.

I catch up to him and gently touch his forearm. "Ommo, take care yourself. If you see more helpless baby seals beached here, do not steal their hope. Please give them hope, like you did for me today."

Ommo nods. "Take care of yourself and Dolly."

***

Today there will be a ship to take us to a refugee camp. It will mean one step closer to getting my family to America. I wake earlier than usual this morning and join Tree for a swim while others sleep. I wade out to the warm water and immerse my body under the gentle waves. These same waves once rocked our little boat so violently, it made us throw up, and brought us pirates that changed some of our lives. These harsh waves claimed the life of three of our boat members. How many countless more? These waves that could not quench our thirst when we were dehydrated or feed us fish when we were starving. Today I elect to forgive these waves.

Tree and I enjoy the peaceful morning. We splash around and try to outswim each other, playing games to see who can swim faster or submerge further and longer. He teaches me to spot for blue swimmer crabs and how to catch them. We have a contest to see who can catch the most. Of course, he wins. Together we fill the five-gallon bucket with crabs in an hour, with me catching fourteen of the sixty blue swimmers. We get out of the water and spot a bask of crocodiles sleeping with their mouth open to release the heat. Tree and I stay clear of them and walk back to the group with our catch. I cannot wait to leave this little island.

This morning will be our last crab and coconut feast on the beach. I am grateful that we did not starve the past two weeks, but am sick of the same meal every day and cannot wait for rice, meat or fish. I daydream about fried frog legs and the crepes that Sister Six makes, only this time, with lots of shrimp and pork. By 1:15 p.m., the group stands clustered together on the beach. There is a lot of excitement this morning. The big Norwegian ship is here and larger than I imagined, at around fifty or sixty meters. It waits for us far in the distance and drops down smaller boats into the water to retrieve us. Group by group, we are ferried to the glorious vessel while the Indonesian military supervise. I find myself searching for Ommo but he is not here today.

Alongside the massive steel cargo ship, we are hoisted up with ropes and nets. Sơn, Tùng, Minh-Tú, Biện and other men climb the ladder. A man throws a large canvas bag down to me and directs me to put Thủy-Tiên in it. My four-year-old is hoisted up into the boat. Her body bangs against the ship a few times on the way to the top. My arms are raised in case I have to catch her. Thủy-Tiên is trusting in what is happening at the moment. *My brave girl.* Tree and Snitch

183

climb the rope and I follow behind them. Hồng-Mai and others wait for the net.

I grab hold of Tree's arm. He pulls me in. I survey the deck and see there are already four hundred other refugees onboard, all rescued at sea. I am so elated and speechless. It is heaven on water! Announcements come over the speakers, first in English, then in Vietnamese, that we are all going to the island of Pulau Galang. We all cheer. Volunteer firefighters, doctors, nurses, and counselors walk to our group and offer assistance. They give us fresh water and a bowl of noodles. A young woman with blonde hair and blue eyes, wearing a knitted Marius sweater around her shoulders, hands Tree and me a metal utensil with a long handle and four sharp, narrow tines that curves upward at the end.

"It is a type of cutlery, called a fork," she says. "You spear the food and put it in your mouth." I find her accent darling and sing-song-like with the different inflections. I especially like the way she pronounces the word "food". Although her mouth is stiff and her lips tense, her eyes shine. I can listen to her all day.

"I want chopsticks. I am not putting these sharp spikes into my mouth," says Tree.

She finds Tree's appalled expression amusing and laughs. "We use it like this." I find her charming and her pronunciation of "we" as "vee" endearing. She takes Tree's fork, stabs the noodles, spins it in circles until a layer of noodles is wrapped around the utensil, and hands it back to him. "Linguine with herring." I give it a try and take a bite of the noodles. It is delightful. She points to the front of the boat. "Over there, we have clothes that have been donated by various charitable organizations. Take what you need."

I realize we are safe and with tears of joy in my eyes, I hug Tree. "We are not going to die."

Tree's face lights up. "No, and we are no longer government property."

After eating, I take Thủy-Tiên over to the pile of clothes. She selects a white cotton shirt with a print of *Raggedy Ann and Raggedy Andy* on it, and another black shirt that says *"Barbie"* on it in pink lettering. We pick a pair of shorts to go with them. A yellow shirt with a pretty woman on the front of it catches Thủy-Tiên's eyes but it is too big for her. She insists I wear it. The woman on the t-shirt has long black hair. She is wearing a bathing suit in colors of red, yellow and blue. Her bikini bottom has white stars on it. Below her picture are the words *"Wonder Woman"*. I take the shirt because the colors remind me of Việt Nam's flag but also the American flag. A purple blouse catches my eye and I take that one as well to compliment the jeans and polyester pants I have slung over the crook of my elbow.

With our new clothes in hand, I take Thủy-Tiên to the washing station and wait in line. Soon it is our turn. I rinse her down with water and wash her hair and body before scrubbing myself clean. I feel human again. I put on my clean yellow Wonder Woman shirt and slip on the same crooked black pants I had sewn years ago, afraid of losing the emerald engagement ring that Sam gave me. I search for it in the elastic waist and smile knowing the ring is still there. Sam, my first love. I promise myself to never sell his ring. I smile again and imagine myself as ragamuffin chic with my bright yellow shirt and crooked black pajama pants. Or should I say, refugee chic, since I am now a refugee? I imagine myself walking the runway in Paris wearing my uneven pants, one pant leg wider and shorter than the other, stitched together with three different colors of thread. I giggle out loud imagining Sister Six's shocked face to see my horrible pants make it to fashion week. I spend the next few hours enjoying the boat ride, embracing the breeze on my face, and watching the sea come to life with fish jumping out of the water. Thủy-Tiên makes friends with some of the other children on the ship. They run around making up games and laugh with childhood innocence. I make small talk with some of the families sitting around me. Before long, we arrive at the harbor and get ready to disembark on the gangplank.

Who should be waiting for us at the dock but Ommo?

# 33 THE CAMP

Uniformed men stand to attention and wait for all four-hundred forty of us refugees to get off the Norwegian vessel. I catch a glimpse of the pretty blonde woman who taught us how to use a fork and wave to her. The Indonesian military search everyone's bags and take what they want. An uneasy feeling settles in my chest. I want to run back to the ship and be a stowaway, maybe end up in Norway. Now, the idea of waiting at the refugee camp until sponsorship to America feels like an impossible dream. Ommo, Gus, and a few other soldiers ask the group questions and separate us into clusters.

Ommo points at me and waves me over. "Your name please."

"You know my name," I say.

"I need your full name," he demands in a serious tone.

"Lê Ngọc Tuyết." I give him my maiden name. "Surname Lê. First name Tuyết."

"I thought it was Snow?"

"Tuyết means 'snow'."

"Spell your name." I spell my full name for him. "How many are in your group?"

"Three," I respond.

"Spell their names for me." I comply with his request. "I thought your daughter's name is Dolly?"

"It is a nickname I call her, just like Tree is my nephew's nickname. Why you separate people in groups, Ommo? I do not--"

"What are their ages and relationship to you?"

"My daughter is four-years-old and my nephew is sixteen." Ommo annoys me. He is the eyelash adhered to my eyeball, the loose insole in my shoe, the run in my pantyhose. I want to crumple him up like paper and toss him in a trashcan.

"Are you the head of the family?"

"Yes. You cannot separate--"

"Your birthdate and theirs?" He cuts me off again.

"July 30, 1974, and December 16, 1962. My birthday April 13, 1939."

"Please take your family and sit over there in group A. You will be given instructions."

"Ommo, there is another boy, Thành. He travel same in our boat but he have no family. I want him with my family."

"He will be in group D with the unaccompanied minors."

There are a lot of children sitting in Group D and more joining them. Children as young as eight or nine years old wait to discover their fate. They are with other children and teenagers. Somehow, they got separated from their family. I need to work on getting Snitch to join us or at least be with Sơn. I do not want him alone.

Tree, Thủy-Tiên and I sit down on the dirt and rocks with the rest of the families classified as Group A. I am disheartened when my group is called to be transported to the camp. There are still hundreds of people being interviewed and every face appears the same. The boat people of trawler 93752 have been separated and are lost in the crowd of black hair and polyester clothes.

The bus ride to the camp is a loud one. People talk over each other, making plans to write to their family back home or ask for money from relatives who have settled in other countries. Some are nervous and fear they will never receive sponsorship. Others are excited to be on land and dream of endless possibilities for the bright future ahead. I am vexed about what this camp means for my family. I am hopeful it is a bridge to a better life and the chance to forget the recent past.

There is a longing in me to return to the old Việt Nam. I miss my country that is lost forever. I miss my family whom I may never see again, at least, not until it is safe to return. I am nothing more than a homeless person stuck between yesterday and tomorrow and two countries that do not want me.

I see mangos growing on the island and wild monkeys swinging on the trees. If I allow the green foliage to blend together into a blur, maybe I can convince myself that I am in a rural jungle near Vĩnh Bình. Perhaps on the other side is a nice beach, with a bustling market nearby, and if I try, I can convince myself that my family is sitting around the table playing tứ sắc, the Chinese four-colors card game. I envision Sister Six cooking bò lúc lắc, a French-inspired Vietnamese cuisine of cubed beef marinated in sesame oil, garlic, oyster sauce, soy sauce, salt, and sugar, then sautéed and enjoyed with a salad tossed in a lime vinaigrette dressing. I yearn for a different life, one that has Tâm, Hải and Sam in it.

The bus stops and I exit with the rest of the passengers. Tree and Thủy-Tiên get off before me. A big sign "Welcome to Pulau Galang" stands prominently.

A man with a large mole between his eyebrows strides to the front of the covered shelter where we congregate. He carries a megaphone and is wearing brown-tinted sunglasses, large like aviator goggles. His bell bottom pants are too short for him and his shirt a bit tight. "Hello, friends. My name is Don. I am a representative with the office of the *United Nations High Commissioner for Refugees.* Welcome to Pulau Galang." A young Vietnamese woman with long black hair, wearing a floral dress, lifts up her megaphone to translate his message. "The UNHCR is here to help you with resettlement into a participating country or repatriation if you voluntarily would like to return to your country." Don pauses so the woman can translate. "Everyone here has been assigned to Group A because you are traveling with your family and have a small child. We currently have two thousand refugees in the camp and hundreds more coming each day." He pauses for the translator. "Unfortunately, we do not have enough barracks for everyone so we will assign by lottery. You will be reassigned into a barrack as soon as a family vacates. Until then, you will need to find a spot anywhere within the camp borders to call home. We have minimal supplies available and more will be received next week. If your family's name is not called for an assigned barrack, please make use of the tents and tarps provided by the *American Red Cross.*"

The longer the representative speaks, the more desperate I feel. It dawns on me that I am essentially in prison. The camp border is outlined with barbed wire. Indonesian soldiers and guards dressed in green or tan uniforms stand by, on alert to pounce and maintain order if they need to. As far as I can see, there is no running water or sanitation system. I see a well and am suspicious it has contaminated water in it. Beyond the barracks is a small hill with rows and rows of dilapidated structures and makeshift shelters. There are huts put together using tarps, weathered pieces of wood, blankets, palm or bamboo leaves, corroded aluminum, or rusty tin parts.

Clothes hang on ropes or drape over partitions to dry. There are so many people loitering around, so bored that they find chewing on their nails entertaining. Some are asleep on a hammock with their arm draped over their eyes to shield the glare of the sun. I see mothers tending to their babies, all of whom are either topless or bottomless.

"Aunt Eight, he called your name." Tree taps my hand. "We are in barrack two."

I am relieved our family has a room rather than a tent to sleep in. Tree, Thủy-Tiên and I receive a welcome kit that includes soap, utensils, towels, and a kerosene stove. We report to our assigned barrack with the clothes on our backs and whatever articles we selected on the Norwegian ship.

Each barrack has a row of five living quarters on top and five open spaces below. The barrack is held together with bent nails and crooked boards affixed to some rotting wood. There are five sets of stairs leading to the door of each living quarter. Down below, the open space is bare, with three walls and no door. In the corner are a pot, a few cooking utensils, a plastic water basin, some plates, bowls, cups, and cutlery. I suspect these items were left by previous inhabitants. I walk the ten steps up the stairs to the second level and stand at the platform. I take a deep breath and open the door.

I am greeted by hot, stale air, with a hint of dust and mold permeating my senses. The room is roughly twenty square meters and other than the wood platforms with mattresses on them, it too is bare. There are six pads to sleep on, three on the floor and three on the wood shelves. The thin mattress pads are lumpy and stained. A thin blanket sits on each. Only two have pillows and one pad actually has a sunken box spring. Tree claims one of the beds on top with the box spring. It is closest to the window shutters.

"Alô?" A young Vietnamese woman greets us from the doorway with her husband and their twin daughters.

"Hello." I nod to the family. "Is your family assigned to this room as well?"

"Yes," she answers. "I believe we are sharing. My name is Mai. This is my husband, Khải, and our daughters, Mỹ-Kiều and Mỹ-Loan."

"Your daughters are so lovely. How do you tell them apart?" I ask.

"We can see their differences," says Khải, "but others can tell them apart by their ears. Mỹ-Loan is the older one by two minutes and she has her ears pierced."

"Yes, I see," I say. "Mỹ-Loan, how old are you and your sister?"

"Yes, Auntie, we are eleven and will turn twelve next month," answers Mỹ-Loan politely.

I introduce myself and the family and tell them to call me Eight. We spend the rest of the day getting acquainted with each other and the families in the other rooms. I learn that Mai and her family have been at the camp a month. They stayed in a tent at first. I understand the Red Cross, the Indonesian Red Crescent Society, and other world relief organizations keep the camp operational, offering services in health, education, and social welfare. The UNHCR manages the resettlement programs but it is the Indonesian government that implements them. The military guards the camp and limits people entering or leaving. Many of them can be bribed and a lot of the single women who have relationships with them find their application for resettlement approved much faster than others. And if you have a large family, you can expect to live in the camp for a long time before your whole family gets sponsored.

One of my neighbors, Bảo, was a successful business owner and is a highly educated man. He speaks good English, French, Mandarin Chinese, and Vietnamese. He and his large family of thirteen have been in the camp for a year. Like many others, after the war ended, his family's rice plantation, cars, and scooters were seized by the government. He risked arrest many times by purchasing food in his town and reselling them in Sài Gòn for ten times the price. His family was starving. The communists transported all the rice from the south to the north to feed their people. He saved enough money to buy a boat thirteen meters long for nine taels of gold. He even spent three million đồng on fishing nets to pretend he was a fisherman, but their boat captain ended up changing his mind and staying back. Luckily they had no problems getting past the border. They were in international waters for seven days with only a toy compass and a letter from a friend that detailed the navigation route. Eighty-eight people were in the boat in the beginning. They survived on raw squid and fish that flew onto the boat during the tempest rainfall. Everyone was miserable and cold. Politeness and social order quickly vanished as everyone fought for space. They were attacked by pirates four times and nine people were murdered. Eventually they were rescued by a Dutch merchant ship that hoisted them up onto the boat with a suspended gangplank. I conclude that we both knew Dr. Đức and his wife as they helped both our families escape.

"You have a higher power protecting you to be so fortunate to have a barrack already," says Bảo. "I hear the UNHCR is building two hundred barracks on Galang to accommodate twenty-thousand people, and there will be a hospital, administrative offices, and community facilities."

"I hope they build bathrooms with running water so we can take showers," I say.

"I would like to see a church or a pagoda. There are many monks, nuns, and priests here," says Bảo, "but each day I drift further from spirituality."

"I hope your family gets sponsored quickly."

"I have a large family so it will be some time before someone pays for all of us. We can separate and go at different times or places, but I insist we stay together."

Mai and Khải grab a chair and join Bảo and me.

"How do things operate around here?" I ask.

Khải lights up a cigarette and exhales before answering. "If you are hungry, there are some basic items that are provided to us, such as rice, canned fish, salt, sugar and cooking oil."

Mai provides additional insight. "Rice is brought in every week or two but there is never enough. It will last your family two days. Sometimes there are meat or fresh vegetables. Many of us try to grow our own vegetables."

Bảo surrenders to the temptation of Khải's cigarette and bums one from him. "You will find that life here is monotonous and the only thing to do while you wait for your application to get approved is to sleep and garden, but the soil here is hard and dry." Bảo takes a deep drag of the nicotine and exhales. "There is no running water so we rely on catching the rain. One other thing. My advice to you, when you are cooking your rice, is to fill the kerosene half way. Otherwise, it will expand and leak out. If you need help getting the wicks started and lighting the burner, I can show you. It is a little fickle."

"Thank you. Tell me, Brother Bảo, how do I apply for resettlement? Is there an interview process?" I ask.

"There are announcements daily over the loudspeakers. Your family will be called to the interview office. It will take some time before you learn of your status. They will announce the names of people accepted to leave but then you have to wait again for the country to make arrangements to receive you. There is a lot of paperwork and travel planning, medical inspections and shots…Hundreds of people arrive here each day, more than the number of people leaving. You will see. Life here is hard."

"Where did you get your mosquito net?" I ask.

"You can ask the guards to get you things but they will expect you to pay three times the cost. Each family receives a monthly subsistence allowance from the UNHCR for necessities. If you have family who can send you money, I suggest you write them. You can have my net after I leave, if you need it."

I chat with Bảo, Mai and Khải for another fifteen minutes. They are full of information but Bảo is the storyteller.

# 34 A TORNADO

It has been two weeks since we arrived at the camp. Time drifts slowly here. Bảo was right, life is hard on Galang. There is no clean water. On the weekends the guards let us go to the beach to swim, bathe, and do laundry. Our daily menu consists of sardines or tiny dried shrimp stir-fried in soy sauce, and a cup of rice to cook. It is never enough and we are always hungry. The whole camp is rat and snake-infested. I fight to keep our rice and food supplies sealed. At night there are swarms of mosquitos and without a net to ward them off, we become a buffet feast for them. The worst part is the stench. The crowded shanty town of poorly-constructed barracks and makeshift tents is nothing more than a large pot of rotting flesh, urine, and feces. Many people have scabies or are sick with malaria or some ailment. Every day people die as more become ill. There are as many births as there are deaths here.

Thủy-Tiên passes her time playing made-up games with children nearby. Her favorite one is dropping the handkerchief on top of another child's head and then having that child chase and catch her before she runs a full circle around their group of friends and sits down in the empty seat at the circle. Tree passes time by climbing like a monkey over the fence and disappearing for hours at a time. At night or in the early morning, he hops out of his top bunk, slithers through the window, and scales down the railings. He says he is fishing and hunting for wild boar, but sometimes he comes back smelling like alcohol, which is illegal to have in the camp. Christmas and Lunar New Year are the only two holidays in which it is permissible to imbibe. I ask him about his disappearances and he dismisses me like a nosy neighbor. He is growing distant from me, becoming disrespectful, and either angry or sad all the time. In not so many words, he is telling me he yearns to return to Việt Nam and resents his elders for forcing him to leave. This morning I lay awake on my mattress and read the carvings on the walls. There are names and dates scratched on them from previous tenants. I resist the urge to carve my name because years from now, what will it matter? Who will see it? Who will care?

"Shit!" Tree scrambles off his mattress and jumps down.

"What is the matter?" I leap up to see what is wrong.

"This is disgusting!" Tree pulls back his thin mattress to expose the sunken box spring. Crawling out of the cracks of the walls and covering his bed are hundreds of tiny rice-size bed bugs. Tree scratches his back frantically. I lift up his shirt and see red welts covering his entire back where the bloodsuckers dined. Tree flips the bed to the floor and we both get to work stomping on them. Our roommates join the blitzkrieg.

Thủy-Tiên wakes up from the ruckus. "Black pepper?" She mistakes the dead bugs for ground pepper.

"I cannot stand it here!" Tree screams. "How much longer are we staying in this hell?"

Before I can answer, he sprints out of the door and down the stairs. Mỹ-Loan and Mỹ-Kiều run after Tree but cannot keep pace with him. They abandon their quest and return back to the barrack.

Mai tries to comfort me. "Give him time. Both of our families have a good chance of getting sponsored soon. We are a small family with young children."

"Mai," I say, "I had my interview with the administration office to see if we are eligible for refugee status and can be resettled. I told the authorities I wanted to go to America and they asked if I had friends or family there. The only person I know is my friend, Sergeant Skyler Herrington, who served in the U.S. Army. He was born and raised in the Seattle area."

"Maybe the UNHCR will track him down. Maybe he can sponsor your family." Mai shakes the dust from her blanket out the window.

"I hope so. I wrote to my family back home. Thủy-Tiên's dad wrote to them and they included his letter in their mail to me. He is in South Carolina but will soon be moving to a town called Houston in the state of Texas. He is doing well. He will be working under a division manager for some company, managing one-hundred-fifty employees, but his goal is to open his own machine shop."

"You belong in Houston, not Seattle." Mai's husband, Khải, restores Tree's mattress to the top bunk.

"He is married to an American woman and they now have two sons."

"You should write to your husband and ask him to send you money," says Mai.

"I do not want him to know where we are," I say. "We each have chosen different paths and it is best we live separate lives."

"Do you think that is fair to Thủy-Tiên?" Mai gives me something to think about.

"And how are your family doing?" asks Khải.

"My sister is paranoid with the government. She calls them all Việt Cộngs and does not dare venture outside after 8 p.m. curfew. There are always people patrolling the streets and the perimeters of the towns, waiting to catch you doing something illegal. People's crops and livestock are still being seized. My sister has had some luck selling cakes and pastries so she is starting her food business. My sister-in-law is learning to perfect her sewing skills and wants to be a seamstress with her own tailor shop someday. My brother is still driving a truck each day and my brother-in-law is trying to get his hands on a chicken and a rooster. He wants to raise and sell them or fight them. They are doing anything they can to live."

"My family back home is struggling as well. They eat rice soup and sweet potatoes every day, once a day," says Khải.

"Yes, my family does not have enough money to buy anything and depend on what they can grow or raise," says Mai.

We watch the twins teach Thủy-Tiên how to play a game with chopsticks. They toss a small ball in the air and pick up as many chopsticks as they can before the ball drops.

"We should go to the beach for a swim and let our daughters play," I suggest.

"Yes, I can use the distraction. Let me grab our laundry," Mai says.

***

Bảo's family joins us for the afternoon. We walk the one and a half kilometers to the beach. There are a lot of people frolicking on the sandy shore today. Families, teenagers, and small children take advantage of the sand to exfoliate their skin and run into the crashing waves to wash themselves clean. Several children are standing naked in the shallow banks of the beach, splashing each other gleefully. A woman shrieks in the distant shoreline. A handful of people run to her and gather around to see what is going on. Curiosity beckons me to follow.

A young woman's body has drifted to the coastline. Her waterlogged body shows signs of severe maceration. Her skin and nails are detached and most of her hair has separated from her head. There is a dead crayfish entangled in her hair. The palms of her hands and soles of her feet are wrinkled. The body is green and black. Her eyes have been picked over by birds or sea creatures and what is left cannot be distinguished. And yet, I recognize her clothes. It is Thảo's body, the young mother who was brutally raped by the pirates and who took her and her baby's life at sea. My heart shatters into a thousand pieces but my tears do not flow. My heart grows cold and my anger rises. It is a perfect recipe for a tornado of emotions as I flash back to the Thai men dragging the women to their boats to violate them and toss them into the sea like a used tissue. The face of Tý and Minh-Hoàng form a funnel cloud in my mind. It swirls angrily and collects the faces of all the bitter melon men and pirates who harmed my friends and family and caused destruction along the way.

The Indonesian Navy arrives to take the body away. They load Thảo into a car with a red cross symbol on the side door. Everyone is asked to return to the

194

camp.

\*\*\*

I replay over and over Thảo's body washing to shore and I cannot sleep. I quietly get out of bed and notice Tree is not in his. My little dolly is sound asleep. I walk down the stairs and stand outside. Next door Bảo and his wife are having sex. I brave the walk alone and resolve ten minutes away from my daughter should be fine, since Mai and Khải are here.

I walk toward the perimeter of the camp until I can make out the outlines of the barbed wire fence. There are two people smoking and drinking but I cannot make out their faces.

"What barrack are you in?" asks the smaller of the two shadowy figures.

"The second one," says the taller figure.

I recognize their voices and crouch down to stay hidden.

"I am in sixty-eight, near the guards' barrack," says Snitch. "There are one-hundred-twenty of us unaccompanied minors crammed in there. There is one man living with us to take care of us. He is nice. Have you been on the outskirts of the camp?"

"Fuck, Thành, I go anywhere I want on this Shit Island," says Tree. "This camp is sitting in the middle of a cleared forest. The harbor is five kilometers from camp. I am guessing there are ten thousand people here."

I am appalled he is using foul language and smoking. This is a new side to him that I do not like. Where is my caring, loyal and resourceful nephew I helped raise?

"Have you heard about Hồng-Mai or seen her brother?" asks Snitch.

"Fuck, it is terrible what happened." Tree takes a drag of his cigarette and chases it with some beer.

"I have not run into any of the other people from our boat, have you? There must be a hundred barracks here."

"Sơn and Minh-Tú are in barrack fifty-eight, I think. Have you been sponsored yet?"

Snitch takes the last gulp of his beer and throws the can on the ground. "Germany is taking a lot of the unaccompanied minors. I am going on the next boat."

"Shit, send me a letter when you get to Germany so we can keep in touch. Otherwise, I will not fucking recognize you when you call my name with a German accent."

The two boys laugh.

"I heard every week a ship comes to take people to Australia or Germany or America," says Snitch.

"My aunt wants to go to America. I want to volunteer for repatriation, but I am a minor under her care so I am fucking stuck. I miss our country even if it is infested with Uncle Hồ's legion of Cộng Sản."

"Why would you want to run back to Hồ's legion of communists?"

195

Tree laughs. "The rice is better there."

"There is a rich Chinese woman who is selling jasmine rice that her family sends here. You should get some. It is the same quality we are used to. Meet me here tomorrow at noon and I will take you to her."

"Shit, that rice better be good," says Tree. "It is almost 3 a.m. The guards should be having wet dreams by now. I am going to get us more cigarettes and with some luck, more alcohol."

The two boys part ways. I am scared he will get caught and beaten. Tomorrow I will have to beat him first.

***

The announcement comes over the loudspeakers. "Lê Ngọc Tuyết, you and your family are to report to the administration office in fifteen minutes. I repeat. Lê Ngọc Tuyết, please bring your family to the office in fifteen minutes."

My heart races. There can be only two reasons why I am being called. Either Tree got into trouble or we are going to America. I grab Thủy-Tiên's hand and run to the office. It is raining heavily today. The dirt walkways are muddy. There is standing water and large puddles to slow us down. I pray Tree also heard the announcement and will meet us there. On the way, I notice a woman smiling brightly at me. Her mouth showcases her wide row of white teeth and a wider row of gums above them. She points to her handwritten sign, advertising a cup of jasmine rice for four hundred thousand đồng or two hundred fifty rupiahs. She must be off her hammock to charge that extortionary price.

We burst into the refugee camp office and startle the people in there. I announce myself. A woman hands me an envelope and directs me to the resettlement processing center. We run to the UNHCR center drenched in rain and breathing heavily. I sweep my hair out of my face and recognize the three people sitting at the table in front of me. The first person is Don, the UNHCR representative who welcomed us to Galang. The mole between his eyebrows appears darker and larger than I remember. Next to him is the Vietnamese woman who translates for him. She wears a name tag that says "Mary". The third person, to my surprise, is Ommo. The same Adonis face I remember, but softer and kinder today. He waves to Thủy-Tiên and she waves back.

"Mama," my daughter says excitedly, "it is the man who plays that instrument."

I nod to her and we take a seat. The third seat is empty and I desperately pray Tree will show up. I hand Don the envelope.

"Where is your nephew?" Don opens the envelop and reviews the documents.

"He coming," I say nervously in English.

"We have reviewed your application," says Mary. "Your first choice is the United States, second is Canada, and third Sweden. We are happy to inform you that you have been approved for resettlement in Sweden."

"Oh, I am happy," I respond. "I pick Sweden because my friend, Minh-Tú, you know him? He say there is Swedish embassy in Hà Nội and he hear they help bring my family in Việt Nam to reunite with us."

"I cannot confirm that Sweden can help your relatives back in Vietnam emigrate to Sweden." Don hands the documents over to Mary for further review. "Let's worry about your family first."

"Your nephew needs to be here. We need to do a complete medical examination and give you some vaccinations," says Mary. "We need to prepare travel arrangements and visas."

I hope Ommo is not the one doing the medical assessments. He notices my eyes on him and smiles. *Why are you so handsome when you smile?*

"Yes, you need to be immunized against smallpox, hepatitis, tuberculosis, tetanus and a couple other diseases," says Don.

"But if your nephew does not arrive for this appointment, your application will be recycled back into the waiting pile." Mary flips open an ink pad. There are two stamps in front of her. One says "APPROVED" and the other one says "REJECTED".

I panic. I do not want to stay at this camp longer than I have to. Being here for two weeks is nothing compared to others who have been here months. Tree has never failed me. I am hopeful he will come any minute now.

"If Sweden does not work out, we have an opportunity for you while you wait for a sponsorship." Don slides me a folder. "We need volunteers to teach English to refugees who have been approved for resettlement. While they wait for the transfer, they will be learning English and basic cultural information about their host country. We chose you because your application indicates you used to teach math and your English is good. You and your daughter would be living in staff housing. Your nephew can live in the unaccompanied minor barrack until your departure. And Ommo here is assisting the camp commanding officer. He will help you--"

"No," I say.

"No?" Ommo's kind face now grows cold and upset.

"My English not so good and my nephew cannot separate with me," I say. "He will come."

"If he is not here in five minutes, we will have to reject your placement with Sweden," says Mary. "You can appeal."

We sit in awkward silence. I avoid eye contact with Ommo but Thủy-Tiên is enamored with him. She waves to him and asks him in Vietnamese where his rebab instrument is.

After five minutes, Don stands up. "We cannot wait any longer."

"Please, two more minutes. He will come," I plead.

"I am sorry. We have another family to meet with." Don hands me the folder on the table. "Consider teaching while you wait."

"I will escort them back." Ommo grabs a large umbrella and ushers me out the door. "It is raining hard outside." The warmth of his hand on my back comforts me but the hurried push of his fingers contradicts this security. I sense his impatience to leave the processing center and cannot understand why he is upset. I would rather slither in the mud than walk with him back to the barrack and listen to his reprimands.

# 35 TREE

Ommo and I walk down the row of vendors in zone two of the camp with Thủy-Tiên wanting to hold his hand not mine. On either side, there are people selling various items in the stands. There is even a café under a blue tarp and a small restaurant nearby. Some of the strangers stare at us inquisitively, while others, judgmentally. I am paranoid they will spread rumors that I am sleeping with this man to get special treatment. I pause to smell the coffee beans and close my eyes to enjoy the aroma.

"Would you like a cup of coffee?" asks Ommo.

"No," I lie.

"Sit. I want coffee." Ommo orders two cups of coffee and warm tea for my daughter. "Why do you hate me so much?"

"I no hate--"

"I have been trying to make things right with you ever since we met and I apologized for hitting your boat mates. I was following Abu's orders. I played music for you--"

"Not for me, for--"

"No, for you, Snow, and I brought you sapodilla fruit from my mother's tree. I pulled favors to get your family into a barrack and got your application processed with priority."

I am stunned and speechless. He is exasperated with me. He throws his hand in the air as if to say "I give up" and rubs his palms on his knees.

Our drinks arrive. I take a sip of the hot coffee. If only every moment in life is like the first sip. "Thank you."

Ommo relaxes his shoulders. "You are welcome."

"I need to find my nephew."

"I will help."

"I wish to see my friends too. Do you know where they are?" I ask.

He takes out a pen and small pad of paper from his shirt pocket. "Write down their names and I will find them." I write down Hồng-Mai's and Tùng's name, as well as Sơn's and Minh-Tú's. "I need more than their first names. I need surnames. There are thousands of people here with the same names."

"I sorry. I have only first names. Maybe you check names of everyone arrive to Galang on same day as me."

Ommo sighs. "I will see what I can do." He abruptly whips his head around and addresses curtly the two women working the coffee stand. He says something to them in Indonesian and they stop speaking to each other.

"They are spreading rumors about us," he says.

"What they say?" I am upset.

"They think we are lovers." He winks at me.

I blush and divert my attention to Thủy-Tiên. We spend the next ten minutes enjoying our beverages and talking about my daughter's health and what heart surgery would mean for her. Ommo escorts us back to the barrack via a longer route. He walks leisurely and is in no hurry to get out of the mud and rain. We arrive at my barrack the same time as Tree.

I lunge for my nephew to grab his ear. I am furious he has been out all night and caused us to miss the opportunity to go to Sweden. Before I can yell at him, he collapses to the ground.

Ommo carries Tree into our room and places him on my mattress. "He is burning up."

I grab a towel and run down the stairs to the drum of fresh rainwater. With the towel soaked in cold water, I run back and apply it to Tree's face and neck. "We need a doctor and medicine."

Thủy-Tiên, Mai, Khải, and the twins stand by helplessly.

"There are none that will come to you," Ommo says. "If he had a minor illness and the strength to stand in line, he can visit the Red Cross tent for treatment."

"He cannot die." I am terrified. "So many people get bury here and their site have no sign. No dignity for them."

"He will not die." Ommo places a reassuring hand on mine.

Tree is conscious and shivers. "I am cold."

I wipe the moisture off his face. I do not know if the beads are from his sweat or the rain.

Ommo offers a diagnosis. "It is possible he was bitten by a snake in the forest or ate something bad." Tree writhes in discomfort and it reminds me of Tuấn, when he had pinworms in his body. "Try to keep him cool and as comfortable as possible. I have to report to work after my lunch break." Ommo reluctantly leaves our side with the promise to return later with medicine for Tree's fever.

***

My defiant nephew has been sick for over a month but he is getting stronger. Headaches and abdominal pains are frequent visitors, so is vomiting and diarrhea. Khải helps Tree downstairs whenever my nephew needs to throw up or have a bowel movement. Sometimes, they are not fast enough or Tree is not strong enough so Mai helps me clean up. I pray several times a day.

*Dear Lord, in Your light I entrust You with our lives. Please Heavenly Father, wrap Your protective arms around Tree and place Your healing hands on him. Keep us safe from harm and deliver us to freedom. Please also bless the friends and families in our lives. In Thy holy name I pray, Amen.*

I have learned that Tree has been infected with malaria. Sometimes his body will convulse and he passes out from exhaustion. I feed him water with a spoon to keep him hydrated and sleep next to him to try to keep him warm. All day and night I keep vigil and have no energy for myself. I give Tree the malaria pills that the Red Cross gave us. The pills bring back haunting memories of Mrs. Trần overdosing on chloroquine. My roommates are a blessing and help with Thủy-Tiên. They take her with them to the dining hall to eat and bring back food. They help her go to the bathroom and take her to the beach for bathing and distractions. The twins have become her older sisters and play with her. They cleverly take stones they find and scrape the edges on the cement to smooth the surface into round balls and shoot them like marbles. With the subsistence allowance from the UNHCR and through Ommo's kindness, I am able to buy two mosquito nets.

Ommo and I have become friends this past month. The twins and Thủy-Tiên adore him. He brings them a treat when he visits or plays marbles with them and talks to them like little adults. I want to trust him but my experience with Minh-Hoàng reminds me to never let my guard down. I want to love him but every man I try to love ends up gone from my life. Mai is smitten with him and says he looks like a movie star. Khải is not happy when Ommo visits, mainly out of jealousy, but he tolerates him, probably because Ommo is in a position to make life either comfortable or difficult for us.

"I have some news for you today," says Ommo. "Can we talk outside, the two of us?"

I leave Thủy-Tiên with the twins and Tree with Mai and Khải. We walk outside towards the church that the other refugees are erecting from supplies provided by humanitarian organizations. The sun shines brightly so we find a tree to sit down against.

"I have made contact with your four friends," Ommo says.

"That is wonderful. I want to see them," I say.

"I informed Sơn and Minh-Tú you were in barrack two and they will visit."

"Thank you. What about Tùng and his sister?"

"I do not have good news about Hồng-Mai. Last month she was raped while heading to the toilet. She cannot identify her assailant. It could have been a guard or a refugee at the camp. Her brother is quite distraught."

The shock of this news shakes my core. I can only imagine the pain and shame Hồng-Mai is going through and how alone she must feel. I burst into tears.

Ommo wraps his arms around me. "You need to go see them today. Her brother is beside himself with worry and cannot comfort her. She will not talk to him or let him touch her. She will not eat or bathe."

I give in to his comforting embrace. "Take me to her. We go now."

"The police are investigating the incident. I requested a caseworker and a legal officer--"

"Now, Ommo. We go now. I need to see her."

\*\*\*

Hồng-Mai's face is barely recognizable. She lies on the clay floor in a trancelike state of mind. She is emaciated and smells bad. I suspect it has been a couple of weeks since she last bathed. She exhales. The foulness of her breath makes me cringe.

Tùng also looks lethargic. "I am weary of living." Tùng drops his head into his hands. "I am going insane here."

"Your sister needs you to help her get through this." I gently touch his hand. "We need to be strong for her and I will be strong for you."

"We do not want to suffer anymore." Tùng grabs hold of my hands and squeezes. His tight grip of desperation cuts off my circulation.

I notice my fingers turning red and try to extract them from his grip. "Everyone here is in their own tormented hellhole, but if you wait a little longer, you will find light again."

Tùng sobs. "There is too much darkness to find light." He leaves his bamboo hut to cry alone. Ommo exits to follow him and leaves me with Hồng-Mai.

I slowly caress Hồng-Mai's head. "We will get justice for you and destroy the man who did this to you. Do not be ashamed." I remove the strands of hair from her face. "You did not cause this. Let me be your strength, Hồng-Mai. Lean on me. You are not going through this alone. I am here with you. Do you understand me? We will take it one day at a time. Together." Hồng-Mai clings to me and cries uncontrollably. The tighter she squeezes, the tighter I squeeze back. "Be strong and persevere. Is that not what Buddha teaches you?" I rub her back and soothe her as if she were a child. "Negative thoughts will lead to more suffering. I will find some incense to burn. We will ask a monk or a nun to chant for you to purify your mind and meditate with you, so you can find enlightenment." I lift her face up so she can see mine. "Hồng-Mai, remember, it is wrong to take a life, so eradicate those poisonous ideas."

Hồng-Mai weeps louder. I hold her tight and rock her. Together we share her sorrow.

\*\*\*

A week has passed. Tree's energy is rising to the peak of his recovery and he wants to go for a swim. I am comforted by his enthusiasm and appetite. Even Hồng-Mai appears to be healing although the emotional scar will always be with her. I help her bathe daily by wiping her down with a wet washcloth and scrub her scalp and hair with a bar of soap before rinsing it. Today, I leave Hồng-Mai for a couple hours to sit with my nephew on the beach and enjoy a bowl of rice and pâté while Thủy-Tiên slurps on her porridge.

"I am sorry for disrespecting you and ruining our chance of leaving here to go to Sweden," says Tree.

"All is forgiven. I understand how much you miss home. You are becoming a man and you were dealing with everything the best way you could. I have put a lot of pressure and demands on you and that is a heavy burden of responsibilities."

"I enjoy being helpful. It makes me feel worthy, but I miss my parents and my little brother."

"I strongly believe we will go to America one day," I say. "I hope we can sponsor them."

"Are you sure that is still what you want? I mean, you can have a life here." "In the camp?"

Tree laughs. "No, I mean with Ommo. He likes you and you like him too but will not admit it."

"I hung my fishing net a long time ago, Tree. I do not want a man to complicate my life. You and Thủy-Tiên are my life now. You both come first."

"More refugees arrive every day and live in makeshift houses. It will be only a matter of time before they build a second camp and we take over this island. Ommo can take you away from all this"

"It is turning into a tent island for sure. There are rice bags and tarps hung everywhere for shade, and fishing line or rope to hang clothes. Ommo is a convenient solution but it would not be right to take advantage of him. And I am not in love with him."

"In time you can love him. He is a good man in the wrong uniform. He serves Indonesia but his heart serves you. I am sure of it."

I laugh. "Tree, you are a romantic. Come, we need to swim."

The three of us splash around in the water for the next hour to forget our problems. Thủy-Tiên finds a crawfish and wants to keep him as a pet. She is mad and pouts when I tell her no.

# 36 REUNION

Sơn and Minh-Tú stroll up to the barrack and call out my name. I poke my head out of the window. Their faces greet me with impatient grins.

"A reunion with my brothers." I fly down the stairs. We keep our formal custom by shaking hands but if there were no eyes around, I am sure we would have hugged like relatives. We sit on the stools outside and catch up.

"Thành got resettled in Germany," says Sơn. "Did anyone get a sponsorship yet?"

"I am happy for Snitch," I say. "We got approved for Sweden but Tree missed the interview and health inspection so we are now waiting again."

"I was sick with Malaria." Tree reminds me.

"There was a lady near my barrack who failed her resettlement interview. She wanted to die when they rejected her application," says Minh-Tú in his thick northern accent.

"She can appeal." I pick up a stick and draw figures of us in the dirt.

Sơn kneels on the ground and uses his finger to give my stick figures hair. "She has three options – appeal, get sent back to Việt Nam or die here."

"If she was pretty or had money, she would have received approval," says Minh-Tú. "There are twice as many men than women here and all the pretty single ones are having relationships with the guards to get their resettlement approved."

Minh-Tú's comment makes me uneasy. It was because of Ommo that I was assigned a barrack upon arrival and because of him that my application for resettlement was processed so quickly.

"I hear the price to bribe the papas is one thousand U.S. dollars if you want a ticket out of here." Sơn now adds shoes to our stick figures in the dirt.

"This makes me wish I was a rich, pretty young girl." Minh-Tú laughs at his own comment.

"What is a papa?" I ask.

"That is what they call the Indonesian officials," says Sơn.

"Why?"

Sơn shrugs his shoulders. He and Tree focus on drawing a family portrait of us.

"I do not ask questions either," says Minh-Tú. "I am sticking to myself and cultivating a garden to grow squash and chilies. A friend of mine sent me some clothes and I traded them for supplies with another refugee in the camp."

"I want to run a coffee shack," says Sơn. "A relative sent me money so I plan to build a coffee stand to pass the time. My coffee stand will be the only one with music. There is someone who is selling his *Sony CF-210L* portable stereo cassette recorder."

"Fancy. I will be your biggest customer," I say. "The administration offered me a teaching opportunity. I would be teaching English to prepare people for resettlement, but I declined."

"Why?" asks Minh-Tú. "You would be great at it and I would be your worst student." We laugh together at his confession.

"What if I get sponsored soon and have to leave before I make any traction teaching you to say 'Hello, my name is'?" I giggle, happy to be sitting with my honorary brothers, talking about whatever subject the breeze brings.

"At least I would have learned something when I get to Canada or Australia." Minh-Tú beams.

"I bet you will end up in Australia," says Sơn. "There is less red tape and a shorter waiting period."

"But Australia only takes professionals with special skills," proclaims Minh-Tú. "I am a farmer and a fisherman."

"Yes and I was in the army and then an unsuccessful thief trying to steal boats to leave our country," says Sơn.

"Denmark and Switzerland would take you both. They take refugees with special needs," I joke. We all laugh. I wish we had some fried squid and *Heineken* beer right now to ăn nhậu, the pastime of socially eating and drinking with friends.

"Have you seen any of the others who were in our boat since we landed on Galang?" Minh-Tú takes my stick and draws a frame around the family portrait.

"Whatever happened to Biện, the man who stepped on the sea urchin?" asks Sơn.

Minh-Tú and I shrug our shoulders. I tell them about Hồng-Mai and Tùng. We agree to visit them. Perhaps the reunion will do them good and they will not feel alone having friends who care about them. The boat people of trawler 93752 are my new family and I am excited to reconnect.

Tree and Thủy-Tiên join us on the walk. We stroll past the coffee stand that Ommo took me to in the rain. The same two women who were talking rumors about Ommo and I being lovers give me disapproving glares. Am I the camp slut to them? I try not to be disturbed by what they may or may not be thinking about me.

We pass a merchandise stand selling daily sundries. One of them is pushy trying to sell me a sun umbrella. On our walk to Tùng's and Hồng-Mai's hut, we talk about the police brutality Sơn witnessed when some of the refugees staged a hunger strike to protest the unfair treatment here. The military came in with tear gas and dogs. Those protestors were arrested and thrown in jail. He claims the military wants to make life unbearable here so that we want to return to Việt Nam.

Tree shares what he does at night, sneaking out of the camp and running through the forest to get to the beach so he can swim and fish.

"You will be beaten if you get caught," cautions Minh-Tú. "They only let us go on the weekends."

"Why you cannot be like the other kids, Tree, I do not understand. There are safer ways to pass the boredom, like painting one of the shacks or playing soccer or making paper boats to float," I say.

"I am not a kid and I like to sleep and swim," answers Tree. "That is it."

Sơn and Minh-Tú shares with us how they survived in the re-education camps. Minh-Tú ate mice, crickets, and frogs raw, and rotten vegetables, spoiled rice, and wild bananas. He got so constipated from the tannins in the bananas and developed dysentery. He almost died. Sơn said leeches feasted on the prisoners and there were snakes and lice that shared the prison space. Many died from diseases like beriberi and malaria and illnesses like tetanus. Minh-Tú says every week prisoners had to stand naked in their cell while the guards hosed them down with water. Sơn shares how he once caused problems by speaking negatively to the guards. They beat him, twisted his arms and stepped on his head.

"Life in prison was debilitating and tragic," says Sơn.

My thoughts skip to Hải sitting in prison and rotting there because he tried to protect me. Then there is my sweet niece, Tâm, and I worry about her sufferings too. My good spirits become eclipsed by the gloom.

We arrive at Tùng's and Hồng-Mai's hut. We step inside and receive greetings from angry swarms of flies. The odor cripples me and I gasp at the sight of Tùng and Hồng-Mai lying on the cold clay floor, their fingers laced together, with a bottle of *Malathion* between them.

Minh-Tú picks up the bottle of insecticide. "I thought this went down with the boat."

I fall to my knees and wail out the feelings of anger, hurt, betrayal and deep sadness in the loss of my fellow brother and sister. "Why did you do this? Why?" I pound my fists against both of the lifeless bodies before me. I am angry that others did not even care to check on them and that the smell of their death melted in with the sour smells of the camp.

Sơn tries to pull me away and Tree shields Thủy-Tiên from the scene. I cannot take any more deaths. I have to leave this terrible place.

# 37 GOODBYE GALANG (FEBRUARY 1980)

Life in the camp this past year has been a struggle. I can almost equate it to the Stockholm syndrome. I have become accustomed to the daily grind and the routine of accommodating more refugees each day. Usually the refugees are ferried from Malaysia, Thailand, or Singapore, but not too long ago, there was a boat from Việt Nam that washed directly onto the shores of Galang Island. I am able to coexist with the Indonesian military and have learned that not everyone is bad.

Thủy-Tiên is now five years old and Tree is seventeen. In two months, I will turn forty-one. Today is Lunar New Year, February 16, 1980. It is the year of the monkey.

Earlier today I visited Hồng-Mai's and Tùng's grave and prayed they found enlightenment in another consciousness. Many of the graves are unmarked but theirs is not. We used scraps of wood from the church that was being built and Tree nailed them together into a Buddhist swastika. We painted it red and staked the symbol into the mound of dirt. Minh-Tú planted a chili plant at the base of the marker so sometimes I take a chili to the barrack to spice up a meal.

Refugees continue to come and go and when there is a group leaving the camp, there are always people to wish them well at the harbor. Bảo's departure was bittersweet. His family all got sponsorships, but unfortunately, got split up and went to different countries. He was so insistent about keeping them together. Indonesia continues to take volunteers who wish to repatriate back to their country of origin. A second camp will be built several miles from this first campsite and will be opened next year, mid-1981. People who get accepted for resettlement will transfer to the second campsite while they wait three months for all the arrangements to be made. If I am not sponsored by next year, there is a good chance my family will move to the second site. English and cultural orientation classes will be mandatory there and I intend to volunteer for the *Save the Children* organization to help teach English in the camp schools. I get a t-shirt if I do. Through donations from various organizations, my wardrobe has expanded to more than a *Wonder Woman* shirt, a purple blouse, and my ragamuffin chic pants. There is an American man named Gaylord Barr who served in the *Peace Corps* in Morocco and will soon come to Galang. He is going to interview and select volunteers to teach English as a second language to those resettling. He is from Washington State, like Sam and Skyler. Hopefully, my English is good enough and he will select me as one of the teachers.

Social networks have developed here but also rivalries and disputes. Life here is generally mundane and bearable. Sometimes it is even fun. The camp now has many more facilities than when we first arrived. There is running water but we are only allowed to run water an hour each day. A few showers and toilets have been installed and in addition to the camp administration office, Indonesian Red Cross hospital and UNHCR offices, there is a youth center, sports center, and music center, places of worship, a post office, and a cinema that shows Chinese movies dubbed in Vietnamese.

We plan to be entertained by one of the Chinese movies in the cinema today and then celebrate the New Year with some beer and tea in the youth center.

"Aunt Eight, her lips look blue to me," says Tree.

I kneel down and take a hold of Thủy-Tiên's hands in mine. "Is it hard to breathe?" My dolly nods. Her lips are indeed blue and so are her fingertips.

"We should take her to the PMI," says Tree.

"No hospital!" Thủy-Tiên sits down in protest. "I want to see the movie."

"She looks tired and her fingers are swollen," says Tree.

"You enjoy the movie, Tree. I will take her to the PMI."

"No!" Thủy-Tiên punches the ground with her tiny fists. "No Red Cross! No hospital!" She works herself up into a tantrum and instantly turns on the water faucet. Tears pour from her eyes and her face is flushed pink. I pick her up and she fights me. "No PMI!" Her writhing body makes it difficult to hold her. I lose my grip and Thủy-Tiên falls to the ground. She runs from me. "I want to see the movie!"

I grab her wrist and drag her in the opposite direction of the cinema. My daughter stomps on my foot and slaps me in the face. I am surprised that for a sick little girl, she is quite strong. Tree tries to pick her up but with her kicking and punching, he loses balance. They both fall to the ground. Together we drag her away as people gawk. We barely walk two hundred meters before her body goes limp. Thủy-Tiên passes out from the exertion.

The line at the Indonesian Red Cross, known officially as *Palang Merah Indonesia*, is long. There are pregnant women and people with toothaches, snake bites, fevers, and all kinds of illnesses.

I am impatient to stand in line and run to the front. "Please help. She sick. Not breathing!"

Tree is right behind me. People grumble, swear, and push us as we rush past but I do not care. One of the nurses points to a room and tells me to wait. A man standing in line curses at the nurse and argues he has been standing in line for an hour with a deep cut in his arm. I lean close to my daughter's face and can feel the faint exhale from her nostrils.

Minutes later a doctor comes into the room. He listens to her heart. "Her heartbeat is faint and I can hear clearly a swooshing sound. It is erratic. She definitely has a hole in her heart."

"Will she live?" I ask fearfully.

"Sometimes the problems will resolve on their own," says the doctor.

"She have this since she born," I say.

"Then she will likely need surgery to patch the hole. The blood between the two chambers of her heart is mixing and if left untreated she will have heart failure."

Tree is worried. "What is he saying? Her color is worse."

"There is not much we can do for her, except let her rest and monitor her the next few days," says the doctor.

"No surgery here?" I ask in a panic.

"This is a basic hospital. I am sorry."

"She cannot die here!" I scream. I grab his shirt and beg him to save her.

\*\*\*

Two days go by and Thủy-Tiên's health has improved slightly. My daughter's tiny frail body is motionless but she is sleeping peacefully. Sometimes she wakes up and asks for water.

Ommo comes to visit. "Has there been any change?"

I nod. "She better. I was scared to bury her here."

He caresses my cheek. "Snow, marry me. Let me take you all out of here. You can finally say goodbye to the camp."

"I want to leave Galang, but…" I am conflicted, torn between wanting to say yes because it would mean we would be taken care of, and saying no because I am not in love with him.

"I know you do not care for me the way I care for you," says Ommo. "But I can make you happy and take care of you, Dolly, and Tree. Please say yes."

His handsome face draws me to touch him. For the first time, I feel the velvet softness of his skin. Ommo puts his hand over mine. The warmth of his fingers radiates through mine. His eyes hold me captive. He leans in and I can smell his minty breath. Our lips touch and I find myself responding to his sweet kiss.

"Yes," I whisper.

\*\*\*

This morning my name is called over the loudspeaker. Tree carries Thủy-Tiên on his back and we run to the United Nations resettlement processing center.

"Ommo knows how to work his magic," says Tree. "I cannot believe we are leaving this refugee camp."

"We have been here for a year. Can you believe it? Soon we will say goodbye to the Galang camp."

"We aimed for America and we could have landed in Sweden, but here we are, about to permanently call Indonesia our home." Tree gallops like an excited horse and my dolly loves the ride.

"God works in mysterious ways." I slow down to a walk to catch my breath. "Soon I will marry Ommo and we will be much closer to our family and you can return when it is safe to do so."

We check into the office to receive papers from the refugee task force then head to the UNHCR office.

"Hello, Don." I greet the UNHCR representative, who is sitting in the same seat as the last time I was here. I notice the mole between his eyebrows is definitely larger.

"You have all members of your family with you this time." Don shakes my hand. His excitement mirrors my own.

"Yes. We are very excited." I sit down and hand Don my papers. I steal a glance at Ommo, sitting in the third seat, looking very dapper in his uniform. There is a radiant glow coming from his eyes and his smile.

In the middle seat is a man I do not recognize. His name tag says "Joseph". *What happened to the translator, Mary?*

Don picks up on my curiosity and queues the introduction. "This is Joseph. He is a VOLAG representative."

Ommo arches his eyebrow and delivers a questioning glance at Joseph. "What do you mean VOLAG? You are not the translator?"

Joseph snickers. "Of course not. We all know she does not need a translator." Joseph dismisses Ommo and turns his full attention to me. "Hello, Ms. Le. I am with a private voluntary agency and I am extremely pleased to inform you that you have been accepted to resettle in the U.S."

"What do you mean?" Ommo stands up and glares at Joseph and Don. If shuriken stares could penetrate through the skin, Don's and Joseph's arteries would be shredded open right now. That radiance I saw earlier from Ommo has been ignited by a flame that is going to explode.

I am thankful I am not on the receiving end of Ommo's fury. "We go to America?" I divert Ommo's attention away from them.

"Yes, Ms. Le." Joseph is not intimidated by Ommo towering over him. "My job is to provide placement services for you and your family in the United States. There is a church in Seattle, Washington...well, Kent, Washington actually, that has accepted sponsorship of your family. We received a letter from--"

Ommo pounds his fist on the table, making everyone jump. "No, this meeting is to inform her that she is no longer a refugee and--"

"I am sorry but it has already been arranged." Joseph lowers his voice an octave. He rotates his body a few degrees towards me, as if to send Ommo a message that he does not appreciate Ommo infringing upon his business. "Your family leaves in two days."

Ommo kicks back his chair. He clenches his fist but refrains from showing his rage. "What are her options here? She can decline and not accept your services, right?" He sits down and pleads with his eyes for me to reject the placement.

Tree grabs my hand. "What is happening? Why is Ommo so upset? Are we not permitted to stay in Indonesia?" My nephew who never asks questions is now asking all of them at once.

My head is spinning. I am elated about the news yet devastated for Ommo and me. I was mentally prepared to marry him and start a new life with him. I even imagined Ommo playing his rebab for Thủy-Tiên before bedtime. I was getting used to the idea of having a husband and convinced myself I could love Ommo enough to be happy with him.

Joseph ignores Ommo's tantrum and talks to me. "Ms. Le, we received a letter from Skyler Herrington. He is a member of a Presbyterian church in Kent. The church has raised enough money to sponsor your family of three to the United States. I have been working with him and the church to ensure they assist you with housing, community integration, and job placement. They will be there at the airport to receive you in Seattle."

Don stands up, walks around the table, and leans on the edge of it. He is directly in front of my chair. "You can, of course, reject the placement, but your application would not be recycled back into the resettlement process. Your family will be sent back to Vietnam."

"Snow." Ommo intercepts Don's speech. "We are going to marry and start a life together here. Tell them."

Don does not give me time to think. "We need to do a health inspection and give you all the necessary vaccinations today. Your travel arrangements are being processed. In two days, there will be a boat at the harbor to take you and others who have been approved for resettlement to Singapore. It is a five-hour boat ride."

Tree stands up. "He said Singapore. Are we going to Singapore? I do not want to go to Singapore."

I ignore Tree. "Tell me more, Mr. Don." I find it difficult to meet Ommo's eyes. His heart must be breaking and desperate for reassurance that I will choose him over America. I cannot give him the comfort he seeks. My head and my heart are not in agreement.

"You will be in Singapore for two weeks before flying to Hong Kong, then Japan, and finally, to Seattle."

My nephew is now livid. "Hong Kong? What is in Hong Kong? What is happening? Tell me!" I let the news sink in and then tell Tree. "We are staying here." Tree crosses his arms defiantly across his chest. "You accepted Ommo's proposal! Thủy-Tiên is so fragile she might not make the trip. If we stay in Indonesia, we can be closer to our family. We cannot go to America. Either you reject the placement and we get sent back home or you marry Ommo."

I try to calm him down. "Tree--"

"You can go! I am staying." Tree imitates Ommo's actions and kicks his chair back. "I can live with the unaccompanied minors and volunteer for repatriation."

As if Don can understand Tree, he says, "Your nephew cannot stay here by himself. Either you all go or you all stay, or return to Vietnam."

"We never go back to communist country," I say.

Tree stomps toward the exit door. I stand up and block him from leaving. He challenges my authority and pushes me aside. In one quick advance, Ommo slams the door shut and tells Tree not to disrespect or hurt me, but of course, my nephew does not understand English. Ommo restrains Tree and forcefully pushes him back into his seat. I am determined not to let Tree ruin my chances for America. I reach out and take hold of Ommo's hand.

He gently extricates himself from my grip. "There is nothing to say, Snow. Your eyes cannot betray your heart and I already know your decision."

"You are being selfish." Tree's voice is cold. He crosses his arms and looks at me with so much hatred. "You are breaking two hearts if you take us to America."

"This escape was never about your heart or Ommo's. It was about Thủy-Tiên's. I am sorry you feel this way. My heart is broken too, but I am not the selfish one here. My decision to flee our country was not made lightly but I never misrepresented my intentions to go to America." I swallow the lump in my throat and force back the tears. "Mr. Don, Mr. Joseph...I accept the placement to Seattle."

Ommo shuffles over to Thủy-Tiên and lifts her up into his strong arms. "I will escort them to their medical examination and make sure they receive their immunization."

"It is settled then." Don claps his hand together. "The church was adamant that we processed quickly."

Joseph shakes my hand. "Congratulations. I wish you a safe journey. I will be in touch to assist you once you're in Seattle."

Tree does not make it easy for the nurse to check his head for lice, get a blood sample, or give him vaccinations. A physician is called in to finish the medical evaluation and Ommo prevents Tree from leaving the examination room.

"I am not going to beg you to stay." Ommo pins Tree down with the weight of his body. "But please think about the uncertainty that awaits you in America. If you stay here with me, you will be safe. You do not have to work, or if you want, you can teach again. I will make sure your daughter gets help from the best doctor, whether it is in Thailand or Singapore, or here in Indonesia. And Tree can go to school...be close to his parents and return when the conflict is over."

I feel so conflicted right now. One moment I am sure I need to stay and the next, I am determined to leave. "I care for you. I know you be good husband to me. I understand your heart, Ommo. It loves my daughter and nephew very much. But I risk everything to go to America. Now I have chance. My friend Skyler will help us."

"I love you. I want to spend the rest of my life taking care of you. Just give it some more thought."

I nod. Tree springs up and bolts out the door.

***

Wednesday morning I wake up early to the sounds of laughter outside the barrack. I open the shutters and appreciate the view of so many familiar faces. I wave to them. "I will be down shortly." I check to see if Tree is in his bed and am thankful he did not run off in the middle of the night. His eyes are red from crying all night. He jumps off the top bunk, shoves our clothes into a plastic bag, and storms out of the room without saying a word to anyone. I hand Mai my mosquito nets. "I know Bảo gave you his when he left, but you can have ours too. Maybe you will want to sell them."

Mai, Khải, and the twins hug Thủy-Tiên and me, but we save our tearful goodbyes for later. We walk down the stairs and into a crowd of cheers and applause. Sơn, Minh-Tú, and all who are left from trawler 93572, including Biện, are here. Even Tiền and her husband, Trương, came with their daughter, who is now ten months old. Together we walk to the entrance gate of the camp where a large group is already waiting to leave. The school shut down today and there are students and teachers congratulating those of us who are leaving. Personnel from UNHCR, the Red Cross, Red Crescent Society, and other humanitarian organizations wish us the best. There is a lot of excitement today but also sadness to be leaving this camp that has become a home. The military is here to escort us to the harbor. I scan the area but Ommo is nowhere to be found.

The walk to the harbor is leisurely and will take us two hours. There are thirty of us leaving today. I assign Tree the task of walking with Thủy-Tiên and the twins, Mỹ-Kiều and Mỹ-Loan. Perhaps the responsibility will prevent him from running away. I keep searching to catch a glimpse of Ommo but instead I catch sightings of monkeys in the trees and faces of strangers dressed in tan uniforms.

To keep my mind off of Ommo, I chat with Tiền and her husband, Trương. "I cannot believe a year ago, you were pregnant and our lives were so bleak. Now you have a daughter and next month you are going to America."

"It was not long ago that we were fighting over drinking water and I was throwing punches at Sơn." Trương chuckles at the memory.

Hearing his name, Sơn joins the conversation. "I told you all to bring your own provisions. At least I brought jicamas." We laugh now looking back on how we behaved.

Tiền can hardly contain her excitement. "Life is full of surprises. My cousin left in '75 and was at a refugee center in Fort Chaffee, Arkansas for a while before she resettled in Oklahoma City. She is sponsoring us to Oklahoma with the help of a Catholic parish."

Trương hands their daughter over to his wife. "Your turn to hold her."

"No, let me hold her." I fight over their daughter. "She is deliciously chubby. You gave her the perfect name. It is very suitable."

"We thought naming her after the empress, Nam Phương, would be perfect," Trương declares proudly. "She will be the bridge between East and West."

"Tell me more about Oklahoma," I say to Tiền and Trương. "What did your cousin say in her letters?"

"Not much, other than it is fairly inexpensive to live there. She opened a restaurant and it is starting to do well. There are many refugees settling there. We are going to help with the restaurant and eventually, we want to open our own grocery store," says Tiền.

"She also said," adds Trương, "those streets are not paved in gold there. Maybe they are in Seattle, but not Oklahoma City. What was the street she mentioned? Classic? Claston?"

Tiền corrects her husband. "Classen."

I chat some more with my friends on our walk to the harbor and divide my time between them. Son and Minh-Tú are still waiting for sponsorship but California and Texas are looking promising. Mai, Khải, and the twins have been approved for resettlement in Canada, but they will be in Galang for another three months while arrangements are made. As for Biện, he has his heart set on Australia.

We finally arrive at the jetty and wait on the dock. The military inspects our bags once again and I notice a few of them take liberties to pocket what they want. My nephew stands solemnly holding Thủy-Tiên's hand. He has barely spoken to me the past two days.

I wrap my arms around Tree. He resists at first. I persist and hold him tighter. "Let me hug you." He eventually gives in. I feel his muscles relax. He weeps. "I love you so much. When we left Vĩnh Bình, I told myself I had to be strong and brave for all of us. When your father asked me to take you with me, I was so scared. I thought, I can barely take care of myself. When Uncle Tý left, I did not know how I was going to take care of Thủy-Tiên. And you know what? You were my partner all along. I drew my strength and my courage from you. You were the one who taught me to take risks. We have come so far and survived so much together. This is another new beginning for us. It is not the end."

Tree squeezes his arms around me and lets go of all the emotions he had bottled up inside. His body shakes and I let him cry until there are no tears left. We stand together with the others who are departing Galang today. There are a lot of hugging, kissing, and handshakes taking place. Displays of yin and yang sentiments pour from everyone, with tears of joy and tears of sadness. Even some of the guards who have built friendships with us are emotional.

A large blue and white ferry boat arrives. The crowd cheers and I am overwhelmed with jubilation. I give Mai and her family another hug and let the tears flow freely. Sơn and Minh-Tú cannot hold back their tears either. One of Abu's men, Gus, announces through a megaphone that we can begin loading. Tree, Thủy-Tiên, and I stand in line with our papers and belongings. To commemorate the day, I wear my *Wonder Woman* shirt. The line moves and we step onto the plank. I turn to wave goodbye. The roar of the crowd gets louder. And then, I see him.

Ommo smiles and waves. I break free from the line and run to him. My handsome, beautiful, kind Adonis. Ommo pushes through the crowd to meet me. He pulls me close and holds me. I stand in his embrace and breathe in his scent.

He kisses my head and hugs me tighter. "The boat is not going to wait for you."

"It will," I say with confidence.

"Write to me. Send pictures." Ommo kisses my forehead. "Come back and visit."

"I will."

Ommo leans down and grazes his lips against mine. His minty breath consumes me and I pull him down to my hungry mouth. I have no cares that people are watching and gasping. I have to take a piece of him with me.

A gentle breeze blows and I reluctantly let go of him. We run together to the plank so that Ommo can say his goodbyes to Tree and Dolly.

I board the ferry boat with my family and the others. As we pull away from the island of Galang, I blow Ommo a kiss. There is only one word to describe this exhilaration. Euphoria.


# THE END

We hope you enjoyed this book. Please consider writing a review to help other readers enjoy SNOW IN VIETNAM. Thank you!

Want to know more about Amy or her next project? Subscribe to Amy's monthly newsletter, *Amy's Monthly Yodel!* You could win a monthly giveaway just for subscribing!
https://mailchi.mp/a8bd3ead7647/authoramymle

Follow Amy on social media!
#SnowinVietnam

https://www.facebook.com/authoramymle
https://twitter.com/amy_m_le
https://www.linkedin.com/in/amymle/
https://www.pinterest.com/amyle2/
https://www.instagram.com/amy_m_le/
Website: http://www.amy-m-le.com

## About the Author

Amy M. Le was born in Vietnam and immigrated to The United States in 1980 at the age of five with her mother and cousin. She graduated from Western Washington University with a degree in Sociology and worked in the technology and telecommunications sector for twenty years. After her mother's death in February 2017, Amy left her corporate job to write her debut novel *Snow in Vietnam* as a tribute to her mother's heroic decision to flee Vietnam after the fall of Saigon. Amy calls the Pacific Northwest and Oklahoma her home. Her greatest joy is spending time with her husband, son, and pets.

Made in the USA
Middletown, DE
29 August 2020